Berkley Sensation Titles by Anya Bast

WITCH FIRE
WITCH BLOOD
WITCH HEART

Heat Titles by Anya Bast

THE CHOSEN SIN

WITCH HEART

ANYA BAST

B

BERKLEY SENSATION, NEW YORK

THE BERKLEY PUBLISHING GROUP
Published by the Penguin Group
Penguin Group (USA) Inc.
375 Hudson Street, New York, New York 10014, USA
Penguin Group (Canada), 90 Eglinton Avenue East, Suite 700, Toronto, Ontario M4P 2Y3, Canada
(a division of Pearson Penguin Canada Inc.)
Penguin Books Ltd., 80 Strand, London WC2R 0RL, England
Penguin Group Ireland, 25 St. Stephen's Green, Dublin 2, Ireland (a division of Penguin Books Ltd.)
Penguin Group (Australia), 250 Camberwell Road, Camberwell, Victoria 3124, Australia
(a division of Pearson Australia Group Pty. Ltd.)
Penguin Books India Pvt. Ltd., 11 Community Centre, Panchsheel Park, New Delhi—110 017, India
Penguin Group (NZ), 67 Apollo Drive, Rosedale, North Shore 0632, New Zealand
(a division of Pearson New Zealand Ltd.)
Penguin Books (South Africa) (Pty.) Ltd., 24 Sturdee Avenue, Rosebank, Johannesburg 2196,
South Africa

Penguin Books Ltd., Registered Offices: 80 Strand, London WC2R 0RL, England

WITCH HEART

A Berkley Sensation Book / published by arrangement with the author

PRINTING HISTORY
Berkley Sensation mass-market edition / January 2009

Copyright © 2009 by Anya Bast.
Excerpt from *Witch Fury* copyright © 2009 by Anya Bast.
Cover art by Tony Mauro.
Cover design by Rita Frangie.
Interior text design by Laura K. Corless.

ISBN 978-0-425-22553-0

BERKLEY® SENSATION
Berkley Sensation Books are published by The Berkley Publishing Group,
a division of Penguin Group (USA) Inc.,
375 Hudson Street, New York, New York 10014.
BERKLEY® SENSATION and the "B" design are trademarks of Penguin Group (USA) Inc.

PRINTED IN THE UNITED STATES OF AMERICA

10 9 8 7 6 5 4 3 2 1

For my mom,
thanks for your support in everything I do.
I love you more than I can say.

ONE

Twenty-three years as the handmaiden of a *daaeman* had prepared Claire for many things, but not this. Nothing could have prepared her for this.

She huddled back against a brick wall, the cold seeping through her thin dress, and watched the inky shadows grow on the building opposite her. Discarded paper disturbed by the wind rustled over the pavement and a sudden bloom of voices and laughter came from the mouth of the alley and gradually faded away.

Still the shadows grew.

Claire glanced at the street beyond the pocket of shadows in which she'd secreted herself, where pale yellow light from street lamps pooled on the sidewalk. She didn't think she could make it. She didn't think she could outrun them.

There were few people in the world—any of the worlds—who could outrun a determined *daaeman*, especially an *Atrika*.

The alien earth sighed and shuddered far beyond the concrete beneath her feet, reacting to her dulled and confused magick. This place, this Earth, was nothing like she remembered. The place she barely recalled was green, soft, and redolent with fragrant, growing things. This place was hard and chilly. Too loud. It hurt her eyes with sharp edges and bright lights.

Part of her had longed to return to this place, even while most of her had feared it. Claire knew now she'd been right to fear.

Pass me by. Please, pass by.

The odd dry tang of Rue's magick still flavored the back of her mouth. The hot rush of it had faded to something bitter. It tingled through her body, giving her the shakes from time to time as her body struggled to contain this thing that was so much bigger than her. She wasn't meant to hold this power. She wasn't made for it. It wasn't hers. The elium, the most powerful weapon of the *Ytrayi*. Or at least, that's what she suspected it was. Whatever it was, the *Atrika* wanted it and that could only mean her death.

The only question was whether it would come slow or fast.

She squeezed her eyes shut, remembering. It had only happened yesterday, but it seemed like years had passed. When the *Atrika* had breached the palace defenses, Rue had taken her to the portal room with the intention of destroying the interdimensional doorway that bridged Earth and Eudae.

But when the *Atrika* had broken into the chamber, Rue had blasted her with a ball of magick so strong it had momentarily taken her sense of sight, smell, and hearing. As he'd meant it to, the blast had catapulted her backward, into the doorway. Rue had meant to destroy the portal after she'd fallen through, and undoubtedly he had, but not before two *Atrika* had lunged in after her.

On the Earth side of the portal, she'd taken one single moment to orient herself and then had lurched forward into a run for her life, knowing the *Atrika* would be fast behind her. Even though her stomach had been heaving with the aftermath of her fall through the doorway, even though her head had been ready to split like a too ripe melon, she'd run.

But not fast enough. Not far enough. And she certainly hadn't hidden well enough.

Last night she'd climbed a set of metal stairs and curled up on the top of a building to sleep with the sounds of a city she almost remembered, but not quite, below her. In the morning, forced to find food, she'd climbed down and had done her level best to avoid the two *Atrika* she'd known were hunting her.

In all her years on Eudae she'd never even seen an *Atrika* up close. Rue, the *Cae*, leader of the *Ytrayi daaeman* breed, had treated her as a pampered pet. He'd protected her from anything that might hurt her . . . until now. With Rue, she'd wanted for nothing, never gone without food. This, all of this, was utterly foreign to her.

She needed to find Thomas Monahan and the *aeamon*, half-breed *daaeman*/humans, who resided on this planet. They called themselves elemental witches here. They were the only ones who would understand what had happened. They were the only ones who could help her now.

Claire knew little of them, didn't know where to find them, or how they functioned in this world. She couldn't even use her magick, not with Rue's gift fluttering inside her. She had no idea how her power would react. If it was elium Rue had imbued her with, accidentally tapping it could mean utter destruction. The inability to use her power was perhaps the worst thing about her current condition.

Worse than the cold. Worse than the hunger or the fatigue or the fear.

In every way imaginable, she was hobbled.

Claire had never been so cold. In all the demonic winters she'd spent on Eudae, where the temperatures ranged into the bone-shattering range for an *aeamon*, she'd never been this miserable. The wound she'd sustained on her foot the first day as she'd run from the *Atrika* hadn't so much healed up as it had frozen up. Hunger constantly distracted her and made her weak. By now she was so bedraggled, people on the street gave her a wide berth and pitying glances.

Never had she been so humiliated.

Today she'd walked down streets, not knowing where she was headed. She'd only known she had to keep moving since the *Atrika* might be able to track her magickally.

People had pressed paper and coins, which she recognized as money, into her palm once in a while. However, when she'd inquired where she could find the elemental witches, they'd only given her strange looks and hurried away. Inquiries as to how to protect herself against demons—the human's pronunciation of *daaeman*—had met with a similar response, so Claire had stopped asking. These random acts of generosity were few and far between, but they'd already helped her buy a little food, a transaction she'd stumbled through badly. And the resulting piece of meat wrapped in soggy bread had been horrid.

She'd managed to evade the *Atrika* for a while, but then she'd turned a corner and there they'd been. Claire had whirled and tried to go in the other direction before they spotted her, but it had been too late. So she'd run to this alley and endeavored to hide.

Now they were searching for her. She could smell them. *Daaeman* magick had a peculiar sharp scent and these *Atrika* weren't masking their true nature at the moment. Likely they were trying to spook her.

It was working.

Claire opened her eyes just for a moment and glanced up into the dark sky with its odd absence of stars. Nothing but concrete here. Concrete and square shapes. Black, cold sky. On Eudae, in the capital city of Ai, the buildings were made of lavender and rose marble, sometimes black or gray. They all shone and glittered under the sun. Structures built in columns, gentle slopes, and arches. The palace, called Yrystrayi, was majestic in its architecture.

Daaeman were brutal regardless of breed. Even the *Syari*, the scholar class, were more prone to killing before asking questions. The warrior class, the *Atrika*, were the worst. Unlike the rest of the breeds, they dined on rotting flesh, loved to drink blood, and became aroused by torture and pain.

But all the breeds, even the *Atrika*, had beautiful architecture.

Her mother told her she'd been born here on Earth, and Claire did have some hazy, early childhood memories of this place, but mostly she felt like she'd slipped down a rabbit hole. Her mother, before she'd died, had told the story of *Alice in Wonderland* often to Claire. Maybe her mother had felt like Alice when she'd first come to Eudae as much as Claire did now on Earth.

Footsteps crushed refuse underfoot, disconcertingly close. Claire froze, the saliva in her mouth drying up.

The shadowy fingers on the building opposite her lengthened and then halted. Claire caught her breath and didn't blink. Honking and voices from the street barely filtered into her arrested awareness. The fingers reversed and came back in her direction.

Claire balanced, ready to take flight. Run. That's all she could do. She wanted to tap her magick, use her best weapon. Her fingers tingled with the desire to do it.

A *daaeman* face appeared above her. "Got you."

His huge hands came down on her shoulders and squeezed. Tears burst into her eyes from the pain. She struggled and his grip dropped to her wrists making her yelp.

The second *Atrika* grabbed the first around the waist and hauled him back away from her. "She's mine!" he growled.

The first *daaeman* who'd grabbed her—Claire believed he was called Tevan—gathered himself from where he'd been knocked to the pavement. With a low growl trickling from his throat, he launched himself at the second. Both their eyes glowed red and their teeth had extended.

Killing rage.

Claire stood for a split second, watching the *daaeman* face off. If the magick Rue had imbued her with was elium, it was very valuable to them. Of course they'd fight over it. Within her lay all their hopes and dreams of victory against the ruling *Ytrayi*. They would each want control of it.

Lucky her to carry such a treasure.

Claire bolted.

Realizing they'd lost their prey, the *Atrika* stopped their territorial dispute and followed her.

Ducking low and swerving, she just evaded Tevan's grasp and shot out of the alley, dodging tall silver cans, lumpy black sacks, and jumping over discarded boxes. Her shoes, made for the sleek marble floors of the palace, hadn't fared well on the concrete pathways of Earth. Shredded on the bottom, they provided little protection.

Something sharp stabbed her sole and she yelped, feeling a gush of hot, sticky blood. She cursed in Aemni, one of the languages commonly spoken among all the breeds. Now she was leaving a perfect trail for them.

She careened out into the street and nearly collided with a

man. He yelled at her as she dove around him and sped down the sidewalk.

Across the way, a flood of people exited a building, spilling out into the night-dark streets under a brightly lit overhanging sign, talking and laughing. Knowing a crowd was her only chance, Claire detoured, pounding across the road. The shiny fast-moving conveyances—*cars*, that's what they were called—honked and swerved.

She plunged into the crowd on the other side, scattering those directly around her with surprised gasps. Risking a glance backward, she saw the two *Atrika* had reached the street and had spotted her. They made their way toward her.

"Help! Help me!" Her voice sounded rusty and she choked on the English. She'd used it with Rue when he wanted practice and with the earth witch, Thomas, when he'd been trapped in Yrystrayi. Otherwise she hadn't spoken it since her mother had died.

The people around her appeared alarmed. Most didn't look at her. They pretended she wasn't standing there asking for aid in tattered shoes and a torn, dirty dress that provided no protection against the cold bite of the air. Some glanced at her with pity on their faces; others smirked and talked behind their hands. A woman pressed one of the pieces of green paper into her palm. Claire stared down at it, uncomprehending. She'd asked for help, not money.

"Please, the *daae*—demons," she whispered. "The *Atrika* demons will get me."

The *Atrika* would crack the seat of her magick open to get the elium. Crack her like a nut for the meat inside. How had Rue ever expected her to succeed? One *aeamon* servant against two motivated *Atrika daaeman*?

She closed her eyes, reliving the moment when the *Atrika* had forced the door of the *Ytrayi* portal chamber down. The burst of brilliant magick, the bellows and war whoops, the *Atrika* all in a killing rage. Rue could even now be dead. There was no help in her immediate future. Even if Rue had survived, it would take a long time to open another doorway, even longer for Rue to track her down.

A hand curled over her shoulder, startling her. She looked up into a handsome male face. Elegant, sloping brown brows, green eyes, a smile. "Come with me," the man said. "There's a diner just up the way. We'll get a meal and see what we can do to help you."

Her gaze flicked back to the *daaeman* crossing the street. They were growing very close now. She grabbed the man's arm. "Yes, let's go."

He patted her hand. "It's all right. Calm down now, okay?"

She glanced backward at her pursuers. "Let's stay with the crowd. Do you mind?"

"Of course not. Will the crowd keep the . . . demons . . . away?"

Oh, thank all Four Houses and the Patrons! He understood. She nodded emphatically. "They won't hurt me if I'm with humans. They don't want to incite an interdimensional incident."

He raised his eyebrows. "Ah. Let's go then. What's your name?"

"Claire."

"Claire, what a lovely name. What's your last name?"

She didn't answer because she didn't know it. Her mother had never told her. She only shook her head and glanced away, embarrassed. Were surnames very important here? A mark of class, perhaps?

As they walked, the man flipped open a small black object, punched some buttons and spoke into it. Claire didn't pay attention to what he said, she was too focused on the *daaeman* following them. They kept their distance now, but they would stalk her until they found her alone and vulnerable. All she'd done was buy herself some time.

Claire hoped the humans had some way of dealing with *Atrika*. She'd heard one had been stuck here without a doorway for many years. The witches had dealt with that one. Perhaps the elemental witches were rulers in this place. It would make sense, considering their abilities. Although that didn't explain all the blank looks she got when she asked about them. At least she'd found one man who understood about the *Atrika*. Hopefully, he'd know how to find Thomas Monahan.

The good news—if there was good news—was that there were only two *Atrika* and no more could follow, since Rue had destroyed the doorway.

A hysterical laugh bubbled up from her depths. She was penniless and lost in a foreign world she hadn't walked on since she was six years old and there *only* two *Atrika* who were chasing her. That was the good news?

The man looked concerned when she laughed. He hesitated, then pulled the door of a restaurant open for her. "We're here." Claire's mind had been spinning so hard, she hadn't even noticed they'd reached their destination.

She entered a small establishment, glancing at her surroundings. People sat belly up to a long counter. Others sat in the booths near the large front window that gave a view of the darkened street. Most of the restaurant's patrons turned and looked at her, making Claire self-conscious about her clothing and dirt-smudged face.

"No vagrants in here," said a skinny, sharp-faced waitress wielding a pot of some dark, unidentifiable liquid.

Horror shot through Claire. "I am not a vagrant." She glanced away, knowing full well she looked like one. She'd been— *was*—handmaiden to the *Cae* of the *Ytrayi daaeman* breed. Slave, perhaps, but slave to the *master*. That meant the best of everything, even though she'd been property.

The man set a hand to her shoulder. "Of course you aren't." Then he turned to the waitress. "It's okay. I'm a clinical psychologist and . . ." He pulled the waitress aside and spoke in low tones to her. The waitress nodded and glanced at her.

Claire's intuition niggled. This was not a good thing.

That had not been a good glance.

A clinical psychologist? Her mind sorted through the notebooks filled with English lessons and vocabulary her mother had left her. A psychologist was a physician of the mind. Why had he mentioned that to the waitress? Did he think Claire was crazy?

She sucked in a breath. Her alarm factor ratcheted upward. She had to get out of here. What had seemed like a safe refuge a moment ago didn't seem so anymore. *Houses*, she had no idea who to trust in this world, which meant she could trust no one.

She lifted her gaze to the window and saw the darker-skinned *Atrika* staring in at her. His eyes were shadowed and full of menace. He parted his lips and flashed fang at her—a silent promise. .

The bell on the door behind her jingled and she turned to see the other *Atrika*, masking as human, enter the diner. This one was lighter than the other—tall, blond, broad-shouldered. Ripped with muscle, this one could break her bones with a twist of his wrist. This was the one she thought was called Tevan. If it was Tevan, he was one of the leaders of the *Atrika* uprising. A commander.

Oddly, he looked like Rue. It made her throat close with longing for home—safe, warm home. She had mixed feelings about the *Ytrayi*, but right now the thought of them was a familiar comfort in a world of threat.

Hundreds of years ago, the *Ytrayi*—leading two of the other *daaeman* breeds—had tried to exterminate all *Atrika* from the face of Eudae. They'd missed pockets of them and those survivors had gone underground, vowing to take Eudae for themselves one day. The attempted genocide had fueled an already growing war between the breeds.

The one she thought was Tevan caught her gaze for one long moment and she couldn't look away. Violent promise shimmered deep in his dark blue eyes. He ducked into a booth and pretended to read the plastic menu. He still wore his fighting leathers from head to toe and drew many curious glances.

All of the *daaeman* breeds, there were four of them, could mask their appearance through magick. An *Atrika* could appear to be *Ytrayi* or *Syari* or *Mandari*, for example. They only showed their true faces when angered or on a hunt. At the moment Tevan was indistinguishable from any other male in the restaurant, but for his powerful build.

Claire turned back around, her heart thumping. She pasted a purposefully bland look on her face. It would not help to allow the *Atrika* to know how badly they frightened her. They loved it when their prey was afraid. It made the hunt that much more fulfilling to them, made them want to be more savage once they caught their prey.

Claire took a second glance around her surroundings, noting the entrance to the kitchen and a small hallway leading to two doors nearby. There was probably a back exit, but she couldn't go that way. The second *Atrika* was undoubtedly on the other side of it by now; he'd disappeared from the sidewalk in front. She needed a window or something that let out on the side of the building.

The clinical psychologist turned back to her, a tight little smile on his face. "Please, let's sit down. I ordered a nice orange juice for you."

Claire didn't know what this nice orange juice was, but she wanted no part of it. "I need to, uhm . . ."

He took her by the upper arm and led her to a booth. "Just sit with me a little. I want to talk to you about the . . . demons."

Yes, now she heard the disbelief in his voice when he said the word *demon*, heard the hesitation. Perhaps the witches here were underground. Maybe the humans knew nothing of them or *daaeman*, nothing of their intersection with the people of Eudae in their ancient past.

How could they be so ignorant?

Claire slid uneasily into the booth, feeling the slick plastic beneath the fabric of her dress. At least it was warm in here. A moment later the waitress set a tall glass of bright liquid in front of her.

The man leaned forward, making the plastic beneath him creak. "Claire, do you know what year it is?"

She didn't. Claire stared hard at the tabletop.

"Claire? Do you know what country you're in?"

That one she knew. She looked up. "The United States."

The man smiled. "Very good. Yes, you're here in Chicago, among friends. Do you know who the president of the United States is?"

She could take it no longer. "Of course I don't! I've been trapped in a demon dimension for twenty-five years, since I was six years old! I only just came back a day ago, after being forced to ingest a ball of magick I shouldn't be carrying and then pushed through an interdimensional doorway. I am being chased by two of the most aggressive of the four demon breeds for that magick. They'll kill me to get it." She pursed her lips together and stared at his dropped jaw and wide eyes. "So, you see, sir, I do not want to sit here and answer meaningless questions about who your president is."

Outside a high-pitched whine grew louder. She frowned, glancing out the window. Something approached. What was that horrid sound?

"I've called some people to come and help you, Claire."

Another laugh burbled from her depths. "Help me? No one can help me now. Most especially not you." She slid from the booth and bolted for the kitchen. Behind her, she heard the *Atrika* rise and follow her, his footsteps heavy on the shiny floor.

The man also followed her, yelling at her to stop. She glanced back, seeing Tevan shove him to the side. The human male went sprawling against the counter and careened to the floor while the diner's patrons gasped.

She plunged through the doorway and into the kitchen, immediately becoming engulfed in strange greasy odors. Claire skidded to a stop in front of a cook who stood slack-jawed, loosely holding some sort of food preparation implement.

Claire ran down the stairs near the man, the only exit available to her. Hearing heavy tread behind her, she raced to the only safe place she could see—a doorway leading into some sort of storage room—and slammed the door closed behind her.

She pulled a shelf filled with cans and food sacks over in front of the door just as the *Atrika* hit it on the other side with teeth-rattling strength. Tevan bellowed in outrage even as she wedged the shelving into a space that would prevent him from pushing the door open.

She had one advantage. The *daaeman* wouldn't be able to jump—teletransport themselves—for a couple of days. They needed to find true equilibrium with the vibrational frequency of this dimension before they could do that. The molecules of this place moved slower than those of Eudae, and to bend space to jump before they found a balance might kill them.

She should be so lucky.

Claire whirled, eyes wide and breathing hard. Her magick pulsed within her chest, tingled through her arms and legs, begging for release, but it was in there, mixed with the other, strange *daaeman* magick. She had to deny it.

Copper? Was there any copper here? All the *daaeman* breeds were allergic to it. It was banned on Eudae, even dug up and disposed of in toxic waste areas, but here on Earth it wouldn't be. She saw none in her vicinity that she could identify. Too bad, since likely Tevan and his friend hadn't yet been able to develop any partial protection against the metal.

Tevan pushed and yelled on the opposite side of the doorway. It was only a question of time before he found a way through magickally.

Time to leave. Frantically, she searched for a way out.

There! A small window close to the ceiling, above a low counter strewn with cans of vegetables. Apparently, this room was mostly underground.

Behind her, the door opened a crack and the metal of the shelving bent. "I am Tevan, commander in the *Atrikan* military, and I almost have you, little witch."

TWO

CLAIRE SCRAMBLED ONTO THE COUNTER AND unlocked the window. Her movements made oddly precise from the terror coursing through her, she pushed with all her might until the old window gave and slid upward. She pulled herself out of the opening, standing on cans to boost herself upward.

Immediately, hands clamped down on her shoulders and yanked her up like she weighed nothing. She struggled, kicking and screaming, thinking it was the other *daaeman* who'd come around to guard the window.

"Stay still! We're trying to help you!" demanded a gravelly voice.

Four hands pushed her down to the cold pavement. "Let me go! They're after me. Please!" she cried.

"Yeah, yeah. We know. Demons are chasing you, right?"

Strong arms yanked her to a standing position. She found herself blinking up into the faces of two tall men, one with dark skin and the other with light. They wore uniforms. She struggled for a moment, trying to place it . . . ah, they were policemen. Meant to protect and serve. Guardians of the peace, protectors of the innocent. She relaxed. She was safe.

"Claire, right?" asked the dark-skinned officer.

Glancing around at the dank, narrow passageway between the buildings, she nodded. Where had the *Atrika* gone?

"I'm Officer Adams and this is Officer Evans. We're going to take you in, get you some help." He began to draw her toward the street, but she dug her heels in. The officer stopped and turned toward her with a sigh. "We're going to make sure the demons don't get you, all right?"

His tone. She frowned. He sounded like she was his tenth crazy person that day and he was weary of all of them.

"How can you protect me from the demons when you don't believe in them?"

Officer Evans took out a pair of cuffs on a sigh. "Look, lady. We're almost off shift, you know? Why don't you let us bring you in nice and easy, without cuffs. I understand you were being chased by some man . . . was that your boyfriend, honey? There's another unit around front, dealing with him. You can press charges against him at the station. So, let's just go, okay?"

"I can't go to your station. If I go with you now, the demons will find me and kill me."

"That's it." He grabbed her and forced her arms behind her back. The snick of the cuffs around her wrists declared her truly in trouble. He mumbled a bunch of meaningless words at her while he secured her.

Officer Adams grabbed her by the arm and yanked her forward, toward the mouth of the narrow passageway. Claire could do nothing but follow, casting a long look over her shoulder.

No *Atrika*. That was something, at least.

She'd again been saved by the intervention of a human, though she had no delusions the *Atrika* wouldn't follow her to this station, whatever it was.

She allowed the men to lead her to their car. Lights flickered brightly on the top of it. *How odd*. On Eudae there was no need for such enforcers of the rules. Everyone stayed in line. If they didn't, they died. It was pretty much that simple.

They led her to sit in the backseat of the car, took off her cuffs, and gave her a blanket. A heavy grate separated her from the two officers in the front of the vehicle. She snuggled into the blanket and tried not to be alarmed at how trapped she felt. The darker-skinned officer rummaged through a bag in the front seat and pulled out a plastic baggie filled with two golden sponge cakes.

"Want these?" he asked. "They're all I got. Aren't nutritious, but you looked half-starved."

She had to stop herself from grabbing the package and swallowing it whole. "Thank you," she said, taking the food.

The policeman laughed and shook his head. "You're polite for a crazy girl."

The officers got into the front and slammed their doors closed. On the sidewalk a distance away, the dark *Atrika* glowered.

Claire didn't stare long; she ducked her head and concentrated on the interior of the vehicle. She'd never seen anything like it. Since *daaeman* had the ability to jump to different locations, they didn't need vehicles like these. The only time physical conveyances were necessary was when they needed to move things. Those vehicles were powered by magick and looked nothing like these boxes of metal.

The officer who was driving took a small black device from the dashboard, mumbled into it, and then pulled out into traffic. "What's your last name, honey?"

She pursed her lips together, unable to answer and unwilling to lie. She couldn't even begin to guess at what might be a likely last name here, though Thomas's had been Monahan.

He chuckled. "All right then, I'll let the experts sort you out."

Claire didn't really care where they were going, as long as it was away from the *Atrika*.

Claire ripped the plastic food package open and ate both cakes in record time. Closing her eyes, she moaned with pleasure. They were the best things she'd tasted in her entire life.

By the time they reached their destination, she was nodding off from a combination of heat and having something in her stomach. She felt like she could sleep for a week. When this was over, if it was ever over . . . that's exactly what she would do.

The vehicle stopped and they ushered her into a wide brick building. She still clutched the blanket tightly around her.

They guided her past a bank of desks where other officers were typing, talking, or shuffling paperwork. Finally they reached their destination, a small room with a table and a couple of chairs, and they left her there. A few minutes later a female officer entered with a cup of some delicious, sugary hot drink, which Claire drank down in almost one swallow.

"What is this?" Claire asked the dark-haired woman, Officer Mallory.

Officer Mallory's face screwed into an expression of annoyed disbelief. "Hot chocolate."

"It's good."

She snorted. "What? You've never had hot chocolate before?"

Claire shook her head.

The door opened again and the man from the diner entered. He gave her a long look. "Hello, Claire. I'm Dr. Hitchinson. Contrary to what you may believe, I *am* here to help you."

She said nothing, looking away. She didn't like this man. Through her muted water magick, she sensed he was *bad*.

He sat down at the table across from Officer Mallory and they proceeded to discuss her as though she didn't exist. Claire calmly sipped her hot chocolate and amused herself by thinking of all the different ways she could shock them had her magick been available to her.

Claire had been eight when her mother had died. That's when Rue had taken her as his handmaiden in order to protect her. Every day since, Rue had tweaked her magick—snipping here, grafting there. He'd given her abilities far beyond the earth magick she'd been born with. She was powerful and she wanted so much to show Officer Mallory and Dr. Hitchinson just how powerful she was.

Dr. Hitchinson tented his fingers on the table in front of him. "I was exiting the Livingston Theater on Dearborn and Randolph after a show. She ran into the crowd shouting about demons chasing her. I brought her to a restaurant and called the police. In the diner she expressed her belief once again that she was running from demons and that she was newly arrived in this dimension. That's when she bolted and that man in the diner gave chase. I suspect he was her boyfriend or husband."

Blood surged through Claire's veins at the notion. "He is not my boyfriend or husband!"

Officer Mallory acknowledged her existence. "Then who is he? He managed to evade our officers, Claire. If you want to press charges against him, you'll have to give us his name."

She snapped her mouth shut, unable to explain Tevan's true identity. They already believed she was crazy, ignorant humans. If she babbled any more about demons, it would be worse for her. She crossed her arms over her chest. "I refuse to reveal his identity."

"I thought he was a demon," said Officer Mallory with disdain.

"I don't know what you're talking about. There's no such thing as demons."

Officer Mallory tipped her head to the side and frowned at her. "What is your accent, by the way? I can't place it. What's your native language?"

Claire examined her nails and tried not to tell the truth about her accent. "I was born and raised in Holland." All the notebooks her mother had left her about life in this place were coming in handy.

Dr. Hitchinson pressed his lips together. "No matter what she says now or how rational she seems, she was *not* lucid then. In addition, I believe her to be in danger from that unidentified male."

"I can take care of myself."

That finally drew his attention. "Oh, really? We found you nearly frozen to death and ignorant of your own last name." He turned his attention back to Officer Mallory and pointed. "I want her admitted to the psych ward at Stroger for evaluation. She's a danger to herself, not to mention she's in danger from that man."

Claire's jaw locked. "There is nothing wrong with me!"

Again she was ignored by Dr. Hitchinson. "Lean on her, Officer Mallory. Find out who that man was that pushed me into the counter. I want to press charges." His eyes flicked to her, examining the bruises marking her wrists and lower arms where Tevan had gripped her. "I will if she doesn't."

"Okay," said the policewoman on a sigh. "I trust your opinion, Doc." She closed the file in front of her. "We're taking her to the hospital. They can figure out what to do with her over there."

Hospital. She frowned. A place where they treated the sick, took care of people. Well, that couldn't be too bad. Maybe she would be safe there for a while. Maybe she could get warm, get some food in her stomach.

THE HOSPITAL WAS A NIGHTMARE.

It wasn't a place where they helped people. It was a prison— cold, white, sterile, filled with frightening angular metal implements, and screaming, moaning humans. It stank of cleaning products, but beneath that lingered the scent of fear, blood, and death.

The second they let her out onto the floor where she was to be "helped," Claire had wrinkled her nose at the smell and understood she could not remain there under any circumstances. When she'd tried to leave, they'd wrestled her into a small, blindingly white room. Petite and starving, she was no match for the two hulking human male orderlies who were manhandling her.

"No! Let me go! I cannot be locked up in this place!" Claire had cornered herself, but she wasn't down for the count. She kicked and her foot connected with an orderly's male part. He *oofed*, backed away clutching his groin, and gave her a look to kill.

The second male moved on her with ferocity, while the slightly built blond female doctor looked on like she'd seen it all before and was supremely bored by it.

While Orderly A nursed his privates, Orderly B managed to wrestle Claire face-first onto a long, hard exam table and force her arm out. Panic edged into her throat as the doctor came toward her with a wicked-looking syringe.

"No, don't do this. You do this and you leave me defenseless against them. Please!"

"Now, don't be silly, Claire. This serum is to protect you against the demons and the vampires."

Vampires? What was a vampire?

The needle bit into Claire's arm. Her eyelids instantly

began to feel heavy and her knees weak. "No. This is . . . this is . . . wrong."

As her mind fumbled against the haze settling over it, she lost control and tapped her magick. The action was pure instinct, born of perfect terror, the kind not even the *Atrika* could incite and accentuated by the alien drugs coursing through her bloodstream. It was the one thing she'd sworn not to do until she knew more about what Rue had infused her with.

Power exploded through her, bowing her spine and cracking her head backward to make contact with the orderly's, who released her and yelped in pain. The thread she'd pulled felt violent, alien . . . just like this world she'd been thrust into. It burned through her, searing the seat of her magick.

During the half second she had before the pain and drugs plunged her into unconsciousness, she reached out to any air witch she could.

Please, hear me . . .

She sent her plea only a moment before the thick, cloying darkness closed over her.

THREE

ADAM'S COPPER BLADE CONNECTED WITH THOMAS'S in the newly built sparring chamber on the Coven grounds. Sweat trickled down his bare chest, pooled in his belly button. He turned, met Thomas's blade once more. The impact reverberated up his arm and through his chest and back.

Whoosh. Clang.

It had been a year since they'd gone up against an *Atrika* demon who'd been trapped on Earth, away from his native Eudae. The demon had killed six witches trying to open a doorway before Thomas Monahan, head witch of the Coven, and Isabelle, sister to one of the slain, had offed him.

In the process, Isabelle and Thomas had been pulled through to Eudae. Adam had been there to see it happen, but incapable of stopping it. While Isabelle had been sent home, the demons had kept Thomas for a while. They'd cut his long hair, a source of strength for the earth witch. They'd tried to break him.

Whoosh. Clang.

The force of Thomas's hit crashed down his arm and rattled his teeth. "Fuck, Thomas!"

Yeah, they hadn't broken him.

Since that ordeal, the Coven witches had never stopped training with the copper weapons they'd used against the *Atrika*. The vicious demon breed were allergic to the metal, although they sometimes developed a defense against it, something that Micah, the Coven archivist and all-around geek, was trying to investigate. But for now it was the only weapon the witches knew of.

The absolute *only*.

All of them knew the time they'd have to fight the *Atrika* would come again. The only question was *when*. Adam hoped it wasn't in his lifetime, but he'd be ready if it was.

"Come on, Adam. Don't hold back just 'cause he's the boss," Jack called from the sidelines. "I need you to break him in for me. I'm next up, man. I'll buy you a beer if you can beat him."

It wasn't so much the beer that motivated him, though he wouldn't turn it down. It was more a desire to beat Thomas. Just because, normally, at least in swordplay, he could.

He'd even quit smoking to train. Now *that* was dedication. His fingers still twitched for a smoke now and again, but at least now he could run a bunch of laps and not be wheezing at the end. He'd tried to stop drinking, too, but that hadn't gone as well. Adam figured a man needed a few vices. Kept him interesting.

Adam nodded as he eyed Thomas, who adjusted his grip on the sword handle as if anticipating a renewed assault. "That's a bet, Jack."

Fire roared through his body, his magick tingling through him. Blue flame leapt from his fingers, curled around the grip, and shot up the blade. He roared and engaged.

Swoosh. Clang.

This time Adam was the one who set teeth to rattling.

"There's the Adam we know and love," called Jack.

Adam pivoted, renewing his attack. His blade connected with Thomas's and he pushed him back a few steps. Grunting, sweat streaming, he pressed harder. Adam might be gifted in swordplay, but that didn't mean Thomas was easy to beat.

Swoosh. Clang. Swoosh. Clang! Clang! Clang!

Thomas blocked and defended, but Adam had him on the run now. His muscles bunched and burned. To defeat Thomas Monahan he had to dredge up every last molecule of strength he had. His whole body flexed and sweat poured down him as he beat his opponent backward, up against the wall of the sparring chamber.

He went for the final shot, cutting upward with his blade and lightly touching Thomas in the stomach with the edge of the shiny copper weapon.

Deathblow.

Panting, Thomas dropped his sword to his side in defeat.

Out of breath, Adam dropped his sword, too. "Sorry, boss." He shrugged and grinned.

Thomas regarded him through obsidian eyes and leaned over, bracing his hands on his knees. "I'm really glad you're on our side, Adam."

Jack bounced out into the middle of the sparring mat, obviously relishing being rested and refreshed while Thomas was panting and exerted. "Okay, my turn."

."I don't think so," answered Isabelle, who'd just entered the room. She came to stand near her husband and reached up to finger the short bunch of hair at his nape. "My mom is here for a visit. Thomas said he'd have lunch with us."

Catalina, Isabelle's mother, had been trying to develop a relationship with her daughter after she'd subjected Isabelle to a pretty bumpy childhood. Isabelle seemed happy to finally have a mom she could count on.

"Anyway," Isabelle continued, "Mira needs Jack to help her with Eva."

Eva was Jack and Mira's new baby, a rare and very protected little air witch. Mira was the most powerful air witch around and likely her daughter would be every bit as strong.

"That's married life for you." Adam grinned.

Mira had been involved with a real gem of an asshole during her first marriage and had vowed to never marry again. It had taken Jack a while to wash the taste of that first bad marriage from her mouth, but he'd managed to do it. He and Mira had finally tied the knot after Eva had been born.

"I love it, man," Jack answered with a grin.

Yeah, so had Adam.

"Eva's still fussy, I bet," Jack answered Isabelle. "Mira and Eva—we believe—heard something disturbing last night. It was a cry for help, but it was brief and without detail. We don't know who it was from or where she is. All we know was that it was a female air witch who sent it."

Thomas grabbed a towel and wiped his face and neck. "Mira told me about that this morning. If they hear anything else, let me know right away."

"We will."

Isabelle wrinkled her nose. "In any case, Thomas and Adam both need showers pronto."

"I guess training can wait," answered Jack, dropping his sword. "It's not like there are any *Atrika* loose on Earth this very second."

The *Atrika* were the freight train of the demon breeds, and none of the breeds were exactly fluffy bunnies.

Adam threw his sword to the mat. "Man, don't say that. Every time someone says something like that, it's proved wrong." He shook his head, remembering what they'd gone through with Erasmus Boyle. "I really don't want *that* proved wrong."

Jack held up a hand. "Okay, okay, I'm sorry. I'm out of here, anyway. My family is calling." He walked over to the wall to stow his weapon.

Family. The word squeezed Adam's chest every time, but he'd never let these guys know. He picked up his sword and walked over to put it away. "I'm out, too. I'll be in my room if anyone needs me."

"Got a date tonight?" called Isabelle.

Adam threw a careless glance over his shoulder. "What night don't I have a date?"

Isabelle just grinned and shook her head, leaning against Thomas and wrapping her arms around his waist, sweat and all. Now *that* was true love. Adam was happy that Thomas and Isabelle had found it together. Jack and Mira, too.

Adam knew his shot at it had already blown by and disappeared on supercharged roller skates. He'd just sat there and waved at its retreating ass. There, then gone. Like some kind of really bad—or tragic—practical joke.

"Womanizer," she shot at him.

"Is that supposed to be an insult?"

Isabelle grinned. "You're incorrigible."

He spread his hands and shrugged. His tendency to serial date was a familiar, playful issue between them. "I can't help it if I'm popular with the ladies."

"Uh-huh. If you disappeared from the Earth tomorrow, all womankind would mourn and break out their vibrators in your memory."

He shot her a grin and a wink. "Damn straight."

Isabelle shifted and rolled her eyes. Her shirt gaped a bit, showing one of the tats that Theo had inked her with. Isabelle wasn't an earth witch, able to use tattoos to store spell energy, but she had been scarred in places by the *Atrika* demon they'd fought last year—Erasmus Boyle. At Isabelle's request, Theo had created a few designs around her scars to cover them, or, in Isabelle's words, celebrate them. She'd survived the ordeal by the skin of her teeth.

Adam grabbed a towel and headed up to the room he kept at the Coven.

Women did like him. They always had, even before he'd joined the Coven as primary muscle to the boss and jack-of-all-trades fire witch. His face wasn't handsome in the classical sense and he'd broken his nose twice, which made it crooked, but he was still apparently attractive enough to women. His body was fit, not because he had an ego but because he needed to be in shape for his job.

Their primary enemy, though they'd acquired another recently, were the Duskoff, a warlock cabal run by one bad dude, Stefan Faucheux.

Warlocks were witches gone bad, ones that turned their back on the Coven and betrayed the values it held dear, which meant they were powerful enough to be truly dangerous. The members of the Duskoff broke the covenant of *harm thee none* all the time and used their magick for their own gain, no matter who it hurt.

Normally, the Duskoff kept the Coven on its toes, but they'd gone eerily silent over the last year. Stefan Faucheux had turned up once after the *Atrika* incident, then disappeared. All agreed that didn't bode well. Stefan wasn't exactly the shy and retiring type.

A quiet Duskoff was a Duskoff up to no good.

So even though the last year had been calm, the Coven witches trained—fast, hard, and unrelenting. They could expect trouble to pop up anytime. If not from their new friends, the demons, then from the Duskoff.

Once inside his room, Adam found a slender redhead reclining on his couch. She was dressed in a skimpy black lace nightgown, her long, curling hair cascading over the arm of the sofa.

He pulled the key out of the lock. "Whoa, Jess. I thought we weren't supposed to meet until eight."

She rolled off the couch and sauntered toward him. He and Jessica, a water witch, had been having a nice little affair for the last couple of weeks. She was just coming off a bad divorce and looking to play a little in her newfound freedom. Jess didn't view him as relationship material, just fucking material. That was fine with him. She wanted to sow some post-divorce wild oats and he was reaping the harvest.

Normally water and fire, as far as witchy relationships went, didn't work well. Water and earth had an affinity. So did fire and air, but the Coven could count all the known air witches on two hands and most of them, with the exception of Jack's wife, Mira, weren't very powerful. In his and Jessica's case, since it was all about sex, it really didn't matter.

Adam loved it when it was all about sex. In fact, it was the only kind of relationship he did.

She brought her lips—ruby red, glossy—an inch from his. Her gaze flicked out the window. "It's very chilly tonight. I thought instead of going out"—her hand strayed between his thighs to cup his cock against her palm—"we could just stay in, order some food, have it delivered. We can . . . keep each other warm."

He put his hands on her shoulders and pressed his body against her. "Honey, I need a shower."

"Oh," she pouted. "I need your hands on me now." She caressed him and he tipped his head back on a groan. His cock was swelling under the stroke of her fingers. She bit her lower lip. "I'll wash you later and make it worth the wait."

Adam raised a brow even as he lowered his mouth to meet hers. "Okay, baby, then let's see how dirty we can get."

USING HER MAGICK, EVEN THOUGH SHE'D EMPLOYED just a minute amount, had made Claire ill. Or perhaps it was the drugs they'd been pumping her full of. Maybe it was both.

When she'd regained consciousness she'd wanted to die for about four hours. Luckily, most of the negative side effects had passed and she'd regained her will to live.

Claire didn't know if it was the elium in her that had made her sick or if it was the drugs. She only knew that nausea was her constant companion, along with a head-splitting migraine. Her cognitive processes were sluggish and dull.

And apparently, no air witch had heard her call.

Perhaps Rue had made an error and sent her to some alternate version of Earth, one in which no *aeamon* existed. But that would mean Rue had made a mistake and Rue didn't make mistakes. Surely, there had to be some witches around. After all, the *daaeman* had bred them themselves when they mated with humans eons ago. By now they should have comprised a large portion of the population.

Maybe, for whatever reason, they didn't. Maybe that's why they were underground, a secret. Maybe that's why none of the humans knew about them and why they thought Claire was a raving lunatic.

"Let's talk more about the demons, Claire," said a doctor in a charcoal gray suit.

Houses, she was beginning to hate all doctors.

Claire shifted in the uncomfortable chair. She'd spent most of the last couple of days drugged. This was the first time she'd felt truly lucid and the first time she'd been able to plead her case to someone in charge.

She folded her hands in her lap and looked up at him with an even stare. "I told you, Dr. Charnowski, I don't believe in demons."

Claire knew he could ferret out a lie with her body language and she was definitely lying.

He tipped his silvered head to the side. "Then why were you found screaming about them on the street? We tested you for drugs and found none, so there has to be another reason."

She nibbled the edge of her thumb. "I was . . . going through a bad time, Doctor." She glanced at him from under her lashes.

Claire understood she had to act like the sane person she was, a sane person who didn't believe in demons or witches. She needed to play the system if she was going to get out of this place.

The *Atrika* were probably outside the hospital, waiting for her. She needed to get out of here before they tried to break in and get her. Between these walls, without her magick, she was even more defenseless than she'd been on the streets.

Claire continued her lie. "My boyfriend had just tried to kill me. He was chasing me! I was confused, frightened. I guess, I guess . . . I thought he was a demon."

Doctor Charnowski sighed and set his tablet and pen on his desk. "I understand that sort of trauma can be disorienting, but you suffered a strong delusion if the witnesses are to be believed." He pressed his lips together. "Look, I'd like to be able to release you, Claire, but you won't give us your last name and your fingerprints turn up absolutely nothing in the database. And with this delusion you had . . ."

She leaned forward. "Please, Doctor, I just want to be able to get on with my life. I'm fine."

"Yes, but what life, Claire? It's like you're a ghost in the system."

Should she choose this time to tell him the truth? *Well, actually, Doctor, I'm from an alternate dimension, one where* daaeman *rule. There I have a blossoming career as the handmaiden to the* Cae. *I'm an earth witch, you see, but like none you've ever seen because my magick has been twisted and subverted by my master. I'm like a human guinea pig . . . except I'm not human. Not completely.*

Yes, that would buy her permanent residence on floor eight here at Stroger Hospital she had no doubt. These humans only believed what they could touch and see. There was no room in their minds for anything beyond the mundane.

She only stared at him stonily.

He clasped his hands together. "Look, I understand that you're afraid of your boyfriend. You have reason. We can help protect you. Just, please, help us out a little. Tell us who to contact. You must have family, friends. *Someone* to care for you."

She jerked her gaze away. She had no one. No one anywhere. Not on this Earth, not on Eudae. She was completely, crushingly alone. The emptiness that existed in her chest grew a little wider, a little blacker, with the reminder.

After a moment, Dr. Charnowski sighed. "Fine, Claire, have it your way. A judge has issued a commitment order. You're staying here until we can determine whether or not you're a threat to yourself or others."

Later in her bed, after they'd locked the door and turned out the lights and her roommate lay moaning in the bed beside hers, Claire reached into herself one more time and parsed out a thread of the twisted, heavy magick. She could not take any of her own now without it being tangled with Rue's *daaeman* magick.

This time she did it deliberately. After all, the last time she'd pulled it she hadn't died, she'd just almost died. If she didn't risk it again, she'd perish here anyway.

Immediately, her gorge rose. She lurched to the side and brought up her lunch of spaghetti and Jell-O onto the polished hospital floor even as she used the magick to broadcast a thought to any air witch able to hear her. This time she'd make it more complete.

Please . . . I need help. My name is Claire and I'm at . . .

FOUR

ADAM SAT IN THE LIBRARY, ALSO THE ROOM THAT Thomas had adopted as his office, watching Mira pace in front of Thomas's desk with Eva in a brightly colored sling around her shoulders.

"All of them heard it, Thomas," said Mira. "Every last one of the air witches in the Coven heard her plea, down to Molly, who just has a bare whisper of power." There were only three, not including baby Eva.

Thomas sat back in his chair and rubbed his chin. "It doesn't seem possible that Claire could be this side of the doorway."

Adam stood. "Boss, a year ago it didn't seem possible a demon was running around on Earth killing witches either. We need to go check this out."

"It could be a trap. We haven't heard from Stefan or the Duskoff for months. This seems like just another way to draw us out. We need to contact Darren and Eleanor and find out if they've noticed anything out of the ordinary."

The Chicago coven was the largest of the covens and ruled all of the United States, but there were two smaller covens, too. The one on the West Coast, located in San Francisco, was headed by Eleanor Pickens. Darren Westcott led the East Coast coven in Boston.

"Regardless, we owe it to Claire to investigate," Isabelle put in. She sat on the edge of Thomas's desk, the only one in the Coven able to do that and not be dismembered. "You would have died on Eudae if it wasn't for her intervention."

"I'm aware of my debts, Isabelle. I just don't want to go into this half-assed. We need to plan."

"Look," said Adam, coming forward. "Out of all of us, I have the least personal history with the Duskoff, and I used to be a cop. I'm probably the best one to go in. You create a distraction and I'll get her. If I'm stopped, I can play it off."

Isabelle jerked. "You used to be a cop?"

He grinned. "One of Chicago's finest, and I wasn't even corrupt." Adam averted his gaze. "That was a long time ago, though."

He could feel the weight of Isabelle's stare. They'd become good friends, he and Isabelle, but he didn't talk much about his past, not to anyone. Thomas was almost the only one at the Coven who knew the whole story.

Eva squalled and Mira bounced her a little to quiet her. "I don't think this was the Duskoff. Neither do any of the other air witches. Even Eva heard it. She woke up from a sound sleep and started to cry. It had a strange magick behind it."

"Strange magick?" asked Thomas. "What did it feel like?"

"Odd. Foreign." Mira shook her head of long dark hair and screwed up her face. "Like nothing I've ever felt before. I can't even describe it."

"Almost like earth magick, but . . . twisted?"

Mira nodded. "Yeah, *yeah* . . . exactly. *Waaaay* twisted. Really, only a breath of earth. The rest was just *off*." She paused, thinking. "I could taste a little water and fire, and air, of course . . . but that's not possible."

Thomas surged to his feet. "It's Claire. It's got to be. However impossible that she should be lost on this side of the doorway without Rue around. I became very acquainted with her flavor of magick last spring when I was trapped on Eudae."

Adam stepped forward. "So let me go get her."

"Yes," said Thomas, "and we'll take Theo. He's got some

experience with trauma and Claire's got to be traumatized if she'd been thrown to Earth the way it sounds she has."

"Theo's not exactly the best with personal relationships," Adam replied.

"Yeah, I know, but he's strong as hell. He comes."

THE LIGHTS FLICKERED AND DIMMED. CLAIRE SAT straight up in the chair of her hospital room, panic shooting through her. Beyond the walls of her quarters, the normal sounds of the ward intensified. The lights dimmed once more and shouting reached her ears.

Claire rose from her chair. She was alone in her room. Where they'd taken her roommate the Patrons of the Four Houses only knew.

A fine tremble had begun in her limbs. Were the *Atrika* already making their move? Or had her magick-laced plea for the attention of the witches fallen upon the ears of the air-inclined as she'd meant? It seemed too soon for the latter. She'd only sent her message the night before. Certainly, they couldn't be so close or mount a rescue so soon. Not if they were small in number and as weak as she was beginning to suspect.

By all the Houses, she hoped she was wrong.

Hope flickered and she quashed it. She couldn't afford to hope. She had to be ready for the worst to come through that door if she wanted to survive.

She glanced around, finding nothing she could use as a weapon. Her captors were careful to leave her room clear of such items. The only thing available to her was her tray from this morning's disgusting breakfast of runny oatmeal, dry toast, and thin orange juice served from a chemically flavored plastic cup.

Food here—with the exception of the golden cakes—was even worse than the military *daaeman* breed fare she'd grown up on. *Marzaan* was a standard gruel containing all the nutrients she needed to be healthy . . . except actual flavor.

She flipped everything off the tray and ran to the door.

The lights flickered again. The lock on her door buzzed and her fingers tightened around the tray. The knob turned and the door cracked ajar. Her skin prickled at the presence of *other.* Not completely human, whoever it was coming through. Not a nurse. Not a guard or a doctor.

The door opened enough to admit a human-sized individual and Claire stepped forward, swinging. It hit something solid with a clang. The lights flickered again.

"Ow!"

Gripping the tray, Claire backed away. *Daaeman* rarely said *ow*, especially not *Atrika*.

The door pushed all the way open and a tall, broad man staggered forward holding a hand to his head. "I'm on your side, damn it." He pulled his hand away from his face. A red mark had bloomed in the center of his forehead. "Claire, right?"

She nodded. *Aeamon.* That's what he was. She could feel it now. A fire witch.

His hair was blond and stood up in spikey tufts around his head. His nose had been broken many times. Or maybe it had been broken once, badly, and had never mended right. It sat crooked in an otherwise attractive face along with dark blue eyes and a pair of expressively full lips. He wore a long black leather coat and had a black bag slung over one broad shoulder.

This man was the complete opposite of Thomas's dark, brooding handsomeness. Thomas was the first *aeamon* male she'd seen in . . . well, *ever* and was the measuring stick by which she judged all others.

Response stuck in her throat, she dropped the tray to her side. Smoke curled from beyond the doorframe. Apparently, he'd simply melted the lock on the door.

He held out a hand like she was a wild animal. "Thomas, you remember him, right? He and another earth witch are busy unleashing an arsenal of earth witchy things to create diversions all over this floor. They sent me to get you. Fire magick in a hospital is never a good thing. You coming, or have you grown to like this place?"

She glanced around and shivered. Dropping the tray to the bed, she took his hand. His grip was strong and warmed her cold skin. It was the kind of touch she immediately wanted to trust, to allow to comfort her. It proved how badly she needed someone to rely on right now. However, in her position, such inclinations were dangerous.

They exited the room and stepped into the deserted hallway. The soft-soled shoes they'd given her made no sound on the slick, patterned floor. Voices, raised in alarm, carried over the sound of malfunctioning equipment filtered dully from behind thick closed doors.

He led her toward the reception desk and the bank of elevators at the end of the corridor. "So, do you speak or have they stolen your voice?"

She shot him a look of annoyance. "I can speak. Where is everyone?"

"Distracted. Thomas and Theo are creating problems with the electrical wiring. Just the lighting on this floor, the computers, and some of the nonessential equipment." He glanced at her. "They're not doing anything to machines that keep people alive. It's just enough to have everyone worried about what the hell is going on. Keeps them out of the corridors so we can get you out of here unseen."

She shrugged. "As far as I can tell, there's no one on life support on this floor. Only us crazy people."

"Yeah, that's why we're here. We know you're not crazy, Claire."

"I don't know about that. This world would make anyone insane," she mumbled.

He laughed. It was a rich, rolling sound that made her warm. She hadn't been truly warm since before Rue had pushed her through the doorway.

They approached the elevators and Claire caught sight of Thomas. He looked healthy and strong, so different from the last time she'd seen him when he'd been standing in front of the doorway, holding off three *Ytrayi daaeman*, and begging her to jump with him. Back then, his hair had been shorn close to his head, his eyes had been hollow, and his powerful body grim and gaunt. His hair was still short, but his body was once again powerful.

Beside him stood a darker-skinned man, broad and tall as Thomas. His hair fell past his shoulders and pulsed with a power she could feel even from twenty feet away. Tattoos peeked from beneath the long sleeves of his shirt and Claire could feel that they, too, had been imbued with power. That marked him right away as a fellow earth witch.

Just as she pulled from Adam to run to Thomas—the only familiar face she'd seen since being pushed into this world—the elevator doors opened and Tevan stepped out.

She stopped short, shock coursing sharp and bitter through her body.

She shouldn't have been surprised. Tevan had been drawn by the pulse of magick on this floor, no doubt. Thomas, Adam, and Theo had to be expelling a lot of power to keep these humans behind doors for so long. In the melee, that possibility had escaped her.

Thomas and the others hadn't known what they were walking into, of course. They hadn't known their magick would draw the *daaeman*. They'd simply been focused on getting her out.

Thomas stared at Claire for half a second, then yelled, "Go! Go, Adam! Get her out of here!"

FIVE

CHAOS EXPLODED.

Thomas whirled toward Tevan in combat position even as Adam yanked Claire back hard against him.

Apparently, the tearful reunion would have to wait.

Claire stumbled back and around, watching Adam reach to the nape of his neck and pull a copper blade from the sheath apparently concealed under his long coat. Thomas and Theo had done the same.

Tevan would have his hands full, whether or not he'd ingested the caplium that would make him partially immune to the bite of copper. Claire had taught Thomas how to wield his magick to get it past an *Atrika*'s shields.

"Come on, honey, we've got to go," Adam ground out as he pulled her down the corridor. "Thomas will have my ass on a platter if I don't keep you safe and a fucking *Atrika* demon just fixed his beady red eyes on you with murderous intent."

Claire glanced back at Thomas and the other witch, Theo. They'd engaged with the *daaeman* right there by the reception desk. By all Four Houses, she wanted to use her magick! She hated that she was vulnerable and powerless as any common human right now.

Just like the ones who would soon be spilling out into the corridors as a result of the earth magick no longer being focused on keeping them behind doors. "But what about—"

Adam yanked her down the corridor with a strength she couldn't fight, cutting off her sentence. Clearly, she wouldn't be around to see the looks on the humans' faces if this fire witch had anything to do with it.

Together they ran to the end of the corridor, turned right, and bolted out a pair of double doors with a flashing red sign above it that read EMERGENCY EXIT. Yes, this was an emergency.

They pounded their way down flight after flight of stairs, their footsteps echoing through the stairwell. Adam kept her hand tight in his and gripped the sword handle in his opposite hand.

"What about the humans?" she panted at Adam. "They're going to start coming out of the rooms, into the corridors."

"Yeah, I know. We don't ordinarily open cans of magickal whoop ass where the normals can see. In this case, I don't know. Thomas and Theo will do their best, but it depends more on that *Atrika* than anything else. I doubt the demon cares much if he's seen."

"He does. I don't know why but they don't want attention drawn to themselves. I noticed I was safe whenever I was around humans." She paused, remembering the diner. "Well, mostly."

"That's good. We'll take any advantage we've got at this point."

At the bottom of the stairs, he guided her into a corner and carefully opened the door. Apparently, he found the other side *Atrika*-free because he sheathed his weapon. He threw her the bag draped over his shoulder. "In there you'll find a change of clothes and a wig. Go on and change."

Breathing hard more of pure fear than physical exertion, she doffed her pajama top immediately.

"Oh, fuck," Adam breathed. He turned around.

She wasn't wearing any undergarment beneath.

Oops.

Claire finished dressing, remembering belatedly that Earth customs were different than Eudae customs. Her mother had explained that to her before she'd died. "I apologize, but now is not the time for modesty." She threw her hospital clothing into a corner, having shed all of it but the soft slippers.

Adam turned back around, a grin spread across his mouth. "Did I say I minded?"

Claire's cheeks warmed and she crammed the blond wig over her head. It covered her long, curly dark hair.

She could have forgotten to dress every day on Eudae, walked around naked all the time, and the *Ytrayi daaeman* would never have given her more than a cursory glance. It wasn't that they didn't view her in a sexual way; it was more that they respected her female status in such a formal, regimented way that they would never allow their libidos to get out of control. They would never note their arousal or comment on her beauty out loud. She'd been totally safe from them.

It was important to remember that *aeamon* males were different. They would view her in a way the *Ytrayi* didn't—as a sexual possibility—and did not, by all accounts, have the same restraint and discipline an *Ytrayi* had.

That was something to get used to. Something important to remember.

He grabbed her hand and opened the door a crack again. "Okay, come on. We have to get out of this building. Hell's breaking loose." Adam pulled her along behind him as he slipped out into the corridor beyond the door.

Two policemen bustled down the hallway past them toward the elevators, hands on their service revolvers.

"Thomas said to go out the emergency room exit if we got split up." Adam steered her down a corridor past people in wheelchairs and on gurneys who were accompanied by nurses and doctors.

They made their way through the emergency room waiting area. Claire got an eyeful: there was a woman with a bloody leg, a flushed, tired-looking child, and a man holding his stomach among the waiting throng. Adam guided her out a pair of automatic sliding doors and into the blessedly fresh air.

A shiny silver vehicle pulled in front of them, tires squealing. The dark earth witch, Theo, sat in the front seat. Thomas drove.

"Get in quick," Theo commanded.

Adam opened the back door, pushed her in, and quickly

followed her. She ended up with her cheek to the leather upholstery and Adam's big body pinning hers as Thomas sped away.

The fire witch helped her sit up and she found herself tucked against his side, his arm around her. His heat calmed her, so she didn't move away.

Thomas glanced at her in the rearview mirror. "Hi, Claire." His gaze was warm, affectionate. Like a brother's.

Her heart plummeted to her toes and she realized she still nursed, way deep down, a little flame for this man. Stupid. She knew all too well his heart belonged to another.

Claire reached out and fingered his blacker-than-obsidian hair. In spite of everything, she grinned. "It's growing back in."

"Everything broken heals. It's good to see you."

Her grin broadened. "Well, that's a lie."

"Okay," he amended with the shrug of one broad shoulder and a disarming smile flashing in the rearview mirror. "I'd prefer it be under different circumstances." He paused. "What are you doing Earth-side and can you tell me why we just had to evade two *Atrika* demons, Claire?"

She drew a breath, pulled the blond wig from her head, and told him everything that had happened to her in the last forty-eight hours.

"I can't use my magick," she finished. "Rue gave me this ball of . . . this . . . this power that the *Atrika* want so badly and then pushed me through the doorway. I don't know how to wield this *daaeman* magick yet. I think it's a weapon called the elium and it could kill me or those around me if I try. I only used my own magick in the hospital to reach out to air witches out of pure desperation." She twisted the fake hair in her lap. "You remember how hard it was to kill one *Atrika*—"

"Now there are two Earth-side."

She nodded.

"But no more. If Rue crashed the doorway, that means no more than two came through. At least there's that."

Claire raised her gaze to meet Thomas's in the mirror for a moment. "Rue crashed the doorway, which means no one comes through . . . or goes back. Not until he gets it up again, which is time-consuming and difficult to do." She pressed her lips together. "If he's still alive."

"We know how hard it is to create a doorway, Claire. We've been trying to do that for the last eleven months, to pull you through." She started in surprise, but Thomas went on. "I know you declined to come back with me, Claire, but you looked uncertain about your decision to stay."

She dipped her head and studied her jean-clad knee. "I was afraid to leave the life I knew, but a part of me did want to return with you that night."

"I thought so."

"Fear won," she finished, swallowing hard. "I missed the Earth I remembered, but I was afraid to leave Eudae."

He met her gaze in the rearview mirror. "And now here you are, despite your fear."

"Yes."

"Were you punished for helping me escape, Claire?"

That night was burned into her memory. She'd spent weeks nursing Thomas through the torture Rue had inflicted on him, weeks planning his escape. On the night her plans had come to fruition and she'd helped Thomas from his cell to the portal chamber, the *Ytrayi* had discovered her betrayal. There had been a battle, but she'd taught Thomas how to fight *daaeman* with his elemental earth magick and they'd fought their way down the corridors of Yrystrayi successfully.

She'd betrayed the *Ytrayi* out of allegiance to the *aeamon*, because she was one. She'd done it to show Rue she was not *his*, that he'd never broken her and shouldn't take her for granted. She'd done it to show the *Ytrayi* she *could* do it, to prove her strength to them. Finally, she'd done it in honor of the love Thomas and Isabelle shared.

"Yes, I was punished, but not badly." She reflected. "Well, it was bad enough. Rue hobbled me magickally for six months."

Thomas glanced at her in the mirror. "But they didn't hurt you? I was very concerned they'd hurt you physically."

She shook her head. "Rue would never allow me to come to harm, no matter how dire my crime." Claire paused. "Until now, anyway."

"You're valuable to Rue, aren't you?"

She shrugged a shoulder. "I'm a magickal oddity on Eudae. A diversion, an . . . entertainment for him."

"What, like a pet?" Adam growled beside her.

"No, I'm more than that. I'm a servant, his handmaiden, but Rue has some emotional attachment to me. I am his property, though."

Adam's arm tightened around her. "Not anymore you aren't."

The realization that she was now free hadn't registered until that moment. Lightness flared briefly in her chest right before the sentiment crashed straight to her toes.

She shook her head. "Rue will come for me." She paused and drew a breath. "I remain his property."

Theo spoke for the first time as he turned toward her. "We need to deal with the *Atrika* demons first. Then we'll think of how to handle your keeper." He bared his teeth briefly, making Claire think he probably already had some idea of what he wished to do with Rue. "But you're only property if you choose to be." He turned back around.

"The *Atrika* will come after me with a vengeance," said Claire. "They can scent me from a long distance because of the nature of my magick. They also freely use blood magick, unlike the *Ytrayi*. I don't know much about blood magick, but they may have access to a tracking spell."

Thomas glanced at her in the mirror. "That's why we're running. *Right now*. When we've put some distance between ourselves and these guys, we'll stop and regroup, figure out where to go from there."

"What? We?" Claire leaned forward. "No, Thomas. I will not allow you to become more involved in this than you already are. What about Isabelle? You need to protect her from the threat I've brought with me."

Adam snorted.

Thomas met her gaze in the mirror. "Protect Isabelle? Clearly, you've never met my wife. Isabelle knows how much we owe you, Claire. She'd skin me alive for not doing all I could to keep you safe."

Adam laid his hand flat against her back. The heat of his palm radiated through her shirt and into her skin. "It's not safe for you to go it alone."

She turned wild eyes toward him. "It's not safe for Isabelle! Or for anyone because of me."

"Because of Rue, not you, Claire." Thomas's hand tightened a degree on the steering wheel. "I've warned the Coven already. Those who are vulnerable to a possible attack have already left the building. Jack, Mira, and the baby, for example. I told Isabelle to go, too."

"Think she listened?" Adam's mouth curved in a smile.

Thomas glanced in the mirror. "You know Isabelle. Anyway, the *Atrika* are hunting Claire. They're not going to the Coven, so everyone there is safe. They're coming straight at us."

She flopped back against the seat. "Stop the car immediately. I'm getting out. I didn't save you on Eudae to send you back to Isabelle only to have you killed by an *Atrika* here."

"Claire," said Thomas in a steel-backed voice. "I'm not arguing with you about this."

She jerked her chin at Theo and Adam. "I suppose both of you have loved ones, too?"

Theo just stared straight ahead and said nothing. Adam looked down at his shoes. Neither of them answered.

"No?" She jerked her hand out. "Well, then, fine. These two are expendable. They can help me get free of the *Atrika*. *You*, Thomas, as head of the Coven most certainly are *not* expendable and shouldn't be anywhere near me right now."

Adam frowned. "Expendable? I'm not sure I—"

Claire leaned forward, gesturing. "I will not be responsible for putting your people's head mage in harm's way. I will not argue about *that* with you, Thomas."

"I actually agree with her," said Theo.

The car went silent. Seemed that this one didn't speak often, but when he did, people listened.

Theo continued. "I believe what she's suggesting is a wise course of action. Adam and I can take her out of Chicago, away from the demons hunting her. You can go back and protect the Coven. They need your leadership now more than ever, Thomas."

"Exactly." Claire sat back with a huff of breath. She cared too much about Thomas to see him in danger's path now, and she wouldn't be the one to put him there.

Thomas's fingers tightened to whiteness on the steering wheel.

"I don't exactly think Theo and I are *expendable*." Adam shot her a glance laced with icicles. "But I have to say that Claire and Theo have a point. We don't need you anyway, boss. Theo and I are totally capable of making sure Claire stays safe."

Thomas glanced up into the rearview mirror at the phrase, *we don't need you anyway*, his lips compressing. "Against two *Atrika* demons?"

Adam leaned forward, a mischievous grin flashing over his mouth. "We all know you're a micromanager and a control freak. Everyone says you need to start trusting your people more. Now's the perfect opportunity."

"I do trust you and Theo." He glowered. "And I'm not a micromanager or a control freak."

The entire vehicle went silent. Beside her, Adam coughed.

"Don't forget the Duskoff," said Theo finally. "Don't ever forget about them. Who knows what's going on here exactly? Who knows whether they're involved or not? You need to stay at the Coven, Thomas. Let me and Adam handle the woman."

"Don't call me *woman*." Claire glared at the back of Theo's head. "I have a name."

Adam leaned close to her. "He has issues with things like normal social interaction."

Well, she did, too, but she still managed to remember people's names.

"Fuck," Thomas swore under his breath. Claire detected a note of defeat in his voice. "You take this car. You take my Coven ATM card. You withdraw a ton of cash and only use that for whatever you do. No credit cards. No paper trail. We don't know what kind of resources or Earth-savvy these demons have yet or whether or not the Duskoff is involved. Keep your head down. Hear me?"

"We hear you, Daddy," Adam answered.

"Head to the Twin Cities," Thomas added.

Adam raised his head. "To Jack's place in Minneapolis?"

Thomas shook his head. "No. To a heavily warded safe house in Saint Paul. For now. Until we figure out what's going on."

Adam gave him a strange look. "Wards don't work on demons. Nothing works on demons."

"Yes, but we don't know yet if the Duskoff are involved."

"Good point. I didn't know we had any safe houses there."

"The Coven keeps at least one in all the major cities. They double as investment properties." Thomas glanced at Adam. "It's heavily insured, so if you have to torch the place, you can, but try not to, okay?"

Adam held up his hands. "Hey, boss, you know me."

"Yeah, I do."

Thomas guided the car into the parking lot of a long building where people went in and out with plastic and paper bags. While Thomas did something in the front of the vehicle, Claire gawked at her surroundings.

Adam caught her eye, probably catching her staring. "We're northwest of the city. Lots of suburbs. This is a shopping mall. People come here to buy things."

"Oh, like a marketplace."

"Sort of. They sell clothing, furniture, and other household things here. Not food."

"Ah." She stared out the window at the passersby. "On Eudae the women make most everything for the home and for decoration. They are the artisans in that world." She tried to keep the note of wistfulness out of her voice.

Eudae was the only home she'd ever known and she felt a bit sick for it, brutal and cold though it had been at times. These *aeamon* wouldn't understand her feelings, since the *daaeman* were their enemies.

Only the *Atrika* were her enemy. Not the rest. Not the other breeds. Yes, she might harbor some resentment for the *Ytrayi* and for Rue in particular, but her feelings were mixed. They were, after all, the only people she'd ever really known or identified with.

"Micah would love to talk to you sometime," Adam said, interrupting her thoughts.

"Who is Micah?"

"He's the Coven archivist and general all-around knowledge manager. He's the one who has been spearheading the efforts to open a doorway and rescue you these past months. Micah is fascinated with all aspects of demon culture, and you're a direct source. The texts he's got are useful, but aren't complete. Especially when it comes to modern-day culture on Eudae."

She fingered the hem of her shirt. "I would be happy to speak with him sometime."

Thomas turned and handed a folded piece of paper to Adam. "I hope you can speak to Micah in person soon, Claire. For the time being, it's time for you all to get going. Go far. Go fast. All the information you need is on that sheet." He slipped a small rectangular disk from his wallet. "ATM card. I'm out of here." He opened the door and exited the vehicle.

Claire quickly got out, too, and threw herself into Thomas's arms as Adam took the wheel. She buried her face in his chest. "Thank you." The words came from the bottom of her being.

Thomas dropped a kiss on the crown of her head. "No, Claire. You have nothing to thank me for. You saved my life. Now I'm just trying to return the favor."

He released her and strode away, pulling a small black object from his pocket, pressing a button and talking into it.

Claire stood for a moment outside the car, letting the breeze buffet her hair. She stared down the strange street they'd traveled on, watching strange people and smelling strange smells.

Were the *daaeman* on their trail even now?

Dumb question. Of course they were.

SIX

Somewhere near the exit signs for the House on the Rock in Wisconsin, that's when the *Atrika* caught up with them.

Adam was driving while Theo rode shotgun. It was strange seeing Theo in a car, since he normally drove a bike—a Harley Night Rod, to be exact. He looked uncomfortable in something with four wheels, like he had a touch of claustrophobia.

Claire was drowsing in the backseat, her black curls tumbling around her heart-shaped face. She sat up and gasped, "They're behind us."

There could only be one *they're* she could be referring to. Damn, dirty demons.

"I thought we lost them. How did they catch up with us?" She turned around, staring down the black highway behind them. Her accent was odd, overly rounded vowels and flat consonants. It was unlike anything he'd ever heard before.

He caught her gaze in the mirror and narrowed his eyes. "How do you know they're behind us?"

She drew her full lower lip between her teeth. They hadn't had much in the way of orthodontics on Eudae, but her teeth were pretty naturally straight anyway. "I can feel them, like a

tingle in the center of me. It's Rue's magick maybe. The elium."
She shook her head violently, curls flying. "There's so much
about this magick I don't understand yet. I need a quiet place to
explore it."

"Hey, it's okay." He tried to calm the edge of panic in her
voice. "Just answer me one thing. Do you think they can track
you magickally?"

She thought for a moment. "No. I don't think so. I'm actually not totally sure what they can do with blood magick, but
if it was that easy to track me they would've found me in
Chicago before the police brought me to the hospital." She bit
her lip again. "Although I did move around a lot, so . . . I'm
not sure."

"Well, we're about to find out. Hold on." He swerved toward
an exit at the last minute and gunned the engine hard. Beside
him, Theo grabbed the armrest. All the cars behind them, save a
black SUV, passed the exit.

Seeing no other cars and none of the ever-vigilant Wisconsin patrolmen in sight, he ignored the stop sign at the top of the
ramp and guided the vehicle down a small two-lane road into
the hills. Evergreens whipped past in the glow of the headlights.
Evening had settled not long before.

The trees didn't lack for water, Adam could feel it. Fire
witches were always hyperaware of their surroundings and
how well a place would burn. This area had received a lot of
water lately. That was good. He didn't want to use fire against
the demons, but if it came down to it he didn't have to worry
about starting a forest fire.

"Adam." Claire's voice quivered.

Adam pushed the accelerator almost to the floor. The trees
flew faster.

"Adam!"

He looked in the rearview mirror. Claire's blue eyes were
wide, her already pale face paler, and her lips compressed.
Every muscle in her body seemed taut as she stared at the road
in front of them. "What is it?"

Theo shifted in his seat. "This is probably only the second
time the woman's ever been in a car and you're trying to break
the land speed record."

The black dot in his rearview was getting bigger. His gaze

flicked to Claire. "I'm sorry. You can have a panic attack when we're free of these guys, okay?"

She dragged her gaze to his and forced her jaw to unlock. "It's fine. Do what you have to do."

He did. Slowing down just enough not to tip the car, he took a corner fast and hard. Thank the gods for remote parts of Wisconsin. Where they were now was blessedly uninhabited.

They breezed past a motel that would have been a great set for a horror movie and then more trees. As soon as Adam found the right spot, he slowed and guided the car off road.

"Are you all right?" He glanced at Claire.

"Better." Her face was green, belying her answer.

He went slowly now, over huge bumps that knocked his teeth together and enduring the branches scraping the paint off Thomas's Mercedes S550. Finally, he was deep enough in to not be seen. He hoped. Adam turned off the headlights and cut the engine.

He shifted, fingers itching to hold his sword, which he'd stashed behind the front seat. Honestly, going head-to-head with two demons right now was not the wisest course of action. They weren't ready to face creatures who could regenerate limbs, heal almost any wound, and had almost zero vulnerabilities . . . not yet.

It was best to hope that the *Atrika* passed them by, gave them time to plan and prepare. That didn't stop Adam from wanting action, though. Like Thomas had wanted it. Like Theo wanted it. Now Theo sat hunched over in his seat, fists clenched, jaw locked.

But sometimes good sense had to win out over testosterone.

He adjusted the mirror to reflect into the backseat. There, Claire took deep, measured breaths with her eyes closed. For being plunked down into an alien world and into a life-or-death situation simultaneously, Adam thought she was doing exceptionally well.

He let his gaze trace the curve of her cheek. She was brave. Pretty, too, in an unconventional way. She wore no makeup to speak of and, by the looks of her creamy, clear complexion, probably never had. Her dark hair hung to her narrow shoulders in a tangle of natural curl. Her face was heart-shaped, chin coming to a sharp little point. A long—nearly too long for attractiveness—nose sat atop a nicely shaped mouth, bottom lip much fuller than the top.

Adam noticed women. All the time.

Even when he'd been deeply and insanely in love with his wife, he'd noticed them. He'd never been unfaithful in his life, but no woman escaped his eye. Claire was very attractive in a pixielike way. She was small, which made him instantly want to protect her.

His stomach tightened. He wondered what she'd had to endure in her life. It couldn't have been easy to survive as the only elemental witch on Eudae.

Her eyes popped open to find his in the rearview mirror. Their gazes caught, locked. Adam almost fell into the power of her blue eyes. Oh, there was a lot to this woman . . . much more than he'd seen so far.

"They're near," she whispered. Her voice in the quiet sent a shiver up his spine.

Theo straightened and Adam snapped to attention, glimpsing the slow-moving headlights of a car on the road behind them, just barely visible through the foliage.

"Fuck," he murmured. They were trolling for them. The demons knew they'd gone to ground. The car rolled slowly past and he let out the breath of air he'd been holding.

Then the car stopped.

Claire turned in her seat to watch through the leaves. They could see nothing but swatches of light, but the low idle of the SUV's engine reached their ears.

The vehicle backed up a little and halted on the road parallel to their position.

"Out," said Theo in his low, gravelly voice. "We need to get out now."

He was right, there was nowhere for Adam to move the car. He'd gone all in for this poker game, tried for a bluff. Apparently, he'd lost. "Yeah."

Quietly, they opened the doors and slid out. Claire grabbed their sword sheaths and handed them over to Adam and Theo once they were clear of the car. Behind them, the SUV's engine stopped.

Leaves and dead plant matter crunched under their feet as they made their way into the darkening gloom. The chill in the air kissed their skin and showed their breath white in the early spring air.

As they hunkered behind some brush, Claire shivered beside Adam. He channeled a little heat, the seat of his magick in the center of his chest pulsing a bit, and sent it through his arms, hands, and chest. Then he pulled Claire toward him, wrapping her in a close embrace. She stiffened against him at first and started to push away, but then melded to his body like warmed candle wax.

More footsteps on the winter dead Wisconsin ground. Demon footsteps. Growing nearer and nearer.

Motionless, Claire in his arms, Adam watched through the brush as the demons approached the car. One had his hand on the trunk. The other one, the tall blond one, was nearing the driver's side.

Pulling away from Claire, Adam stood and shot a fire bolt in the direction of the car's gas tank. It hit in a white-hot explosion.

Thomas's ninety-thousand-dollar car blew up, the demons along with it.

"Oh, *Houses*," Claire breathed, shooting up to stand beside him.

Adam didn't know what houses had to do with anything.

She cringed against him, covering her eyes from the brightness of the blaze, and Adam held her close, protecting the side of her head with his hand.

Theo's lips curved in a rare smile. "Nice shot. Don't know how the boss man will feel about it, but nice shot all the same."

Adam grinned cheerfully. "Thanks. Let's just hope those bozos left the keys in the SUV. Otherwise, we've got a long walk."

Theo's grin deepened. "No. I can hot-wire it."

Adam cast him a sidelong look and mocked, "Why Theodosius Winters, I declare! You shock me!"

Apparently, Theo's short stint of verbosity had come to an end. He simply strode forward, toward the crispy demons.

Adam and Claire followed. They had to get out of here before the fire was noticed.

As they skirted the vehicle, Adam increased the heat of the

fire. He wanted no trace of that car left to lead back to Thomas Monahan or the Coven.

"God's, demon magick is putrid," said Theo. "I had hoped to never again have that stink in my nose."

"You're not the only one," Adam answered.

Theo raised his hand, also expending magick to clear a ring around the sedan with his earth abilities. It ensured the fire couldn't jump to the nearby trees and bushes. True, this area had received a lot of moisture recently, but better safe than sorry.

The authorities would no doubt wonder about the strange ring, but humans were notorious for finding plausible answers for implausible occurrences.

The two demons had been thrown back in the explosion and now lay burned and smoking not far from the vehicle. Damn it. Adam had been sure they'd been mostly incinerated in the initial blast. One of the demon's legs was on fire. Both lay at unnatural angles, eyes open.

Maybe this whole thing would be over before it had even begun and they could get back to the Coven. Although they needed to do something with the bodies. Humans found answers for the implausible, sure, but if they decided to do an autopsy on these guys . . . There wasn't any explaining away acidic blood.

"They're not dead, Adam, even though they look it," said Claire as they passed. "They've gone into a type of coma that happens when their kind sustains a bad injury. They're regenerating right now and they'll soon recover."

Adam stopped short, remembering Thomas and Isabelle telling him of the motorcycle crash that Isabelle had initiated in an attempt to kill the last *Atrika*. Erasmus Boyle had lain prone on the road for a time, too—thought dead before he'd woken up and *poofed* Isabelle right out of Thomas's arms.

"Really? Fuck." He pushed a hand through his hair and tried to mask his disappointment. "That sucks. I guess thinking this could be over quick was too optimistic. The Terminator has nothing on these guys."

Claire just frowned at him. Pop culture references were a little lost on her.

He drew his sword from the sheath he carried. "Then let's make sure we give them a wound they can't recover from." He grinned. "These fuckers might be immortal, but I want to see one try to regrow its head. Theo, please take Claire to the SUV. I'll be right there."

Theo guided Claire away and Adam turned toward the prone demons. This wouldn't take long. Just a little chop here and one over there, heads would roll, and he would duck the spraying acidic blood. Then he would puke, and they could all go back to Chicago. It was a great plan.

Simple. Clean. Efficient. *Perfect.*

Sword grip clenched in his hand he approached the one whose leg was doing its best to burn to ash and tried not to gag from the stench of baked demon. Ironically, according to Micah's sources, *Atrika* loved the aroma of cooking *aeamon*. Probably serve it up with chutney and a nice white wine.

He stood near Demon One's head, feet spread, and readied his sword for a deathblow. The thing's blue eyes stared blankly up at him. He sure as fuck *looked* deceased. Adam raised his sword.

The thing blinked and his eyes focused on him. A hand snaked out and grabbed his leg.

Damn it! He'd betrayed a cardinal rule of horror movies and now he paid for it! Never go near the monster, even if it looked dead.

Adam brought his sword down fast and hard, but the demon let go of him and rolled to the side. His blade bit soil and dead leaves. From his left, movement caught his eye. The other demon was moving, too.

Damn short comas.

Tires slid on the ground behind him. He whirled to see the back door pop open and Claire, pale-faced, motioning to him. "Come on! Get in!"

His hands tightened on his sword and he looked back toward the creatures. The demon he'd tried to skewer growled and turned his head toward Adam. His eyes were glowing red. That meant the demon was in a killing rage. He remembered that clearly from the last *Atrika* he'd fought. The other one lurched to stand about four feet away, his lips curled back and fangs extended.

When were demons *not* in a killing rage?

"Adam!"

Demon One—the blond one—snarled.

SEVEN

OKAY, TIME TO GO.

Adam lunged for the backseat, careful not to spear Claire with his sword on the way in. Theo gunned the engine and the tires churned up the earth. Magick pulsed and they were out fast. Theo had altered the ground beneath the SUV to make sure they got out of there as soon as possible. Tires hit pavement, squealed, and they were off.

Adam lay crosswise in the seat, draped across Claire's lap. "Damn it!" He threw the sword to the floor of the vehicle. "Fuck!"

"We'll get them, Adam," said Theo. "We have to choose the time and place, though. You remember what the first one was like."

Adam pushed up to a sitting position with Claire's help. He ended up staring straight into her face about a breath's space from her mouth. Her eyes went a little wider and her breath hitched. He levered into a sitting position beside her.

"They were in a killing rage, the both of them," she said quietly. "I suspect strongly they have injected themselves with caplium by now, which protects them against their copper allergy. You could not have won against them alone, Adam. Not even with Theo's help."

"What is caplium anyway?"

"It's a mixture of ingredients, a cooked-up potion, essentially. I only know of it, not how to make it. The *Ytrayi* destroy the copper they find so caplium isn't something they use every day."

Adam stared out the window at the passing scenery. Theo was getting them back on the highway. "How do you kill these things?"

"What Isabelle did was right. Injecting copper straight into their bloodstream works, though it can be slow depending on how much caplium they've taken. Beheading works, blowing them to itty-bitty pieces works."

"Basically, utter destruction. Wounds they can't heal. They're immortal, the fucks. Why couldn't *we* have gotten a little of that genetic goodness, I ask you?" He rubbed his mouth. "Goddamn it, I need a cigarette." His fingers literally itched for one right now.

She nodded. "There are other defenses, magickal ones." She paused. "I need to get somewhere safe. I need to sift through this new power inside me. After I do that and can be sure how to wield my magick safely, then we will have a defense against them."

He turned his head and studied her in the dark car. "Getting you to a safe place is our top concern."

"Then you did the right thing back there. If you'd stayed to fight, you'd both be dead by now and they would have me."

"They want to extract that magick inside you?"

"You have a thing here, something called a coconut?"

"Yes."

"They want to crack me like a coconut and drink the milk within."

He grimaced. "That's vivid."

She shrugged a shoulder. "That's *true*. My magick is like the meat of the coconut, but whatever Rue gave me is the milk. The problem is that in places the milk has soaked into the meat. I need to examine those places, try to extract the milk and isolate it."

"They'd kill you trying to get out Rue's magick, wouldn't they?"

She twitched. "They will simply take bites of meat in order to get the milk. Yes, they would kill me." For a moment, she went silent, her head dropping a bit. "I don't know if there's a way to get the foreign magick out of me without killing me anyway."

"The theory of magick isn't really my strong suit, but we have Micah on our side. If anyone can figure out a way to do it, it'll be him."

She said nothing in response, so he reached out and took her fragile, warm hand in his. They sat in silence as Theo hit the highway. From the other direction, police cars and a fire engine zoomed toward the exit, sirens wailing. Someone had reported the fire.

The car they drove was undoubtedly stolen. Adam hadn't had a chance to check the plates, but he'd bet anything they were Illinois. The driver, he'd make a guess, was probably long since dead. They'd have to ditch this car soon and find another one. No way could they make it all the way to Minnesota in this one. Far too risky. Adam didn't say anything to Theo. He already knew what they had to do.

He glanced at Claire. Her fingers were still intertwined with his and their hands lay between them on the seat. "What was it like over there?"

She studied him in the darkness. "Eudae? Different. Less chaotic. Everything here seems big and . . . unwieldy. It's cold here and all the buildings are sharp." She looked out the window. "The people are sharp here, too, such a mass of emotional contradiction. Some are helpful, like you and Theo. Most . . ." She shook her head. "I can't generalize. I've only been here a few days."

"So things aren't . . . *sharp* on Eudae?"

"The *Atrika* are a horrid *daaeman* breed. The worst. They were made to be killing machines, soldiers for the ruling class. You must understand that the *Ytrayi* are a brutal breed, too, but their world is very ordered, very sane. There are certain protocols that are always followed, behaviors that are expected of them. They have little emotion, unlike the *Atrika*, so there is little unordered violence."

"I'm sorry but I don't understand."

She blew out a breath. "You know what to expect on Eudae, living with the *Ytrayi*. There aren't any surprises. When my mother and I came over—" Claire snapped her mouth shut and looked out the window.

Clearly, she didn't want to talk about that, but he wanted to hear more. "So I guess they don't have cars or TV over there."

"No cars. There's no need. They've mastered the art of dimensional travel."

"Ah. *Poofing*."

She looked at him. "*Poofing?*"

"That's what Isabelle calls it. When they open a mini doorway and travel to another location."

"They *jump*, yes." She pursed her lips. "We use the word *jump*, not . . . *poof*."

Wow, this woman needed to lighten up.

Claire turned to face forward, drawing her hand from his. "Entertainment isn't something the *Ytrayi* engage in. It's considered a waste of time and the *Ytrayi* don't waste time, *ever*. They do play sports sometimes, though. To hone their battle skills." She shivered. "I don't like to watch that."

Adam immediately remembered something Micah had said once about the Mayans and the ball game they used to play. The one in which the losers lost their heads . . . literally. "They almost sound primitive."

She made a scoffing sound. "Hardly. They are farther ahead in terms of technology than you are. They don't believe in frivolous entertainment, but they do appreciate fine art. The *Mandari* breed creates all sorts of sculptures, things that encompass energy, which make them shift and change periodically. The wall coverings in their homes do the same, change color and texture at their whim."

"Wow. That would make interior design a breeze."

Claire was not amused. "They typically own one outfit at a time. They have no need for more clothing because the fabric adjusts to temperature and need. It's keyed to the thought process and environment of the *daaeman*, always changing, always cleaning itself, always protecting with perfection the being within."

There was a note of pride in her voice and almost *wistful-ness*. Did she miss Eudae? It was the only home she'd ever known, yet she'd essentially been a slave there. Perhaps it was Stockholm syndrome.

"That sounds cool, Claire. How come you don't have clothes like that?"

She studied something in her lap. "*Aeamon* are not allowed such things."

He wasn't surprised. "We're considered inferior there." It wasn't a question. He already knew, both from his experience with Erasmus Boyle and from the research Micah was doing. "Boyle, the *Atrika* who tried to kill all of us last year, kept referring to *aeamon* and humans as cattle." He couldn't keep the note of tension from his voice.

"The *Ytrayi* are different than the *Atrika*. Please remember that. However, *aeamon* are still half-breeds, still considered of weaker blood. I was afforded respect because I am female and the *Atrika* honor females. Also because I was Rue's hand-maiden and there I was—"

"You mean like his slave?" The words lashed the air. Adam couldn't have held them back even if he'd wanted to.

"We will talk no more of this." Her voice trembled with anger. Claire leaned her head back and closed her eyes, signaling an end to their conversation.

ADAM KNELT BESIDE THE WOOD-BURNING FIRE-place in the safe house's living room and kindled a small flame in the dry branches until a fire caught and held.

They made it to the Coven safe house in the early morning hours. They'd left the SUV in Hudson right before crossing the bridge over the Saint Croix into Minnesota. From there they'd waited until morning and had taken a taxi to the Minneapolis International Airport, only to stave off suspicion. Then they'd taken another taxi to their destination.

It paid to be careful.

The house wasn't just any house. It was a million bucks easy. Located in the upscale neighborhood of Crocus Hill, it was a three-story renovated home that had probably been built sometime in the late eighteenth century. It was a Queen Anne Victorian with a spindled porch, two large windows flanking it. It even had a turret.

From Thomas Monahan and the Coven he should have expected no less. They'd probably bought this place when real estate here was cheap. Hell of an investment. Now he had a good idea of how the Coven had amassed its fortune.

It was a gorgeous piece of architecture and Eliza would have known more about that than he did. What little he knew came from her. She'd always been blabbing on about her work. She had loved being an architect. And, fuck, Eliza would have loved this house, too.

As soon as they'd pulled up to the structure thoughts of Eliza had crowded Adam's mind, eliminated all others and plunged him into a very dark place. He hated it when things reminded him of Eliza, yet every day something did.

Adam, Theo, and Claire spent the first day getting to know the house, putting their financials in order, buying food, and most importantly, finding a new car. They'd paid cash for a used 1970 Dodge Challenger that had been owned by a speed freak. The car's innards reflected it. They'd figured the ability to go fast wasn't such a bad thing. In fact, it was a priority.

It was pretty. In his book, it was prettier than the house. No way in hell was he blowing *that* car up.

The big question on everyone's minds was whether or not the demons could track them magickally. Tonight they'd probably find out.

Soon after they'd settled down for the evening, Claire procured one of the guest rooms on the main floor as an area to play with that bastard Rue's bundle of stashed joy. The elium.

Theo had retreated to the bedroom he'd chosen on the second floor for the night, his store of comaraderie apparently used up. He wasn't exactly an outgoing guy. Sparkly personality had passed him by when he was born. Or maybe it wasn't because of genes, but rather the ordeal he'd gone through when he'd been a teenager.

Theodosius Winters was one of the more powerful earth

witches that the Coven knew of. When Theo had been seventeen, the Duskoff had kidnapped him because of his strength.

The Duskoff did that sometimes, took more powerful witches when they were vulnerable in order to break them young and use them for their own purposes. If they were air witches, sometimes they used them in blood rituals or other really distasteful things.

A good rule of thumb was to never allow yourself to be taken by the warlocks.

In any case, they'd tortured Theo until he was almost dead, trying to break his spirit and turn him. They'd never succeeded and had intended to kill him. But the Coven had sent a rescue party, a young Thomas Monahan included, and broke him out before they could do that.

Theo hadn't escaped without being scarred, though, mentally and physically. He'd been in a psychiatric ward for a while after the hospital had discharged him. Eventually, he'd come to work for the Coven, having a special grudge against the Duskoff.

Deep furrows marked the skin of Theo's chest, shoulders, and back, probably made by a bullwhip. Adam had seen him bare from the waist up, seen how Theo had riffed off the scars with black tribal-like tattoos all over. The tats were charged with power the way earth witches stored it. Theo packed a lot of magick on him now—all kinds of spells he'd cooked up and stored. He was the Arnold Schwarzenegger of magick.

Adam knew Theo was itching for an *all-out* with the Duskoff, but these days the warlocks were nowhere to be found. At least, not the head honchos, not Stefan Faucheux and his inner circle. They'd disappeared after the battle with Erasmus Boyle. Stefan had called to taunt Isabelle with the fact he'd escaped Gribben, the magick-free prison on the Coven's property, and then vanished.

Duskoff International, a conglomerate with headquarters in New York, ran like any other evil corporation these days, manufacturing goods in sweatshops, outsourcing their labor, and laying off employees. No human knew warlocks sat in the executives' chairs, of course. No human could feel the warding that circled the Duskoff building or understood the tongue-in-cheek elevator music: "I Put a Spell on You," "Black Magic Woman," "Season of the Witch," and other assorted cheesiness.

So, yeah, Theo had a hell of a grudge to bring to bear on the Duskoff these days. Most of the Coven witches did. Adam didn't. Not specifically. Adam just had gratitude to the Coven, lots of it. Gratitude and loyalty.

The grudge he bore was only against himself.

Memories rose up, coloring his vision as red and hot as the fire he'd kindled in the hearth. His hands began to grow warm and the seat of his magick tingled. He closed his eyes and forced himself to cool down.

"Adam?" came a small female voice to his left.

"What is it?" His voice came out as a growl.

Silence.

He opened his eyes to find Claire gripping the back of the fancy couch, her face as white as the fabric. Adam stood. "What's wrong?"

She only shook her head. Her knees gave out and he was there in a flash, helping her to sit. "I tried to separate the magick . . . but it was like pulling off my own fingernail. The elium is seared to my seat." She went green and he pulled her against him, resting her head on his chest. "I can't extract it. Not on my own."

"So don't try. Wait for Micah, okay? Pulling off your own fingernail is not cool."

"I would do it in a heartbeat if I really thought it was something so minor," she whispered. "The more I tried to separate the energies, the more it hurt. I don't think I can live though the extraction."

"Can you control it? Rue's power, I mean. Do you think you can wield your magick and the elium together?"

Claire didn't speak for several moments, only drew shuddering breaths. "I don't know yet. The one time I did it involuntarily, I passed out. Tomorrow I'll start experimenting."

"I want to be there when you do."

She flinched. What an odd reaction. "Thank you. Really, this . . . searing of the elium to my seat, it isn't so different from the experiments that Rue did on me. He grafted *daae-*

man magick onto my earth magick and I had to learn how to manage it. He totally altered my power that way. This is just on a larger scale, and I need to be sure of what he gave me in order to proceed. Tomorrow I'll find out what this is for certain, whether it's the elium or not."

He nodded. "I'll start talking to Micah about your problem tomorrow." He glanced at the clock. "Now it's time to get some sleep."

She made a scoffing noise. "Sleep? Tonight? I don't think so."

"Yeah, I know what you're saying." He rubbed his chin. "You have to be hungry. Want something to eat?"

She grimaced. "Almost all the food I've had so far has been disgusting."

He recoiled as if in shock. "Whoa! That's only because you haven't tasted my famous banana pepper sandwich." He drew her to her feet. "It'll help you sleep, promise."

"Banana peppers will help me sleep?"

"Yeah, it shocks your body right into a deep slumber. Kills all your dreams for the night as an added bonus. Works like a charm."

She laughed. It was a nice sound, full of joy. It was the first time he'd heard her do it. "At this point I'm willing to try anything."

Fifteen minutes later he slid his creation to the center of the breakfast bar in the middle of the kitchen and dug into his own sandwich with relish.

She eyed the hoagie bun dubiously. He'd scooped out the innards of the thick bottom half and replaced it with a mixture of salt, olive oil, capers, and diced banana peppers. On top, he'd layered a little bit of prosciutto and some aged Monterey Jack cheese.

"What did you eat on Eudae?" A memory of the contents of Erasmus Boyle's refrigerator flashed into his mind. "Scratch that, maybe I don't want to know."

She picked up the sandwich and studied the end. "Actually, probably nothing you would find abhorrent. The *Atrika* are the ones with the nasty diet; raw, rotting meat is their favorite. The *Ytrayi* and other *daaeman* breeds eat very healthy things. Some cooked meats. Lots of nuts, berries, and vegetables. I ate what they ate. It's quite good for you. Not, what do you call it? Junk food."

"You've never had junk food? Oh, man, you've missed out on part of your heritage. I've got a whole world of Ho Hos and Ding Dongs to show you."

"I had some yellow cakes with filling my second day here. That was good."

"Twinkies?"

She shrugged. "Maybe." Grimacing, she bit into his sandwich and chewed while Adam waited for her reaction.

Claire closed her eyes for a moment and sighed, a look of rapture passing over her face. "This is delicious."

Adam couldn't help the slow slide of his gaze over her plump lips, the curve of her chin leading to her throat, and the way her long eyelashes lay against her cheek.

She smiled at him. "If this is junk food, bring on the Ding Dings!"

Adam grinned. Gods, she was cute. He was trying not to look at her sexually, him being her protector and all. Ordinarily, it probably wouldn't bother him so much, but Claire was different. She seemed so innocent, new to this world. Of course, she wasn't. She was a grown woman in her early thirties. A woman who had seen and heard things so far beyond his comprehension he could barely imagine them.

He wondered if Rue had ever forced himself on her. Adam's fists twitched at the mere thought. He wondered if she'd ever had demon sex, voluntary or not.

There was no tactful way to ask that question.

"Ding Dongs," he corrected.

"What?" She batted long, dark lashes and crossed her legs. They'd bought her a few clothes today, so she wore a pair of new jeans. She grinned. "Oh, yes. Sorry."

She was starting to warm up. That was good. It was *not* good that he was starting to warm up, too, and the reason why had nothing to do with his abilities. He watched her polish off the sandwich and practically lick the plate clean.

He cleared his throat. "We'd better at least try to get some sleep tonight." He took another bite of his sandwich.

Claire pushed the empty plate toward him and stared down at it. "About that." She drew a breath. "I haven't had one good night of sleep since I was pushed through. Well . . . if you don't count the times I was passed out or drugged." Her lips quirked.

"What can I do to help you?" he asked around a mouthful.

She raised her gaze. "Sleep with me."

EIGHT

Adam choked on his bite of sandwich and coughed. "Uh, what do you mean?"

"Since I was eight I've slept on the floor near Rue's bed. Every single night. I'm not used to beds or to sleeping alone. I've been having nightmares."

Claire. In his bedroom. When he was already fighting an inappropriate attraction to her? He wasn't such an uncontrolled cad that he couldn't resist her . . . he didn't think. Still, it wasn't the best scenario.

"Don't you think your nightmares might have more to do with your situation, Claire, and less to do with your sleeping arrangements?"

She pursed her lips. "No."

He sighed. "Look, no way am I letting you sleep on the floor. What was wrong with this guy Rue anyway—"

"Nothing!" she shot back. "It's just the way things are done there."

He stared at her for a moment, wondering how else things were *done* there. Adam wanted to ask her about Rue and if she'd ever been taken advantage of by him, but he didn't know her well enough to ask. It wasn't his business, even if his hands heated with anger at the thought of this woman being forced by demon scum.

"Look, that's not the way things are done *here*, okay? We'll move one of the twin mattresses into my room and you can sleep on that. No way am I letting you sleep on the hard, drafty floor of this old house."

"But—"

"No way." He used his cop voice. He hadn't used that one in a long, long time.

Her lips compressed for a moment. "I can try it."

"Trust me, you'll get used to sleeping in a bed. It's much more comfortable. Can I ask why he made you sleep you on the floor, Claire?"

He figured it was to show her she was lesser. Adam wanted her to say it. It was the first step in breaking through that weird Stockholm syndrome shit.

"The magick. Even at night his experiments worked in me. I slept on a cushion, not the floor, but it allowed me to be at the correct elevation for him to wake and make adjustments as I slept."

Adam bit back the lab rat comment poised on the tip of his tongue and nodded curtly. Hell, her sleeping in his room was probably a good idea anyway. They still didn't know if the dynamic demon duo had tracked them out of Chicago magickally or not. It was probably best she was near one of them in case they showed up during the night.

He nodded. "Let's move the bed then."

Between the two of them, the task was done quickly. Adam knew Theo would get the wrong idea because Adam had a certain reputation among the witches. That was something to deal with tomorrow. Tonight they needed to get some rest.

Adam came out of the bathroom, rubbing a towel through his hair. He'd barely managed to remember to put on a T-shirt and a pair of boxers before he'd exited. Normally, he didn't wear pajamas to bed. Probably better he did these days, anyway. He didn't want the experience of fighting demons in the buff.

Claire sat on the edge of her bed with her back to him. She was just pulling a nightshirt over her head. He got an eyeful of slender, creamy back tapering to a waist any man would want to nip at. He glimpsed the curve of a breast and the flash of one pretty pink nipple before the fabric sheathed her.

He stopped short, towel nearly dropping from his suddenly loose grip.

Fuuuuck him.

Unaware he was there, Claire stared out the large window that backed the king-sized bed. It was dark now, but in the daytime it overlooked a private backyard with lots of trees and a small heated pond teeming with goldfish. The look on her face was so forlorn that Adam completely forgot about sex . . . for a moment. For him, that said a lot.

"Hey, are you all right?" He dropped the towel on some prissy red and black upholstered chair and walked toward her. "We don't know each other very well, but I'm a really great listener."

She pulled herself out of her stare to look at him. He tried hard to ignore the black curl that had been caught on her shoulder and how it had sprung into a ringlet when she moved. "I'm so messed up. Is that the expression? I'm disturbed." Her voice sounded heavy with emotion. "I miss Eudae, can you believe it?"

"It's the only home you've ever known. I don't think it's strange that you're feeling a little lost here."

She motioned with her hands. "Yes, but I was basically a slave there. A well-treated one, but still without freedom, without choices. I was denied the life I would have had here—a regular childhood, a normal education, my first car, my first boyfriend." A smile flickered briefly over her face. "Ding Dongs. There's part of me that's really happy to be here because this is my home, but I feel like I don't fit. I feel like I was made for Eudae and that's the only place I'll ever be comfortable."

"Do you want to go back?"

"I *did*. I did want to go back when I first got here." She hesitated and then shook her head. "Now . . . no. But that doesn't stop me from missing it."

"Claire, you're only thirty-one, right? You have a lot of years to make up for everything you've missed out on."

"A lot? Shouldn't it be many? Many years to make up for everything I've missed out on."

"Uh?" He raised his eyebrows. "Are you an English teacher?"

She shook her head. "Sorry, I'm just clarifying. My mother taught me the language and she was very particular."

Her mother. Interesting.

By the way Claire's face had shuttered and how she'd looked away from him at the mention of *mother*, it was clear he shouldn't press. He would, though, just as soon as he felt he could.

"Yeah, well." He sighed and pushed a hand through his short, damp hair. "I didn't exactly get the best education out there, you know? I was born and raised in Cicero, a suburb near downtown Chicago, by a single mother who had no money to send me to college. As soon as I could, I joined the police force." He almost went on to explain how lucky he was that his wife had been brilliant and had made lots of money, but he stopped himself.

He never talked about his wife to anyone. With Claire, he sensed it was important he open up a little. Claire needed a personal connection with someone like him—an *aeamon*. Talking about Eliza pricked too much, though.

Her gaze traveled over him slowly, as if just noticing him for the first time. There was a sexual heat in her eyes that he'd believed her impossible of just moments ago.

Well, hello . . .

Then, as soon as it had appeared, it flashed out. "Anyway, about experiencing life"—she turned away—"maybe. Depends on how much of it I've got left."

He sat down on his bed, just a few feet from her. He didn't want to invade her personal space. Okay, that wasn't true. He *really* wanted to invade her personal space, that's why he kept his distance.

"You're here now, Claire, where you belong. We won't let anyone take you back there if you don't want to go. Not those fucking demons, not Rue, not anybody."

The fire of that conviction burned through his body as he spoke the words. He hadn't known how much protecting her had meant to him until he'd said it.

"I would like to believe that." She glanced away. "But you don't understand how strong they are. Rue will go to the ends of this Earth to retrieve the magick he stored in me. The fate of the *Ytrayi* and the other *daaeman* breeds depend on it."

"Yeah. Well, they don't scare me. I've hunted worse things to the ends of the Earth."

She looked back at him. Mentally, he tripped and fell into the serious, beautiful, dark pools of her eyes. "No. You haven't."

CLAIRE HAD WATCHED ADAM SLIDE THE LONG COP-per knife under his pillow before he flipped off the light. Did he really think that would work against these *Atrika*?

She stared at the silver moonlight bleaching the light from the planes and hollows of his muscular body, sprawled blanketless on the bed above her.

Of course, even as she sneered, she knew exactly where the copper sword in the room was—nudged up against the wall between Adam's bed and the night table. If the *Atrika* showed up in the night, it would be the first thing she went for.

At least until she got her magick under control. *If* she could get it under control.

In the bed above her, Adam shifted onto his back and groaned. The deep, masculine sound shot through her body like a bullet. Adam was intriguing.

Claire squeezed her eyes shut. What in the Houses was wrong with her? She couldn't go around being *intrigued* by every male she met.

It was true she'd had little enough romance in her life. Hardly any, in fact. And the first—and last—time she'd had sex, it had ended very, very badly. *Bloody* badly. It made her gorge rise to remember.

Maybe, since she'd had such a lack of contact in that way, she was a little affected by every man she met. She frowned. Okay, that wasn't true. She'd come into contact with lots of policemen, doctors, orderlies, and other males since Rue had pushed her through and she hadn't been attracted to any of them. She hadn't thought of Theo in that way, even though he was physically very good-looking. Only Thomas and Adam had pushed her buttons so far.

Thomas was off-limits. She knew that only too well, having saved his life and sent him home from Eudae for Isabelle. Plus, he was married.

Anyway, Adam intrigued her more.

When she'd been in her early twenties, she'd longed for sex. Wanted more than anything to feel a man's skin sliding against hers, his breath on her throat, lips on her stomach, thighs, breasts. Every night she'd fantasize about it until she could barely function during the day.

She'd hidden her desires from Rue, who would have told her what she already knew—it was just hormones. Silly chemicals in her woman's body driving her to procreate. A throwback to the caveman days to ensure the survival of the species. Then Ty had shown interest in her, answering all her carnal wishes.

Ty had been a wonderful male. A *Syari daaeman*, he'd known so much about the world, taught her so much. They'd had long conversations and spent as much time as they could together without being discovered by Rue or anyone else.

She'd fallen in love with Ty even though she'd known their relationship couldn't go anywhere, not really. It had gone against every cultural norm on Eudae, and Ty had risked much by just associating with her . . . much less having sex with her.

He'd risked everything and lost.

She squeezed her eyes shut, deliberately altering the path of her thoughts. It had been so long ago she could barely remember what it was like to have sex. It had been five years since she'd been with a male.

After what had happened with Ty, she'd turned her sexuality off. Just shut it down. She'd had no other choice. It had been Thomas's arrival that had made it flicker to life once more, but it was Adam who truly piqued her curiosity.

How would Adam's skin feel against hers? What would his mouth taste like? How would the curves and hard planes of his body feel under her exploring hands?

Houses, she was so stupid! She had more important things to worry about right now than sex. She had to turn her silly, base desires off for now—*again*—and concentrate on surviving. Tomorrow she'd start poking at the jumbled mess inside her and untangling the threads.

Damn Rue for doing this to her!

She'd been loyal to him since the moment her mother had died and she'd been turned over to his care . . . with the exception of a few minor rebellions and the rather large one of her helping Thomas escape.

Claire had understood that Rue had never felt much emotion for her, not like an *aeamon* would, but he'd treated her with respect and understanding for all those years. Surely, he had *some* regard for her. Yet, when he'd slammed that thunderbolt of magick into her, he'd not hesitated. Not blinked an eyelash.

It was true he'd had no choice. If her assumption about the magick inside her was correct, it would mean the end of the other three *daaeman* breeds if the *Atrika* gained control of it. Yet, Rue had known he'd been sentencing her to death, most likely, and he hadn't cared.

Men.

She sighed noisily and tossed, turning her back on the sight of Adam.

NINE

"IF THEY'RE TRACKING US MAGICKALLY, THEY'RE biding their time," Adam said into the phone to Thomas.

It was a warded call and a warded call would work to keep privacy from a warlock. From a demon, all bets were off. But Claire was of the opinion that if the demons were watching the house, they wouldn't monitor the phone lines.

"Does Micah have anything yet on Claire's problem?" Adam asked.

Silence. "Not yet. He needs to talk to her."

"She's going to start poking around in the magick today. I think she'll know more soon."

"Call us whenever you have more information, or e-mail. There's a computer in the study." Thomas spoke low to someone near him, hand covering the mouthpiece. "Isabelle wants to know what she's like."

Adam's gaze strayed to Claire. She stood in the kitchen, sipping her very first cup of coffee with cream and sugar. Her eyes were closed and her facial muscles slack. Her dark hair, mussed from sleep, curled lazily around her shoulders and her lashes shadowed perfect, alabaster skin that had never known makeup and didn't need it.

"Gorgeous." Mentally, he slapped himself. "I mean—"

"Adam." Thomas's voice held a hint of warning.

He blew a frustrated breath and whispered into the mouth-piece, "You'd have to be dead not to notice. I'm not a total pig. I noticed she's intelligent, too. To go along with it, I noticed her magick, whatever it is, is mad wicked strong. Once she gets it all under control, she's going to be a force to be reckoned with. She's any witch's dream girl."

"Okay. How's she doing emotionally?"

"Emotionally?" He reflected. "She seems a little cold. It's hard to tell. It's not like she's opened up a lot. I know she's confused by the fact she misses Eudae and feels like a foreigner here. That's all I really know, though."

"Consider where she's grown up. The *Ytrayi* aren't known for displays of feeling."

"Exactly. I think she's had to learn to repress a lot of that. Anyway, she's warming up slowly. I think it's just going to take some time. Other than that she's feeling a little out of place, but she's eager to experience all the earthy things she's missed out on."

Silence. "Don't show her too many *earthy* things, Adam."

"I mean like *food*, boss." Now he was irritated. "Like TV. Like driving fast. Like just having fun." *Fuck, and sex, too, maybe.* Claire was a grown woman and could make those decisions for herself. "I'm not going to take advantage of her. Shit. Who do you think I am?"

"I think you're Adam Tyrell, who never met a woman he didn't want."

Mark him down for wanting this one, too. Guilty as charged. Still, he was annoyed. "Gotta go, boss. Things to do, demons to fight."

"Stay in touch, Adam."

They hung up and he walked into the kitchen. Claire still sat at the breakfast bar sipping the steaming cup of coffee, her eyelids heavy with pleasure. She noted his approach, gaze flicking over his chest, down his legs, then back to her coffee. Interest there, then gone.

Theo stood at the stove, wearing only a pair of pajama bottoms, black tribal tats inked all over his dark skin. The delicious aroma of eggs and bacon wafted from his efforts. Adam's stomach rumbled.

"Micah has started working on Claire's problem and if we know him, he'll be up twenty-four/seven until he makes progress. Otherwise, it's the usual. Head down, eyes open. He told us to hunker down here for a while."

Theo turned, fry pan in hand. "Did you tell Thomas about his car?"

Adam sat down at one of the place settings at the bar. "Yeeeeah, I think I forgot to mention that."

"Uh-huh." Theo scooped eggs and bacon onto all their plates, set the pan aside, and sat down to dig in.

Adam took a sip of his steaming coffee. "Hey, it was a good gamble. It would've solved all our problems if it had worked."

"Yeah, but it didn't work and now Thomas is out his car." Theo put a forkful of eggs into his mouth.

Claire picked up a piece of bacon with a grimace, nibbled a bit, and then set it aside. The eggs she seemed to like, though, and ate those with relish.

"So do I want to know what you ate in Eudae?" Theo asked before he forked more egg into his mouth.

Adam laughed. "I asked her that last night."

"The *Ytrayi* and other breeds aren't like the *Atrika*. They eat like you do." She glanced at him and shrugged. "It's all just different meat, vegetables, and fruit. The soil is different there, the water, everything."

"Is it true demons are cannibalistic?" Adam asked.

"Do we have to talk about this right now, Adam?" Theo replied. "Anyway, we already know they are, right? Or is your memory so short?" He swallowed hard. "Mine isn't."

"Well, sure, they eat *us*, Theo. I'm asking if they eat *each other*. Anyway, you brought it up."

Claire tried nibbling at a piece of bacon again. "In battle or in times of war all *daaeman* breeds are cannibalistic, even the *Syari*, the scholars. They eat their enemies alive as an intimidation tactic, but also to consume their magick and essential life energy. The *Atrika* were bred to be the ultimate warrior. They are always cannibalistic, no matter if it's in a time of war or not, and will eat their prisoners or any other *Atrika* that crosses them badly enough."

Theo laid his fork down and pushed his plate away.

"When you say *bred*, what do you mean?" asked Adam.

Claire's eyes widened. "You don't know the *daaeman* are genetically engineered?"

"No." Both he and Theo said it at the same time.

"We don't know how or by whom. They suspect some alien race tampered with the indigenous species of Eudae millions of years ago. Either that or another race did it and the *daaeman* breeds wiped them out, just as they wiped out every other race on the planet."

Adam set his fork down and sat back in his chair. "Wow. So the demons are like . . . super-enhanced beings."

She nodded. "That's why they're so hard to kill. Whoever bred the *Atrika* made them nearly indestructible. Even their blood is a weapon."

"Acidic," answered Theo. He was being positively extroverted this morning. "So it's only the *Atrika* who have acid for blood, not the other breeds?"

"Yes, that's why my favorite theory is the one that says the *daaeman* breeds were created to serve. The *Atrika* to fight. The *Ytrayi* to run things. The *Syari* to keep records. The *Mandari* to build. But the creators did their job too well and were taken over by their creations and were annihilated."

"So, basically, we're genetically engineered, too," answered Adam.

"I guess you could say that."

"Crossbred from demons and engineered by default. Thomas is going to love this," Theo murmured.

"And how jealous will Micah be that we got this information first?" Adam grinned and Theo grinned back.

Damn. The man was making progress.

PAIN LANCED THROUGH HER, MAKING CLAIRE'S vision dim for a moment. Wincing, she pressed her hands between her breasts and gasped.

"Are you okay?"

She popped an eyelid open. "I'm fantastic. Peeling back the foreign magick seared to mine is tons of fun."

"Sarcasm isn't necessary."

Claire closed her eyes again. "Just let me work."

When she'd tried to go into one of the bedrooms to do this alone, Adam had forbidden her. He'd insisted on accompanying her even though she'd told him it could take her well into the night to accomplish this.

He sat on a chair, one long leg thrown over the arm, reading a book. She sat cross-legged in the center of the bed trying to separate the magicks. Theo was off being Theo somewhere. He was undoubtedly good in a fight and his power pulsed strong and palpable inside him, but she'd never met a more silent, gloomy man on Earth or Eudae.

Adam held up a hand. "Hey, that's great. Next time you turn white, gasp, and nearly pass out, I'll just leave you alone, all right?"

"Thank you."

Adam raised an eyebrow and went back to reading his book.

She closed her eyes again and returned to peeling apart the powers. It was, indeed, what she'd thought it was. Now that she'd had a few hours to fully explore it, she could tell. It was the elium. A mass of violent energy so great it was amazing she'd been able to absorb it all. No normal *aeamon* would have been able to do it. It was only because her magick had been tweaked and transformed by Rue that she'd been able to carry it.

And, oh, how she didn't want to carry it.

Now her goal was to extract the tendrils of it from her own power, to bunch it into a ball in the middle of her seat and build high walls around it. It was imperative that she regain control of her own elemental abilities, since she was more powerful than any *aeamon* on Earth. Her magick would be the most effective in coming battles. Truly, she was the only one able to fight the *Atrika*.

Two questions haunted her. Provided she was able to separate the magicks and bind the elium, would she be able to use any part of it as a weapon against the *Atrika*? Also, could she shed the elium and still live?

Claire was trying not to be pessimistic about either of those answers.

In fact, it was better not to think about it at all. Nausea having faded, she tried a new tactic. Instead of prying the magicks apart, she would call her magick away from the elium. Like to like. Focusing her attention deep into the earth below her, she pulled directly from this foreign place itself. Dark and deep. Solid and strong. It filled her until her body became heavy and immovable as a mountain.

The magick came slow and sluggish since this was not the natural home of the *aeamon*. The magick of the elemental witches came from *daaeman*—from Eudae, not Earth. So it was harder to pull directly from the elements here.

Once she had a good draw on the earth below, the pulsing heart of her, she moved to water. Casting tendrils of exploring power in a way no non-tampered-with witch would be able to do, she found moisture in the earth and tapped into the base source of its power. She pulled the essence of it within her until her mountain became soaked with dew—cool, life-giving, and refreshing.

Next she went for air. It was all around and easy to draw from, filling her with a lightness to counteract the mountain sensation of earth.

Last, she sent tendrils out to seek fire, usually the hardest of the elements for her to locate. Here, though, it was easy. The day was chilly and many people had fires lit in their hearths, just as Adam had lit one the previous night. She located one and trapped its unpredictable, destructive, fascinating energy and brought that, too, into her. It flickered to life in the seat of her magick, as warm and wonderful as she found a certain man who wielded it.

All four elements woven together mimicked her own special brand of magick. Tears slipped down her cheeks as she realized just how much she'd missed it. The elium had muddied everything, cut her off from her own power. It was like she'd been an amputee but now had miraculously regrown her missing limb.

Houses! She wanted the elium gone. If it couldn't be gone, she wanted it contained.

Using the borrowed power, she held it inside her, luring her own magick to it. Like to like. Bait to quarry. Nothing happened and Claire's hope sank to her toes.

Then, a flicker.

A pulse.

Like a great beast raising its head and sniffing the air for the scent of food, her magick took notice. And pulled. Hard.

The magicks began to separate. A blinding white-hot flash of pain—as if someone was skinning her alive—ripped through her. Her spine bowed backward under the force of it and her facial muscles contorted.

Underneath the agony, she vaguely understood that she could thrust the borrowed elemental power away and allow her magick to re-adhere itself around the elium. It would stop the pain, but she wanted the elium to lose its hold on her own power so badly that she held on to the bait and endured the separation. The pain was so great she couldn't even cry out. Her mouth opened in a soundless gasp of unbearable anguish.

Adam was there, but even though her eyes were open, she couldn't see him clearly. Claire saw only a dark shape. Strong hands eased her down onto the bed, stroked through her hair. He said things to her—soft, quieting, reassuring things—but it was like another language.

Darkness closed its fist around her. House-blessed nothingness . . . She sank into it willingly.

THE SPECIAL WOODSY, CLEAN SCENT OF SOAP AND shampoo teased Claire's nose—the smell she'd come to identify as Adam. Her eyelids flickered open and Adam's face came into view. He'd bundled her in a blanket on the bed and tucked her against his body. She should have been toasty warm, but her whole body quaked with chill. The center of her chest throbbed dully and she remembered the peeling away of the magicks and shuddered.

"Hey," Adam said softly. "Okay?"

"I think so." She tried to get up, but he held her tight against him.

"Just relax a minute. You scared the shit out of me."

She frowned. That had to be just an expression.

"I was across the room and your entire body went tense.

You tried to scream but couldn't, and all the blood drained from your face." His voice took on an awed quality. "Your *magick*, Claire, it pulsed like the explosion of a tiny nuclear bomb. I absorbed the shock of it clear across the room. It shook the fucking walls. I got to you and a second later you were out like a light. What happened?"

She sighed, trying to organize her thoughts. Within her, her magick pulsed, just as it had done every day of her life before Rue had imbued her with the elium. A little to the left and up lay the elium itself in a hard little ball of ultimate power. A cancer within her. It was still connected to her power by snaky, sticky tendrils, but less than before.

"I pulled energy from the elements around me to coax my magick away from the elium." She swallowed hard and trembled, remembering the agony. "It worked better than I anticipated. It was fast and very painful."

"You've got your mojo back. I can feel it."

She concentrated, drawing the moisture from the air around her until she had a ball of it. "Yes." She smiled. "It is back."

"Fuck, Claire," Adam breathed, staring at the small, condensed orb of water floating above her hand. She kept it suspended there using air magick. "You're an earth witch. How the hell are you doing that?"

Kindling energy underneath the water, she engulfed the whole thing in a blast of white-hot flame, evaporating it. "I'm like no witch you've ever met, Adam."

It wasn't ego that made the words spill from her lips; it was truth speaking. For better or for worse.

Adam only stared down at her, apparently at a loss for a response.

She pushed up and faced him, holding his steady gaze. It hit her all at once. Her confidence, recently shaken by events, had returned. The heat of him, his scent, his proximity—all of it excited her. It made her body quicken, become lush and alive in a way she had not allowed in many years.

"I hold the magicks of all four elements within me. All those years with Rue, that's what he did. He experimented with the power inside me, my earth magick. He drew in the other three elements and changed my base earth power in a way that has never been done before. I don't have to store charms like a regular earth witch. I can draw from all four elements, sometimes two at a time—but never all four at once."

He stared at her for a long moment before speaking. "Claire, that makes you more powerful than any other witch on this planet."

Her mouth quirked. "Kind of a change of pace since on Eudae I was one of the weakest individuals."

"One of? There were demons weaker than you?"

"Some of the *Syari* class are fairly weak. Some in the *Mandari*. The rest . . . not." She grinned. "But don't worry, I can kick *daaeman* ass when I want to. Just ask Thomas. He watched me do it at his side on Eudae."

"I can feel the air magick." He shook his head. "You know about the draw, right? Air and fire, water and earth? I mean, I was attracted to you before, but now it's more . . . intense." His gaze flared hot.

Yes, she felt it, too. Fire and air held a natural attraction. Now that all her elements were unmuddied by the elium, she could sense the flicker and spark of her air and his fire meeting, checking each other out, rubbing up against each other.

The powers would find balance soon and the artificial attraction would ease, but she'd been drawn to him sexually before the elium had relented so it made the whole thing more extreme.

And, by his own admission, he'd been attracted to her, too. *Wow*.

She lifted her gaze to meet his smoldering expression with interest. With her heavy-lidded gaze, she showed him *exactly* what she was thinking about. Sweaty things. Carnal things. Skin-on-skin things.

He cleared his throat. "Listen, if you're all right, I should leave. Thomas would kick my butt into next week for acting out any of the things currently going through my head."

Adam moved to rise and she put a hand on his forearm, stopping him. "Don't leave."

"I really should."

"I hate that word, *should*. It's ugly in any language."

He hesitated, and then settled back. After a moment, he reached out and touched her cheek. "Wow. Beautiful, intelligent, strong, and a powerful witch. You've got it all, baby."

She blinked, her smile fading. "You think I'm beautiful?"

"You're kidding right? I think you're gorgeous."

Her cheeks heated. "It's been a long time since anyone told me I was pretty."

"What's wrong with those demons?"

She smiled. "They're *demons*."

"Oh, yeah." His head dipped toward hers and the heat of him chased the chill from her bones a bit. "This is such a bad idea," he murmured. His gaze centered on her mouth.

TEN

"It's the worst idea ever," she agreed. Her breath had a little hitch in it and her heart sped its pace. Her hands found his upper arms and clenched there, feeling the bunch and flex of his muscles. Strength. Power leashed for the moment.

He repositioned himself over her, pressing her down against the mattress. His gaze still searched her face, lust flickering in the depths of his dark blue eyes—lust for her. At the moment Claire felt like the most beautiful, most desired woman on the face of the planet—both of them.

"I shouldn't kiss you," he murmured.

"There's that stupid word again."

He grinned for a fleeting moment. Adam's head dipped and his mouth came nearer hers. "If it were up to me I'd tell you you were beautiful every day." The words came out a whisper and Claire sensed they were sincere. His lips brushed hers, just barely, sending a wave of pleasurable shock through her.

Claire wanted.

Oh, how she *wanted* with every molecule of her being. She wanted him to pull away the blankets between them, undress her slowly, and make love to her. She wanted to know what his bare chest was like under her fingers and tongue. How would his thighs feel pushing her legs wide open? How would his cock feel tunneling deep inside her? She could barely remember the experience.

Oh, now she remembered. Ty. She jerked and stiffened.

Luckily, there *were* blankets and clothes between them. Luckily, she had all those years of practice locking away her sexuality.

Before he had a chance to do anything more than barely brush her lips, she pushed him back, but with effort. "Wait. Rue would kill you, and I don't mean that figuratively."

Adam leaned in again. "Rue doesn't have jurisdiction here." He jerked. "Or . . . are you and Rue . . ."

"No!" She shook her head. "He would never consider me in *that* way. I mean, he thought of me as a woman, but I was more like his protected ward or magick experiment than anything else. He never saw me sexually and I never thought of him that way either."

He grinned again. "Then I'm not seeing the problem."

"But—"

His mouth caught hers, slid over it. *Ah, Houses.*

She melted against him, her lips parting of their own accord against the flick of his velvet tongue that promised beauty and pleasure. His teeth gently grasped her lower lip and rasped the sensitive flesh. Much farther down, her sex noticed and reacted, growing warm.

With one kiss he'd awoken her completely. Like the fairy tale her mother used to tell her when she was a child.

Mustering up every ounce of willpower, she pushed at him again. This time she also swung her legs down and bolted from the bed to the middle of the room, away from his devilish mouth and hooded, lust-filled eyes.

"I want to," she gasped, "but this is not a good idea. Rue will—"

"Rue will what?" Adam stood and walked to her, an amused smile playing over his lips. A smile like a man confident in his ability to seduce her. "Anyway, I thought you said I was expendable."

"I lied."

"Rue isn't here, Claire. He's off in another dimension. He could even be dead. *Rue* isn't going to do anything, but I might."

"That's what I'm afraid of."

He moved close to her and she couldn't make herself dart away. "As far as this being a bad idea, well, honey, you couldn't be more right about that." He grinned and dimples popped out on each cheek. Adam dipped his head and his warm, sweet breath caressed her lips. "I love to be bad."

His mouth dropped to hers once more and he pulled her up against his chest. The heat of him bled through the fabric of her clothes and made her nipples hard. If this continued any longer, she'd be completely lost. She couldn't let that happen.

But then . . . disaster.

His hand slipped under her shirt and found the small of her back, touching bare skin. His fingers caressed the tense muscles there. And then his other hand slipped up her back to the nape of her neck and cupped it as he tilted her head to the side and deepened their kiss.

Adam Tyrell was a man who could make a woman feel like the most desirable, beautiful person on the planet. Right now, that's how Claire wanted to feel. Facing death, she wanted to celebrate life. She wanted to throw all her concerns to the wind and escape into the sexual oblivion that he offered. Fighting against that powerful escape just dangling in front of her was nearly impossible.

His tongue swiped against hers, sending a jolt through her. Then he settled in to lazily kiss her as his wicked fingers massaged and caressed, dipping lower and lower.

His touch shredded her will until it was gone.

Her hands ran up his arms, concentrating on every luscious bunched muscle from his wrist to his shoulder. He yanked her against him with a little sexy growl in the back of his throat that made her nipples go tight.

Oh, yes, she remembered this . . . and it was *good*.

She wanted it again. Now. With Adam. Forget Rue.

Adam dropped his mouth to the sensitive place below her ear and nibbled. Gooseflesh erupted over her body. Adam kissed his way down her throat and over her collarbone, then dragged her gently back toward the bed.

"It's been a long time," she murmured against his mouth when he caught her lips once more.

"A long time?"

"It's been five years for me, Adam."

He stilled, then jerked and pulled away. "Wait. What are we doing? What am *I* doing? Claire, the last thing I want is to take advantage of you. I told Thomas I wouldn't do this."

She swallowed hard. "So you don't find me attractive after all?"

He blew out a breath. "Honey, you float my boat in every way. That's not it. This is the damn air/fire thing pushing me to do what I've wanted to do since we met."

She walked to him and took his hands in hers. "What's that?"

"Seduce you. Take you." His eyes narrowed. "Fuck you, Claire, until you're so flushed with pleasure you can't even speak."

Her breath hitched and lust pulsed through her body. She ran her fingers through his hair. "I don't have a problem with that."

"I don't want to—"

"Shut up now." Claire went up on her tiptoes and pressed her mouth to his.

He groaned against her lips and wrapped his arms around her.

"Take me to the bed," she murmured against his mouth.

He did. Once he got her there, he laid her on the mattress and hovered over her, still kissing her. She gasped against his lips as he worked the button and zipper of her jeans open. His warm, broad palm spread over her abdomen, teasing the edge of her panties.

He raised his head a little. "So, you're not a virgin?"

She bit her lower lip and shook her head.

"Good. Because the things I have planned for you a virgin wouldn't be able to handle."

Thank the Houses.

"Adam, I've missed this so much. I want—I want—"

"Me to help you make up for lost time?" he murmured against her mouth.

She nodded.

"Claire, I specialize in no-attachment sex. It's kind of my

thing. Has been for years. If you want me to help you go wild for a while, I'm willing."

"That sounds good," she breathed.

He kissed her again, all the while working her pants down and off.

She closed her eyes, remembering Ty, remembering the last time a man had kissed her this way . . . Images flooded her mind. How she'd yearned for him and how he'd given her everything. Ty had been the only person besides her mother whom she'd ever formed a truly deep attachment to. He'd loved her and she'd loved him.

Then one night, Rue had caught them in the weaving room . . . in a state of undress. His anger had been terrible. He'd gone straight into a killing rage, incensed that Ty had dared disrespect not only an unmated female, but his own handmaiden.

Houses, that night Rue had called her his *daughter*.

"How dare you dishonor my House and my daughter this way, Ty!" Rue had yelled, his eyes red and his fangs fully extended. "You have broken all of our laws and I pass judgment on you *now*."

Ytrayi judgment was swift and brutal. Nothing Claire could say would have stayed Rue's hand.

Claire jerked, remembering the carnage. Her heartbreak. After Ty had been killed Claire had never felt so alone, not even after her mother had died.

Adam pulled back. "What's wrong? You're crying. Are my kisses really that bad?"

She allowed a smile to flicker over her mouth. "If Rue ever finds out we were together, he will tear you limb from limb." She paused. "Literally."

Adam sat up. "Claire, are you worried for me?"

She propped herself on her elbows. "Yes."

"That's very sweet, but I've had demons wanting to tear me up before and I've always managed to stop them."

She blinked, looked at him with solemn eyes. "You would not be able to stop the *Cae* of the *Ytrayi*. He's worse than an *Atrika* when properly motivated, when his control has snapped and he scents blood."

"Rue's kind of the baddest of the bad, huh? Why would he want to hurt me for touching you?"

She pursed her lips, thinking how to phrase her answer. "In their culture, the father is responsible for the females until they are mated. Under no circumstances are males allowed to touch unmated females. If a male does so, the father is honor bound to eviscerate them."

"Wow. I've always had a thing for dangerous sex, but that goes above and beyond."

"The catch is that I cannot be mated. It's against their law for an *aeamon* to mate a *daaeman* and since there are no *aeamon* males on Eudae . . . Also, Rue declared himself my guardian when I became his handmaiden. The night he caught me with Ty I discovered that meant he considered me his daughter and, as such, under this cultural law."

"You know, I'm beginning to really not like this guy, Claire. So you were supposed to remain a virgin for your entire life, then? And he would kill anyone who laid a hand on you?"

"Yes. As a female *aeamon*, I was the most defenseless individual in their culture and Rue was very protective of me. I was to remain untouched until the day I died, even though it wasn't fair to me and I did resent it."

"But I'm not a demon, Claire, I'm an *aeamon* male. What if I want to mate you?"

She smiled. "Are you asking to bind my life with yours for all eternity? Death do us part?"

"Uh . . ."

Her smile widened. "Then you cannot touch me. Touch me and be eviscerated."

"Yeah, well, I don't live on Eudae. I don't play by their rules. You shouldn't either, Claire."

"If I did, I would've remained untouched for my entire life."

He gave her a sly look. "And you didn't do that, did you?"

She shook her head and bit her lower lip. "I did something even worse than lose my virginity. I fell in love with a *Syari*, one of the scholar class, and he fell in love with me. When Rue found out—"

Adam made a slashing motion across his throat.

"Not only that, he—"

He held up a hand. "I got it. The fewer details the better."

"I don't want to be responsible for that again, no matter

how much I want . . . *this*, whatever this is that's happening between us now."

Adam said nothing for a moment. Then he began, "I guess if my last lover had been eviscerated for having sex with me, I'd be a little jumpy, too. But, Claire, you're a witch, not a demon. You're home now. Stop thinking like a resident of Eudae."

"As *aeamon*, I'm half-*daaeman*. And I've been playing by their rules since I was six, Adam."

"Yeah, okay." Adam leaned down, pinning her to the bed. He spoke close enough to her mouth that his breath warmed her lips. "But I think you're worth the risk."

She inhaled a little, feeling his words go straight to the center of her. He really believed it. Her empathy, coming from her water magick, picked up that clear, crystal feeling of truth.

He stayed that way, barely touching her. Their gazes locked, held. The heat of his body bled through the fabric of his clothing and into her skin. His eyes seemed to hold pure heat, everything he wanted to do lay there immersed in barely banked fire.

Something in the depths of her chest squeezed a bit. Emotion rose—hers or his, she wasn't quite certain. All of a sudden they were one being. Claire wasn't sure where she stopped and he began.

It was intense and her body responded in kind. Her sex quickened, remembering what it was like to be aroused. She moved on the bed a little, wanting him to touch her like she'd never wanted anything before. Wanted his hands on her again, more intimately this time.

This was a man who could help her explore the side of her femininity that had been neglected for so many years. He could help her revel in the ultimate expression of life while she fought to keep hers.

Yes, this was a good decision. This was a man accustomed to doing this for many women, a man who would use her as she would use him. Perfect. She closed her eyes, waiting for his kiss.

But it never came.

Her eyes opened. Slowly, his gaze fastened on her mouth as he sat up. "As much as I hate to cut this short, we need to tell Theo and Thomas you've separated the magicks."

What? A moment ago he'd been ready to tear her clothes off. She *wanted* him to tear her clothes off! Jolted from her bliss, she also sat up.

Recovering quickly and trying to mask her confusion she replied, "Of course, you're right. Pleasure shouldn't take the place of business."

Adam held her gaze steadily. "Pleasure should always take the place of business, Claire, but it shouldn't take the place of guarding your life."

Suddenly feeling uncomfortable about their whole exchange, Claire stood and went for the door. "I'll go tell Theo."

ADAM STARED AT THE OPEN DOORWAY, LISTENING to Claire's exchange with Theo in the living room. It was true they needed to share information as soon as they got it, but this particular bit could have waited awhile longer.

It had made a convenient excuse.

The addition of her air magick had opened some kind of floodgate. He'd been attracted to her before, but once she'd peeled her magick from the elium, the sexual draw had exploded. He couldn't remember being this attracted to a woman since he'd been with Eliza.

All he'd wanted was to ease her pants down and off, explore and tease every luscious inch of her body until her cries had echoed loud enough to bring Theo running. It had been so, *so* hard to pull away. Especially since she'd been laying there beneath him, nipples hard, chest heaving, lips rouged and swollen from his kisses, and her eyes had been begging him to do it.

Giving in to the passion in that moment had just been wrong. It had seemed like . . . adultery. Adam bowed his head. Gods, how stupid! Yet, there it was, stupid or not.

Eliza had been in her grave for seven years now and she'd slap him silly if she knew he'd pulled away from a woman because of her. Fuck! He'd slept with lots of women after he'd grieved for Eliza and moved on! But none of those women had ever evoked anything like what he'd felt with his wife.

Until Claire.

And there was the problem. *That's* why it felt like adultery.

Adam rubbed his chin and squeezed his eyes closed for a moment, trying to work out the *why* of that. It was probably the air magick. Once that eased up, he could keep the promise he'd made to Claire and help her make up for lost time.

Fuck Thomas and his opinions. Claire was an adult and could make her own decisions. If she wanted to take what Adam offered, so be it.

But it would have to wait until this strange, jarringly familiar intensity faded.

ELEVEN

"*ADAM.*"

Claire moaned and her eyelids fluttered open. One muscled arm was thrown over the side of the bed above her head. She couldn't see any more of Adam's body.

That was a good thing.

She closed her eyes again and slid her hand between her thighs, where the erotically charged dream she'd just woken from still made her warm and achy.

Never had she had a dream like that.

He'd hovered over her, his big body pressing hers into the mattress, breath hot on her collarbone, belly button, inner thigh . . . His spiky blond hair had brushed her skin as he'd drunk from the center of her, driving her fast and hard toward a shattering climax with his lips and tongue.

She'd never even known such acts were possible. They didn't do *that* on Eudae as far as she knew.

Claire fisted the sheets in her hand remembering how, after he'd brought her to climax with his mouth, he'd held her wrists above her head, spread her thighs apart with his knee, pinned her down with his hips, and thrust his cock deep inside her.

It had been so real.

And her climax had almost been real, too. It had fallen just tantalizingly short, leaving her slick and wanting between her thighs. The dream had made her nipples sensitive and her mouth wanting to be kissed again like he'd kissed her last night.

Claire brushed her nipple with her fingers, sending a shock wave of pleasure through her body that made her gasp. Under the pad of her index finger, her clit felt swollen, needy.

She groaned in frustration.

He'd really come on to her the night before, had tried his best to seduce her. She'd gone for it, too. She'd fallen at his feet like some stupid virgin female desperate for a tumble. *Houses*, she'd admitted that she wanted sex from him and had practically thrown herself at him to get it. If he'd worked her pants off and done all those erotic things that had been reflected in his eyes, she would have let him and moaned for more.

But instead he'd abruptly cut short their liaison—that excuse he'd used had been abominable—and had barely looked at her twice since then, even though she was sleeping in the same room with him. All he'd done when it was time to sleep was mutter good night and snap off the light.

Bastard. He was playing some game and she didn't know the rules. So she simply wasn't going to play.

Yes, she still wanted him. Her body ached for more of the touch he'd teased her with, for the caresses he'd given her in her dreams. But she wasn't going to be tempted and then ignored. Damn him if he thought she was that desperate.

If he wanted her, which it appeared he didn't, he was going to have to work for it now.

ADAM WOKE WITH A GASP AND THE BIGGEST GOD-damn hard-on he'd ever had.

He took a labored breath and rolled over, careful of his painfully erect cock. Claire's bed was empty, the sheets and blankets neatly tucked in around the mattress they'd put on the floor for her. Her voice came from the other room, where she talked to Theo.

What the hell!

He hadn't had a dream like that since he'd been a preteen and at least back then he'd come in his sleep and received some kind of relief.

He ground his palm into his eye socket and let out a shuddering breath. Just the sound of her voice right now made his body tight with desire.

"Fuck," he swore low and rolled out of bed. He needed a shower—a cold one.

As he crossed the floor near her mattress, he caught a whiff of Claire—that unique scent of her which was a combination of soap and some kind of flower he couldn't place. It made his knees go weak with desire. It made him want to collapse onto her bed and roll around in it like a feline in catnip.

He double-timed it to the bathroom and ran the water in the shower while he chuffed off his sweatpants and tossed them to the floor in a wad. Then he climbed into the shower and let the lukewarm water sluice down his body, pound on his shoulders and head.

Adam leaned one hand against the tiled bathroom wall and closed his eyes, trying to banish the memory of the dream and failing. He hit the cold water on the faucet big-time, but not even that helped.

The soft brush of her inner thigh against his cheek, the taste and scent of her filling his senses and making him crazy with the need to fuck her. The sweet feel of her clit against his tongue and the way she shuddered and moaned as he brought her to a hard and fast orgasm by sucking that sweet little bit of flesh into his mouth.

Afterward, the delicious give of her thighs against his knee and the feel of her wrists under his hands. The hot, velvet snare of her sex around his hard cock, so sticky sweet and perfect. How he'd fucked her hard and fast—flesh slapping on flesh—until she'd shattered a second time, the muscles of her pretty, perfect sex milking his shaft . . .

He had his hand around the base of his cock before he even knew he was doing it. Adam stroked himself from root to tip, harder and faster, just the way he wanted to thrust deep into Claire. He fisted his hand against the wall as he came, pleasure rising up from his balls and exploding. Claire's name tumbled from his lips as it washed over him.

When it was finished, he leaned his head against the wall and let the water run down his body.

What was it about this woman that had him so goddamned torqued up? He had lots of women in his life. Witches were lucky in that they didn't have to worry about catching diseases. Adam had made damn sure he'd taken advantage of that benefit since Eliza's death.

Drowning his sorrow in pussy. That's what Jack called it.

The point was, he'd never been hurting for women, so why was this particular one affecting him this way? Like he was some thirteen-year-old kid who just found his dad's stack of *Penthouse* magazines under the bed?

Damn it, he couldn't wait until their magicks found a balance and he could relax.

After he'd showered, dressed, and gulped down a cup of black coffee, he filled up another mug and found Claire and Theo out in the backyard.

He was the only one who hadn't dressed in a winter coat and gloves. All he had to do was tap a little magick and he stayed warm. Just like his own private furnace. Adam guessed Claire could do it, too.

"Now, push it," Claire directed.

Earth magick pulsed as Theo pulled up about twenty little sprouts from the frozen earth in the backyard. His breath showed in the crisp morning air with his exertion. Green stalks lifted their sleepy heads and unfurled their leaves.

"Shit." Adam stood beside Claire. He studied the new growth that had sprung from the ice-covered ground. "Have you ever been able to do that before, Theo?"

Theo took a break from staring at the new plants to glance at Adam. Awe had transformed his face. He blinked. "No."

You didn't get *awe* from Theo very often. Disdain. Anger. Silence. Not awe. It was jarring.

"That's crazy." Adam turned to Claire. "And incredible."

Claire shrugged. "These were some of the first tricks that Rue taught me once I became his handmaiden. My magick was stronger in days." She frowned. "Magick is harder to wield on Earth, though. It feels heavier here."

"Do you know tricks for fire magick?" Adam used a little power to heat the cooling cup of coffee he carried.

"Yes, of course. I can't do for you what Rue did for me because I'm not a *daaeman*, but I can help you both improve your elemental skills."

Theo turned toward her. "How did Rue give you the other three elements?"

Theo had been fascinated with her ever since she'd freed her unique power, and it wasn't for Claire's sparkling personality or beautiful face. Theo was a power hound; there could be no doubt about that. He was an already highly skilled witch and was enthralled with her because she was even more highly skilled.

"He did it with *daaeman* magick." She pursed her lips. "Honestly, I'm not sure how. It was a progressive thing, over years. He would augment my power at certain times of the year, day, hour. Grafting spells onto it, twisting it, and molding it. Sometimes even in the middle of the night. It seemed complex and, until recently, I suspected I was very valuable to him because he'd managed it. Then he bounced the elium into me and sent me tumbling down the rabbit hole with two *Atrika* on my tail."

"Not that I want to defend Rue or anything," Adam said, "but it sounds like his hand was forced. He's probably coming after you as soon he can. Of course, if I have anything to say about it, he's not getting you back."

Adam took a drink of his coffee to mask the flash of protectiveness he felt over her. It made his hands clench and his jaw lock.

Claire might have Stockholm syndrome or whatever for Eudae and Rue, but Adam was going to do what he could to break it. It was like a crust of ice coating her and it would kill her eventually.

Claire glanced at him, anger sparking in her eyes. "Yes, well, Rue has been my companion and protector for many years. If he can take the elium from me, I'll let him."

"Do you plan to return to Eudae?" Theo asked.

She gazed up at him. "I don't know if I'll have a choice."

"You're not a slave," Theo answered in a forceful voice. "You are a free person. You can make your own decisions, Claire."

Her laugh sounded harsh in the quiet air. "I think you are

naïve, Theo." She glanced at Adam. "Both of you. You have no idea what you are up against in the *Atrika* or the *Ytrayi*. The *aeamon* of this place have been lucky so far that the *Ytrayi* have ignored them. If they ever set their sights on taking this place, Houses help you all. *Choice*." She snorted. "In the face of Rue's will, I would have little."

Theo fixed her with a gimlet glare, his jaw locked. He opened his mouth to reply, but his cell phone vibrated. Theo took it from his pocket and walked into the house, answering the call.

Adam unlocked his jaw enough to speak. "If they ever come after us, Claire, you'll see just how resourceful we can be." He knew his eyes glittered with anger, belying his smile. "Don't underestimate us."

"I'm sorry if I wounded your pride. So far the Coven witches seem to be strong. I would hope they would be able to defeat the *Ytrayi* or the *Atrika* if it came down to it. I just—"

He rounded on her, coming so close he could smell her skin, feel the heat of her body. Adam hesitated, feeling a little drunk all of a sudden. Damn good thing he'd found relief in the shower. "*They*, Claire? Why do you always draw a line between us and them and put yourself on the demon side? You're a witch. You're *one of us*."

She shook her head, looking away.

He grasped her upper arms, the mask he always carefully kept in place was in danger of slipping from his expression but he couldn't help it. "How can I make you see that you belong to us, Claire?"

"I belong nowhere, Adam. I belong to no one. My mother ensured that when she dragged me from this place when I was six and gave me to the *Ytrayi*."

His grip tightened for a moment and his mouth opened, then closed. He released her. "Damn your mother, then."

She turned and walked away. "Too late."

He grabbed her arm and swung her around to face him before she could leave. His gaze searched hers for some trace of what she might be feeling.

"I'm fine, Adam." Then she turned and walked into the house.

"That makes one of us," he whispered before she disappeared within.

She hesitated, but kept walking.

WHILE THEY WAITED, CLAIRE KEPT HER AIR MAGick open as much as possible to alert her if the *Atrika* came near the house, but after four days the *Atrika* hadn't showed. That was good. It was bad that Micah had made little headway on her problem, and Claire grew even more restless for a way to rid herself of the elium.

On the couch opposite her, Adam lay with his powerful body spread out, taking up every inch of available space. His eyes were closed, but Claire knew he wasn't sleeping. By now she could recognize the changes in his breathing pattern that signaled true slumber. She'd lain awake the last three nights listening to every move he made.

He wore a pair of well-loved jeans that—not that she was paying much attention—defined his thighs and rear really well. Claire liked blue jeans, a garment they didn't have on Eudae. She especially liked them on Adam when they were well worn in all the right places.

She shifted uneasily on her chair, jostling the heavy book in her lap. The dream, even after three days, still clung to her memory. It still made her shiver when she thought about it.

And Adam still hadn't touched her.

The fact that Adam hadn't touched her bothered her a lot less than the fact that she really, really wanted him to.

Irritated, she flipped the book of photography she'd been thumbing through closed. The heavy thump startled Adam, making him jump.

She sighed. "If I could just get to the Coven and work with Micah, maybe together we could figure it out. I need to take a look at the texts he's got, but I can't do anything to help him from way over here."

Adam relaxed again and closed his eyes. "Too dangerous. If the *Atrika* can't track you magickally—which it appears they can't—logic says they're staking out the Coven somehow, watching for some clue about where you are."

She tossed the book to the cushion beside her. "I dislike having a weapon inside me."

"Have you learned how to use the elium yet? Maybe if you learn to tap it and direct it, you'll feel less hostile toward it."

"I'm still trying. I can only poke at it so much during the day before it starts making me feel ill. It's like having a cancer inside me."

"Cancer?" Adam opened his eyes, swung his long legs to the floor, and crossed the room to her. The air/fire attraction that hit them both powerfully four days ago by now should have faded. They'd spent much time together, even sleeping in the same room. By all rights, their magicks should have found a balance and ceased in the incessant brush-and-hum, the give-and-take that was so sexual in nature.

Not to mention the fact that not only did she have air magick inside her, she had water magick. Fire and water were natural repellants and should have cancelled out the air/fire thing.

But, no, it didn't.

Now, even days later, when Adam reached out and she took his offered hand, sparks and shivers of awareness curled through her. With Theo, even though they also shared an earth/water attraction, she felt little, and even that bit of little had disappeared two days ago.

It was Adam who had woken her body from its self-imposed sexual coma. It was Adam who intrigued every inch of her body.

Yet, he'd made no move in her direction since that afternoon. Nothing more than a heated glance had passed between them, or the occasional brush of bodies in the hallway that made her knees weak.

Clearly, she was the only one feeling the attraction and it stung her pride.

After all, it wasn't like they didn't have the time or opportunity. All they did all day was practice magick. She taught Theo and Adam tricks to make them stronger, to prepare them for any confrontation with the *Atrika*. The *Atrika* possessed natural shields against elemental magick, but that didn't mean it couldn't be used as a weapon when wielded a certain way. Put a little twist on a bolt of elemental power and it could be quite effective against a *daaeman*.

When she wasn't giving magick lessons she was poking at

the elium. Unfortunately, most of the time it made her sick to touch it.

Adam came to a halt in front of her, hesitated, then pulled her up flush against his chest.

She stiffened and tried to pull away. "What in Houses are you doing, Adam?" Her jostling only made him hold her tighter. Her air crushed out against his hard chest and her hands clenched on his broad shoulders.

She went still and desperately tried to ignore her body's responses to his proximity. The last thing she wanted was to give him the satisfaction of knowing how he affected her. Not when he'd teased her and then rejected her so thoroughly. Despite his words, Adam didn't find her attractive after all. That was fine. Houses knew she should be used to being found unattractive by now.

He grasped her hand, his opposite arm curling around her waist. Claire fought the urge to pull away from him and bolt from the room. Where was Theo, anyway? The man disappeared so often. Too often. Right now it was damned inconvenient.

Adam flipped her hand over and stroked her palm with the pad of his thumb. It shouldn't have felt erotic, such an innocent thing . . . but it did. "Let me touch it."

TWELVE

She blinked. "*What?*"

"The elium, Claire." His eyelids lowered a little, along with his voice—smooth black velvet. "What did you think I meant?"

Adam tried hard to keep up the façade of a carefree, joking man, but Claire could see through it. All was laid bare in his blue eyes, which teemed with a turmoil and darkness that often contradicted his harmless grin. Perhaps he'd fooled the Coven witches, but he hadn't fooled her.

Adam was a man to watch out for, a man with a temper, a past, and an appetite to do damage because of it all.

"I never know for certain with you." Was her voice shaking a little? Damn it!

"As a fire witch, healing lies within my domain. You say the elium is like a cancer within you, so let me explore it. Maybe I can help." His thumb continued to stroke her palm.

"Stop that," she snapped.

"I'm trying to make you relax."

"It's having the exact opposite effect."

The stroking stopped. "Sorry, baby."

Irritation flashed. "Don't call me baby. I am not your baby. Stop it."

He grinned. "Sorry, *Claire*. Relax now."

"You won't be able to—oh." Her breath hitched and her eyes closed.

His power invaded her senses—spicy, strong, hot. It curled through her body like a velvet ribbon with a mind and a mission. It reminded her of the first time Rue had tweaked her power, but that had been purposeful, matter-of-fact. This was seductive, sexual.

Adam's magick permeated her skin and soaked through her, like a smoky awareness. It wasn't threatening, but rather something subtle and soft. It reached into her body, exploring her within—seeking, seeking . . .

She shivered. "How can you do that?"

"Don't underestimate us lowly witches." His voice was a silken snare. "We all have our specialties. Now relax."

"I don't think of you as low—*oh*." The sleek tangle he wove through her did things that had nothing to do with magick, not the elemental kind, anyway. She was powerless to tell him to stop.

"That's right. Just allow it."

Her knees went weak and Adam helped her to sit on the couch. He knelt on the carpet in front of her and continued the exploration.

Then he found the elium and she jerked, her eyes coming open. What had been the brush of velvet and silk now rasped like burlap. It didn't hurt, but it did jar in comparison. The elium was an oddity, not fitting with the rest of her magick. Adam's gentle exploration brought that fact home clearly.

His eyes were closed. "Ah, there it is." The internal stroking began again, calming her back into relaxation. "I can feel it. It's rougher than the rest of your magick, foreign. It doesn't fit with your base power, like a puzzle piece with irregular edges, but it's still elemental in nature."

Her body had gone heavy and warm. Adam's fingers tangled through her hair and massaged the base of her neck as the tendrils of his power curled through her. She swallowed hard and had to force her vocal cords to work. "It's *daaeman* magick, not elemental."

"Maybe, but it *is* elemental at its core, Claire. I can taste the fire in it. It calls to me. Fire and metal. I can feel cold, hard ore. The tang of it, almost like copper but not quite, coats the back of my mouth. Wood is present, too. It's otherworldly fire, metal that I can't place, and foreign wood. They're—"

"Elements of Eudae."

"Yes, maybe."

She opened her eyes. Adam's mouth was only a breath's width from hers. He'd been staring at her as he worked, his eyes unfocused. Now they focused. His fingers ceased the gentle massage at her nape for several heartbeats, then resumed.

Claire thought for a moment that Adam would close the short space between their lips and kiss her. They held a heated moment between them before Adam released her, the magickal tendril of his power yanking from her with a palpable snap. She let out the breath she'd been holding.

Adam turned away, his shoulders hunched, a slight tremble going through him. "How much do you know about demon magick? Educate me."

She forced her mind into first gear with effort. She cleared her throat and, with it, tried to clear the lazy fog that Adam had settled over her mind and body. "I can't do what you just did. I've never touched any *daaeman* magick with my power, but it seems natural there would be elemental magick in *daaeman* magick."

"Why do you say that?"

She swallowed hard and organized her thoughts. "Our magick was born of theirs, so the elements must be present in their power."

"Yes." He turned to her. His face was once again that mask she was familiar with, but shadows moved through his eyes. "I bet you can touch another *witch's* power, Claire. *Witch*, being the operative word. It's a skill only some have, and with your abilities I bet you have it. Want to try? You never had the opportunity on Eudae. Here you do."

She took a step toward him, intrigued by the possibility. "Can I try on you?"

A cocky grin split the serious expression on his face, but something unsure moved through his gaze. It was gone in a moment and he walked to her. "That was the general idea."

She touched the center of his chest, the seat of his magick. "How do I start?"

"Close your eyes."

She allowed her eyelids to drift down. His hand closed over hers, broad, strong, and warm. It made her jump.

"Shhh, it's all right, Claire." His voice was the barest whisper and she could too easily imagine him using it in bed with her, limbs and sheets entangled. She licked her suddenly dry lips.

"Now, draw a thread of your power," he instructed. "However you do that, from one element or a couple. Parse out just a little and send it into me."

She did as he instructed, feeling the sluggishness of the Earth she now resided on. Working magick here was akin to living on the moon her whole life and then having to get used to gravity. Focusing her power, she eased it to Adam's chest, hesitated for a moment, and then pushed it in.

His breath caught and his hand tightened on hers. "Yeah," he breathed. "You're in."

Her mouth twitched a little at the desire in his voice. It was arousing to feel another's power rub against yours that way. Nice to know he felt it, too. Now if she could excite him to the point of insanity and then walk away, they'd be even.

She would if she could.

Inching a little closer to him, so she just brushed his chest, she allowed her magick free rein in his body, touching the fiery heat that dwelt within his seat. It was dangerous, playing with power like his. You could get burned if you went too far. So she resided just on the edges of it, licking at it with her own magick, rubbing up against it like a cat.

He pulled her against his body with a groan and his hard cock pressed against her stomach. His hands slipped to her waist, sought the hem of her shirt and her skin beneath it.

"Claire, fuck—" he bit off. His hands went to the button and zipper of her jeans, lingered there. The heat of his fingers warmed her abdomen.

Finally, some reaction from him. Maybe she wasn't just chopped liver after all.

The problem was that she was reacting, too; her body was

responding to his interest in her. The game she played with him might cost her considerably. She stroked his magick anyway, calling it to hers to pet.

Suddenly, his hands tightened around her and his magick flashed white-hot. She gasped, snapping her power back into herself as he pushed her away. She sat down hard on the couch behind her.

Then he was there, with his hands on her knees. "Are you okay, Claire?"

"I-I'm fine. What was that?"

"You," his voice sounded ragged. "It was you. It was hard for me to hold myself back. Eventually, I couldn't." He paused. "The draw between us should have evened out by now, but I'm still really attracted to you. Too much."

Her head snapped up. "I thought you couldn't feel it."

"Oh, hell, Claire, I feel it every second you're near me."

That was great, but it still didn't explain why he hadn't been touching her. By all rights, if he was feeling even a fraction of what she was feeling, he should have been all over her. "It should have faded by now."

"I know." His voice came out a low growl. "Goddamn it, I know."

She swallowed hard at the heated look in his eyes. At the moment he looked ready to push her back onto the couch and strip her clothes off right then and there. Not even Ty had looked at her that way—like she was a four-course meal and he hadn't eaten in days.

"Why do you seem so concerned by the attraction between us, Adam?"

He broke his intense study of her face. "Claire, I don't know what to say." Adam turned his head away and rubbed his hand over a jaw that needed a shave. "Look—"

"Hey."

They both looked up to find Theo staring hard at them from the entrance of the living room. Correction, staring hard at Adam.

"Got something to say?" Adam asked. He didn't move his hand from her knee and there was a challenge to his voice. Some unspoken communication passed between the two men.

Theo stared at him a moment longer and then looked at her. "You all right?"

"Why wouldn't I be?"

Theo's shoulders were tense. "If you ever aren't all right, you come to me."

Adam stood. "What's the big deal, Theo? I was helping her with her magick. She got burned by mine and I was making sure she was okay."

"Yeah, well, it looked to me like you wanted to help her with more than just her magick." Theo moved his gaze to Claire again. "Like I said, if he gives you trouble you don't want, you come to me."

Adam shifted, visibly bristling. His lips pressed into a thin line, but he didn't reply.

Claire tried not to smile. These *aeamon* weren't as disciplined as the *Ytrayi*, but the males had just as much testosterone pumping through their veins. "What if he gives me trouble I do want?"

Theo mastered his surprise well, but she still caught it moving over his face like a swiftly moving cloud. He blinked. "That's between you two. I'm not the house mother."

She didn't know what a house mother was, but she surmised he was saying he wasn't in charge. "That's good to know."

Adam shifted and a bored look overcame his face. "Did you come in here to actually say something interesting, Theo?"

"I just talked to Thomas. He's handpicked ten witches to intercept us and help us guard Claire until Micah makes some progress. They're going to trickle out of the Coven, make sure they're not being watched, meet up, and travel here. Thomas said we can expect them tomorrow morning sometime."

"Who?" Adam asked.

"I only know James, Craig, Erin, Tom Blake, Andrea, Lisa M., and Ingrid for sure are coming. He didn't name the rest. Jack fought to come, but Thomas nixed it because of the baby."

Adam nodded. "It's a good crew."

"Just about the best. If Jack and Thomas were in it, it would be."

Claire stood, suddenly feeling cold. She hugged herself. "I don't want the best of the Coven witches put in danger for me."

Theo fixed her with a stare. "This isn't just about you, Claire. We don't want the *Atrika* to have the elium either. That could be dangerous for us."

"You're not worried about the *Ytrayi?*"

Theo shrugged. "The *Ytrayi* are a wild card, but they've gone out of their way to leave us alone." He shook his head. "We don't know what the *Atrika* would do with the elium in their hands. Trust me, this is about self-preservation just as much as it is about saving your life."

"You're awfully talkative there, Theo. Did you get laid last night or something?" asked Adam.

"Fuck you, Adam," he shot back . . . and actually grinned. Claire was surprised the man's face didn't crack.

"I want to take Claire to the park," said Adam. "We need to get out of the house." He turned to her. "Wanna get out of here for a while?"

"You don't have to ask me twice."

Theo's grin had faded.

Adam noticed and held up a hand toward the earth witch. "Hey, man, you know the *Atrika* can come in here whenever they want. We could have Claire locked down in Gribben and the demons would tear through it like tinfoil. The wards mean nothing to them. They haven't attacked for four days, which means they don't know where we are. It's okay if we go out for a while. Claire needs some space and fresh air."

She did. Adam had nicely anticipated her needs . . . in that regard anyway.

"Like I said, I'm not the house mother." Theo glowered a moment longer, then disappeared back through the doorway.

Adam looked at her for a full moment, then grinned and held out his hand. "Let's ditch this place for a while."

A few minutes later they were out in the car. Neither of them bothered with coats, since they both had fire magick to call. The Challenger *vroomed* to life and settled into a low purr, the vehicle humming beneath her with obvious leashed power.

Adam curled his hands around the steering wheel and closed his eyes for a moment. Bliss enveloped his features.

"You love this car," she said when he put it into drive and hit the gas pedal.

"It's a thing of beauty. What's not to love?"

She settled into her seat and watched the scenery pass by—huge, older homes that housed wealthy families. Perfectly trimmed lawns. Careful sidewalks. There were no cold, hard edges here. In this place, Claire felt a little more at ease. Or maybe it was the man beside her that put her at ease. Adam had an alternating effect on her. One minute he made her blind with need, the next she was comforted by his presence.

He turned down another of the pretty streets and they traveled out of the residential area and into a commercial one. Shops twinkled brightly in the early evening and couples walked hand in hand down the street.

Must be nice, she mused, *to have someone all your own.* Someone you could share yourself with, body and soul. Even though she'd learned to live without that, a part of her longed for it. Longed for a person to call her own in this world, or any of them.

"You know this place well," she said, distracting herself from the dangerous, self-indulgent path her thoughts were taking. "You know right where you're going."

"I have ties here. Family." He paused and drew a breath. "My wife's family, actually. They live around here. My wife and I were both born and raised in Chicago, but she had extended family up here, uncles and cousins. I used to come to the cities with her sometimes."

Claire really didn't hear much after the word *wife*. She'd turned and begun to study him with fierce attentiveness. "You're married?"

He glanced at her. "No. Not anymore." His voice had gone tight, as tight as his white hands gripping the steering wheel.

Claire searched her memory, as she so often did, for her mother's teachings. "You're divorced, then?"

"No, we never divorced."

She stared straight ahead, working it out. "Oh, I'm sorry."

"Wasn't your fault." He cast her a sideways grin, but it didn't reach his eyes. Not even close. "Anyway, lots of the

Coven witches have ties to Minnesota. Maybe there was a genetic pool here, some kind of witchy draw or something, I don't know. Ingrid is from around here. Jack McAllister, too. Thomas even keeps an apartment around the cities. Me, I just know it secondhand."

"Might be the water and trees."

"Excuse me?"

"The elements in this state are strong. Lots of water. I can feel it all calling to me."

"They don't call it the Land of Ten Thousand Lakes for nothing. There are a lot of water witches here, according to Micah." He took a left. "Here we are, Cherokee Park."

Adam slid the Challenger into a spot. They got out and walked into the trees. It was a bit cold outside, so there was no one around. The residential street opposite the park was quiet.

Once they were well into the park, Claire felt more at ease. She stopped for a moment by a towering tree. Leaning against it, she splayed her hand on the rough bark and closed her eyes, soaking in the environment. The cool air kissed her cheek and rustled the branches of the tree overhead. The ground was soft beneath her feet and the scent of earth subtly reached her nose.

This was the Earth she remembered from her childhood.

Green, growing, redolent with the scent of the raw element. All of the elements were here save fire, though the possibility of that one existed everywhere, all the time. Ah, yes, *now* the human part of her was home . . . *finally*.

"Thank you for bringing me here," she said, her eyes still closed. Emotion rocked through her, stimulating the water magick in her seat.

The heat of him warmed her, he stood so close. "I thought you might like a little nature in your diet. After I felt your magick, with all four elements combined, I figured you were probably dying for some of this."

She opened her eyes and took a deep breath of fresh air. "And I didn't even know I needed it."

He jerked his head. "Come on, I want to show you something."

She followed him, almost unconsciously locking step with his.

Adam glanced at her, shoving his hands into his pockets. "So what's with the *Houses* thing?"

Claire frowned, then realized he referred to the expression she used. "The Four Houses of the Universe. It's the primary religion of the *daaeman*. I was raised on it. There are four Houses, each with a spiritual Patron, one for each of the *daaeman* breeds. When *daaeman* die, they live between lifetimes in their respective House, awaiting rebirth." She pursed her lips. "Where they figure the *aeamon* go, I've no clue. I suspect they think we're soulless."

He missed a step. "Demon religion. That's wild."

"Why? They have a culture just like you. Religion, laws, art."

"Yeah, that's what Micah keeps saying. It's just strange. I mean, here demons are a part of *our* religion. They're the bad guys, the devil's pals. They're the ones responsible for all the evil in the world and are the creatures some people blame for their own bad behavior. Demons possess people, make them do malicious things."

Claire went silent, thinking on what he said. "The breeds once dwelt here, a very long time ago, during your biblical times and long before. They coexisted with humans, even had babies with them."

Adam nodded. "That's what created witches."

"Yes. Now, I don't know for certain, but I'd make a guess that because the *daaeman* were so otherworldly, so like gods, that they became a legend in your culture. Eventually perhaps they were made into these creatures that spread evil. I can see how they would be perceived that way by humans."

"But *Atrika* really are pure evil."

She nodded. "Yes. The *Atrika* are living weapons, created only to fight wars on a scale that has likely never been seen on Earth. The *Ytrayi*, *Syari*, and *Mandari* lived with the humans in harmony. The *Atrika* hunted them and occasionally fathered children on the females, oftentimes through rape. The bridge was open to all the breeds back then, before the *Ytrayi* tried to rid Eudae of the *Atrika*."

"Too bad they weren't more successful."

"It's true the *Atrika* are bloodthirsty, every last one of them. They were designed to be that way. They're the most emotional of the breeds, too. The emotion makes them even more dangerous because they act from impulse and on selfish whim. Ever since the wars on Eudae ended, they've been bored. The other breeds—mostly—think of the greater good of their race before making decisions."

"A bored *Atrika* is a dangerous *Atrika*."

"Any kind of *Atrika* is a dangerous *Atrika*."

Falling into silence, they walked through a copse of trees in the darkening twilight. Leaves crunched under their shoes and their breath showed in the cool evening air.

Claire caught her breath as the view emerged.

Adam came to a stop beside her. "The bluff overlooking the Mississippi."

"It's gorgeous."

Adam had known what she'd needed more. All he'd had to do was touch her power and he'd understood her better than anyone else had in a long time. She closed her eyes for a moment and inhaled deeply. "You really do know how to heal people."

"That's my thing, strangely enough. Odd skill to have in such a destructive element." The edge of his mouth crooked upward. "Healing is my greatest strength. Thomas would say my greatest strength is demolition and I'm pretty good at that, too, but healing? Yeah, that's really my thing."

She stared at him for a long moment, looking past the surface of the personality he put on display and straight into the center of him. Claire tipped her head to the side. "So you heal everyone but yourself?"

His slight smile faded and he shifted a little. "Everyone's got wounds."

She redirected her gaze to stare out over the bluffs. "True, but some people's are deeper than others."

He jerked his gaze away from her. "Mine aren't."

She didn't believe him.

The sun sank below the horizon, tangling the sky in hues of red, orange, purple, and yellow until full dark settled over them.

"Maybe this place can be beautiful after all," she murmured.

"Claire?"

She turned toward him and opened her mouth to answer, but he pulled her up against his chest and settled his lips over hers.

THIRTEEN

Her breath rushed out of her at the slow, erotic drag of his mouth across hers.

Adam didn't kiss her, not at first, he just rubbed his lips compellingly against hers. Slow. Thoroughly. Like he was about to devour her, but was biding his time. Tasting. Savoring.

Making her crazy.

Her fingers curled into the fabric of his shirt at the shoulders and she held on for dear life as his sensual assault on her mouth continued. His kiss alone promised wonder in bed. Her breath hitched a little in her throat. Then he slanted his mouth across hers and *really* kissed her.

Claire's toes curled in her shoes.

His teeth raked her bottom lip and her lips parted for him. She allowed her tongue to softly brush his, but the slight touch seemed to make him crazy. Adam crushed her to him and kissed her deeper, until his kiss drove all thought from her mind.

He slipped his hand beneath the hem of her shirt and massaged the small of her back with one strong hand, then brought it up to finger the clasp of her bra.

He broke the kiss and rested his forehead against hers, breathing heavily. "I want you, Claire."

"For the last few days, I thought I'd done something to repulse you." Her voice held a quaver.

He laughed, a raw, gravelly sound. "Like I said, I'm too attracted to you. That's the problem."

"I don't see any problem. I'm attracted to you, you to me. We've got time to kill. We're both of consenting age. I've gotten over my fears that Rue will rip your head from your neck. Where's the problem?"

"You don't care if my head is ripped from my neck?"

She pretended to think. "Well, maybe a little. You wouldn't be able to give me those incredible kisses if you had no head."

He chuckled a little and then stared down at her for a long moment, his face shadowed in the half-light. "Let's go back to the house. I think we have some unfinished business."

BY THE TIME THEY GOT BACK, THE HOUSE WAS dark save for the spill of light under Theo's bedroom door. Adam had taken her by the wrist as soon as they'd cleared the front steps and she practically had to jog to keep up with his steady progress toward their room. If Theo had been standing in their way, Adam probably would have just run him down.

Once inside the room, he bustled her past the mattress on the floor to his bed. He flipped on the bedside light as soon as they got there.

She flipped it off.

He flipped it on again.

When she went to turn it off once more, he reached out and caught her hand, kissing her fingertips. "Uh-uh," he murmured. "I want to see you, every beautiful inch."

Her cheeks heated, but contentment flared through her.

He knelt on the floor between her spread legs and pushed the hem of her shirt upward, kissing over her stomach as he went. Finally, her shirt was gone and he drew a sharp breath.

She was clad in only her bra, a pretty pink lace one that she'd bought on their shopping expedition the first day. It pushed her breasts upward and showed her nipples through the filmy fabric. She'd purchased it because she'd never in her life owned something so feminine.

Adam looked like he wanted to gnaw it off her.

He drew his finger over the plump swell of one breast, then brushed his knuckles over her nipple through the fabric. She shuddered in pleasure and her nipple instantly pebbled. Farther down, her sex reacted.

"Pretty," he murmured, then lifted a brow. "Wonder what else is?" He dropped his hands to the button and zipper of her jeans and made quick work of them. When he slid her pants down and off her, along with her shoes and socks, he found the matching panties.

He made quick work of those, too.

She gasped in surprise when he spread her thighs and the cool air of the room bathed her sex.

"So fucking pretty," he murmured, staring down at her. He held her spread with a hand to each thigh. Then he leaned in and breathed over her.

She trembled with pleasure, her hands-fisting in the blankets on either side of her. He rose then and kissed her. At the same time, he pushed her onto her back with the pressure of his mouth. His clothing rubbed roughly against her bare skin, sending shivers through her.

There was something very erotic about being nude while he was clothed, but that didn't change the fact she wanted him naked. She pulled at his shirt.

"Let me touch you, look at you," he murmured against her mouth. "We have time. There's no rush. Let me savor you."

His hand planed her thigh slowly, spreading her once more for him. He kissed his way down her body, over her collarbone, then over the swell of her breasts still in the pretty pink bra. He ran the tip of his tongue down her solar plexus, dipped it into her belly button, dragged it over the swell of her stomach.

Finally he pinned her thighs to the bed with his two broad, strong hands and kissed her between them.

"Adam!" she gasped, her body jerking off the mattress in a combination of acute arousal and utter shock.

He raised his head. His eyes were heavy lidded with lust. "What's wrong?"

"What are you doing?"

"I'm going down on you, Claire. I wanted to see if you taste as sweet as you look, and you do. *Better*. I want more."

His voice was a silken snare, roughened velvet. His own passion rolled off him in intoxicating waves.

Houses, she hadn't been wrong when she'd thought he looked ready to devour her.

"Don't tell me Ty never did this to you."

She shook her head, cheeks heating. Claire didn't think *daaeman* did *this* at all. It was like what Adam had done to her in her erotic dream.

"Lie back, Claire. Relax. Let me enjoy you." He yanked her down an inch, forcing her to recline. With a firm grip on her thighs, he kept her spread and open to his devilish lips and tongue. If she had wanted to move, which she didn't, she wasn't sure she'd be able to. She was essentially at his mercy . . . and it excited her.

His lips worked over her, weaving an intimate dark magick that she'd never before experienced. He nibbled on her labia, drawing them between his lips. He slid his tongue against her clit, which had fully plumped out from its hood, pouting for attention.

Adam gave it what it wanted. Over and over. Harder and faster.

She grasped fistfuls of blanket and hung on as he sucked it between his lips and caressed it with his tongue. Just the sight of his blond head between her thighs was erotic enough to push her fast to the edge of an orgasm.

He slid a finger deep inside her sex, thrust a few times and then added another, stretching her sex in a deliciously pleasurable way. She let out a low moan.

"Does that feel good, baby?" he asked softly.

"Yes."

"I can't wait until I can slide my cock in there."

Her climax shattered over her, stealing her breath and her thought. Her back arched from the bed, but he remained latched to her, riding her through an intense pleasure that swamped her body and mind.

When it was over, he loomed over her, looking more feral than she'd ever seen him—every muscle in his body tense. His hand was on the button of his jeans and his gaze, which had gone dark and intent with arousal, focused on her face and held there. Then he hesitated and swore low and long under his breath. He punched the mattress beside her and then rolled away to sit on the edge of the bed, head in his hands.

Alarmed, Claire sat up. "Adam?" She touched his shoulder.

After a moment, he stood and pulled his shirt off. The muscles of his back rippled with the movement. "Sleep with me tonight, Claire. In my bed."

It wasn't the first time she'd seen him shirtless, but it made her mouth dry nevertheless. He was leanly built, not overly muscular, but just enough muscle to make you think he'd win any fistfight and would probably fight dirty to do it.

"That was the general plan," she answered in a shaky voice, drawing her knees together.

He took the rest of his clothes off, save the black boxer briefs that outlined the curve of his rear and the jut of his long, wide cock. Adam was still aroused, she could see it clearly. Her fingers itched to touch him, stroke that long, hard length.

Adam snapped off the light. He put her under his blankets, her back flush up against his chest and his arms around her. A satisfied sigh escaped her at the strength of his embrace, the scent of his skin close to hers, and the feel of his groin against her bare buttocks. "But Adam—"

"Shhhh . . . This is called spooning. It's something we *aeamon* and humans do. Do you like it?"

"Yes, very much."

He kissed the shell of her ear. "I wanted to feel you, skin to skin. I wanted your warmth tonight. Is that okay?"

"Yes, but you never—"

"I'm just fine," he murmured. "Better than I've been in a long while and that pisses me off a little, that's all. Get some sleep, Claire. Tomorrow the other witches will get here and this place will melt into chaos."

Despite herself, the warmth of his body, the low rumbling sound of his voice, and her own fatigue were too much for her to fight. Her eyelids drooped and she relaxed into sleep within the circle of his protective arms.

THE SWEET FLAVOR OF HER STILL LAY ON ADAM'S tongue. It was just an appetizer and he wanted the full course.

She'd come so sweetly for him, just the way he'd imagined she would.

Adam had come close to dropping his jeans right there and sliding his rigid cock into the hot velvet clasp of her sex. He still couldn't believe that he hadn't done it. She'd been there, beautiful, wanting him, her sex willing and spread for him . . . and he'd resisted.

Sex with Claire still felt like it would make him unfaithful.

He couldn't put a finger on why Claire was different, but she was. His feelings for her on all levels were intense. As intense, maybe even more so, than they'd been for Eliza. And that was just wrong. There could never be another Eliza.

Adam had to wait until this strange, intense attraction he had for Claire faded. He just hoped it faded before he exploded from sexual need. Jacking off in the shower was becoming very unsatisfying.

Once that intenseness was gone, he could fuck Claire without feeling like he was cheating emotionally on his dead wife.

"Hell," he muttered into the night, disturbing the soft tendrils of Claire's dark, curling hair. "I really am insane."

Maybe so, but he owed Eliza that much. *More*.

ADAM WOKE TANGLED IN CLAIRE. HER LONG, SLIM leg had somehow inserted itself between his thighs during the night. Her cheek pressed to his chest and the silky tendrils of her hair brushed his lips.

He ran his hand up her arm as his eyelids opened, over her smooth, sleep-warmed skin, and she murmured something incoherent, nuzzling his pectoral.

Arousal gripped him like a vise. He became painfully aware of the state of his cock, hard and wanting the woman whose limbs were currently intertwined with his.

She wasn't wearing any underwear.

If he rolled her to her back, tugged her beneath his body, spread her thighs with his knee, would she protest? If he slid his cock deep into her sleep-hot sex, would she sigh and moan for him? If last night had been any indication, Claire would welcome anything he did to her.

And he'd dreamt of her again.

That was why his body had awoken in such a state of intense need. Dreamt of her hands gliding down his chest, her lips brushing over his stomach, closing over his shaft—tongue wet—willing and exploring. In his dreams he'd played out every one of the things he'd wanted to do to her the night before . . . and what he'd wanted her to do to him.

Ah, gods, this was going to kill him.

Carefully, he untangled himself from her delectable body and sat on the edge of the bed, resting his head in his hands. He focused his attention on the carpet underneath his bare feet and tried to ignore the naked woman in the bed beside him.

Having her sleep with him had been a bad move. At the time he'd craved the feel of her against him and the warmth of her body. He'd asked her into his bed on a whim, not thinking about the price he'd pay in the morning.

And those damn dreams! He'd never had any so vivid in his life. Having Claire in his bed was a definite *no-go* from now on.

Claire roused and touched his shoulder. Her fingers on him were like an electric shock through his body. He shot from the bed, mumbled that he had to take a shower, and got the hell out of there.

CLAIRE WATCHED ADAM RETREAT AS IF SHE'D burned him. Frowning, she collapsed back against the pillows and watched him close the bathroom door.

The remnants of another sexual dream still clung to her mind and body. Last night in dreamland, Adam had done things to her unlike anything Ty had ever dreamed up. She'd done things to Adam, too, things that made her blood heat and gave her shivers simply to recall.

She'd put his cock in her mouth, made him tremble and groan her name. In her dreams she'd brought Adam—a big, strong man—to his knees with the bare swipe of her tongue and the kiss of her lips on his shaft.

Afterward he'd taken back control and forced her to her knees. He'd taken her from behind, his cock thrusting deep into her sex harder and faster, his hand stroking her clit, until pleasure had burst over them both.

It had been a wonderful dream, but she wanted the real thing.

Sex with Ty had been incredible. Back then, he'd satisfied all her needs, in every way. However, Adam was proving to be far more inventive. For example, she'd never known a man's tongue could do *that* to a woman.

The man intrigued her, even if his moodiness was somewhat off-putting.

Claire's brow knit as the shower in the bathroom turned on. She had no idea where she stood with him. The man ran as hot and cold as the water he now washed with.

She rose, got dressed, and went in search of the lovely warm drink they called coffee. The invigorating jolt to her veins was fast becoming the only thing that truly woke her all the way up in the morning.

Theo sat at the kitchen table. Pots, bowls, and a mortar and pestle sat on the counter. The kitchen was still redolent with the dry tang of herbs and Theo's spell book was open on a counter. The earth witch had been busy that morning.

She poured herself a cup, fished out a container of strawberry yogurt from the fridge, got a spoon, and sat down near him.

He laid the paper he'd been reading aside, replacing it on a stack of others. His long dark hair fell over one carmel-colored shoulder. "I've been checking the papers from here to Chicago. No crimes worthy of an *Atrika* have popped up, not even in the city."

She spooned up the yogurt. "That's good and it's bad. Good that no one has died that we know of." She hated to have to add that last bit to the end. *That we know of.* "Bad that the *Atrika* have gone quiet."

"What do you mean?"

"If the *Atrika* aren't leaving carnage in their wake, that means they're stalking. Stalking someone or something. They're calculating, trying to be quiet and unobtrusive."

"Yeah."

"When the other *Atrika* was loose here, the one your warlocks pulled through so many years ago, what did you say he called himself?"

"Erasmus Boyle."

She nodded. "That's right. Did he kill many people?"

He took a sip of his coffee. "Six witches, including Isabelle's sister. We know about those for sure. Micah went through all the police records since Boyle was pulled through. I think Micah's number at last count was one hundred and fifteen likely kills of humans."

"That would make sense. On average that's about five kills per year since his arrival. That's more or less what an *Atrika* will take normally, just to stave off boredom. He was not stalking."

"At least not until he started picking off the witches for his magickal blend. He stalked those witches." Theo paused. "Ask Isabelle. He stalked her."

Claire slid her half-finished yogurt cup across the table, suddenly not hungry.

Adam sauntered into the kitchen with his hair wet and sticking up in blond tufts all over his head. He'd shaved, and he wore a pair of close-fitting jeans, a black cable-knit sweater, and a pair of black boots. He mumbled something unintelligible at them and poured a cup of coffee.

"Witches aren't here yet," commented Theo.

"Yeah, I noticed that." Adam lifted his cup. "Thanks for pointing out the obvious, man."

Theo gave him an exasperated look. "Somebody woke up on the wrong side of the bed. I'm just saying, they're not here and they should be."

Icy cold fingers of dread eased up Claire's spine. She opened her mouth to inquire further, but Adam's cell phone vibrated in his back pocket.

He fished it out. "Hey, Thomas." Pause. "No, they're not here." Adam's expression turned grim. "I've been helping Claire parse out her magick." Pause. "Yeah, yeah." Pause. "Okay."

He snapped the phone shut and looked at them. "They lost communication with the Coven witches in the middle of the night, while they were on their way here." He rubbed his chin. "The *Atrika* may have caught them en route. If they did, it's possible they know our location."

Claire stood, throwing her air magick wide open. She glanced at Theo's spell book. "How many charms are you holding, Theo?"

Theo stood, pushing a hand through his long, power-saturated hair. "I couldn't sleep last night. I was up until dawn brewing. I have as many charms as I can store."

"You both remember what I taught you about using earth and fire magick on *daaeman*, right?" She walked into the living room, to the window, and looked down the street.

They followed her and both answered in the affirmative.

"Good. You might have a . . . what's it called? A pop quiz soon."

The *Atrika*, if they'd gotten to the Coven witches, could be at the house anytime. They could be there now, just waiting for the right moment to spring.

She reached with her mind, using the air magick she possessed . . . *listening*. She heard low conversations, leaves blowing in the wind, the murmur of a couple talking on a front porch, the gentle purr of a car engine, a baby crying. She couldn't hear anything out of the ordinary, but that meant little.

And then . . . nothing. A cloud of silence enveloped the world.

Oh, Houses.

She turned, sorrow spiking through her. "I'm sorry about your friends."

Adam took a step toward her. "Claire, what do you—"

"We need to leave. Now."

The *Atrika* burst through the front door.

FOURTEEN

THE BEAUTIFUL WOOD AND GLASS OF THE FRONT door shattered. All three of them dodged to avoid chunks of dangerous flying debris.

The close proximity to the *Atrika* made the balled-up, concentrated elium suddenly sing to life like a tuning fork inside her chest. The jarring sensation drove her to her knees.

Scenting blood in the water, Tevan's blue gaze latched onto her and his eyes narrowed. He spoke in Aemni. "Kai, I'll take care of our own. You take the *aeamon* males."

"Agreed, Tevan."

Tevan took a step toward her and a wall of white-hot fire sprang up between her and the advancing *daaeman*. *Adam*. Tevan's roar of outrage could be heard even over the snap and pop of the spreading blaze.

Claire fought to drag herself to her feet, summoning her own magick around and past the demanding, grasping elium as she went.

Adam grabbed her arm and hauled her out of Tevan's reach as both *daaeman* simply stepped through the wall of fire to come after her.

The air filled with the heavy press of *daaeman* magick,

turning it acrid. Both Tevan and Kai were raising it. It combined with the cloying choke of smoke to suffocate her. A bomb waiting to explode.

Theo pulled power to counter and the addition of wet earth filled her nostrils. As Theo let loose, Adam pulled her down to the floor, covering her with his body.

Dark tang. Hot rush. White, painful blast of air.

Daaeman magick and Theo's earth magick collided in midair. The entire house shook. Bits of the ceiling rained down on Claire's head.

Adam and Claire scrambled to their feet and all three of them retreated backward toward the kitchen. She knew that Adam and Theo could throw as much fire and earth at them as they wanted, but she was the only one with the ability and knowledge to slow them down.

Once they cleared the kitchen doorway, she pushed away from Adam and turned toward them. "*Dars vo. Valdencti ami sae,*" she told the *daaeman. Take me. Leave my friends alone.*

Tevan stopped short, his handsome face twisting with amusement. He answered in Aemni. "Are you asking us for mercy for them?" He gave a short, brutal laugh. "They offend by merely drawing breath, little witch. The only mercy they'll get is a swift death." He took a step forward, his voice lowering to a gravelly, silken murmur. "But you we will treat well."

"Until you get the elium."

He stopped again. "You are not one of them, *vae* Claire." Her eyebrows rose at the use of a formal *daaeman* title for females. "You lived nearly your whole life on Eudae. *Aeamon* or not, we will treat you with respect."

But for an *Atrika*, that still meant death. A respectful killing, but death all the same.

That was not agreeable to her.

Her magick came in a flash, exploding from her chest and her fingers. She couldn't do it any other way; they would feel her raise it and counter it.

The kitchen blasted into chaos. The chairs and table flew at the *Atrika*. The appliances shook free of their mooring and rocketed toward them. Air magick picked up everything it could and turned it into a maelstrom, all targeted at the *Atrika*. The floor beneath their feet shook, making them lose their balance. Superheated water erupted from the pipes and sprayed them. The fire that Adam had started, she fed, sending it in a racing arc toward them.

She couldn't draw all four elements at once, but she could pull a thread of each one by one to create absolute destruction.

"Go!" she screamed at Adam and Theo. "I'll hold them off."

"I'm not leaving you, Claire," yelled Adam over the screaming of her magick and the bellowing *Atrika*.

"I'm the only one who can keep them busy. Go!"

"And when you get tired, what then?" He grabbed her around the waist and hauled her backward.

Theo threw the kitchen door open and they made a flat-out run to the Challenger. The *daaeman* wouldn't take long to shake off the assault. Claire hoped they wouldn't follow up with *daaeman* magick. Not here in the middle of this idyllic neighborhood in broad daylight.

Theo slid behind the wheel and Claire climbed in the front while Adam melted the tires of the sleek gray sedan on the street, presumably what the *Atrika* had used for transport if they hadn't jumped here.

Once Adam had lunged into the backseat, Theo slammed on the gas and the car took off, tires squealing on the pavement. Claire held on as the car shot down the street and took a corner too fast. Behind them, the pretty Victorian in the lovely non-magickal neighborhood burned.

Claire tried to catch her breath and keep her heart from beating faster than the car was traveling. She closed her eyes and assured herself that the *Atrika* couldn't jump into the vehicle with them. As long as they were moving, the *daaeman* couldn't get a fix on them. To jump they needed an *exact* location.

A fire truck passed them going the opposite direction. The fire hadn't been too out of control when they'd left. They should be able to take it in hand before it threatened any other properties. As they'd left, she'd felt Theo moor the land around the house, to help keep the fire from spreading.

Adam slammed his fist into the driver's seat in front of him and swore. "That was Ingrid's car out front."

Ah, the gray sedan.

Theo's hands tightened on the wheel. "I know." His voice was low, grim, and resigned.

"How the fuck did they find the Coven witches? Thomas told me they all left the property separately and at different times. They did that in case they were being watched. So what the f—"

Claire turned and speared Adam with her gaze. "You're dealing with the hunter incarnate, Adam. You can take all the precautions in the world, but they'll still find you if they want to badly enough."

"They got our location out of Ingrid or one of the other Coven witches."

She stared at him for a moment, trying to repress the lump of emotion that had sprung into her throat. She felt responsible for this. "Yes." She swallowed hard. "You should prepare for the worst."

"I know." Adam shifted his gaze past her, to the road.

Theo pulled out his cell and punched in a number, waited, then snapped it closed. "Ingrid's cell. It was worth a try." His voice was tight with a trace of emotion.

She leaned back against the seat, tears blurring her vision.

"We're heading south, into Iowa," Theo said after several long moments of just the sound of the road under the Challenger's tires. "We're going to keep moving this time. From place to place, until Micah gets something on how to remove the elium. So settle back. We have a long drive."

THAT NIGHT THEY STOPPED AT A MOTEL THAT SAT on the edge of a cornfield. The stalks were demolished and dry, harvested long ago for their corn and then ravaged by deer and other animals.

Adam got out of the car, the gentle rustling of the remaining stalks sounding around them in the cool night air, and glanced at the backseat. He'd thought Claire had been sleeping, but she raised her face and her eyes were wide open. She was pale and her expression a little shell-shocked.

He frowned. "Are you okay?" Pause. "Yeah, that was a dumb question." He opened the back door and helped her out. Her hand in his, only that touch alone, sent a tremor through him.

She shivered a little and he fought the urge to draw her close to him. "I won't be okay until this is over."

"Ditto. Come on, we both need food and a good night's rest. Tomorrow we can go shopping again. Maybe this time we'll get to keep everything we buy."

As they made their way through the parking lot and into the lobby behind Theo, Adam noticed uneasily that the lot was full. When they reached the counter, his fear was confirmed.

"We can do two rooms, not three," said the man behind the counter. "All the hotels are booked up for miles around. There's a big game at the university this weekend."

Theo turned back to look at them. Dark circles marked the skin under his eyes and he looked haggard. "Claire shouldn't stay by herself anyway."

Claire stiffened. "I'm more powerful than either of you. Both of you put together!" She glanced at the hotel employee and drew a breath. "I don't need your protection. I need your *guidance*, but if I must stay with one of you, I prefer Adam." She paused and looked apologetic. "No offense meant, Theo."

Theo blinked. "None taken. I'd rather have a room to myself anyway." He turned back to the man behind the counter.

Adam had been looking forward to the possibility of a night on his own, too, if only to keep his hands off Claire. He didn't know how much longer he was going to be able to do that. Especially not with the vivid dreams that had been plaguing him.

Once he and Claire made it to their room—it wasn't like they had a lot of luggage—Adam pulled the phone book out of the desk drawer and called the first pizza place with delivery he found. After he was done, he put the phone back into the cradle and started to make himself comfortable.

Claire was sitting on the bed, shirt cuffs pulled down over her hands and staring at the faded green carpet at her feet as though it held all the mysteries of the universe.

"You hungry?" he asked, pulling his shirt over his head and tossing it over the back of a chair.

"Famished."

"Ever had pizza?"

She looked up at him. "Pizza? No, but my mother told me it's delicious."

"It is. I guarantee you'll like it."

She returned to staring at the carpet. "I don't deserve

pizza. It's my fault those witches were put in danger. If they die—"

He walked to her and put his hands on her shoulders, forcing her to look at something other than the floor. "Stop it, Claire. You heard what Theo said about keeping the elium out of the hands of the *Atrika*. That's for the good of everyone. The Coven witches signed on for this gig. They knew the risks, just like Theo and I do. Anyway, we don't know what happened to them yet. Maybe they got away."

"Maybe. Adam, I got the feeling Theo knows Ingrid personally."

Adam dropped his hands from her shoulders and rubbed his chin. "Yeah, they're sleeping together. I don't know much more than that, though. Don't know if their relationship is about more than just the sex or not. Theo isn't the sharing type."

She swallowed hard. "Do you know any of the missing Coven witches personally?"

"They're all friends, yes. I know them all."

Claire turned her face up to his. "Tell me about them. I want to know these people whose lives I've affected."

Adam sat down beside her and told her everything she wanted to know. He told her about Ingrid and how she had a brutal temper, but a very good heart. How she'd slept with lots of the witches at the Coven, even Jack McAllister for a while, before he'd met his wife and the mother of his child, Mira. He told her about James and how he loved to snowboard and ski. And about Tom and his nasty habit of drinking milk straight from the carton in the Coven's kitchen.

He talked until the pizza came and then while they ate. Claire devoured her share, washing it down with Coke. She'd developed a taste for junk food pretty quickly.

"How about you?" he asked as they polished off the remains. "You have any friends on Eudae?"

She thought for a moment. "Their culture isn't like here. It's not so informal or friendly. There were some that I spent time with, weaving magick or performing certain tasks, but you don't joke around there. You don't order pizza and sit around talking until early in the morning."

"You were really lonely, weren't you?"

She nibbled a crust a bit, then threw it onto the box. "Yes. I didn't realize it then because living there was all I knew. Now I understand how lonely I was."

Adam took a chance and brought up the subject that had been on his mind from the beginning. "Jack McAllister, he's a fire witch back at the Coven, says he knew you when you were little."

She stiffened. "What?"

"His father, William Crane, was the head of the Duskoff. Crane was the mastermind behind opening the doorway and casting the demon circle that pulled Erasmus Boyle through all those years ago. Jack was just a kid back then, but his shit of a father demanded he be present for all gatherings of the Duskoff. Jack says he remembers a little girl named Claire running around his father's mansion during those meetings. You must have been about six, he told me—curly dark hair and blue eyes."

The blood drained from Claire's face. "This man is William Crane's son?"

"Yes. Estranged son, anyway. The day they cast the circle that brought Erasmus Boyle through from Eudae was the last day Jack called William Crane his father. Crane adopted a little boy later on, a fire witch named Stefan. But biologically, yes, Crane was Jack's father."

"Was? Crane is dead?"

Adam nodded. "Mira, Jack's girlfriend, got to know her air magick really well one day and pushed him through a forty-story window. Why all the interest in William Crane?"

Claire had regained the color in her face thanks to the conversation and the pizza, but now it was gone again. "My mother used to talk a lot about him. She was a member of the Duskoff and was personal friends with William Crane. My mother was a warlock."

"I figured as much."

"We spent a lot of time at William Crane's mansion. I remember a little of the house, but I was very young. Mostly I remember the gardens. Sweet-smelling flowers everywhere, tall trees, green grass. My strongest memories of Earth are from right before we walked through the doorway, so that garden has always shaped my vision of this world." She paused, shaking her head. "I do have vague memories of a little boy with large eyes. That's probably Jack." She shook her head, remembering. "He never smiled."

"He says you did. He says you ran around the house, charming everyone, smiling all the time, and getting into everything." He drew a breath, plunged ahead. "You don't smile all the time anymore, though. Is that because your mom took you away the day they cast that demon circle?"

Her jaw locked and she glanced down at the demolished pizza. "Yes. After the circle was cast and the *daaeman* had come through, my mother summoned me from where I played in the garden. While the warlocks dealt with the enraged *Atrika*, she took advantage of their distraction and walked us through the doorway. That's how we got to Eudae."

"Jesus, Claire. That's practically suicide. Why did she do it?" Rage made fire spark in his palms. He closed his hands to hide it from her. How could a mother pick up her young daughter and just walk straight into hell?

Claire looked down at the blanket and picked at a stray thread. "My mother was impetuous, sometimes more like a child than an adult. I suspect mental illness, but I was so young when she died. I'm just not sure. She told me she'd fought with Crane earlier in the day about how to handle the *daaeman* they would bring through. My mother had—" She swallowed hard. "She had—"

"Hey, look, Claire. It's okay if you don't want to tell me all this."

She shook her head and raised her gaze to meet his. "Just know two things before I say this. Know that I loved my mother more than anyone in either of these worlds. Also know that I am nothing, I mean, *nothing*, like her."

Adam nodded. "Okay." He knew that already.

She lowered her head again. "She had aspirations of allying with the *Atrika* and bringing them back here. She wanted to take over with their help." Claire looked up at him, her pretty eyes wide and shining with tears and shame. "Adam, my mother wanted chaos and bloodshed so she could have power and prestige."

Adam didn't even blink. "Claire, your mother was Duskoff. She was a *warlock*. It's what they all want. That's why they break the rede."

She went back to studying the crust-strewn pizza box. "Anyway, she'd fought with Crane. He'd disagreed with her about how best to employ the *daaeman* they'd pulled through. My mother was angry, so she walked into the portal, thinking she'd find the *Atrika* on the other side and do it her way."

Adam couldn't reply.

He got up, paced across the room and back before he could speak. "So she just gathered her six-year-old daughter from the garden where she'd been playing and walked through an alien doorway not knowing what would happen on the other side?"

Anger simmered under the surface of his skin. A thousand licks of flame. Protectiveness of Claire, even twenty-five years after the fact, swelled.

While he'd been having the training wheels taken off his bike and having birthday parties at Chuck E. Cheese, Claire's mother had been busy taking her away from everyone and everything that was familiar to her. Not to mention knowingly putting her daughter into harm's way—directly into the arms of demons.

Claire raised her head, protective anger to match his crossing over her pretty features. She opened her mouth to retort and he held up a hand. "Okay, I'm sorry. I know. You loved your mother."

"I did."

Of course she had. Her mother had been the only human being—*aeamon*—in Claire's entire existence.

He pushed a hand through his hair and desperately fought to get a handle on his emotions. Adam had no idea why Claire made him lose his grasp on them so often. "What happened once you got over? Did she ever find the *Atrika*?"

"No, thank the Houses. Rue found us first. He was set on killing us because he understood that my mother had come to try and make an alliance with the *Atrika*. Instead, because we were females, he took pity on us."

"But he never sent you back."

She shook her head. "No. He didn't trust my mother not to make trouble with the warlocks. I thought he might send me back after my mother died, but I'd become too valuable to him by then."

"Gods, Claire."

She shrugged. "You asked."

"Do you know who your father is? Do you have any family at all that you know of here?"

She went very still. "I have long suspected my father to be William Crane."

Again, Adam was speechless.

"I don't know for certain. My mother died when I was eight. It was sudden. An illness took her in the space of a week. I suspect Crane because of how often she talked of him." She licked her lips and her voice grew quieter. "And the *way* she talked about him."

"If that was true, Jack would be your half brother." Maybe there was some kind of DNA test they could do when all this was over . . . *if* all this ever was over.

She looked up at him. "Yes, wouldn't that be crazy?"

Adam was sure Jack would think so.

FIFTEEN

Claire curled her shaking hands under herself on the bed. She'd never talked about any of this to anyone before. She'd certainly never spoken aloud her suspicion that William Crane was her father. There was something about Adam that made her open up, something about him that made her trust him.

It was time she started trusting someone.

At any rate, it felt good. Like she'd oiled some rusty hasp on the box containing her secret self. Now she could open it easier and share the contents if she chose.

She watched Adam clean away the pizza box and turn the bed down. He'd taken off his shirt, so she watched with interest the way his muscles flexed as he moved.

Adam seemed deep in thought about what she'd told him and didn't notice her staring. He knew he was gorgeous, though. Adam was a man who understood the effect he had on a woman and used it to his full advantage.

Well, with all women but her anyway.

He looked up at her. "I guess we're sharing the bed tonight?"

Damn it. He sounded *resigned*.

Claire looked away from him. "Yes."

"We have no toothbrushes, nothing to sleep in but our clothes. In view of the situation, not knowing if the *Atrika* will track us here, we should probably sleep fully dressed." He spread his hands. "We don't know if they'll show up in the middle of the night. We don't want to be caught with our pants down. Literally."

She sighed. "Look, Adam. I can take care of myself. As I must keep pointing out, I'm stronger magickally than you or Theo. I need you two mostly to guide me through life here, not really to protect me from the *Atrika*. *Houses*, I'm strong enough to do that myself. Anyway, I'm fine with sleeping in the car—"

Adam was in front of her within the blink of an eye. He pulled her to her feet. "You're staying in this room. With me. Tonight. Don't give me any bullshit about me not being able to protect you." He paused and his lips twitched. "It offends my male arrogance and stirs up all my testosterone."

"Adam—"

The trace of amusement faded. "No. *Really*, Claire. All joking aside."

She tried hard not shiver at the touch of his hands, which now rested on her waist. "You just seem so reluctant to touch me." Claire did her best to keep the note of pain from her voice, but she couldn't manage it totally. "I thought I would spare you."

He glanced away and swore under his breath. "Claire, you're killing me. You know that? You're totally fucking killing—"

He kissed her.

His mouth came down over hers with such heat and possession that it pulled the breath right out of her. He didn't coax her lips apart, he demanded. The first touch of his tongue on hers was like a brand and it sent tremors of sexual need rocketing through her. He owned her mouth, every inch of it. With this kiss he made all question of his desire vanish.

Adam pushed her backward, onto the bed, and followed her down, still kissing her. He crawled up her body, sliding his hand beneath the hem of her shirt and up to cup her breast through the material of her bra. She gasped into his mouth.

"Claire, I want you. I'm fucking taking you this time, too."

"Finally," she whispered against his mouth and then nipped his lower lip. "I want you, too."

He shuddered and nipped back. "I have no condom."

"I'm an earth witch at the core and very familiar with my body's rhythms. I won't get pregnant tonight."

He kneed her thighs apart and pressed his cock against her through their clothing. "I guess we won't be staying fully clothed after all."

"It could be dangerous when we fall asleep."

He dragged her lower lip between his teeth. "I don't think we'll be doing much sleeping," he drawled in a honeyed voice. He slipped his hand to the waistband of her pants and unbuttoned them. "Let's get rid of these." Adam had them off her in a matter of moments.

She kissed over his chest as he worked her shirt up and over her head, leaving her clad in only her bra and underwear.

Her hands slid over his skin as she undressed him—over his shoulders and down his arms—velvet pulled tight over sinuous steel. Bit by bit, his clothes dropped to the floor, revealing his mouth-watering chest, his narrow hips, and—*finally*—his long, wide cock.

It was beautiful.

Claire closed her hand over it at the root and stroked upward, running her fingers over every delectable vein up to the smooth crown. Adam jerked and groaned against her mouth, dragging her lower lip between his teeth.

Pressing her backward, Adam braced himself above her on the bed and kissed her mouth, along her jaw, and the sensitive spot just below her earlobe. Then dropped to the swell of her breast.

Claire arched her back and her breath hissed out of her. Her fingers curled into the short strands of his hair when he drew her bra down low enough to lave her nipple. Ripples of pleasure shot through her as he explored the peak thoroughly— every ridge, every puckered valley. Her legs closed around his hips and he ground against her while he did the same to the other nipple.

What he did excited her whole body, clouded her mind with want. Her entire world became his hands on her skin, his lips trailing down her stomach, teeth nipping as he went.

Five small licks of heat flared against her skin—two on either side of her hips, two on her shoulders, and one between her breasts. She glanced down and saw that he'd stripped her of her bra and panties using fine, controlled bursts of fire.

He nipped the curve of her waist. "I'll buy you a whole new wardrobe tomorrow if you want." His gaze flicked over her bare breasts and his voice took on a tone of reverence. "Gods, you are so beautiful, Claire." Kneeing her thighs apart, he dropped his head to her inner thigh and laid a kiss high on her leg. "And you taste too damn good to resist."

"Adam!" she yelped as his hot mouth closed over her. It was the last word she was able to utter for a while.

He laved her clit until she couldn't see straight, until the pressure to climax had her arching off the bed. Yet, he didn't let her tip over the edge. With his skillful tongue, he kept her suspended in the delicious space right before an orgasm. Claire moved her hips, trying hard not to beg him. She wasn't sure she could form the words anyway.

Adam slid one finger within her, then added a second. Deliberately. Methodically. *Diabolically*. He began to thrust.

The pent-up, withheld energy of the orgasm exploded through her. Claire fisted the blankets and cried out as it washed over her. Adam rode her through it, extending it, until Claire's body went boneless and her knees were weak.

Adam climbed up her body and found her mouth, kissing her deeply. His knee slid between her thighs and parted them, his hips settling in the cradle of her spread legs as though they'd been made to fit there. The head of his cock pressed against the entrance of her sex and she rolled her hips, trying to force him inside.

"Hush, Claire," he whispered against her lips. He stared down into her eyes. "We have all night." Holding her gaze, he gathered her wrists and pressed them down onto the mattress on either side of her.

Just like in her dream.

"I've been waiting a long time, Adam," she murmured.

He held her gaze steadily, his expression serious. In his eyes roiled dark emotion, but his body was taut with lust—desire—for her.

"What's wrong?" she asked, frowning.

Adam shifted his hips, bearing down on her wrists at the same time, and thrust the wide head of his cock inside her.

Claire's eyes widened. It had been so long since she'd had a man inside her. The fact he held her gaze as he came within her made the moment that much more intimate. Her muscles stretched as he worked himself slowly within—inch by mind-blowing inch. Her breath caught once he was seated root-deep within her. She felt possessed by him, filled up by him . . . and she liked it.

"Claire," he murmured.

Her name sounded so full of emotion that it momentarily pulled her out of the sensuality of the experience and brought a lump to her throat.

Never, *never* had a man looked at her the way Adam now looked at her. Never had a man, not even Ty, said her name like she was the center of everything. Tears pricked her eyes.

And then Adam began to thrust.

Her fingers curled around his shoulders as he dropped his head and kissed her mouth and then her jaw and then her throat. As he pumped inside her, letting her feel every glorious inch of his cock from root to tip, she let her hands trail over his back, waist, and the gorgeous curve of his rear.

When she finally came the second time, Adam did, too. Pleasure poured over them both and Adam whispered her name over and over into the damp curve of her neck.

They lay tangled together on the bed, breathing heavily for several moments, before Adam rolled to the side and tucked her against him. He trailed his fingers down her arm and over her breast, making her shiver with delight and her nipples pucker.

"I keep having dreams about you, Claire. Sexy dreams. Gods, I've never had dreams like these, not even at the height of my hormone-filled adolescence."

She turned onto her back. He drew lazy circles on her stomach. "That's strange. I've had sexy dreams about you, too."

His circling finger paused, then restarted. "That is strange. What exactly did you dream?"

She licked her lips and felt her cheeks heat. "They're pretty erotic. Are you sure you want to know?"

"Do I *not* want to hear about an erotic dream you had about me?" He gave a low, rough chuckle and moved back to her nipple, teasing it with his fingertip. "You really have to get to know me better."

"Okay, I'll tell you." She closed her eyes and sighed, enjoying the play of his fingers over her body. "The first night I slept in your room, I dreamed you made me come with your lips and tongue. You sucked my clit until I screamed your name, then you mounted me and held down my wrists as you took me. Just like you did now."

"Mmm . . . I like that dream. What else?"

"Another night while we were at the house in Crocus Hill, I dreamed I took you into my mouth. I explored you with my tongue and it was fascinating. I licked up and down your shaft and I wanted to make you come, but instead you flipped me to my stomach and came inside me from behind."

His hand slid down her stomach and between her thighs as she spoke. There, he wove a spell of dark erotic magick that made her breath come faster. The pad of his finger stroked her clit, making it spring to life with pleasure once more.

"Uhm . . ." She picked up her lost train of thought. "I could feel your chest against my back and you pressed me down . . . *oh* . . . against the mattress with your body as you thrust inside me. You slid your hand between my body and the bed to stroke me—"

"Stroke your clit?" he purred. "You mean, like how I'm doing right now."

"Uh, yes."

"And then what happened?"

She licked her lips. "I came. In my dream, I came."

"And now, Claire? Are you going to come now?"

She did. It rolled over her slow and easy, beautiful and gentle in contrast to the two explosive ones she'd already had. Her back arched under the spell of it. Adam sealed her mouth with his and ate up every sigh and moan she made—hungry for them.

Claire curled against his body once it was over and closed her eyes, exhaustion settling over her.

"I had the same dreams, Claire."

She lifted her head. "What?"

"Exactly the same dreams, I bet even on the same nights. Probably at the same time."

"How?"

Adam shrugged a shoulder. "That's a question for Micah."

"Magick." She kissed his shoulder. "It had to be magick. Some kind of psychic bleed-through. Maybe it was my air magick reaching out for you in my dreams."

Adam held her closer. "Baby, everything about you is magick."

CLAIRE ROUSED IN THE MORNING TO ADAM RE-turning to the hotel room. Between his teeth was a white bakery bag. In one hand he held several plastic shopping bags and in the other he had a cardboard holder with two coffee cups.

He set everything on the table. "I got you some new underwear."

She sat up, letting the blankets fall away. Claire hid a smile at the way Adam's gaze roved her bare breasts hungrily. "And coffee."

He picked up the white bag. "And doughnuts. I figured they'd go well with the pizza we had last night. We have to make sure all four food groups are represented in our diet—fat, sugar, carbs, and caffeine."

She smiled. "Excellent."

Adam walked to the bathroom, pulling his shirt over his head as he went. "I'm going to hit the shower. Let me know if I bought the right stuff for you." He disappeared past the doorway.

Claire stared at the closed door. Adam's mask was firmly back in place this morning. Now she could easily recognize it. Something was bothering him, but he didn't want her to see what it was.

The man wore his emotions on his sleeve, but he didn't think he did. Adam obviously thought his mask was seamless, no cracks at all. And perhaps he had managed to hide himself and his feelings from his fellow witches all this time.

But she could feel the darkness in him and see it in his eyes. She saw it pass over his face in unguarded moments and could hear it in his voice. Adam kept secrets, ones he didn't want anyone to know.

She slid from the bed and wandered over to the bags. He'd bought her a few changes of clothes, not just underwear—a couple pairs of jeans, a couple sweaters, a few shirts, and some socks. There were three sets of soft, satiny pajamas, plus various sundries—toothbrush, toothpaste, shampoo, and the like.

He'd also purchased many pairs of panties and several bras, all silk and lace, feminine ones like she'd selected the first day they'd gone shopping.

Had he understood her need to feel such soft, girly articles of clothing against her skin? After so many years of serviceable gray *Atrika* underclothing, the frothy bits of almost nothing available to women here seemed downright decadent—lovely. Or maybe Adam was simply being a man, and hadn't thought past what he wanted to see on her. Claire could hope it was the former. Adam was insightful enough to manage it.

She stuffed the clothing back into the bag. Houses, she was thinking way too much about Adam and his intentions toward her. Under the current circumstances, such frivolities hardly mattered. Why was she even wondering about this? She had a demonic weapon inside her and two *Atrika* on her tail.

Putting the shopping bag to the side, she pulled out a doughnut to nibble on and sipped her coffee while Adam finished up in the bathroom. The doughnut was so good she thought for a moment she'd pass out.

Adam exited after a few minutes with a towel around his waist. In the doorway, he halted, comb halfway through his hair. "Claire, if you sit around the hotel room naked, I can't be held responsible for what I might do."

She set her coffee cup to the table and stood. "Oh, I hope so." Keeping her gaze on him, she took the bag with the clothes and sundries, walked past him slowly into the bathroom, and closed the door.

It took Adam exactly five seconds to follow her.

He caught her by the arm and pressed her against the bathroom counter, facing the mirror, and bracketing her on either side with his hands.

He met her gaze in the reflection. "That sounded like a challenge."

Her lips curved in a smile so mischievous, she wondered for a moment who the woman in the mirror was. "You gave me a taste of everything I've been missing out on for the past five years, Adam." Her sly smile widened. "Can I be blamed for wanting another helping?"

Adam slid his hands up her body to cover her breasts. She watched in the mirror as his skillful fingers plumped and teased each nipple into a hard peak. Her breath came faster and her sex heated. His touch did that to her.

Adam's touch made her body *want*. Action. Effect.

Still holding one breast, he dragged his other hand down her flesh and between her legs. Eyes wide, she watched him stroke her sex in the mirror's reflection. His big hand moving so softly, so slowly. All to pleasure her. The gentle, giving action seemed so at odds with the sight of his forearm and upper arm, which was muscled and powerful—built to be a weapon, yet now bestowing soft erotic pleasure.

Her eyes fluttered shut and her head fell back as the now-familiar haze of lust began to swamp her mind.

"No," he commanded roughly. "Watch me touching you, Claire. *Watch*."

She opened her eyes again and focused on his hand between her thighs. The pressure of her impending climax building, she watched him ease a finger inside her and press his hand against her clit as he thrust in and out. He held her tight against his bare chest, other hand around her breast, fingers playing on her nipple.

Claire's cheeks were flushed and her lips parted. Her eyes were heavy-lidded, languorous, and her hair lay against her shoulders in lazy disarray. Her body tensed as she reached the maximum threshold and her orgasm washed over her. Claire's knees went weak as she came, and she gripped the edge of the counter with trembling fingers.

He flipped her in a heartbeat and had her up on the counter. Adam ripped his towel away and slid her rear to the very edge. Then, setting his cock to the entrance of her sex and tangling his fingers through her hair on either side of her head, he pushed within her to the root of him. His stomach muscles rippled with the long, easy thrust.

There was a mirror behind him, too, one that stretched

from the floor to the ceiling. In it she watched in fascination as his buttocks and the muscles of his calves and thighs flexed as he pushed his cock deep into her body. Her legs, paler than his, were spread wide and dangling on either side of his narrow hips.

Claire gasped at the delicious stretch of her muscles and wiggled a little on the counter. He dropped his hands to her waist and held her still as he thrust.

She curled her arms around his neck and he dropped his head to suck one of her nipples into his mouth. His hands roved her body along with his lips, tongue, and teeth. The man loved to use his mouth, always gently biting, claiming. Always kissing, always licking. Every drag of his lips left a trail of fire behind.

He buried his face in the curve of her throat. "Gods, you are beautiful, Claire. So fucking pretty. And you feel so good." He paused. "In every way. Good enough to melt my heart."

She came first, again, impossibly. It was like her body was making up for all those lost years. Then he came, murmuring her name and kissing along her jawline before claiming her mouth.

He stayed inside her, arms around her and face buried in her curls, long after they'd both found their bliss.

SIXTEEN

IT RAINED. NOT JUST AN ORDINARY RAIN, BUT THE cold kind you get in the winter. Constant drizzle with periods of actual rain. Frigid damp just on the verge of freezing. At times the rain obscured their vision and made all of them a little cranky.

Of course, Adam was cranky for other reasons. He couldn't keep his mind off Claire. He'd given into his libido the night before. Given in and done exactly what he swore he wouldn't do.

Not since he'd first met his wife had he been so emotionally drawn to a woman. Giving in to that draw had dishonored Eliza's memory when Adam owed that memory his life.

At the time, Adam had thought perhaps giving in to temptation just once would eliminate it. He'd scratch his itch and give Claire what she wanted, too—one of the many fundamental human experiences she'd been missing out on. No harm, no foul.

In the back of his mind, Adam had known it wouldn't work that way. His attraction was too strong for such a simple solution. All the rules of engagement were different with this woman. He'd known, way deep inside, that he was just using it as an excuse to touch her.

He'd touched her all right. Thoroughly. Repeatedly.

And in the morning, he'd only wanted to touch her more.

After she'd gone into the bathroom, invitation in the lilt of her voice and the sway of her hips—Claire was fast learning to leverage her feminine allure—he'd stood beyond the door and fought with himself for a full five seconds before following her.

It really hadn't been much of a fight.

All his encounters since his wife had died had lacked a deeper connection, one that was alive and well with Claire. That deeper connection made sex so much fuller and satisfying—just like how it had been with Eliza.

But it also made the low, throbbing bite of grief he was so familiar with flare back to life—a dog worrying his heart like it was a juicy bone. After their encounter in the bathroom, the grief had intensified to pain.

Adam didn't know what his attraction was to Claire. Pheromones? Some unfathomable biological undercurrent? A metaphysical connection? Adam had no idea; he just wished it would fucking stop.

He wished he could get away from her for a while, try to break it. Yet the thought of being away from her made something hard, hot, and unpleasant flare in his chest.

Gods, he was so unbelievably screwed.

And he wanted a cigarette, goddamn it. Or a drink.

They drove through the rainy morning, heading south. Adam and Theo had decided to do a wide circle around Chicago. Every day they'd move somewhere else, but close enough to the Coven so that if they had to get back they could do it in under ten hours. The Challenger was up to the task—sleek, muscled, and fast, it rumbled beneath them, tires sure on the slick, uncertain roadway.

In the afternoon they stopped at a restaurant in a small town past the border of Missouri. While Theo went next door to a bookstore to buy a newspaper, Adam followed Claire inside and sat down in a booth.

She studied the menu in front of her, long lashes dark against her peaches-and-cream skin. A curl, caught on the fabric of her sweater, sprung free. She wore no makeup and styled her hair completely naturally. Claire was honest and clean, in appearance and personality. What you saw was what you got.

Claire was *not* his type. Not at all like Eliza, who'd been polished to perfection at all times and far out of his blue-collar, lifelong working-class league.

And yet Adam still held the scent of Claire in his nose— that beguiling alien flower that clung to her hair and skin. He still had the ghost touch of her on his fingertips, against his body, around his cock.

He wanted more.

The thrill for Adam had always been in the chase. Not that many of the women he pursued he'd had to chase very far. He made sure the women he picked wanted to be caught . . . and let go. Even so, normally, when he'd had them once, his infatuation ended. It was like that old saying: *you always want what you can't have*. Once he'd had it, that was it. The allure was gone.

Isabelle would have said it was brutal of him, and maybe it was. He always tried his best not to hurt a woman's heart. He was always careful to choose women who were looking for the same thing that he was in a relationship—sex, companionship for a short time, friendship. Love was never on the table. Strings were strictly forbidden. Real relationships? Totally out of the question.

The Adam he had been before Eliza's death would never have wanted any of that casual bullshit. He and his wife had been able to finish each other's sentences. They had laughed together every single day of their lives. Shared all. Eliza had been his other half.

But then she'd gone and died. It had been his fault. And everything had changed.

So how was it that this woman, Claire, had gotten under his skin? She was like some sweet addiction that, once sampled, he needed regular infusions of. Adam had been with many women, and yet Claire's responses in bed—so honest, so gently surprised, and so very, very erotic—were arousing beyond belief.

And it wasn't just her sexual responses that drew him. He loved the way she opened like a flower to this world. How, at first, she'd been so unsure and cold, but every day she blossomed to the possibilities around her. Found her place on Earth, even under these circumstances.

Every day she became the human being she partly was, yet had been taught to suppress her whole life.

He liked the way she laughed. He wanted her to do it more often. Adam wanted to be the one to make her laugh, wanted to be the one she looked at—eyes sparkling—while her mirth flowed.

He loved the way her curls moved over her shoulders, too, inky dark against her pale skin. It fascinated him, made him want to plunge his hands into her hair and pull her toward him for a kiss. Her teeth, a little bit crooked in front, he thought were charming. He wanted to trace that little bit of imperfection with the tip of his tongue. His fingers curled to stroke her soft skin whenever he saw large amounts of it exposed, and he loved to run his lips over it.

In fact right now, as she tipped her head to the side and her hair fell away, exposing the long line of her throat . . . his cock hardened. He studied that vulnerable expanse of flesh, thinking about how soft it was under his teeth, wanted to give it the lightest and barest of nips.

She looked up. "Adam?"

"Hmm?"

"You're looking at me that way again."

"What way is that?"

"Your eyes are all heavy-lidded and you're staring at me like you want to eat me."

He leaned forward. "That's because I do."

She shivered a little and he hid the pleasure zinging through his body at her response. Claire glanced at the menu. "Know what you're going to order?"

"No. I was too busy staring at you to look."

She glanced up at him, smiled a little. Blushing, she studied the menu ferociously.

Theo showed up with a thick paper in his hand. He slid in beside Claire, set it aside, and scanned the menu.

The waitress showed up and they ordered. Then Theo sat back and opened the paper in front of him. The three of them read through it in silence while they waited for their food to arrive—a silence of dread, like a vigil.

They found nothing. There were plenty of murders, some massive fires, lots of robberies, and even more corruption, some of it not even political, but no mention of a mass killing of ten individuals that could be marked as a demon slaying.

They each closed their sections of the paper with marked relief and yet . . . where were they? If they'd escaped, the ten witches sent to intercept them should have checked in by now. That fact tainted Adam's mind with the edge of dread. It was only a matter of time before they learned what had befallen the Coven witches. It would not be anything rosy and sweet.

The food came and Adam had the pleasure of watching Claire have her first cheeseburger and french fries which, clearly from the look of rapture on her face, was a sensual experience for her. At some point they'd have to talk about cholesterol, but for the time being he intended to let her enjoy all the culinary delights on Earth that she wanted to try.

"So, Adam tells me you were once kidnapped by the Duskoff," Claire mentioned to Theo between bites.

Adam almost choked on his burger. She hadn't learned much about social nuances and reading people's body language. That topic, thrown in Theo's lap, was the equivalent of a grenade with its pin pulled.

Theo laid his sandwich on his plate and shot a dark, glowering look at Adam before glancing at Claire. "When I was a teenager, yes, they got me for a time."

She set her half-finished burger on her plate and studied him. "They thought they could . . . enslave you?" Her eyes glittered with undisguised interest.

"They've done it before. They had an air witch for a while. His name was Marcus. They got him young and since he wasn't all that strong, they were able to control him. They kept him drugged most of the time. Air witches are a hot commodity, even weak ones, because they can overhear things at a long distance. The Duskoff try and take them all the time."

"But you're an earth witch. Those are a dime a dozen, right?"

"An earth witch," Adam broke in, "yes, but you can feel how strong Theo's power is, right?"

She glanced at Theo. "So that's why they wanted you? They wanted to manipulate you, bend you into a shape they could use to their advantage." She paused, thinking. "Hone you, like a tool or a weapon."

Theo stared at her for a long while before answering. When he finally did, his tone was as gentle as Adam had ever heard it. "Yes, like you, right, Claire? That's what the *Ytrayi* did to you."

She clasped her hands in her lap. "Yes, but instead of a tool or a weapon, I was a curiosity, an experiment to them."

Gods, were they making progress? She'd used the past tense and spoken of the *Ytrayi* for the first time with dread in her voice.

"Maybe the *Ytrayi* aren't so different from the warlocks. I was just lucky to have the Coven witches to back me up." Theo jerked his chin at Adam. "He wasn't with the Coven back then, but I know he would have come in after me if he had been. It's good to have people in your life you can count on. People you can trust."

It was the most that Adam had ever heard Theo say about his kidnapping.

Claire stared down at her plate for several moments, then excused herself to go to the bathroom. Adam watched her disappear down the hallway. Was she thinking about how she didn't have anyone to back her up, didn't have anyone to trust?

She did, but she didn't know it. Not really. Not yet.

Adam eyed Theo across the table. "You like her."

"Yeah, sure I do." Theo glanced at him and shrugged. "Why do you sound surprised?"

"I didn't think you liked anyone."

"Normally, I don't." Theo took a bite of a fry.

Claire emerged from the bathroom and stopped by a small television mounted behind the restaurant's bar. The volume was down too low for Adam to hear, but whatever it was made her stiffen. She wrapped her arms around her chest.

The waitress came by with a pot of coffee and filled Adam's cup. The older woman shook her head sadly and glanced at Claire who still stood transfixed in front of the television. "You all hear about that horrible tragedy? I never thought I'd live to see something so heinous happen around these parts."

Theo glanced at Adam. "What do you mean?"

She stood with her elbow braced on her waist, balancing the coffeepot. "It started yesterday up in Saint Paul. That's where they found the first body." She shook her head. "Murdered like something out of a horror movie. They found another body this morning just shy of Ames, Iowa, killed just the same way and found on the side of that highway there." She motioned toward the door of the restaurant and, presumably, the road that went past it with her coffeepot." The same one I take to work every day."

"Do they know anything about the victims?" Adam asked. His voice sounded hoarse and a little shaky. His fingers had gone icy, all the fire sapped from them.

"Both from the Chicago area, one man and one woman. The police think it's a serial killer." She shook her head. "You all be careful out there." The waitress walked away.

Theo stared at him, mouth set in a grim expression. Barely banked rage clouded his eyes with magick—turning them a deep, earthy brown. A tornado turning up topsoil.

"She said a woman, but we don't know if it's Ingrid or not," said Adam, finally.

"Doesn't matter who it is, they're all friends. *Fuck.*"

It mattered. Adam could see it in Theo's eyes. A normal person didn't sleep with someone and then not flinch when they heard they might be dead. Not even Theo was that cold.

"Is it a message or is it magick?" Theo asked. "Are they using the witches for some kind of tracking spell? Or do they know what direction we took and they're leaving a grisly message to inform us?"

"I have a feeling it's both." Adam pulled his wallet out and threw some bills on the table. "Either way, we'd better get moving." He stood.

Claire walked to them, face pale. "I have to tell—"

"We know." Adam pulled her against him, wanting to protect her against everything coming their way. "The waitress told us. We have to get the fuck out of here." He turned and walked toward the door, pulling her behind him.

"No!"

Adam stopped and turned.

She shook her head. "I'm not running anymore. The *Atrika*

are probably using the *aeamon* for spell-work. That means the others could still be alive. We have to try and get them back."

"Yeah, I suspect the same thing. I'm through running, too, Claire."

"It's a trap," said Theo, standing. "They're using them as bait."

Adam rubbed his chin, thinking about a strategic course of action. "I know. It's time we made a stand." He turned on his heel and walked out of the restaurant.

SEVENTEEN

ADAM GLANCED AT THEO AND STUFFED HIS HANDS into the pockets of his jeans. "As a witch, I don't feel good about stopping in a place named Salem, even if it's in Missouri."

Claire had to think for a moment before she got the reference to Salem, Massachusetts, and the witch trials. It had been a part of her education, stuffed away in the back of her brain.

She often felt one step behind everyone else. In the car between Ames, Iowa, and the restaurant in Missouri where they'd received the bad news, he and Theo had talked about something called a *Slinky* and it had perplexed her for a good half hour.

They were making their stand in a rented cabin out in the middle of the woods near Salem. A town selected because it had a store that dealt in rare weaponry and antiquities. Theo had found that out by searching for stores that met their needs on something called *Google* accessed from a small electronic box he called a PDA.

They were fortunate enough to locate a mecca for collectors, a store that boasted lots of copper weaponry, among other things. Adam was delighted to find a copper sword. All the copper weapons Theo and Adam had brought from the Coven had been left at the house in Crocus Hill.

Their shopping spree left them well armed, but Claire knew it would come down to magick, not swords or knives.

Since they couldn't go to the *Atrika*, they were going to let the *Atrika* come to them. The cabin in the woods meant they'd be able to fight freely and not draw attention from non-magickals.

"I think it's kind of fitting," announced Theo as they brought in the last of what they'd purchased from the car. "Witches are always burned in Salem."

"Sure, now he gets a sense of humor," muttered Adam.

From what Claire knew of the kind of dark magick the *Atrika* used, most likely the *Atrika* already knew their position. They'd probably used the first two witches for some kind of tracking spell. She believed the *Atrika* would keep the remaining witches alive in case they needed them later for blood magick.

She hoped.

"They'll be driving some kind of van or large SUV. Tinted windows, so no one can see in." She'd been giving them her thoughts on the situation as they worked. "They'll be keeping the witches in stasis."

Theo halted. "Stasis?"

"All *daaeman* hold venom in their fangs. When they're in a killing rage, the fangs extend. They're like spiders. They bite their victims and render them immobile. Depending on the strength of the venom, the victim may not retain all their senses, but they will stay alive."

Adam took some food out of a brown paper sack in the kitchen. "Boyle bit Isabelle last year, right before he was going to kill her."

Claire shuddered. "Yes, they can keep a victim in stasis for long periods of time with regular doses of their venom."

Adam walked to the huge fireplace that dominated the open living room and started a fire on the logs with a burst of magick. "How long can they endure that without bad side effects?"

Claire shrugged. "On an *aeamon*, I have no idea. Isabelle is the first I've heard to undergo stasis. The *Ytrayi* have never used it on me, so I don't know."

Adam's cell phone vibrated and he took it from his back pocket. "Hey, Thomas."

Thomas yelled so loud that Adam jerked and held the phone away from his ear.

"Yeah, I know," answered Adam, "but they're going to catch up with us sooner or later. This way, at least we've got a chance of saving the other witches." He listened for a while and then glanced at her. "I got her covered. Got that covered, too. Yeah, yeah." He snapped his phone closed.

"Thomas not happy with our plan?" asked Theo.

"Nope, but I don't see another option at this point and neither does he. If we keep running, they'll keep chasing and killing witches while they come. Plus, when they catch us, we won't have our heels dug in and be ready for them. Anyway, being chased around goes against my grain. I'm not the running type, are you, Theo?"

"Nope."

"Didn't think so."

Adam walked over and gave her the cell phone. "Micah's going to be calling in a few minutes. He wants you to go somewhere quiet for the call. You can take one of the bedrooms while Theo and I finish getting set up."

"All right." She took the phone from him and he grabbed her wrist, deliberately stroking his warm fingers over the inside of her hand. His gaze held hers. There seemed to be a world of emotion and unsaid things in his eyes.

All she wanted right now was to find the couch or a bed and curl with him. He made her feel safe, loved, protected— *cherished*. She wanted the world to go away, the *Atrika*, all of it.

In that one moment she wanted Adam with all she was.

With effort she pulled from his grasp. "Thanks." The phone felt smooth and warm from Adam's hand. She walked into one of the two bedrooms off the living room and shut the door behind her.

The cabin was posh. It was rented out to rich people who liked to hunt or go for romantic interludes, according to Adam.

It was just a vacation spot, but she'd happily make it her home if she could. It was a pity it was so nice, since with the *Atrika* on the way it was likely to be badly damaged.

There were two bedrooms, both decorated in dark primary colors. Overstuffed furniture with lots of pillows and throw blankets were scattered throughout the space. This bedroom had a king-sized bed, a long carved wood dresser, numerous brightly colored area rugs covering the hardwood floors. It even had its own bathroom.

As soon as she'd sat down on the bed, the cell vibrated in her hand. "Hello?"

There was a long pause on the other end. "Claire?" queried a rich, low voice on the other end.

"Yes?"

"It's such a privilege to finally talk to you." Pause. The man sounded a little awed. "Wow. I have so many things to ask you I can't even pick one thing."

Claire smiled into the receiver. His voice quavered with excitement. "I'm told you're sort of the Coven archivist and you've been studying as much of Eudae and the *daaeman* breeds as you can."

"Night and day. It's my obsession. I'm the Coven's walking encyclopedia of all things demon. We didn't know very much before the ordeal last year with Erasmus Boyle. Since then our base of information has really exploded, but there's still lots of things we don't know."

"Well, Micah, I'd be happy to add to your knowledge whenever you like."

"Thank you *so much*." He blew out a hard breath. "Okay, let me organize my thoughts a moment. I called about the elium, specifically. The rest will have to wait. Our goal is to keep you alive and the elium out of the hands of the *Atrika*."

"I would appreciate that."

"Over the last year, ever since Thomas was in Eudae and we were trying so hard to get him back, I've been amassing texts. Lots of them are ancient, books of legend and myth that the world thinks are just legend and myth. Many obscure religious texts. Among the books I've been procuring, there's one called the *Dai Codex*. In it, I found references to elium. What it is. How it works."

"How to get it out of me?" Metallic desperation coated the back of her tongue at the question.

He didn't answer for a moment. "I'm still working on that one, Claire."

She closed her eyes in defeat.

"But we do know more about elium, so we're getting closer."

She opened her eyes. "It's a weapon. I know that much. Adam reached in and sort of . . . tasted it and it's made of elemental Eudae."

"Demon magick."

"Yes."

"It *is* a weapon. Claire, you're carrying a magickal weapon big enough to destroy all the magick on Earth and probably Eudae, too, if it's used toward that end. It can kill, as well, render death to thousands if employed with that aim."

She touched the bone between her breasts—over the seat of her magick—with shaking fingertips. On some level, she'd already known that. The heaviness of it weighed her down inside. Death. Destruction. All hiding within her. Resonating like a tuning fork to the energies of the *Atrika*.

Like to like.

"It's the equivalent of a supercharged EMP blast," he continued. "Only in this case it would render all elemental magick hit by it null. It would also affect all the elements within the strike radius in a negative way—earth, air, water, and fire. The world would be plunged into utter chaos if the elium was ever fully deployed.

"You make it sound like I'm carrying a nuclear bomb."

"You are. Essentially for witches and *daaeman*, you *are* carrying a nuclear bomb. I expect that the *Ytrayi* probably used the elium as a threat against the *Atrika*. Rue probably carried it himself. But Rue probably also understood that while the *Ytrayi* wouldn't use the elium as anything other than a way to press the *Atrika* into certain behavior, the *Atrika* wouldn't hesitate to deploy it in order to wrest control of Eudae from their enemies."

"So when they broke into the palace, he panicked and passed it to me."

There was a long pause that made Claire's stomach tighten.

"A normal witch—a normal *aeamon*—wouldn't be able to carry the elium, Claire. I wonder how much of his tweaking of your magick over the years was in preparation for just such an event." He drew a long, slow breath. "I also wonder if he imbued you knowing that no one, not even the *Atrika*, would be able to extract it."

Her hand tightened on the phone. Had Rue done that? Had he planned since the day he'd made her handmaiden at the tender age of eight to give her the elium in the case of an *Atrika* uprising? Had he allowed her to sleep next to him all those years with such coldhearted intentions?

"You said you're still working on finding out if you can get it out of me." Her voice was barely a whisper.

"I am. Claire, *I am*. Everything I just said, it's a theory. Not proven. I just don't feel like I can keep you in the dark about the possibilities in play."

"I appreciate that."

"I am doing all I can to discover a way to take the elium out of you. Until we make progress on that front, you might be able to use the elium against the *Atrika*."

She shook her head, even though she knew he couldn't see her. "Every time I touch it, it makes me sick."

"Let Adam help you."

She frowned. "What?"

"You said he tasted the elium. That's one of his special skills. We all have them, nuances in our magick. One of Adam's is being able to touch other people's power, make small adjustments, and do healings. If you work with him, he might be able to help you acclimate your magick to the elium and get past the sickness. Once you do that, I have no doubt that with your strength, you'll be able to tap and use it."

"Okay, say Adam helps me past the sickness and I can pull threads of the elium, what if I pull too much? What if I nuke the world?"

Pause. Then, he said, "Yeah, don't do that."

She laughed. She couldn't help it. It was the stress, maybe. It bubbled out of her irrationally until tears streamed down her face. It probably didn't do a lot to reinforce Micah's faith in her.

"Look, Claire, I don't know you. However, judging by how

I'm told Rue shaped your power over the years, I'm betting you have both the control and the ability to do fine work with the elium. You're probably the only witch on Earth who does."

She sobered. "We'd better hope so."

"Yes, because the elium may be the only real weapon you have against the demons hunting you. Also, you should start now. No time to lose."

Nothing like putting a countdown clock on trying to control an alien power that could destroy the world.

Claire drew a steadying breath. "Thank you for calling, Micah."

"It was my pleasure to talk to you, Claire. We'll meet soon at the Coven, I'm sure of it."

Claire wished she could be as certain.

ADAM SAT CROSS-LEGGED ON THE BED FACING Claire, her palms resting lightly on his. She closed her eyes and opened herself to him, allowing him to thread a bit of his power through her.

Beyond the room, Theo kept watch. The *Atrika* could show up at any time, but Adam tried hard not put any additional pressure on Claire to perform. She needed to be relaxed to accomplish this.

When Adam had touched the elium at the house in Crocus Hill, he'd noticed that it was wildly off balance with her normal power. He couldn't do more than brush the elium, but he might be able to regulate Claire's natural magick into alignment with it. That might take away the cause of her sickness and allow her to work with the demon magick.

Theoretically, anyway.

"Okay, Claire, I'm going in."

Her body stiffened and her hands jerked on his almost imperceptibly.

He stroked his thumb across her palm and endeavored to make his voice soothing. "Hey, baby, it's all right. Just take it easy."

She drew a breath and relaxed a little.

"There you go. Now close your eyes and let me in."

Her eyes drifted shut and he drew a tendril of power from

the center of his chest. It was easier to find a way into her this time than it had been before. Somehow, someway, she was more open to him now.

Adam found the seat of her magick and was surprised—for the second time—at its strength and vitality. Claire had been a powerful earth witch before Rue had tinkered with her. Now she was the bionic woman of magick. He found the core of that strength and enveloped it with his own power, steadying it.

She tapped the elium, very lightly. The tap resonated outward like a tuning fork, vibrating against his power through the tendrils the elium had wrapped around Claire's seat. He held on tight to her power and felt her magick cringe at the resonating vibration of the elium down the length of those tendrils.

The level of her magick was so out of balance with the elium that it made it back away, sensing a threat within her. That was his theory, anyway.

Using his fire magick, he nudged her seat, forcing her power to swell and defend itself. It worked. His natural healing instincts coming to the fore, every time Claire touched the elium, he adjusted her power using various tricky methods.

Her hands tightened on his. Adam opened his eyes and saw that she was grimacing. "Claire?"

"You're helping, Adam. You are. Normally, I would be passed out by now. But—" She drew a shaky breath. Her face was pale and her forehead glinted with a fine sheen of perspiration.

Panic rose in his throat. "Stop, Claire. Release any hold you have on the elium right now."

"I can't." She shook her head. "I need to learn how to control it."

"Yeah, but not at this high a price. It's making you sick."

She drew another deep breath and her body trembled. He couldn't let her power free of the cradle he was holding it in until she'd completely backed away from the elium. "It feels like it's sucking my life away."

"Let it go." He growled the words. "*Now*, Claire."

He felt her release the light hold she had on the elium. Immediately, her eyes fluttered closed and she collapsed backward onto the bed. Adam's thread of power snapped back into him like a rubber band and he was over her in a flash, holding her in his arms.

She lay, shaking and cold. Her shallow breath made his heart beat fast in his chest. "Claire, can you hear me?"

After a moment she nodded, licked her dry, white lips. "Give me a moment."

He stroked her hair. It tickled his nose and he breathed in the scent of her gratefully. "You're scaring me, baby."

She gave a shallow laugh. "I'm scaring myself." She swallowed hard. "It's taking little chunks of my life from me."

"It's not," Adam said in a fierce voice. If it was, he'd kick its ass.

He lay down beside her, spooning against her—her back to his chest—and wrapped his arms around her, trying to get her warmed up. He pulled a thread of power and wrapped her in it, but all the heat he poured into her seemed to just evaporate.

She shivered. "I feel so cold, so dead."

Her words made fingers of dread crawl slowly up his spine. He held her closer and increased the amount of heat in his embrace. She shivered once and then went still.

"Claire?" He sat up, trying to look at her face.

In answer, she rolled to her back, lifted up, and kissed him. But it wasn't just any kiss. This was a full-on fuck-me kiss with all the trimmings.

Her tongue meshed to his, mouth slanted and aggressively pressed to his lips. His body responded like a shot. What had been fear for her only moments ago melted easily into passion.

"Damn it, Claire. You're going to make me crazy with a kiss like that," he whispered against her mouth. "Stop it. You're playing with fire."

"I know I am. I'm trying to make a spark." She studied his face for a moment. "Make me feel alive again, Adam."

Whoa.

"Baby, as much as I want you, now is not the time. We have no idea when the *Atrika* might show up and—"

She kissed him again, cutting off the rest of his sentence. Finally, she set her forehead to his. "*Exactly.*"

Claire nipped at his lower lip and slipped her hand between their bodies to fondle his already hard cock.

There really was only so much one man could take. Especially, Adam was chagrined to admit, when it came to Claire. She was already like some dark, magickal addiction. When she went after him like this, so aggressively, kissing him this way . . .

The demons could fucking wait.

EIGHTEEN

HE CAME DOWN OVER HER BODY, KISSING HER BACK with even more heat and pressing her against the mattress.

If she wanted him, he was hers.

With his free hand he undid the button and snap of her jeans, pulled them down and off her legs, along with her underwear. Her flesh was pale and cold everywhere.

Pushing the hem of her shirt up, he kissed along her breasts and stomach, then urged her to roll over on her stomach so he could run his lips and hands over the chilled skin of her back. She moved restlessly beneath him, pressing the curve of her perfect ass into the cup of his groin.

He dragged his hand down between the cheeks of her rear and found an area of her body that was a far cry from cold. Hot and slick, Claire's sex was eager for the touch of his hand. He found her clit and rubbed it, making her moan.

Her fingers clutched the blankets as he slipped one, then two, fingers deep inside her velvety, tight sex. Her muscles rippled around his fingers as he thrust in and out. Her hips moved, too, as she met his movements as though he fucked her with his cock.

The last remnants of the control Adam possessed shredded.

He unbuttoned his jeans and forced them, along with his briefs, to his ankles. Claire pushed up again, fitting her ass to his groin in invitation. He grabbed her hips and met her there, pushing the head of his cock into her entrance and feeling the stretch of those satiny muscles, the hot fist of her sex around his shaft.

"Hell, Claire, you feel so fucking good. I'm not going to last long."

She glanced back at him, breathing heavy. "Make my blood pump again, Adam."

Pulling out of her, he held her hips and thrust back in. Harder. Faster. He set up a rhythm that would drive them both to climax in minutes.

Claire dug her knees into the mattress and met him thrust for thrust. Together they fell into a physical harmony that made his magick pulse in the center of his chest, made fire tingle along his skin in hot little bursts. No other woman he'd ever been with made his power flare like that during sex.

Claire's magick answered and it wasn't the elium, it was *her* power—a clear, beautiful pulse of element that momentarily took his breath away.

Knowing he wasn't going to take long to come, he threaded his hand between her body and the mattress, pushed between her soft thighs. Finding her clit, swollen and aroused, he stroked it over and over.

She shuddered, the first clue that he was touching her the way she liked. He kept it up—steady, firm, relentless pressure driven by his thrusts. It made her body shiver, then go taut.

Beneath him, she orgasmed. The muscles of her sex tightened and released in pleasurable spasms, milking his cock. Her cries, soft and heady to his ears, filled the air. Her body relaxed as the climax took her over, her magick flaring in an arc around them.

It wasn't long until he followed her. Pleasure rocketed up from his balls and overtook him, mind and body. He came inside her, her name falling over and over from his lips.

Afterward, they lay on the bed together, tangled and sated. Claire was breathing heavily now, deeply. A healthy flush tinged her cheeks and her body was warm to the touch.

Sex had done the trick. Sex as a reaffirmation of life to counter the taste of death on Claire's tongue.

"You feel better?" he asked, rolling her once again in a position to spoon.

She snuggled against his chest and sighed. "So much better."

"There are strange things about you, Claire. The dreams for one thing." He paused, thinking, his fingers trailing over her skin. "And when we make love, you trigger my magick."

"Make love?"

He opened his mouth and closed it. "Doesn't seem right to say fuck, even though I like to fuck you."

"You think there's a difference between fucking and making love?"

He stroked her upper arm. "Yeah, I do. I've done a lot of fucking in my life and it's been good. I've spent a lot less time making love, but making love is better. Deeper."

"What happened to your wife, Adam?"

He stiffened at the question, his fingers halting the stroke of her soft skin. It was like a punch to his gut when he least expected it.

She rolled to her back. "I mean, how did she die?"

Adam sat up, yanked his jeans on, buttoned them, and pulled a hand through his hair. "She died during a burglary."

"I'm sorry."

He gave a harsh laugh. "Twenty-five brownstones on the block and the guy had to walk into ours."

Adam still remembered it vividly. He always would. He'd just arrived home after his shift. It had been late, around midnight. He'd gone upstairs where Eliza had already been in bed. She'd woken and wanted a bottle of water for her night table. He'd offered to get her one—*Gods, he'd offered to go instead of her*—but she'd told him to take a shower, go to sleep.

He'd just been unbuttoning his shirt when he'd heard the gunshot.

The fear running through him, hot and thick, had been nothing he could control when he'd raced downstairs to find Eliza lying in a pool of her own blood.

He hadn't hesitated, not for a moment. He'd raised power and blasted it at the middle-aged, scruffy-looking thief. He'd been a warlock with earth abilities. Later he'd found out that the warlock had targeted his house specifically; he'd been targeting lots of witches around Chicago, breaking into their houses. He'd already killed three people.

Adam hadn't known all that at the time, though. All he'd seen was a strung-out low-life warlock who'd just shot his wife and didn't look a fucking bit upset about it.

Adam's fire magick had risen unbidden. He'd been out of control, his rage perfect. The warlock had tried to raise power, but Adam had been ten times stronger and faster with his abilities. He'd burned him alive where he stood. A flash of white-hot flame, then just a charred thing on the carpet, smoke curling up in lazy tendrils.

Ashes to ashes.

Once it had been done, Adam had lifted Eliza in his arms and she'd died. The memory still choked him up.

Since Adam had reached for magick instead of his gun, dealing with the aftermath had been a problem. The killing had been in self-defense, since the thief had had his gun pointed at him. But how would he explain the charred remains to the authorities?

Adam had called the Coven and they'd helped him conceal the nature of the killing. They'd helped him dispose of the body, clean up the mess in his house, all of it.

He'd told the police the burglar had gotten away.

Wracked by grief for Eliza, Adam had quit the force the next day and gone to work for the Coven. Thomas Monahan had earned his complete devotion from that day forward, and the Coven had gained themselves a loyal and skilled hunter, someone who tracked down warlocks and dealt with them.

"It happened in the middle of the night. I was just off shift. I had my uniform on for fuck's sake. I had my gun." He let his voice trail off. "But I was too late. She went downstairs to get a bottle of water. I heard the gunshot. By the time I got there, she was on the floor. She died in my arms."

Claire's hand was on his back. She'd probably put it there a while ago, but he only noticed it now. It was warm. The heat of her palm bled through the fabric of his shirt and branded his skin. The touch of her comforted him.

"What happened to the thief?" she asked softly.

Adam spread his hands. "I burned him, burned him practically to ash."

"Your wife wasn't *aeamon*?"

He shook his head. "As human as human could be. She knew about me, though. About us. I could never keep any secrets from her."

Claire was silent for a long time. Finally, she asked, "Do you still love her?"

He looked at her. "Not like that. I'm not in love with a dead woman, Claire. She's gone and I know that. I've grieved her and moved on, but I feel in debt to her. I was responsible for her death." He swore low. "I was *there*! There with my gun, there with my fire. I was in the house and she still died. I was a fucking cop and the burglar still got her right under my nose."

"Adam—"

"So, I'm sure that makes you feel really safe with me, Claire. Considering I'm supposed to be protecting you and I couldn't even keep my own wife from being shot in our home."

She shook her head. "Adam, I do feel safe with you. Sometimes bad things just happen. Sometimes—"

He shook his head and yanked away from her. "No, don't tell me not to feel responsible, Claire. Damn it. I get the stages of grieving and all the psychobabble. It still doesn't change how I feel."

"Okay." She paused, pressed her lips together. "But I do trust you Adam. I trust you more than I've ever trusted anyone."

He shook his head. *Poor woman.* "You're one of the few people other than Thomas who knows any of this."

"I won't tell anyone."

He studied her sitting there with the blankets drawn up around her body. Adam wanted to hold her, *needed* to hold her. Needed her warmth and her closeness in a way he couldn't remember needing a woman for a long time. He wanted her skin to skin, but that wasn't wise.

"Get dressed, Claire. Just in case. Theo said he'd take first watch, so let's try and get some sleep, okay?"

She nodded.

"Even put on your boots." He'd bought her some good steel-toed ass-kicking boots because sometimes magick wasn't enough.

He watched her dress, repressing his very strong desire to pick her up, sling her over his shoulder, and kidnap her. Take her somewhere far away and lock her there, so that he and Theo would be able to fight the demons themselves and she would stay safe.

Adam's jaw locked. Somewhere between then and now Claire had become his to protect, to shield, to care for. Every protective male fiber of his body fought the temptation to simply drag her off by her hair to a cave somewhere so she'd be safe.

The problem with that was threefold. First, Claire was stronger than either of them, so to handicap themselves in battle that way was sort of silly. Second, Claire would never allow him to protect her in that way and she would probably kick his butt royally if he tried. Third, it would just be wrong. Claire's future was at stake; she deserved control over it.

But it was fucking hard to deny that caveman part of him.

After she'd dressed—a pity—he lit a fire in the fireplace, flipped off the light, and lay down with her on the bed. The blaze in the hearth made shadows lick the walls of the room and filled the space with a warm glow.

Even though he'd just had psychological and emotional shit stirred up, and even though they were waiting for two killer demons to come knocking on their door, Adam couldn't help but notice the serenity that stole over him as soon as Claire was in his arms.

She fit there perfectly. Head tucked under his chin, arms around his chest, one long, slim leg resting in between his. Even their breathing meshed.

Adam let out a slow, uneasy breath. The problem staring him in the face was ugly. He'd failed to protect Eliza. Eliza had died.

His arms tightened around Claire. No way in fucking hell, or Eudae, would he fail twice.

THEY CAME IN THE EARLY MORNING.

Claire sat straight up in bed. Adam was already at the door, wicked-looking copper sword in hand. Every nerve in her body seemed to flare to life in an odd psychic awareness. Deep within her, the elium throbbed, making nausea burn bitter on the back of her tongue.

They were here. They were angry.

Adam threw the door open to find Theo already going head-to-head with Tevan and Kai. Earth magick pulsed the way she'd taught him to use on the *daaeman*—with a little twist and a whole lot of punch. Fire magick burned subtly across her skin as Adam drew power.

Claire threw the blankets away and tucked a copper dagger into the waistband of her jeans at the back. Then she rushed after Adam, raising her own elemental magick to join theirs.

As soon as she cleared the threshold, she sent the room into chaos, leaving clear an area around Adam and Theo. Furniture flew, dishes crashed.

The *Atrika* stood at the doorway. They'd just strolled right in, it appeared. While she kept them busy knocking away the projectiles she sent toward them, Adam and Theo lobbed earth charms made to pummel and bolts of fire at them.

Kai bellowed as Theo found a way through his shields and hit his stomach with a bolt of earth magick so strong it made her nostrils tingle with the scent of dry ground. The *Atrika* turned and screamed at her, eyes bloodred and fangs extended. "Come with us and we will not make the male *aeamon* suffer."

"Fuck you," yelled Adam. "You're going to have to kill us both to get to her."

"Stupidity!" shouted Tevan over the din of magick and crashing debris. He lifted his hand and threw a bolt at Adam.

Claire blocked it just in time with earth magick, but the elium—tingling in violent resonation to the *Atrika*—drove her to her knees.

Tevan took the opportunity. A cold, hard thread of power wrapped around her leg. Claire cried out in surprise at the strength of it. Tevan tugged her forward and she went down on her stomach, searching desperately for purchase on the rug.

The rope of energy around her leg tightened painfully, and he pulled her toward him. As she neared Tevan with increasing speed, her fingernails dug into the wood floor, scratched at another area rug.

"Claire!" Adam ran to her, but Tevan yanked her out his reach, toward him, just as Adam's fingers brushed hers. She screamed as she suddenly shot over the polished hardwood floor like a bullet, straight toward Tevan's open arms and sharp fangs.

Adam bellowed in frustration and shot fire magick at Tevan, but he just blocked it.

Hard fingers closed around her legs and flipped her. She lay on her back with Tevan looming over her. He smiled, showing fangs. They were bone white and tipped in red.

She couldn't let him bite her. One bite and she was done for. She'd be unable to use her magick, not to mention move. She couldn't let him jump her anywhere either.

Claire brought her foot up fast and hard, kicking him square in the face with the heavy sole of her boot. He went careening backward with an *oof* of surprised pain.

Adam came from her left and swung his sword at Tevan, striking his thigh. Tevan howled in pain. Acidic blood sprayed from his wound, which popped and sizzled from the copper exposure. The demon went down on his knees.

Taking advantage, Adam swooped his blade upward, aiming straight for Tevan's throat. At the very last moment, Tevan jumped and disappeared. Adam's blade *whooshed* through air.

Tevan jumped back into the room right behind Adam.

"Watch out!" Claire yelled, raising air magick and sending a chair careening into the *Atrika* to knock him off balance.

Adam turned, dropped the sword, and tackled the *Atrika*. Together, they rolled across the floor, punching each other.

To her right, Kai and Theo were locked in a magickal battle. Claire rolled to her feet and sent the couch crashing straight into Kai, giving Theo a chance to regroup.

Then she turned and refocused her attention on the tangle of Adam and Tevan. Tevan pushed his hands into Adam's chest and Claire screamed, knowing what was to come.

Daaeman magick pulsed, scorching the air with its thick, acrid scent. Adam flew backward. He hit the wall behind him with a sickening thump, collapsed to the floor, and lay still. Cold terror crawled up her throat, but she had no time to dwell on it.

Tevan turned toward her and Claire raised a thread of earth to block and fire to parry with. She used both as soon as she pulled them, preventing Tevan from wrapping her in another tight coil of power. She couldn't allow him to drag her toward him again.

Aeamon magick didn't work very effectively on the *daaeman*. It worked as a distraction, or as a sideswipe—magick used the way Adam had done in Wisconsin, blowing up a car and managing to get the *Atrika* in the blast.

But it did work sometimes when you twisted it just right— a thing Theo and Adam had already grown good at and Claire had mastered.

She hit Tevan dead-on with her thread of fire—perfectly executed. He blocked the stream, but it still sent him careening backward into a window. Glass shattered. The scent of charred *daaeman* rose in the air.

The shock of using two separate threads of earth and fire at the same time weakened her knees and sent her collapsing to the floor.

Rue's voice echoed in her mind. *You still haven't learned to integrate the elements, Claire. Learn!*

She drew a shaking breath, knowing she had no time for rest or recovery. Taking the opportunity to help Theo while Tevan was down, she whirled and drew two more threads.

Kai anticipated her action and shot a massive blast of power at her. She dove to the floor just as it hit. It scorched her back, singeing her clothes and sending a flare of pain through her.

She heard a very human grunt and the sound of fists hitting flesh. Claire army-crawled to the edge of the overturned couch—she'd landed behind it—and peered around to see Theo and Kai rolling on the floor, locked in a fistfight.

She understood Theo and Adam's desire to throw punches instead of magick, since their power was not totally effective against *daaeman* shields, but fistfights with an *Atrika* wouldn't go well. She shot to her feet, gathered her strength, and aimed it at Kai.

If only they would separate a little to give her a clear shot . . .

Ironlike hands clamped down over her shoulders, making her yelp in surprise and pain.

Tevan.

He yanked her back hard enough to give her whiplash and she reacted from some primal, animal-like survival instinct. She thrust her hands back and funneled all her earth magick into Tevan's massive thighs, twisting a little and forcing it hard to get past his natural shields.

All it did was make him yelp and release her, but that was enough; she rolled to the side and gathered more power.

Not enough.

He was on her again in an instant, pulling her to the ground and straddling her. Acidic blood dripped onto her clothes and burned through the fabric to her skin from the cuts he'd sustained from the window. The pain made her cry out and writhe beneath him.

Houses, that probably excited him.

Huge hands closed around her neck, closing off her screams of agony. His body braced, preventing her from thrashing, hitting, and scratching in her frenzy to be away from the burning.

His head lowered, fangs extended, toward her throat.

NINETEEN

SHE WENT STILL, HER BREATH *WHOOSHING* OUT OF her. Terror sang through her blood like vinegar—fiery, bitter.

Adam grabbed Tevan and pulled him bodily from her, just as his fangs brushed the tender skin where shoulder met throat. For a moment she lay there, drawing a shuddering breath of relief before pushing up from the floor.

Tevan and Adam had lain to rest all magickal law and had engaged in another old-fashioned fistfight. Tevan was a *daaeman*, and therefore bigger and stronger than Adam.

But Adam knew how to throw a punch.

He connected solidly with Tevan's jaw and sent the *daaeman* careening backward.

Claire sprawled on the floor, parts of her blood-spotted skin screaming with fiery pain, and gaped at Tevan knocked out on the floor. Adam turned, shoulders hunched, expression of absolute rage on his face.

Like something out of a nightmare, Tevan rose behind him and pulled him down.

Claire screamed and *acted*. Without conscious thought. Definitely without planning.

The elium, just the tiniest thread she'd pulled, exploded out of her, rocketing her into darkness.

"CLAIRE?"

She came awake slowly, held and rocked in Adam's arms. Her wounds burned, but his warmth made it all right. Houses, was she still alive? The blast that had propelled her backward had felt like the end of the world and she'd only used the barest amount of the elium. Claire didn't want to imagine what it would be like to use more.

"Baby, are you okay?"

Her eyelids fluttered open. He sounded panicked. She raised her hand and touched his face. "I'm all right," she managed to whisper.

"You almost *died*, Claire. *Fuck*. The elium almost killed you. It was only my healing ability that brought you back." His voice sounded shaky, thin.

She hurt everywhere, but especially her chest where the elium dwelt side by side with her own magick. Nausea curled through her stomach and her head pounded. Her whole body felt cold and shivers wracked her.

Adam's fire magick enveloped her in an effort to stave off the deathlike chill the elium produced, but did little to improve the coldness that had overtaken her.

Claire tried to sit up. "Tevan. Kai. Where are they?"

Theo's strong hands pushed her backward, into Adam's arms. "The elium vanquished them, Claire. It zapped their ability to use magick, as well as ours. They seemed shaken that you'd been able to use the elium and jumped out of here."

She shook her head. "They'll be back."

"That's for certain, but maybe not for a while. It gives us a chance at least."

"We couldn't use our magick for a time either," Theo continued. "We thought you were going to die on us."

She tried to sit up again. This time, Adam helped her. She drew a deep breath and pushed away her pain and discomfort. Her head swam. "The other witches. Have you found them?"

"Take it easy, Claire," said Adam. "The demons *poofed* out of here and then we had to take care of you. We're going to look for them now, but we had to make sure you were okay first."

She tried to push up, but Adam held her firmly. "I'm fine. Let's go."

"Are you sure?" Adam looked doubtful.

"I'm feeling better," she amended. She stood with Adam's help and staggered forward. "We don't have time to lose."

The three of them headed out the door, Claire aided heavily by Adam but regaining her balance quickly. She had no choice. If the witches were out there somewhere in the woods, they needed help.

The charming vacation cabin that Claire would be happy to call home was now trashed. The floor was warped and distorted where Theo had altered it with earth magick and tried to drown Kai. Fire had burned in several places, leaving behind ash, cinder, and the heavy smell of smoke. Between her air magick and the combined *daaeman* magick of Tevan and Kai, almost all of the furniture was smashed beyond repair. Some of it was now beyond recognition as well.

To top everything off, the elium had apparently shattered all the windows in the cabin. Cool early morning air rushed into the room. At least it took the edge off the smoke smell. One had to look on the bright side sometimes.

Not far from the front of the cabin, they found an unlocked white cargo van. Kai and Tevan hadn't expected to be defeated, so they hadn't even bothered to hide it. Claire was betting the kidnapped witches were inside.

Adam stopped short. "Well, we didn't have to go far."

Theo hesitated, then went for the van. "The *Atrika* jumped and just left them behind. I figured they were more valuable than that."

But they all knew the cold, hard truth. The *daaeman* had an unlimited supply of unsuspecting *aeamon* they could use for blood magick. They could just pluck them off the street and use their life force to cast finding spells. No one was safe, not her, not any elemental witch within the grasp of the *Atrika*.

Inside the unlocked cargo van, they found four witches bound, gagged, and lying on the floor. Only four. That meant six were still missing, presumed dead.

Claire's hopes plummeted to her toes. *Four.*

All of the four suffered the effects of a *daaeman* bite. They lay mute and staring, eyes wide open. Claire knew they could see and hear what was going on, but couldn't speak or move.

"She's not here." Theo's voice was ragged from more than just the recent battle.

"I see that." Adam sat down heavily. "Lots of them aren't here. That means . . . Ingrid . . . shit." He looked up at Theo. "I'm sorry, man."

Intense sorrow enveloped Theo's face for a second and then was gone. Like a cloud passing over the moon. His expression steeled into businesslike resolve. "Let's get them untied. We can grieve Ingrid and the others later."

Together they freed one witch at a time and got them into the cabin. Other than almost being *daaeman* food, they looked no worse for wear. Not even a bruise marked them.

James was the first to rouse. He rolled to his side on the bed where they'd laid him and put his hand to his reddish blond head. "Fuck . . . me." He fell silent, then rattled off a string of curses.

Before they barraged him with questions, they allowed him some time to rouse and recover. Claire snuggled back against Adam's body, which was taut with tension. He eased his hands down her upper arms and embraced her, laying a kiss to the top of her head. The circle of his arms gave her safety and strength.

After they'd dealt with the witches, Adam had stripped her clothes off and treated her burns with both his healing ability and good old-fashioned antiseptic and bandages. She would probably bear some scars, but at least she'd not lost her life.

Yet.

Theo returned from the living room where he'd been using earth magick to clean up the battle site as much as possible. Leaning against the wall, he crossed his hands over his chest and waited, as they all did, for James to recover and tell them what had happened.

As they waited, the other three witches began to stir. They'd brought in glasses of water for each of them and a little bread. They probably hadn't eaten for a couple days.

Finally, James sat up and dragged in a few deep breaths through his nose and into his powerful chest.

Claire leaned over, took a plate of bread and a glass of water, and handed them to him. He pushed them away.

"You should," she insisted. "It will help you recover from the venom and we need you strong."

He hesitated, then accepted the glass and plate with mumbled thanks. He drank the water down and took a couple tearing bites of the bread. They didn't want to give them anything more substantial until the effects of the venom had completely worn off.

"They killed them," James finally gasped, setting the plate on the mattress beside him. "They ambushed us right on the other side of Wisconsin, after we'd all met up again. I think they'd been following one of us. When they attacked, they killed two of us right off. The rest of us beat them back, retreated, but they followed. They kept coming and coming all night long until we were too weak to fight anymore. When the dust cleared, two more of us were dead and the rest of us were mute and paralyzed. They left us in the middle of the woods while they went to get the cargo van and then came back for us."

James rubbed his shoulder and winced, looking over the other three witches, who were groaning and sitting up. "Where are Ingrid and Tom?" His voice was flat. He probably knew.

Theo shifted against the wall, grief passing over his face. He said nothing.

"You didn't see what happened to them?" Adam asked.

James shook his head, his face ashen. "They took Tom first, Ingrid the next day."

Claire pursed her lips, not wanting to say the words out loud. But it was her responsibility to do it. "They used the witches for blood magick, James. They used their life force in finding spells to locate us." She paused. "To locate me."

He stared at her for a moment, then lowered his head and closed his eyes.

So Ingrid had been killed in a spell-casting, not in the battle. Claire glanced at Theo, who was staring at the floor in front of him, hands thrust deeply into his pockets. She snuggled back into Adam's arms and he laid a gentle kiss to her temple.

"You're Claire . . . right?" asked a diminutive blonde with

a sharp chin. She winced on every word, her hand pressed to her head.

"Yes, I am."

The woman's gray eyes went flat and hard as gunmetal. "So you're the reason for all this."

Claire flinched.

"Look, Andrea," Adam said, pulling Claire against his chest. "I know you've been through a lot, but shut up. Okay?" His voice shook with anger.

Andrea looked away from him.

"I feel every death like a weight on my soul." Claire licked her lips. "I-I can't even—"

Andrea kept her head turned away. "I'm sorry. It was wrong of me to say that. I didn't mean it. I'm just . . . pissed off. Pissed they took six of us. Pissed we weren't better, stronger, faster." She lowered her head and a tear dropped into her lap. "Pissed I've lost my friends."

The other two witches finally recovered enough to speak. They nibbled at bread, sipped water, and talked about what happened until it grew late in the day.

All of them were shocked by Ingrid and Tom's death and Claire watched each realize in turn how close they'd come to the same fate.

They stayed at the cabin. Relocating—running—was silly since the *Atrika* only had to snag another witch from the street and locate them anyway. The assaulted witches needed rest. They needed food, a bath, and sleep—*sanctuary*. So did Claire, Theo, and Adam.

ADAM CAME AWAKE TO THE SMOOTH SLIDE OF Claire's hand over his thigh and lower stomach. Despite the excitement of the night and despite how far his mind should've been from such things, his body reacted to her touch. He wanted nothing more than to pull her down against him, roll her beneath his body, and caress every one of her curves carefully, methodically, and thoroughly.

He wanted one night of freedom from all this mess to spend with her. Just one night to completely immerse himself in her body, her scent, *just her*. One night to assuage this deep ache he had for her, to sate himself, and subdue it forever.

Instead, he grabbed her hand and pulled her toward him for a quick, deep kiss that only teased him. Having her near him and not being able to completely indulge himself was the worst kind of torture. "What's wrong?"

Her lovely full lips parted. "We need to get out of here before the others wake up. You and me, alone. The *Atrika* will track me, Adam. I don't want to be responsible for any more deaths."

"Claire, if this is about what Andrea said—"

She shook her head. "It's not. This was on my mind long before she brought it up. I understand the nature of Theo and the other witches; they'll fight until they die."

"It's a fight worth dying for. I saw what the elium did, Claire. I felt it. It's important we keep it from them."

"And we will, but we can do it without endangering the others."

He pulled her up, tucking her against his body, and kissed her temple. "You're not used to having friends or allies, Claire. I understand that. You're not used to having people want good things for you, to protect you. Just relax now, okay? We need their magick to help guard you from the demons. Leaving here takes that away and endangers you. We'll teach the remaining Coven witches how to use their power against the *Atrika*. Protecting you means we protect ourselves. So, please, just try to sleep a little now."

Claire's body lost its tension. She sighed and he felt the echo of her weariness and stress through his own body. "I don't like this."

He laughed a little—a soft, low, raw sound. "What's to like?"

Around them the sound of the sleeping witches' breathing filled their ears and the shadows cast by the firelight danced on the walls. There were only two bedrooms, so Adam and Claire had given up their bed to the other witches in favor of bunking down on the cushions from the couch and some folded-up blankets. They were both so weary they hardly noticed the lumps at all.

Claire moved against his body and he gritted his teeth, his

cock hardening. She slipped her long leg between his thighs and her hands under his shirt to smooth over his chest. The blanket covering them rustled with her movement.

He rolled her over and beneath him, then parted her thighs with his knee and settled himself between them. As he slanted his mouth across hers and slid his tongue between her lips, he ground his hard cock against her sex to show her what she was doing to him.

Claire sighed into his mouth and rubbed her sex up against him aggressively, causing delicious friction along his shaft beneath their clothes. It broke the last thin thread he had on his control. Fire jumped in the center of him in response to his arousal. "Are you trying to push me, woman?" he growled against her lips.

"I need you right now, Adam," she whispered back.

She didn't have to ask twice. He reached down and yanked her pants down to her ankles and savagely pushed her panties down and off under the cover of the blankets. All the other witches were sleeping, but even if they hadn't been sleeping, Adam wasn't sure he could've stopped. The scent of her, the movement of her silken skin against his, it all made him crazy.

Claire fumbled for the snap and zipper on his jeans, apparently desperate to feel him inside her. It seemed that foreplay wasn't what she had in mind. When he touched her sex, he found her ready, silky and slick, her clit blooming against his palm. His hands shook he wanted her so badly.

Adam spread her thighs and pressed the head of his cock into the entrance of her sex. Claire sighed and moved her hips, trying to lodge him deeper. He lowered his mouth to hers and kissed her as he pressed farther into her. The slick satin muscles rippled and pulsed along his shaft as he hilted inside her.

Her hands found the flesh under his shirt as he began to thrust in and out of her, setting up a rhythm that would send them both into pleasure fast and hard. This was urgent sex, a joining driven by the need to connect.

He placed a hand to her hips and angled the head of his cock to brush against her G-spot deep within. It wasn't long before she whimpered and her body tensed. As the muscles of her sex milked his cock during her climax, she sank her teeth into the skin of his shoulder to keep from crying out.

Pleasure exploded through him just a moment later and he shot deep inside her, kissing her deeply to muffle his own groans. He collapsed on her, careful not to crush her, and buried his face in the sweet-smelling curve of her neck. His breath came fast and hard as her fingers stroked through the short hair at his nape.

Together they lay tangled for a long time, the low, dying light of the fire flickering over them and the gentle sounds of sleep coming from the bed above them. Adam didn't want to pull from her body. He liked it too much when they were joined. So he remained buried within her even after his cock had gone flaccid.

Fuck, he was growing to care for Claire a lot.

Finally, he rolled over and adjusted himself. Then he pulled her against him, wordlessly. She tucked her head beneath his chin, face against his chest, and eventually fell back to sleep.

Adam tried hard not to think about what a perfect fit she was in his arms.

TWENTY

THEY SLEPT THROUGH THE LATE AFTERNOON AND into the night. Thankfully, no demon came to interrupt their well-needed rest. Claire had made an educated guess—the *Atrika* needed even more time to recover from the elium than they did. When they all awoke, they made breakfast in the remnants of the ruined kitchen and the surviving witches all ate well.

Adam watched Theo lean against the counter and sip his coffee. He'd slipped back into being a ghost, not talking, not interacting much at all. Ingrid's death had affected him badly. Now that Adam had spent some time with the man, he knew him better.

The mood was somber in the kitchen as they ate. Claire perched herself on a stool near the breakfast bar and talked to the witches about how she would train them that day. Her words, quietly spoken, could not cut through the pall of grief that had settled over them all.

Adam's cell phone vibrated in his pocket. He pulled it out and flipped it open, walking away from the solemn group so he could hear better. "Yeah?"

It was Thomas. "How is everyone?" His voice sounded strained.

"Like how you'd think, boss. Not good."

Thomas went silent for a moment, the weight of his sorrow palpable through the cell phone. If Claire felt responsible for the death of the six witches, Adam could only imagine how Thomas was feeling. And, yet, Adam knew that Thomas had taken no chances. He'd done all he could to ensure that the witches had left the Coven undetected. Blame could not be placed on his shoulders.

Adam's hand tightened to pain on the cell phone. Blame lay with the demons, with Rue. His blood heated—literally—and rage clouded his vision for a moment. There was nothing in the universe he wanted more than to make them pay for it.

"Micah has had a breakthrough. You need to bring Claire in."

His blood cooled and his vision cleared. "Booya for good news. Did he figure out a way to extract the elium?"

"Maybe. We're not sure it's going to work, so don't go getting her hopes up yet. This will be an experiment, but we need her here to try it."

"We'll leave this morning."

"Not so fast. Micah also got together with the Coven earth witches and worked up a masking spell. Here's our plan. You cook up this spell over there and use it on the remaining witches. Then you take Claire and go alone, travel back to Chicago."

"What do you mean? The spell will act as a decoy, in case the *Atrika* throw more blood magick at us?"

"Yeah, that's exactly what it will do . . . we think. We're dealing with demon magick and we're never sure how it will react. If Micah is right, if the demons try another locating spell, it will lead them to the Coven witches, not to Claire. It gives you enough time to bring her in."

"Fuck, Thomas, it's like serving the witches up on a platter."

"It's not. You told me yourself that Claire has taught you and Theo to effectively wield elemental magick against demon magick. Teach the Coven witches how to do it. You're not leaving them defenseless."

"Claire isn't going to like this. She won't agree. She already feels responsible for the deaths of the six witches. Last night she was ready to leave the cabin just to draw the demons away from the rest of them. No way is she going to agree to making them into bait."

Thomas's voice grew hard. "Then you fucking kidnap her, Adam. Do whatever you have to do to make this work. We need that elium out of her. We need it destroyed. That's more important than anything else."

Adam glanced at Claire, who still sat on the stool, still spoke in low, serious tones to the others. Her hair slipped over her shoulder in a barely kept tangle of dark curls. Her face was pale and drawn, the stress of the situation wearing on her visibly.

Fuck, he just wanted her safe. He wanted that more than he wanted anything else—even revenge on the demons.

He turned away. "Yeah, I'll get it done."

Adam handed the phone over to Theo per Thomas's request and Theo took down the ingredients for the bait spell. Theo did it unobtrusively, so Claire wouldn't notice.

After Theo snapped the cell phone closed, he slid the paper under a bowl filled with fruit. "I think I'm going to let you and Adam teach the techniques, Claire. My charm stores are badly depleted, so I'd better cook today."

Claire frowned at him. "Are you feeling all right?"

"Yeah, I'm fine. I just feel naked without my charms. I need to spend some time recharging."

"Okay." Claire shrugged.

"We should do this outside, don't you think, Claire?" Adam asked, walking to the door. "It's warm today and it smells like smoke in the cabin—distracting."

"That's a good idea," Claire answered. They headed outside to work, leaving Theo alone to cook up the "bait" charm.

As twilight fell, Adam grew apprehensive about how to get Claire out of the house. He knew all too well she wouldn't go willingly, but he wouldn't—couldn't—kidnap her as Thomas suggested.

By nightfall the spell was in place, accomplished stealthily by Theo using a variety of herbs and minerals. The kitchen still stank heavily of mugwort and winter cherry and it had been difficult to keep an observant Claire from noticing what was going on.

When she asked what all the mugwort and winter cherry was for, Theo had claimed an ordinary charm for deception, but she hadn't looked convinced. They'd been constantly drawing her out of the cabin and into the woods, feigning a desire for fresh air and room to move while they trained.

"What the hell is going on?" Claire demanded, rounding on them all in the living room. "What do you take me for, a novice witch? I felt a powerful spell snap into place about a half hour ago and everyone keeps dragging me outside. I'm freezing!" She turned to Theo. "Mugwort and winter cherry, according to my mother's spell book, *are* for deception spells, but I know you don't need that much, Theo! The kitchen still stinks of it."

Adam's jaw locked. Damn it.

She crossed her arms over her chest and fixed her gaze on Adam. "Well?" She glanced at Theo and cocked her head to the side. "Theo? Either of you have anything to tell me?"

Adam dragged in a breath and told her.

"It's what I wanted last night," she said when he'd finished. "But not like this. I refuse to run away and leave these witches to be found and picked off by the demons."

Lately Claire had begun using the *aeamon* pronunciation of demon. Adam counted that as a positive sign of her becoming more accustomed to life on Earth.

"With all due respect," drawled James from the corner. "We're targets whether you stay or go."

"And it's you they want, not us," Craig chimed in from the kitchen. "Maybe if they find out they've been duped, they'll leave us alone and go after you."

Claire shot him a look of annoyance. "Yes. They'd come for me *after* they'd killed or recaptured all of you."

"They won't," Andrea said. "Today you taught us how to use our magick against them. Now we're not defenseless. I don't want to go up against the *Atrika* again, but if we have to battle them I feel confident that *this time* we have a fighting chance."

"You do, but our chances would be even better if we stuck together." Claire turned and stared down Adam. "You convinced me of that last night, Adam."

"Look, you're valuable," Adam replied, feeling his throat tighten with the words. Valuable in more ways than one. "We can't afford to put you at risk. It's a direct order from Thomas. You're coming with me tonight, Claire. No matter how I have to do it."

She set a hand to her waist and tipped her chin up. "You really think you can best me magickally?"

Nope, he didn't think that at all. He gave her a slow blink and spoke in a lazy drawl. "Well, now, honey, I'm counting on your desire not to injure me."

"You really think you know me so well?"

He grinned. "Yeah, I do." He advanced on her and she took a hasty step backward.

"I could fry you where you stand, freeze you in place. I could lift you up and slam you against the wall."

"But you won't."

"*Houses*, Adam, don't do this."

He kept coming.

Claire raised her hand and drew power. Adam kept walking toward her, sure that she wouldn't injure him. Power flared, shot toward him, and was blocked by Theo, who threw up a shield just in time.

Adam's steps faltered. Okay, that had been *strong*.

She turned and pierced Theo with narrowed eyes.

Before she could get up another shot, Adam walked to her and threw her over his shoulder in one smooth move.

She pounded on his back. "Adam, if you do this, I will never forgive you. Do you hear me? Never!"

"I don't believe you. Anyway, I'll pay that price if it means you're safe." He slapped her ass and she spewed verbal venom.

Adam walked out the door with her slung over his shoulder. Her bag was already packed in the Challenger. They'd leave the cargo van for the others.

She struggled when he put her in the passenger seat, but didn't bolt from the vehicle when he walked around to the driver's side.

Claire slumped in the seat as he started the car. "Been planning this all day, have you?"

"Yep."

"Great."

"Theo even had a charm to render you unconscious. I'm glad we didn't have to use that one," he commented as the car purred down the road away from the cabin.

"Lovely, Adam," she snapped. "Thanks for letting me know."

"What was that blast of earth going to do to me, Claire?"

She glanced at him and muttered, "Render you unconscious."

"Ah. Well, then, in my book that makes us even."

"Not even close."

THEY DROVE THROUGH THE NIGHT, TREES HURTLING past the window where Claire rested her forehead. She was exhausted, but sleep eluded her. Worry for the witches they'd left behind ruled her mind. She faked sleeping, though, just so she didn't have to talk to Adam.

The fact he'd forced her to do this made anger curl through her stomach in long, hot tendrils. Made her want to say things she knew she'd regret, so she didn't say anything at all.

By the time early morning light tinged the world, they were pulling through the heavy iron gates of the Coven. It was amazing they'd never been pulled over for speeding. Adam had made fine use of the vehicle's ability to travel fast.

He gunned the engine once they were past the gates and raced up the curving tree-lined road toward the towering structure she could see in the distance. The Coven looked like a house—a huge one. It was not unlike some of the architecture one might find on Eudae, though that wouldn't be something she'd be sharing with anyone. Claire doubted the *aeamon* would take such a comment in the positive way she'd mean it.

The Coven appeared to be a mansion, like the residence of a very wealthy celebrity she'd seen on television. All white stone with arching windows, fireplaces, domes, and towers. The place was unique and quite attractive.

Thomas stood on the front steps watching Adam guide the car to a stop in the circular driveway.

Unwilling to give Adam even one syllable, she dashed from the car, up the steps, and into Thomas's arms. "It's good to see you."

He held her at arm's length and studied her face. "Are you all right, Claire?"

Adam came up behind her and she spared a scornful glance at him. "Considering all that's going on, yes."

"Hey, Adam," Thomas greeted. "Nice driving. You made it in record time."

"Yeah, well, let's do this. I want that elium out of her yesterday."

Thomas studied the Challenger. "Where's my car, Adam?"

"Yeah, about that." Adam shifted and pushed a hand through his hair. "Your car met with an unfortunate accident in Wisconsin."

Thomas's mouth tightened into a thin line. "Did this accident involve fire magick?"

"It was a chance to kill the *Atrika* and I took it."

"It's true. It would have been a good move if the *Atrika* weren't so hard to kill," Claire said without glancing at Adam. She couldn't resist the urge to defend him a little. "Adam took a gamble. It would have solved all our problems if it had paid off."

Thomas just grunted something about good insurance and guided them into the Coven. The foyer was gorgeous—airy and open, but she didn't have much opportunity to gawk.

They were ushered into a large library, where a tall woman with strawberry blond hair and a broad-shouldered man with reddish brown, shaggy hair and a green eyes sat.

The woman jumped up immediately, came to Claire, and hugged her. The light scent of expensive perfume enveloped her.

"You must be Isabelle," Claire said.

"Yes," Isabelle said, her brown eyes shiny with tears. "I have been waiting a long time to thank you for helping Thomas on Eudae. Without you I don't think he would have made it back."

Claire smiled. "Don't be too sure about that. It might have taken him a long time, but I feel certain Thomas would have made his way back to you no matter how long it took, no matter how hard he had to fight. I just hurried the process up a little."

A tear slipped down Isabelle's cheek and she hugged her again.

Claire laughed. She couldn't help it. She felt good about helping Thomas get back to Isabelle. It was clear they both loved each other very much. Claire allowed herself to melt against the other woman and close her eyes. Just for a moment. The hug felt good.

And she was so tired.

The green-eyed man cleared his throat. "Yeah, as much as I love to watch two hot women hugging, it's time to do this."

Claire disentangled herself from Isabelle and looked at the shaggy-haired guy. "And you must be Micah." The voice had been familar.

He stood. "Yep, I'm Micah, and if you don't want to be demon chow, you should come with me right now."

Fear lanced through her. Houses, she hoped this worked.

Adam walked over and reached out to her. Claire regarded him warily for a moment. She was still angry at Adam, but his hand offered warmth and strength. Regardless of what had happened back at the cabin, she *needed* him right now. She took his hand.

He held her gaze for a moment, hand warm and strong in hers. Her breath hitched at the emotion in his eyes. She stepped to the side, breaking the moment, and her face flushed. Just a look from that man made her knees weak.

All of them, save Isabelle, walked down one of the posh corridors of the Coven to a smaller room that smelled of bitter herbs. Within stood a table that held a spell pot and an open grimoire. On another small table rested a large oval container, like an oversized jar, of some sort of blue-green material. Claire walked to it and ran her fingers down the roughened side. It appeared handmade.

"It's where we'll store the elium," said Micah, close to her.

She glanced at him. "How do you know it can be stored in

such a container? It rested in a demon before the demon put it in me."

Micah pushed a hand through his hair and sighed. She noticed the deep, dark smudges under his eyes that marked his lack of sleep. "I've studied demon lore day and night since you arrived. If the texts I've been able to amass are correct, the combination of elements we blended into this container, along with the earth magick we've woven in, should keep the elium in stasis until we figure out how to destroy it."

Claire stared at the fragile jar for a moment longer, then turned to Adam. "Did you explain to them what it was like when I tapped the elium at the cabin?"

He nodded.

"So they know it was like a mini nuclear blast, zeroing out all magick within its reach? Blowing out windows? Nearly killing me?"

Adam nodded again.

"And that I only barely touched it, drew the thinnest and tiniest of threads to wield?"

"I told them everything, Claire."

She locked her jaw. How could this possibly work? What had she been thinking? There was no way that elemental witches, clear on the other side of Eudae, could ever even comprehend demon magick, let alone successfully manipulate it. All the hopes she'd been nursing in order to survive popped like the frailest bubble.

"This is crazy," she muttered.

"It's not only crazy," said Thomas. "It's our only shot. You know better than we do that the elium cannot stay inside you. The demons will just keep hunting you. When they find you, they'll take the elium and probably your life with it. If we can get the elium out of you, we save your life. We plan to mask the container in some way, hide it from them until we figure out what to do with it."

Claire looked at him. "You don't understand the magick that I'm carrying. Doing this spell and trying to move the elium is like trying to carry a brimming teacup of nitroglycerin barefoot over a bed of hot coals without spilling any."

Micah made an impatient gesture. "I've done the research, Claire, this is our only option."

She tipped her head back and closed her eyes. He was right, of course. Unless Rue showed up right this second and took back the weapon she'd never wanted to possess, she had no real choice to make. The elium had to come out of her or she would die and all the elemental witches on Earth would be in danger, not to mention all the demon breeds but the *Atrika* on Eudae.

She couldn't outrun Tevan and Kai forever. Eventually, she would tire, as she already was tiring. Eventually, her luck would run out.

It went like this: if the spell backfired and the elium was released into this world, all would be lost. If the spell worked, all their problems were solved. It was a hell of a gamble and Claire was not the gambling type.

Her stomach grew cold. That coldness inched up into her throat.

She opened her eyes. "Fine. Let's do it."

Adam was there. He had moved to her side while she'd been having her mini crisis. With a firm, strong hand, he guided her to the small reclining couch that sat in the corner and helped her lower herself onto it. Then he knelt at her side and took her hand in his.

Micah went to stand at the table, near the spell pot and open grimoire. The spell was so complicated he couldn't even memorize it. Great.

"What do you need me to do?" she asked.

He flipped through the book, frowning. "Relax."

"You could ask me to drag down the moon, too; it would be just as likely I could do it."

Micah chewed his lip for a moment, then looked up at her in surprise, as if what she'd said had just registered. "I really do need you to relax, Claire. I need you to let go of the elium when the time comes. You'll know when that time is because you'll feel a tug on the condensed magick in your chest. Until then, just let the spell float you. It's designed to put you at ease, a little like a drug. It actually should be pleasant." He paused. "For a time."

"Lie back and close your eyes," said Thomas. "Micah will do the rest."

Relax and close her eyes? Right.

She glanced at Adam, who looked pissed off. She frowned. Why was he pissed? His eyes swirled with rage, his jaw was locked, and his shoulders hunched a little—tense.

"Is this going to hurt her?" Adam growled at Micah.

"Huh?" Micah glanced up again, a distracted look on his face. "I don't think so."

A muscle in Adam's jaw twitched. "You don't *think* so?"

Micah understood the warning in Adam's tone and gave him his full attention. "Obviously, not hurting Claire is my primary concern, Adam, but we're dealing with alien magick here. I don't even know if this spell will work. It's not like we could test it beforehand. It's the result of days of meticulous research and preparation, not years. I can't read the future."

She squeezed Adam's hand. "It's okay, Adam, I'm willing to take a risk to get this junk out of me."

He turned to stare deeply into her eyes. "You might be willing to risk your well-being, Claire, but I'm not willing to risk you."

The words, the warm, honeyed tone of his voice, and the emotion in his eyes left her speechless.

Adam turned to Micah. "You know what I will do to you if you hurt her, right?"

It was the threat of an alpha male in a situation in which he felt powerless. Adam wanted to control things and couldn't, so he threatened. Claire recognized the behavior immediately, having seen it often in *Ytrayi* males. Adam cared for her enough to be terrified right now, maybe even more terrified than she was.

"Cut it out, Adam," Thomas growled. "You know the last thing Micah wants is to harm someone."

Claire cleared her throat. "Let's get on with this. Every moment we wait is another moment the demons could be tracking the other witches." She leaned back and closed her eyes, thankful for the steadiness of Adam's hand around hers.

Paper rustled, items on the table were picked up, set down. A wooden spoon hit the side of the spell pot. Low words were muttered in a masculine voice.

Lethargy.

It stole over her body slowly, moving from her toes up her

body like some super-enhanced meditation. Her muscles, tense from stress and fear, relaxed one by one, giving up their strain to a curious, irrational peacefulness.

It was a little like when she'd been a child with a bad appendix and the *Ytrayi* healers had been forced to remove it. Back then they'd used a spell like this one to put her mind elsewhere while they cut the offending part from her body.

What Micah did now was also a kind of surgery and the sensation she felt was her anesthesia. It was so powerful that even if she'd wanted to fight it—and a part of her did from simple instinct—she could not.

Her body went limp and heavy, as though in slumber. But she could still hear what was going on around her, still feel sensation in her body and the steady, reassuring clasp of Adam's hand.

The first touch of the foreign tendril of power entering her wasn't even a shock. The curling bit of earth magick went for the seat of her magick first. Inwardly, she pulled herself around it, protecting it, though she knew that was not what Micah sought.

After a moment of exploration, the tendril moved on, this time brushing against the elium. Despite the deep relaxation she was immersed in, she jerked at the light touch. The elium was like an open, unhealed wound inside her and every slightest stroke against it seared her with shock and pain.

Another brush, another. Each got successively more aggressive. She heard a low moan and realized it came from her. Adam's grip grew tighter and low, angry words she couldn't understand bubbled through her limited consciousness.

Pain.

It ripped through her and bowed her spine. The tendril no longer brushed, it gouged. Like a scoop made from a flattened sword, Micah's magick tried to cut the elium from her body.

Claire's eyes opened and she screamed. The pain immediately stopped.

Darkness, then light. Dark. Light. Unconsciousness wove in and out.

Her eyes flickered open and across the room she caught a

glimpse of Adam with his hand around Micah's throat, pushing the earth witch up against a wall. Thomas was bellowing and trying to haul Adam off.

Darkness closed around her for good and she fell back against the couch.

TWENTY-ONE

"IT WASN'T WORKING ANYWAY," MICAH GRUMBLED. He rubbed his throat and Adam glanced away, almost sorry he'd leapt across the room and pinned Micah to the wall. At the time he hadn't been able to stop himself. Claire had been in obvious pain and he would have done anything to make it stop.

Thomas glared at Adam. "So Adam didn't interrupt the spell."

Micah shook his head. "I need to tweak it. There are some anomalies in Claire that I hadn't counted on, stuff related to her magickal structure and her power level. I presumed the core of her was earth with the other elements tacked on, but that's not true. Claire's core is all four elements combined. It's like nothing I've ever seen before. Rue altered her down to her very DNA."

Adam looked down at Claire, who lay pale and unconscious in the bed where they'd moved her to recuperate. "Great."

"At least we didn't blow the Coven up," Micah muttered. "Let's look on the bright side. I'll try again with an altered spell."

"The fuck you will," answered Adam. "I'm not watching Claire go through that again."

"That's for her to decide, isn't it?" Thomas asked.

Adam just locked his jaw and stared down at Claire. Her hair lay tangled against the pillow and her face was pale and drawn. All he wanted was for everyone to leave the room so he could crawl into bed with her, hold her close, and sink into the fact she was *alive*.

During the last part of the spell, right before he'd lunged across the room to force Micah to stop it, Adam had not been convinced she was going to live through it. He was fucking sick of almost watching her die. That was twice now.

No, he wasn't going to let her endanger herself again. He just wasn't. Ultimately, he didn't care what the cost would be.

Adam unlocked his jaw long enough to speak. "Can you both leave now?"

"Sure," answered Thomas. "Doc Oliver says she should be waking up soon. She'll probably want to see you first anyway."

Adam followed the two men out and closed the door behind them. He still felt raw, hostile, from watching Claire undergo the spell. And the stupid thing had failed! The elium still dwelt within her.

The room was much like any other guest room at the Coven. The first room was a small living room, complete with an entertainment center and a hotel-sized refrigerator. Off that room a short hallway led to a bathroom and one or more bedrooms. Some people, like himself, lived at the Coven full-time. They had full apartments, complete with kitchens. Claire's guest room wasn't far from his place.

He slipped back down the semidarkened hallway, shedding clothes as he went. Once in her room, he slid into bed beside her and pulled her close, inhaling that odd foreign flower scent her hair always held. No amount of shampooing seemed to make it fade. He suspected it was something found on Eudae, yet it seemed like a natural part of her.

Her body was warm and soft, her breathing deep. If he closed his eyes he could almost pretend she wasn't unconscious from a backfired spell, but that she merely slept. If he concentrated just a bit harder, he could imagine away the demons, the elium . . . Rue. He could forget about all the things that lay between them, all the things that separated them.

But he couldn't forget about Eliza.

Adam's eyes snapped open as her face flashed on the back of his lids. On the night Eliza had been killed, he'd felt a bit like he did now—raw, frayed emotion leaving a bitter taste on the back of his tongue, anger at himself over his inability to keep her safe. Grief.

If he parsed out all the threads of feeling forming the tight ball in the center of his stomach, he was sure he'd find love tangled up in there—unwanted, unwelcome, uncontrollable—love for Claire.

He couldn't be sure when the first stirrings of it had begun to affect him. It had been like sickness. He'd been exposed to the germ of it unknowingly and days later the fever of it had hit him.

Even though he knew it was irrational, it still felt like the worst kind of cheating. Admitting he had these emotions for Claire meant he was betraying the seven-year-long vigil he'd been keeping for Eliza.

Gods help him, there was nothing he could do about it. He was being swept away in the currents, too tired to fight any longer.

He didn't sleep, not even when the light outside filtered to darkness and enveloped the room in its inky, velvety protection. All through the night, he held her, ready to strike away any danger that came near, but no demons came but the ones he held inside himself.

Sometime just short of daylight, Claire shifted against him, roused, and opened her eyes. She gasped in pain and blinked.

"How do you feel?" Adam asked immediately, even though he knew from the gasp it couldn't be good.

She made a low sound. "My chest hurts. It feels like someone punched me there." Her voice sound rusty and rough. "How are the witches?"

"Last I heard, fine. I told Thomas to come get me if they were attacked. So far, nothing. Maybe your trick with the elium was more effective than we thought."

"Maybe." She paused. "The spell didn't work. I can still feel the elium inside me."

He kissed her temple. "Yeah, we know. Just try to relax

now, okay? The spell Micah used really punched you a good one."

"Is Micah going to try again?"

He pressed his lips together. "Not if I have anything to say about it."

She said nothing for several moments, then turned to face him. Shadows played over the silken skin of her cheek and caught around the curve of her lip. "It's my only chance, Adam."

"He could've killed you."

She shook her head. "He didn't. You were there to stop him before he took it too far."

"What if next time I can't stop him before you really get hurt?"

"Adam, if the spell Micah brews up doesn't take the elium from me, the demons will do more than just hurt me. You know that. We have to be rational about this."

He pulled her close to him. "Yeah, well, let's just take it one moment at a time, okay? Micah hasn't even cooked up a new spell yet."

"It was wrong what you did back at the cabin, forcing me to come here and leaving them behind as bait." Her voice had gone hard and tight.

He dropped a kiss on the top of her head. "I did the best thing I could to keep you safe."

She lay unresponsive in his arms, not answering. Her breasts rested against his arm and the rise and fall of her breathing calmed him. Her presence was warm, comforting, a little arousing, too, if truth was told, even though he understood she was pissed at him.

His hands slid over her curves, gentling her, trying to make amends without using words. Her breathing hitched and she sighed, her breath warm against his chest. She snuggled in closer to him and her body gave up some of its rigidity.

He let his hands explore a little more until they were both breathing heavier and their bodies were growing warmer, tangling a bit closer.

Neither of them spoke. Adam preferred to use his hands and lips to do that, to make Claire his in the one way he knew best. Little by little, he removed her clothes—got her hot and bothered with his stroking hands and the nips and kisses he landed on her body.

He built her up slowly, gently, aware that she was recovering from a bad trauma. His hands slipped over her breasts, teased her nipples, and explored every peak and valley of them. She parted her thighs for him when he murmured he wanted her to, and his hand slid between them.

He traced every inch of her sex, warm and slick from her growing excitement. Sliding within, her muscles clenched around his thrusting fingers, milking them for the pleasure he gave her as little moans and sighs fell from her lips and her dark eyelashes feathered down against her pale cheek.

Her clit had extended from its hood, swollen and begging for attention. In her sexual abandon, Claire had lain back against the pillows, her hair a tangle around her pretty face. Her hands explored his chest and petted his cock, but he wanted satisfaction for her right now. He wanted to put his mark on her body, if he couldn't put it on her heart. Adam wanted to remind her that he had power over her—the power of pleasure.

So he lowered his mouth to her breast to lick and suck one hard, beautiful nipple while he stroked her aching clit over and over. He drank in the little sounds she made, every one of her sighs. He loved it especially when she moved her hips as though looking for something to fill her and murmured his name.

Finally, her orgasm bloomed over her body with a burst and a long sigh. He rode her through her climax, stroking her steadily to extend the shudders of pleasure as long as they would go.

When it was over, she sagged against the mattress and made a sound of contentment, like a cat in cream. Then she rolled to him, tangled her fingers around his neck, and kissed him.

"Make love to me, Adam," she murmured.

He gently nipped her lower lip and smiled. "Later. You need to recover now. I just couldn't resist touching you a little."

Claire closed her eyes for a moment and he saw her fatigue. "I like to make love with you. It makes the worlds go away for a while. It's like an escape."

"Sleep is an escape, too, and you need sleep more right now."

"Will you stay with me?"

"Of course."

Claire was silent for several moments, fitting her body close to his. "I can't get my mind off the witches, Adam. I don't know if I can sleep."

"Yeah. I'm thinking about them, too, but my primary concern is you at the moment, Claire."

"I will never forgive myself if harm comes to Theo and the others back at the cabin."

His hands slid up her arms, warming her. "You never forgive yourself for anything. You carry the weight of two worlds on your shoulders. Relax a little."

"You aren't the one to be giving advice in that area, Adam. Not with the burden of your wife's death on your heart."

Adam went rigid. "Let's not talk about Eliza." His voice carried a clear note of warning. He meant it, too.

Claire apparently hadn't heard it. She pushed up and leaned back against the pillows, crossing her arms over her chest. "Not talk about Eliza? Adam, I think it's long past time you talked of her. You can't go into the future wearing glasses that taint everything in the present by an event in the past."

He bolted from the bed and pushed a hand through his hair. "I knew I never should have told you about her."

"And what then? You'd have gone on without telling anyone? Just wearing that silly mask of yours to hide the guilt you feel over her death? Adam, *it wasn't your fault.*"

"Claire—"

"If you don't let it go, you'll never have another relationship like the one you had with her." She paused, her lower lip trembling. "You'll never know love again, Adam."

Adam stopped and stared, the words on the tip of his tongue—*but I do know love again.* But he wasn't going to say that. Not now. Not when she was pushing so hard on issues he didn't want any part of.

Because while he had found love again—totally against his will—he knew he was still holding back. And, gods, he was terrified he'd lose that love again—not be able to hold on to Claire when she most needed him, not be able to protect her even though he felt like he'd been born to do that job.

Claire sat with the blankets clutched in her narrow hands,

moonlight spilling in and bleaching the color from her already pale skin. Her dark curls hung around her shoulders like silk and her expression was tight, worried.

Adam whirled and stared at the door, wanting to leave the room with every fiber of his being. He couldn't. He couldn't leave her alone tonight—or at all. There was no escape from her words or the truth in them.

"Adam?"

He turned, realizing he'd been staring at the door for some time. He'd told her he'd stay and he must. The demons could show at any time.

But for the first time since he'd met her all he wanted was to get away from her. She said things he didn't want to hear—and would never want to hear.

CLAIRE AWOKE TO ADAM'S BACK. HE'D SLEPT THAT way all night. She knew because she hadn't been able to sleep much at all, falling into a fitful slumber only toward dawn.

It was funny how males—*aeamon* or *Ytrayi*—could just roll over and go to sleep after a heated disagreement. Emotions and tempers could rise and it mattered not a bit to them; they just fell right into uninterrupted snores.

She'd been up all night fuming.

What a stubborn man! And so maudlin, too. High-strung. That's what he was. He tried to put on this easygoing, joking face to the world. No one understood the emotional heart of the man within.

Emotional, yes, but he could still fall right to sleep after a fight.

She flopped onto her back and blew out a frustrated breath. He still held on to Eliza so tightly—to his grief and to all that imagined blame and responsibility. The ghost of Eliza wouldn't let him move on into other serious romantic relationships. Claire wasn't sure when she'd decided that maybe she wanted more from Adam than just sex, but at some point her feelings had changed, deepened. But maybe Adam only believed he had sex to offer her.

Maybe he was right.

Claire sighed as a weight settled in her chest. Turning her

thoughts away from unpleasant things, which seemed to be most everything these days, she glanced out the window. She could tell by the pale, cold light filtering into the bedroom that the leading edge of dawn approached.

Well, she couldn't sleep another moment. It was time to get up, get dressed. Adam stirred beside her, coming awake. She shot from the bed, gathered her clothes, and went into the hallway bathroom. She'd leave the bedroom bathroom for Adam.

Claire didn't want to face him just yet.

She showered and dressed. Afterward, she eyed a drawer filled with unopened makeup packages. She picked up some eye shadow in shades of brown and held them up to her face. Then she tossed the package back into the drawer. She had no clue how to put the makeup on. Anyway, she didn't need to look extra pretty for Adam, and she definitely didn't need to look any more alluring to the *Atrika*. Claire studied her reflection. Adam apparently found her attractive just the way she was. Amazing, but true.

When she left the bathroom, she found Adam not too far away. He sat in the living room of the guest apartment, already showered and dressed.

He stood when she came into the room. "Ready?"

Wow, he'd spoken a whole word to her. They were making progress.

She nodded—not quite sure she was ready to speak a whole word to *him* yet—and they left.

Once they reached the main floor, the eerie sensation of *Atrika* nearby assaulted her. She stumbled and caught herself against a wall, the elium within her singing to brilliant life at the proximity of a more suitable host.

Adam caught her arm and steadied her. "Claire, what's wrong?"

She raised her bowed head and stared at him through stray tendrils of her hair. "*Atrika*."

Thomas came down the corridor toward them. "You have to get out of here now. Adam, take Claire and get out. The demons attacked Theo and the witches at the cabin and are undoubtedly on their way here."

They'd already arrived. They were somewhere in the Coven.

Claire went stock-still for a moment—perfectly panicked. They had to get out of here, to the car. They had to become a moving target so the demons couldn't jump to them.

Adam grabbed her arm and dragged her forward, toward the entrance of the Coven.

"How are the witches?" Claire yelled at Thomas, picking up the pace beside Adam.

"Injured. One dead," Thomas called after them. "Now go! Run as far as you can, pick no destination so they can't track you. Just keep driving. Never stop."

Houses, she hoped Adam had remembered to fill the gas tank of the Challenger.

Tevan jumped right in front of them.

TWENTY-TWO

CLAIRE SCREAMED AND ADAM THRUST HER BEHIND him.

"Get out of my way," Tevan bellowed.

Kai popped in behind them. He loomed over her, staring down at the shocked expression on her face and smiling as if he savored the encounter. The *Atrika* loved it when their prey was terrified.

She and Adam were cornered in the hallway. No way to go forward, no way to go back. Nausea rose to bite the back of her throat with sharp, bitter teeth. So this was the end, then.

Kai reached down and grabbed her shoulder. She didn't think, she just reacted . . . but this time she didn't reach for the elium. Magick exploded from her—air, earth, water, and fire. It was the first time in her life she'd managed to bring all four tendrils together at once. It snapped out like a thick, deadly whip, the cattails aimed at Kai and Tevan. The air around them pulsed once, made her ears pop, and then the world blurred.

When her vision cleared, Kai was on his ass in the corridor

looking stunned. Claire was just as surprised, magick still tingling pleasantly within the center of her chest. She'd reacted straight from a place of fear and instinct, and she'd defended herself and Adam perfectly.

Adam yanked her hard down the hallway, past a shocked Tevan who had also ended up on his butt, and out the door to the car.

She tripped going down the stairs and Adam barely kept her upright. They made it to the car and Adam started it, slamming on the gas and making the tires squeal on the pavement of the Coven's circular driveway and onto the narrow road leading off the Coven grounds.

Glancing in the rearview mirror, she saw both demons jump out of the Coven and run down the road after them. They disappeared and reappeared, every time a little closer to the Challenger.

"Adam," she cried in alarm.

"I see. Put your seat belt on," Adam shouted, gunning the high-performance car down the drive toward the front gate. Someone had called ahead—Thomas most likely—and the gates were slowly opening.

She scrambled to comply and it wasn't a moment after she'd heard it click in place that Kai appeared on the road in front of them. Claire screamed in surprise.

Adam didn't flinch or hesitate, he just ran him down. Kai's big demon body hit the grill of the Challenger and flew upward, making hard contact with the windshield and cracking the glass before rolling off to the grassy yard of the Coven that lined each side of the long driveway.

Shaking, she gripped the armrest and turned around, seeing Kai roll to his feet, apparently unharmed. Beside her, Adam didn't falter in his steady press of gas pedal to floor.

They sailed through the open Coven gates, out onto the street, and into traffic. Horns blared as Adam corrected the car's course and did his best to break the world's land speed record.

As long as they stayed moving, the demons couldn't track them and they couldn't jump into the car.

When she was able to stop shaking and focus, she turned to Adam. "Oh, shit." *Houses* just didn't seem strong enough for what they'd just endured. Maybe she was becoming a real earth witch.

Adam's jaw was locked and his hands were tight on the steering wheel. He didn't even glance at her. All his attention was focused on the road. "That was a little too close."

"Where are we going?"

"Right now, I don't know. Thomas said not to keep a destination in mind so they can't pull blood magick. As far as I'm concerned, we're going to keep driving for as long as we can. Don't care where. My objective is to keep you safe."

One witch dead, that's what Thomas had said. Her fingers gripped the armrest so hard it shot pains up her arm. Foiled by their fast getaway, what were the demons doing now? Were Thomas, Micah, Isabelle, and the others under siege at the Coven at this very moment?

Would any of *them* die?

Adam glanced at her. "What was that thing you did back at the Coven? That little pulse of magick that sent them flying? It wasn't elium, I could tell that much, but it wasn't any one element either."

She shook her head. "I don't know. I did it without thinking. I just grabbed four threads of power, wove them together, and lashed out at the *Ytrayi* with the whip they made."

She pressed her lips together and closed her eyes, remembering the room where Rue instructed her, remembering his words: *Pull the threads together, Claire. Unite them.*

She'd never been able to do it, had never even understood what he'd been talking about. At least, not until today.

"So you used all the elements together, at once."

"Yes, essentially that's what I did."

"It was like demon magick, Claire. It even smelled a bit like demon magick, although not as bitter."

Claire swallowed hard against a suddenly dry throat. "Really?"

"Yeah. Can you do it again?"

"I don't know."

"I hope you can, Claire. I really do." He took an exit onto the highway, headed south.

CLAIRE SHIFTED IN HER SEAT, TRYING TO GET COMfortable on her already numb posterior.

Adam was heading for Florida, but just as a general goal. They had no specific town in mind. They weren't going by a straight shot either, but by a meandering, lazy route.

It wasn't like they didn't have time to waste.

They'd talked to Thomas several hours ago. The demons had, like Claire had feared, attacked the Coven after realizing their prey had once again slipped through their fingers. There were some injured witches, but no fatalities.

The next question out of Claire's mouth had been about the witches with the bait spell on them. It had been Craig who had died. Tevan had crushed his spine and broken his neck.

Tears had rolled down Claire's cheeks as Thomas had explained that the rest of their injuries had thankfully not been severe, all but Theo's. Theo had ended up with a broken leg, cracked ribs, and a concussion. Unwilling to go to the hospital in Missouri, Theo had forced them to bring him back to the Coven, alongside Craig's mangled and dead body.

When they'd reached the Coven, of course they'd found more chaos.

The demons had primarily been interested in destroying all traces of Micah's spell lab once they'd discovered his attempts to draw the elium from Claire. They'd done a thorough job.

It was a setback.

Not only would Micah have to re-create the spell he'd been working to alter, now he would have to once again gather all the ingredients he would need. Some of them were very rare and hard to come by.

The demons had not located Micah's library of carefully procured ancient texts. Micah had those well hidden. That was one bit of good news. The other piece of optimism came from the attack itself. Thomas figured that the demons would not have cared about the lab or the spell at all if Micah hadn't been on the right track.

So for now, while they waited for Micah to fix all that was broken and call them home, they drove.

Claire's heart was swollen with tears and she wished for the numbness she'd been able to achieve on Eudae. Coming to Earth, meeting Adam, had unthawed the ice she'd been able to build up over the years. She missed the cold armor of the lack of emotion she'd had before, though shedding it was probably far better for her in the long run.

Well, if she had a long run.

The road whipped along under the tires of the car, the white lines in the center glaring in the car's headlights. She shifted again in the passenger seat. Somewhere in Kentucky her butt had gone to sleep and she couldn't seem to wake it back up again.

She glanced over at the fuel gauge. It had been full when they started, but now it was getting down to empty. "When you stop for gas, I can drive for a while."

Things beyond the demon issue were still a bit tense between them. They hadn't talked much during their journey.

He glanced over at her. "Ever driven a car before?" Doubt tinged his words.

"You know I haven't, but it looks easy enough to me. Touch the gas pedal to go forward, then brake to stop. I'll figure it out."

He stared hard at the road. "I'd better drive."

She sighed and crossed her arms. "Adam, we're in perpetual, nonstop motion here. There's no way you can keep driving and driving without any sleep. There's a term I heard recently to describe people like you—*control freak*."

A smile tugged at his lips. "You should know that better than anyone," he drawled in a low, warmed-honey voice. "I do like to be in control."

She shivered, her body responding to his tone and the insinuation. Claire shook it off and hardened herself. "It's dangerous for you to keep driving this way, Adam."

"It's dangerous to stop, too. Do you know how long we can stay in one place before they can track us?"

She chewed her lower lip. "Sorry, this is *Atrika* demon

magick we're talking about. I know a little about it, but not everything. Not enough to know how certain individual spells work. Not blood magick."

"Well, we'll have to risk it soon. We need gas and food."

"And a bathroom."

"That, too. Let's pray the pretty car never has any engine trouble."

That was a sobering possibility.

"Fine, so when we stop, I'll take over driving for a while and you can get some sleep."

His hands tightened a degree on the wheel. "I'm fine to drive a little longer."

"Adam, you are not. Don't fight me on this one, you'll lose."

"You can't even drive—"

She drew a thread of air and sent it under the hood. The whole car shuddered. "I don't want to hear another word about it, Adam."

He closed his mouth and said no more.

Of course he waited until the car was on fumes. They stopped at a gas station on top of an exit with plans to take as little time as possible refueling, going to the bathroom, and grabbing some food from the convenience store.

Claire got out of the car and stretched in the crisp, cool night air. It felt good to shed that steel skin for a while.

Peering down the overpass leading away from the gas station and into the country, she had an urge to run—feel the pound of the concrete under her shoes and allow the cool night wind to fill her lungs and play in her loose hair. Freedom from the prison the Challenger made.

She glanced at Adam, who was filling up the car. His shoulders were hunched, his head down in the face of a strong wind. Stress sat clearly in the way he held his body, in the hunch of his shoulders and the tightness of his jaw. He was so incredibly worried for her.

For the first time in her life, apart from her mother, she had someone who cared for her. She stood for a long moment staring at Adam, a smile playing over her lips. In that moment, despite all that was happening to them, despite facing death that morning, Claire felt better than she ever had in her entire life.

"Adam."

He looked up at her, the wind blowing his hair across his forehead. Tension sat in the jut of his jaw and in the lines bracketing his mouth. Trouble clouded his eyes and laid bare in the rigid set of his lips.

Claire smiled.

Adam looked confused for a moment and then the storm clouds cleared. Heat replaced the hardness in his expression, chased away the grim set of his mouth. Love dwelt in the curve of his lips now, warmed his eyes to a darker blue.

They held each other's gazes for a moment longer and then she turned and walked into the store to use the bathroom. She felt Adam's gaze on her like a palpable stroke on her skin as she strolled away. When she turned at the door, he was still staring at her, a smile playing over his mouth. Pleasantness trilled through her body.

Houses, was this what love felt like? If it was, she liked it.

The lights of the store blinded her after driving in the dark for so long. She blinked in the fluorescents, her eyes gritty from lack of sleep.

The man behind the counter glanced at her, then went back to reading his magazine. She passed the Slurpee machine and the racks of packaged cakes and bags of chips, her stomach rumbling. After she used the bathroom she was going to buy out half the store. Junk food, she'd found, was golden.

After she'd used the bathroom with great relief, she stood at the sink letting the warm water run over her hands. Adam had probably finished fueling the car. They could grab some food for the road and start off again, but *she* was driving. They needed to be partners in this, not—

"Claire."

She looked up and saw Tevan in the mirror's reflection. Her stomach clenched. She whirled, drawing power. He laid his hand on her shoulder just as she punched him with her fistful of magick.

She was too late.

The world imploded. Her body tore apart at a molecular level and scattered over the universe. When she came back together, she knelt on a cold, concrete floor, retching.

The toes of a pair of black boots were inches from her nose. Someone was groaning not far away—Tevan. At least she'd managed to hit the bastard before he'd jumped her. Still, she knew all too well that Kai's demon eyes gazed down upon her with satisfaction.

She'd been taken.

TWENTY-THREE

"Claire?"

Adam pounded open each of the bathroom stall doors with rising fear. The back of his throat tasted bitter and his stomach was in a hot, tight knot. Adrenaline-fueled rage rushed through his veins. She'd been too long in the bathroom and he knew with an eerie psychic certainty that something had happened to her.

Empty. Empty. Empty.

The store clerk had seen her go in but not come out and every one of the bathroom stalls were empty. His throat constricted.

Claire was gone.

"Calm down, Adam."

Adam rounded on Thomas. "Calm down? I'm not fucking going to calm down anytime soon. Did you not hear me, Thomas? Tevan and Kai have Claire."

"I am aware."

Adam stood in the middle of Thomas's half-destroyed Coven library office trying to get a handle on his emotions.

The demons had hacked away at the Coven, destroying what they could and starting fires in some of the wings. The Coven witches had waged a war against the *Atrika* between these walls and had managed to drive the demons from the building.

Score point one for the witches; they'd been able to drive them back without any fatalities and they'd not needed the elium or Claire's odd elemental magick to do it. That was a win in a situation in which the Coven was always one step behind demon-kind.

But the cost had still been high.

Theo was in the infirmary, being treated by Doc Oliver. He'd live, but he had even more scars now than before. He'd caught some bad burns in the battle at the cabin along with the broken bones.

Thomas pressed his lips into a straight line. "You need to calm down so we can think clearly. Think clearly and act accordingly."

Adam pushed a hand through his hair. "Wouldn't it be great if we *could* act?" He snorted. "They could be anywhere in the world right now. We have no way to track them."

Thomas had no reply. He knew Adam was right.

Wild grief and fear rose up within Adam, making him feel half-crazy. He couldn't lose Claire. Not now. Not after he'd realized just how much she meant to him. *Fuck.*

And they'd fought. He'd been so stupid. Claire was alive and breathing—warm, sweet, and loving. How could he let his time with Claire be diminished by the memory of a woman long dead, cold, and in her grave?

"Fuck!" he yelled.

If he didn't act soon, there might be two ghosts to haunt him instead of one.

Adam shook his head. "I'm not giving her up." He turned and bellowed, "*I won't let them have her!*"

Thomas held out a hand like Adam was a rabid dog he intended to stave off. "None of us intend to allow the demons to kill Claire."

Adam turned and paced across the room. "We need Micah. He's got to be able to do something, figure out the most likely place they'd take her to try and remove the elium or something. There's got to be something we can do."

"I've already got him on it."

"Can I help? I can't stay idle on this one, Thomas. I need to be doing something . . . anything."

Thomas nodded. "Yeah, you can help Micah by telling him all there is to know about the demons and Claire. Any bit of information that you haven't told him would help, even if it seems totally mundane."

Adam nodded, glancing away and rubbing a hand over his chin. He really did feel half-crazed. Uncontrolled fire jumped from finger to finger. He tamped it down and took a deep breath. "Okay. I can do that."

"Adam?"

He looked at Thomas, tried to focus. "Yeah?"

"You really care about Claire, don't you? This isn't just about losing your charge to the demons, is it?"

He rubbed his chin again, looked down at the ground. "I think I fell in love with her."

Thomas went silent.

"I've only done that one other time in my life, Thomas, and you know how that turned out."

"Yes." He paused. "I remember that night."

Adam raised his gaze to Thomas's face. "I can't let it happen again. Claire can't be harmed. It's just . . . not in the realm of possibility."

"I understand how you feel, Adam."

Adam nodded, going to the door. "I'm going to find Micah."

CLAIRE MOVED AN INCH AND FELT HER STOMACH heave again. She allowed her cheek to descend back onto the cold floor of the building they'd jumped her into. The mode of transport had made her horribly ill, but at least her sickness was keeping the demons at bay—for now.

The walls of the place they'd brought her to had some significant demon-made wards. Wards that prevented her from using her magick. She wondered if the elium was still accessible to her, being demon magick and not *aeamon*. Just as soon as her stomach stopped roiling and her head stopped beating out a symphony of pain, she was going to check that out. At the moment she could barely move.

Cruel hands grasped her upper arms and hefted her. Her head lolled and her stomach heaved. But she hadn't had anything in her stomach to bring up before and nothing had changed. That didn't make her body want to do it any less, however.

Kai lifted her in his arms and laid her on a tall table with a padded top. She blinked, seeing the room for the first time. The beige tiled ceiling was decayed and deteriorating in places. A single light in the center of the ceiling dangled from frayed electrical cords. It cast a sickly pale yellow glow that left the room half in shadow.

She glanced around, seeing water trickling down one wall. Vaguely, she could tell it came from a broken pipe, her water magick flickering faintly in response under the heavy press of the wards. Smashed hospital equipment, chairs with mold on them, and other refuse lay around her like abandoned skeletons from an earlier time. Graffiti painted the walls.

Where the Houses was she?

"If you try to fight us," said Kai in Aemni, "I will bite you. Do you understand? If you so much as brush the elium or attempt to use your magick, I will bite you."

"Wards," she croaked. She couldn't access her elemental magick anyway.

"Wards, yes. We prepared this area just for you," answered Tevan, stepping from the shadows at the far end of the room. Tevan, with his soap-star-chiseled face, made her flesh want to get up and run away without her. He frightened her even more than Kai. "But you still have fight in you. *Do not*. You will only suffer if you try. You're alone here and under our control. You have no friends to aid you, no backup. You cannot expect to prevail against us."

Her jaw locked. Did they really think that would keep her from trying to get away from them? Maybe they didn't understand the strength of an *aeamon*'s will to live. Especially now that she had something—*someone*—to live for.

"And if you don't obey us in this," drawled Kai, "remember that we know where your fire witch is. The man, Adam, we could easily bring him here, easily dismember him in front of you, limb by limb. Don't tell us that he means nothing to you. You have traveled with him for many days and have undoubtedly formed a bond with him. *Your kind* is annoyingly prone to that."

Yes, well, she could hardly deny it. Especially since her mouth and throat had gone dry from Adam's name merely passing Kai's lips. They wouldn't hesitate to make good on their threat. Murders like that were entertainment to the *Atrika*— sustenance for their violent souls.

She turned her gaze from him and stared up at the half-destroyed light. "If you leave Adam alone, I won't fight you."

"That's good." Kai nodded. "Don't expect any rescue either. You are in a place where no one will find you. Hope is lost for you."

"Rue is dead," Tevan added.

The words held such a finality, such a surety, that her chest clenched painfully. The notion that Rue could be dead clawed at her rib cage from the inside, making her realize that deep down she'd been hoping he might show up looking for her. If anyone could take back the elium without killing her, it was Rue.

"You couldn't know that for certain," she snarled at Tevan, who stood like a statue from hell at her feet. "You left Eudae at the same time I did, and when we left, Rue was still living."

Tevan shook his head and laughed softly. "Stop your fantasies, Claire. When the *Atrika* attacked Yrystrayi, we brought so much magick and so many demons to bear that no one survived."

"That's just your ego, Tevan." She spat the words at him. "You have no idea what happened at Yrystrayi after you went through the doorway. Anyway, if you thought the *Atrika* had managed to kill Rue and take over Yrystrayi, you wouldn't be here trying to get the elium from me. In fact, if you'd been so sure of defeating the other demon breeds, you never would have dove through the doorway after me in the first place."

The demons said nothing. Water *plink, plink, plinked* to the floor in the corner.

Time to further undermine their confidence—if the confidence of an *Atrika* could be undermined. "How do you intend to get back to Eudae anyway?" She laughed. "*Idiots!* You followed me here and now you have me, sure. Maybe you'll even succeed in taking the elium from me. But what if you do? What then? You have no way home. You're trapped here just like I am."

She was bluffing a little. They did have a way home. They could use the same method that Erasmus Boyle had used. It required blood magick and the sacrifice of many *aeamon*, but they wouldn't have a problem with that.

However, opening a doorway via that method was tricky. The demons would have to wait for certain astronomical influences to be present, they would have to have the right witches with the perfect balance of magicks, and, lastly, they would have to perform the blood rites at certain times and in certain locations.

The spell was complicated and limited, but it could be done.

"Don't worry about us, sweet Claire," Tevan purred. "We'll find our way back, even should it take decades. And when we return, it will be with the elium in my seat."

Kai stiffened a little at the words *my seat* and Claire tucked that interesting reaction away for later. Tevan planned to control the elium and Kai didn't like it.

"We fully expect that our people will have overthrown the *Ytrayi* and the other demon breeds by now," Kai interjected, his hand tightening painfully on her upper arm, making her wince. "But there are other uses for the elium." His gaze flicked at Tevan.

She frowned. Other uses for the elium beyond wielding it as the ultimate weapon against the ruling *Ytrayi*? What did they mean?

Could Kai and Tevan intend to overthrow the *Atrika* themselves and take rule into their own hands? If that was their plan, there had to be friction between them. No two demons could ever share power. If that was the case, maybe she could use that friction to her advantage. Surely, they were both already considering betraying each other.

Or did they plan to use the elium here on Earth?

Claire shivered.

"What other plans for the elium do you have?" she asked.

"Time for discussion is over," answered Tevan, moving to her head. "We will take the elium from you now."

Bitterness coated the back of her throat. "At least tell me where you've taken me."

"This is not a relevant piece of information for you. Soon you will be dead."

Houses, oh, please. She didn't want to die.

Claire struggled to sit up. They allowed her to move, probably because she had nowhere to go. She swallowed hard at the sudden wave of nausea. "You don't want to give me information, but I have some for you that might be useful."

Tevan tipped his big blond head to one side. "How so?"

"We've established that you can't be sure your people destroyed the *Ytrayi*. No matter what you say, I know that you aren't certain."

Kai and Tevan exchanged a glance that let her know she was correct.

Encouraged, she continued. "Keep me alive and I'll tell you everything I know of the *Ytrayi* and of Yrystrayi. If the *Atrika* haven't defeated the *Ytrayi*, the information could be essential to you. After all, I've lived at Yrystrayi my entire life as handmaiden to Rue himself. I slept in his quarters. I ate with him, studied with him. There is no one who knows him better than I do."

Tevan pursed his lips. "Information from Rue's pet. It's an interesting notion."

"I know all of Yrystrayi's inner workings." It was true, but, of course, she had no intention of giving them the correct information. There was no place in the entire universe, not any of them, where the *Atrika* could be allowed to rule.

Tevan pressed a huge hand on her chest and forced her back down. "You are at our mercy, Claire, and not in a position to negotiate. We will torture this information from you, should you live through the extraction of the elium. The elium is more valuable than your knowledge of Yrystrayi. Do you understand?"

Yes, she understood.

"Now lie back and be still and, for the sake of all the Houses, keep your mouth shut."

Did they expect her to be passive in this?

She reached for the elium, barely touched it, and found hard fingers in her hair, head yanked to the side, throat exposed.

Fangs sunk deep.

Pain flared along her nerve endings and venom rushed through her veins. Hot. Metallic. The taste of it sat behind her teeth, made her gag.

TWENTY-FOUR

CLAIRE SCREAMED. MEMORY FLASHED.

Standing in the center of the bare, well-warded training room with Rue in front of her. His golden eyes boring holes into hers. His magick ripe and hot in the room, tingling through her as he sank his power into the seat of her magick—twisted here, prodded right there . . .

The first time he'd done it, it had almost felt like rape—his will asserted over hers, her protests falling on deaf ears. She'd fought the insertion of his power into her body, had squirmed from him and ran. He'd forced it into her anyway, gentling her with softly spoken words. It was the only time he'd ever spoken so sweetly to her, when he'd wanted her to settle down and allow him to mold her.

Over time she'd learned to accept the sessions with Rue, and as her magick had grown in power, she'd actually started to look forward to them. Although Rue had never provided her with complete answers to her questions, never explained exactly what he was doing.

He'd most certainly never opened up to her emotionally as the parental figure she supposed she'd been longing for. The *Ytrayi* weren't good at that; though in the privacy of their romantic relationships with their mates, she knew there was a degree of shared emotion, caring, even *love*.

But in her relationship with Rue—owner and pet, master and slave—true openness of feeling never evolved. Even though she'd always known—well, she thought she'd known—that Rue cared for her well-being on some level. She'd believed that up until the day he'd imbued her with the elium and sent her tumbling into a foreign world.

Where was Rue now? If he still lived, would he care that she was about to be tortured, probably killed, by these two *Atrika*? And why did she care what Rue felt for her anyway? Why was she even thinking of him in this moment at all?

Probably because he was one of the few people in her life she'd ever formed a relationship with, no matter how dysfunctional.

Probably because it was too painful to think about Adam. Especially about losing him.

Adam.

Pain lanced through her and her spine bowed. Right after the flash of agony, blessed numbness started at her toes and worked its way up her body. Her mind, already befuddled from the venom, flashed again to parts of her life—watching her mother die, meeting Ty.

Then Adam's face filled her mind. Instead of balking from the fear of losing him, she embraced the image and held it close.

Adam smiling at her, Adam glancing at her, annoyed that she was endangering herself. The curve of his lips, the light in his eyes, the warm glow of caring he'd bestowed on her at the gas station right before she'd been taken.

Claire was glad that was the last memory she had of him. It warmed her even as her body went cold from the demon poison making its way through her bloodstream.

Her vision blurred. She blinked and the color of the world bled away to black and white. The numbness and chill in her limbs and body unfortunately did not prevent her from feeling the hard grip of the demon's hands on her arms and legs, or the heat of Kai's breath as he leaned down and examined her eyes.

All sound was muffled, as though she existed underwater. Tevan and Kai spoke to each other in clipped, harsh tones. She could tell by the looks on their faces and the abrupt way they spoke that they were not working well together. The information filtered through the thickness of her thoughts as important and she filed it away.

If she was able to endure what was to come, if she lived through the day, maybe she could use it against them in some way.

Demon magick slipped inside her, like Rue's had so many years ago. Claire closed her eyelids with effort, unable to manipulate any other part of her anatomy. Every fiber of her will screamed at her to *fight, fight, flee!* But, of course, that was impossible. Instead she fought to give in and allow it, the way she'd taught herself to allow Rue's magick inside her.

Claire had learned over the years that when she couldn't avoid something distasteful it was better to bend a little and permit it. If she couldn't bend, she might break.

And she wasn't about to let these monsters break her.

Tevan's power touched the seat of her magick, flicked out, and tasted it like a snake's tongue. She shuddered deep within. Undoubtedly, he found the flavor to his liking, just as he would find her flesh delicious to his taste buds. He hesitated a moment, long enough to make her wonder just how strong a handle he had on his control, then he moved to the elium.

The elium flared under the touch of demon power, thrumming deep within her. The core of the magick nestled in the heart of her, like a pearl embedded in the meat of an oyster. It responded like to like and Claire could tell that the elium wanted to go to Tevan. It reached out like a child wanting its mother, preferring to dwell in the heart of a pure demon than in a mere halfling.

Claire wanted it to go, too.

Tevan stroked the elium carefully, like a mother bird protecting a fragile egg. It was as close to caring as she'd ever known an *Atrika* could get. It made sense, she supposed, that it was a *weapon* an *Atrika* would show tenderness for.

Around the edges of the elium, she sensed how her magick had interwoven with it. Parts of the seat of her magick were tangled with the outer threads of the elium.

Tevan went straight for those threads and started to pull them apart. White-hot needles of pain stabbed through the center of her. Had she not been paralyzed, she would have screamed until her lungs exploded. This was like Micah's spell quadrupled, performed with no finesse or caring.

Unconsciousness threatened but was only snatched away. Claire knew the venom would keep blessed unawareness from her. It was a well-known side effect.

Tevan tried again to unthread the elium from the seat of her magick, and again agony seared her. For every tendril of power Tevan managed to untangle, another wrapped tight.

Her mind swamped with pain, she considered insanity. It might be the only way she could get through this. A wild giggle rose within her, unable to be voiced.

ADAM FOUGHT NOT TO PUNCH THE WALL. LONG gone was the lighthearted man the Coven had known. For years he was the one who joked around with everyone, even under the direst of circumstances.

He could find nothing light within him at the moment, not even a speck. Every moment they spent not finding Claire was another moment the demons had to kill her.

If, indeed, she still lived.

"You need to calm down, Adam."

"I really fucking wish people would stop saying that." Adam turned on his heel and paced away from Jack McAllister. "Easy for you to say; it's not someone you care about trapped with a couple demons who are ready to rip her limb from limb."

"You're right. In your position, if it were Mira in the hands of the demons, I'd be crazed, too."

"And don't fucking tell me that Micah and the others are doing all they can. If one more fucking witch tells me that, I'm going to rip their fucking head off."

"Yeah," Jack said, eyebrows rising. He stood and went to the kitchen, took two short, fat glasses from the cabinet, and poured whiskey into them both. He turned. "Do you want a fucking drink?"

Adam started toward him. "Fuck, yeah." He took the glass from Jack, downed it in one swallow, and then poured another.

"So, it finally happened, then. Adam Tyrell finally fell in love."

He rolled his eyes at Jack and drank down another glass. "Hell, have a baby and get married, and you start going all soft and talking about love."

"You wouldn't be like this if it was anything less. Anyway, what's wrong with love?"

Plenty.

Adam turned and stalked away from him, back into the living room of his Coven apartment. "I was married before, Jack. I'm not unacquainted with love."

Jack went totally silent.

Adam glanced at him. "Yeah, I know. Shocking, isn't it?"

"Yeah, it is."

"Thomas knows. Isabelle knows, but not the details. A few others know. Not many."

"Did you get divorced?"

He collapsed into a recliner with a heavy sigh. Why'd he even bring this up? "No, man, she died."

"*Fuck.*"

"Yeah, fuck."

Jack set his glass down and moved into the living room to sit in the other recliner. "I'm sorry."

Adam tipped his head back against the chair and closed his eyes. "Why do people always say that when they hear someone's died?"

"Because they don't know what else to say." He paused. "How did she die?"

"I was a cop. I bet you didn't know that either. My dad was a cop, too. I followed in his footsteps, just like he wanted. My dad, both my uncles, all of them were Chicago cops. It was in my blood."

"No, I didn't know."

Adam tipped his head forward and looked at Jack. "I was a good cop, too. Never took bribes, never confiscated shit from crime scenes. I wasn't corrupt. Anyway, one night after my shift I got home and a thief broke into our house and killed her." He laughed, a harsh sound. "I was still wearing my holster."

Jack just stared at him. Adam was thankful he didn't say he was sorry again.

"I fried the guy on the spot, right where he stood. You can

guess what I had to do after that. Thomas came in, cleaned up my mess, and I started working for him."

Jack just blinked. "I always wondered how you came to the Coven."

"I loved my wife, Jack."

"I know. I can hear it in your voice and see it on your face."

Adam got up and poured himself and Jack another drink. He needed it. He bet wherever Claire was, she needed one, too. His hand clenched around the bottle as he poured.

If he could confront Tevan and Kai right now he would make fire hot enough to rival the sun, hot enough to get through their shields. When he finally met them again, they were going to taste it.

He finished pouring the amber liquid into the glasses, then braced his hands on the counter and bowed his head as a wave of emotion swamped his mind and body. A trickle of fire jumped down his arm from his seat and sparked harmlessly on the counter. "We have to get Claire back."

Jack, thankfully, said nothing.

Jack had shown up, sent by Thomas, no doubt, to keep him from doing something rash while Micah worked up possible places the demons might have taken Claire. Something about spots in the world where demon magick was likely to be most effective. It had to do with the flux and flow of energy, ley lines, and the basic geographical lay of the land.

Truth was, the demons could have jumped her anywhere, anywhere in *the world*. Their only chance at finding her was divine intervention. Since Adam didn't believe in the divine, they were probably shit out of luck.

After a moment, Adam picked up the glasses and walked back into the living room.

"It wasn't your fault Claire was taken, you know," said Jack as he handed the glass to him.

Fuck it all. "Don't, Jack."

He moved to sit at the edge of his chair. "I mean it, Adam," he snapped. "You and Claire staved off Tevan and Kai against incredible odds. We're dealing with magicks and beings we know little about. There was no way to know they'd be able to track her so fast and pick her up during the five-minute stop you made at the gas station."

Truth was, he did feel responsible for Claire's abduction. "It was like they were just playing with us up until then."

"Yeah, well, Claire pulled the elium on them and then she did something no other elemental witch has ever managed to do and used all four elements on them *together*." He took a long drink. "You'd better believe they were done fucking around by that time."

"Claire is amazing."

"And she might have already escaped. Don't count her out of this yet."

"We shared dreams." His voice sounded a little slurred to his own ears. The alcohol was sending him to a place where he could drift a little.

"What?"

"After I first met her, we had this chemistry—"

"You have *chemistry* with every woman."

"No. It was different with Claire. It was a shared thing, that spark." Adam snapped his fingers in the air and a flame appeared. "And we shared dreams."

"What do you mean, *share*?"

"We dreamt the same dream. A couple times. The exact same dream on the same night, probably at the same time."

Jack was quiet for a long moment. "Huh," he said finally. "That's really strange."

"Claire thought maybe it was magickal bleed-through."

"Like her magick affected yours while she slept, drew your astral self into her mind or something? Mira can let her consciousness walk about without her body. It's something air witches can do. Claire is an air witch, in a way."

"Claire is an everything witch." Adam mulled it over for a moment. "I guess that's what happened. I don't know."

Jack sat forward so fast he sloshed his drink over the rim of the glass and onto the carpet. "That's it, you fucking bastard."

"What's it?"

"You can find Claire that way. You can use the connection you two shared in your dreams to find out where she is."

Adam sat forward. "Are you drunk?"

Jack stood up. "Mira is really into this, Adam. She can tell you more than I can, but I know it's kind of like remote viewing. If you can connect with Claire, you can see out of her eyes and maybe we can tell where she's being held."

Hope flickered to life inside him and then crunched to his toes. "Claire's the one with the air magick, Jack, not me. Didn't you hear a word Micah said? No way do the demons have Claire anywhere unwarded. Wherever she is, she can't access her air magick or *any* kind of elemental magick."

But Jack was already striding to the door. "We don't know that for sure. Anything's worth a shot at this point. The only other thing to do is get drunk; this is time better spent. I'm sending Mira here right now." He turned and pointed a finger at him. "Fucking make some coffee, Adam. She'll need you sober."

TWENTY-FIVE

CLAIRE CAME TO AND CLUTCHED HER CHEST IMME-
diately, rolling over onto her side and groaning.

The elium was still there. She was still alive.

Coughing, she forced herself to sit up and look around.
They'd put her in what appeared to be an old hospital room.

What had happened in the other room, a surgery room in
the abandoned hospital, she'd surmised, was mostly a blur.
That was a good thing judging from what she could recall.

They'd finally given up trying to untangle the elium from
her seat. They'd been close to killing her and they'd probably
been afraid they'd lose the weapon if she died. Eventually, the
venom had worn off and with it the chemical that prevented
her from becoming unconscious. She'd slipped into comforting darkness immediately, and apparently, the demons had
moved her to this room.

Claire had a sneaking suspicion that the method they'd
used to try and take the elium had been gentle by their stan-
dards. She was not looking forward to the next try, which was
probably coming soon.

Now she lay on an old hospital bed which had been covered with new sheets. A new blanket that looked like it had been taken straight from the package was folded at the end of the bed. A plate of steaming food lay on a small, plastic, paint-smattered table by the side of the bed. Other than that, the room was bare save for a small lamp on the floor in the corner, which emitted a weak glow. Rapidly fading daylight came through the uncurtained window.

She rose and went to that diminishing daylight, her muscles protesting every move she made and the center of her chest aching so much it hurt to draw a breath. On her way to the window she passed a small bathroom and wondered about running water and working plumbing. Probably too much to hope for.

They'd put her on the top floor of the hospital. A parking lot many stories down surrounded the building like a concrete moat. Beyond the lot was a stretch of woods, no other buildings or roads that she could see. In the distance she could just make out a few billboards. Maybe they were near a highway?

Judging from the current time of day, she'd been on their table for about twelve hours. No wonder she felt the way she did.

Breathing heavily from just that much exertion, she turned and stared at the food and blankets. It was chilly in the room. There was electricity in the building, it appeared, but no heat. Or perhaps it was demon magick that lit the lightbulbs.

Pulsing all around her in sickening waves, the demon wards dampened her magick and made her power impossible to use. The wards wrapped her seat like a wad of wet cotton. It wrapped the elium, too, but not as securely. She didn't think she could work any of it free, it was so tight. She'd try, though.

It seemed odd that the demons would care enough about her comfort and well-being to bring her hot food and blankets, but she supposed they needed to keep her healthy. If she got sick and died, they might not be able to extract the elium.

She studied the window again, thinking. If she could breach it, she could use her magick because she'd be beyond the demon wards. Her air magick wasn't strong enough to float her to the ground. Otherwise she'd break the glass and leap . . . but maybe there was another way.

The door opened and Kai stepped through. "You're awake."

His powers of observation were keen. She only stared at him, bile from her hatred rising up to bite the back of her throat.

He looked from the plate to her. "You should eat."

"I'm not hungry."

"Then you should drink."

She licked her lips and glanced at the glass of water beside the plate. She was thirsty, but she wasn't giving him the satisfaction of watching her consume anything they brought her. "No, and don't tell me what I should do, Kai."

"You need your strength for the next phase."

Yes, she could only imagine what that would be.

She spoke in Aemni. "What rank did you hold in the *Atrika* military, Kai?"

He hesitated for a moment, surprised by the question. "Captain."

"And Tevan?"

He shifted. That shift in his weight was enough to tell her that he wasn't happy with his answer. "Lieutenant."

Of course, she'd already known that.

"So you take orders from Tevan?"

Kai lifted his chin. "This is not Eudae."

"The *Atrika* don't abandon their military ranking so easily, do they? Surely, a mere change of venue doesn't mean you cease obeying the orders of your superior officer."

The demon's body stiffened. "I did not come here to speak of military order."

She suppressed a smile. It hadn't been a big assumption to make—Kai did not like the fact that Tevan was above him in their pecking order. Now she would do all she could to inflame the discord between them. She had few weapons at her disposal, so she'd use all of them to her advantage.

"Of course." She glanced away and then back at him. "Did Tevan send you here to check on me?" Claire blinked at him and smiled.

"Enough questions!" he roared. "Eat, rest, and drink water.

You will need to be in good condition for the next attempt." He began to close the door.

"When will the next attempt be?" She wanted to know how long she had to try and escape.

He never answered her. He only glared at her and shut the door. The lock turned on the other side.

Claire walked the perimeter of the room, examining the half-destroyed ceiling for places she could pry through.

Nothing.

When she got to the table with the food and water, she kicked it, sending the warmed up canned vegetables and pasta with red sauce over the floor to spread like a bloodstain.

She turned her attention to the window. Maybe there. Claire decided she would try the window first, and experiment with the elium second.

One way or another, she was breaking out of here before the next evil experiment commenced.

FINGERTIPS GRIPPING CONCRETE. TOES BALANCED on a ledge. Chilly wind whipping at clothing, blowing dark hair into her face. Claire glanced down, seeing the steep drop. Her stomach lurched. The wards flickered in and out here; she'd found the boundary.

Back at the Coven, Adam saw and felt it through her.

If Claire knew he'd managed to connect with her through her air magick, she showed no sign, though she was hardly in a place to let him know. He'd hooked up with her in the middle of what appeared to be an escape attempt.

All night and into the morning, Mira had instructed him about how to reach out to Claire using his mind. It wasn't something he should've been able to do, considering he had no air magick to call. Mira had explained that it was a thing that even some non-magickals could achieve. Basic psychic ability—remote viewing. That coupled with Claire's strength in air magick and the fact that apparently he and Claire had some sort of special connection—some emotional and psychic link already—meant that maybe, just maybe, he could reach her.

By midmorning he and Mira had been falling over with exhaustion and they'd still had no luck. Mira had left and told him to get some rest. As Adam had been falling to sleep, so utterly overwhelmed with fatigue, he'd been thinking of Claire, trying to reach out to her. Then, in the murky half awareness of that place between sleep and wakefulness, he'd begun to have flashes of another place.

He'd been so surprised he'd nearly lost his tenuous hold on the images. Adam had sat bolt upright and then laid back down immediately. He'd calmed his breath and closed his eyes, strengthening with all his might the fragile link he'd managed to achieve with Claire.

Gradually, the images had come in clearer and steadier. He'd even begun to get sound and sensation. That had happened after she'd climbed out of the broken window, perhaps because she'd been occasionally beyond the wards that girded her prison, dwelling in the border of them.

Her fingers slipped and adrenaline surged through Adam's veins as it did through Claire's. Fingertips scrabbled for purchase, found it, gripped. She inched to the left, little by little, the side of the building scraping through her clothing, against her stomach and chest. Then Claire stopped, staring at the red brick in front of her. She drew a breath, steadied herself . . .

And leapt backward like a diver off the high board.

Falling. No, *plummeting* toward the ground. Wind whipped at Claire's clothes. Long, dark hair streamed around her head.

Fear rose in Adam's throat. In the bed, his fingernails gouged his palms, drawing blood. Pain surged up his arms.

"*No, no, no, no.*"

It was all he could chant in the two seconds it took for her to fall. Seconds that seemed like forever. He braced for the impact.

Magick flared, tingling through his chest. For a moment he thought he'd called it and then realized it was only a ghost of Claire's body.

She struck. The ground gave like a mound of feather pillows, cushioning her and bringing her to an easy, careful halt.

Earth magick. *Of course.* She'd used magick to make the pavement of the parking lot soft and pliant, like a big mattress.

Thank the gods.

She lay for a moment, undoubtedly recovering from the hard, fast plunge. Blue sky spread overhead. Wind rustled the trees behind her and somewhere from a lofty limb a bird sang. The sun was halfway up in the sky—midmorning. Wherever Claire was, it was in the same time zone. That alone was helpful information.

She got up, the ground beneath her once again hard pavement. One long look at the building she'd jumped from yielded a little more information. It was big, redbrick, and from the looks of the broken, dirty windows and its weed-choked base, abandoned.

She turned and was off. Her boots, still the same ones she'd been wearing when she'd been taken, crunched over the parking lot and into the forest. Dried fallen pine needles gave way to broken branches, leaves, and a tangle of undergrowth as she plunged past trees in an effort to get as far from the building as possible.

Earth magick flared as she used it to help her move foliage out of her way. In the distance, an overgrown road came into view. Farther still a gate, padlocked with heavy chains and a sign . . .

Something behind Claire roared. A monster in the forest, gaining on her fast. Claire's adrenaline spiked, as did Adam's.

Gods, she was so close to getting away.

Claire halted and turned, ready to fight. Tevan and Kai both ran through the forest toward her, murder on their demon faces—eyes red, teeth extended into ripping points.

Claire didn't mess around. She went straight for the elium.

Nausea exploded through Adam as she tapped it. Brutal, shattering spikes of pain blossomed through his body. Still, it was just a ghost of what Claire felt.

That was what it was like to access the elium?

The magick seemed to implode her body. It radiated out in a wave. Tevan and Kai stopped short and another force smashed into Claire, knocking her backward. Her breath *woofed* out of her as she made impact. Darkness flickered over her vision like a curtain coming down.

The last thing Adam saw through Claire's eyes was Tevan standing over her.

Adam rolled off the bed and hit his bedroom floor running. It appeared Claire's escape attempt hadn't been successful, but one good thing had come of it.

He'd been able to read the sign.

TWENTY-SIX

How badly did Adam wish he could fly?

He would've given anything for a pair of fast wings or the demonic ability to jump. It was all he could think about for the entire drive to Tennessee.

It hadn't taken Micah long to locate the abandoned hospital where the demons were keeping Claire. Typing the name of it into Google had brought up a wealth of ghost-hunting websites. Apparently the building was famous for things that went bump in the night and the regional ghost-hunting societies frequently visited to document activity.

How tickled would those non-magickals be to know that real, live demons had decided it was a good place to torture a witch?

In his research, Micah had verified some places over the world where demon magick might work the best. The part of Tennessee where the hospital was located was in just such a place. Micah had mentioned that there were parts of the building itself where Tevan and Kai's magick would also have a greater impact, but he'd had no time to determine where these places might be, even though he worked nonstop in the back of the cargo van, hunched over his books and notes, flashlight in hand, and laptop beside him. If Micah couldn't figure it out by the time they arrived, they would have to search the immense hospital floor by floor.

Adam just itched to get there, itched for action. He wanted into that building so he could do something to find and rescue Claire. Anything. Otherwise he was surely going to go insane.

It would kill him to be too late this time.

Every moment of the trip Adam sat in brooding, silent rage and fear for Claire. Every moment he wished for the ability to fly. And though Adam had not slept even a few minutes since Claire had been taken, he couldn't close his eyes, even for a minute.

They'd brought an army of witches with them, all well fortified with copper weapons. They got there in record time, making a trip that should have taken seven hours in five and a half. It was still too long.

They arrived in Tennessee that afternoon.

When the sun had begun to paint the sky in the rosy hues of dusk, they went in. The Coven witches parked their vehicles at the bottom of the hill where the Our Sisters of Mercy Veterans Hospital was located and made their way through the woods that surrounded it.

By the time they'd reached the building, not a demon had stirred. Adam wasn't sure that was a good thing . . . or a bad thing.

Gods, please let them still be there.

On Thomas's command, they entered the building in well-coordinated groups, all of them groaning when they hit the dampening wards. Adam went on his own, unable to take orders from anyone at the moment, not even Thomas Monahan.

The lobby—or what had been the lobby—was empty save for a few pieces of abandoned and broken furniture, refuse collecting in the corners, and some graffiti on the walls. It looked like teenagers or homeless people had set up a place to hang out in one area. A big moldy green couch sat there and some dirty needles lay on the floor.

"Charming," muttered Jack to his left.

"You don't need to babysit me," Adam muttered, moving across the lobby to the stairs. His boot accidentally kicked an old can and sent it sliding across the floor, making a metallic sound. The sword sheathed to his back felt heavy.

"Who's babysitting? I'm just sweeping like everyone else. You just happen to be in my way."

Adam said nothing. He just moved to the door of the stairwell and opened it. He had to trust his intuition now, that psychic connection Mira thought he shared with Claire.

The landing of the stairwell reminded him of the first hospital he and Claire had been in together. That had been the beginning of the nightmare. Dare he hope this could be the end?

He gazed upward at all the floors. The electricity didn't work here, but light filtered in from somewhere . . . just enough to see by.

"Where do you think she is?" Jack said, stepping in after him.

"Gods, Jack. You fucking scared me." Their voices echoed.

"Sorry. So, where?"

"Up high. When I saw through Claire's eyes, she was probably on the top floor."

Jack whistled, looking upward. "That looks like a good cardio workout to me." He moved to the stairs. "Let's get up there."

ADAM KICKED OPEN DOOR AND AFTER DOOR ON THE top floor, finding nothing. Only more graffiti, a small amount of broken furniture, and equipment too messed up for even the homeless people to steal.

Walking into the hospital, the witches had immediately come up against the demon wards. It had been like entering Gribben, the Coven's prison, where a series of strong wardings built into the very foundation of the building stripped all magickals of their power. This was not quite that bad. Here Adam could still feel his magick, but it was only a shadow of its former self.

He put boot to heavy door once again and found something new. Adam walked within yet another abandoned hospital room. Blankets covered a bed, the first bed he'd found in his search. He went to the rumpled bedding and pulled the pillow to his nose, inhaling. The distinctive scent of Claire's hair filled him. It rocked him back a step, made his knees go weak.

He remained like that until Jack showed up at the door, then Adam dropped the pillow back to the bed and glanced around. Food had been spilled violently on the floor. By Claire or by her captors? The window at the far end of the room was shattered. That, he remembered.

"This is where they were keeping her," Adam said in a dull voice. "I can still smell her on the blankets."

"Come on, let's keep looking, Adam," said Jack, turning from the doorway. "At least we're in the right part of the hospital."

Adam followed Jack out. Throughout the rest of the huge building, the yells and stomping feet of the witches echoed. They thought Claire wasn't here anymore. Jack thought so, too. Adam could tell by the glances of pity he kept earning from his fellow fire witch.

If Jack wasn't careful, those looks were going to get him in trouble. Adam felt volatile. The prospect that they'd come all this way just to find a dead end was pushing him over the edge in the worst way.

Jack and the others could think what they wanted. Adam's intuition told him Claire was still here somewhere. He wasn't giving up until he found her.

Adam stopped in the middle of the corridor, wan light filtering in through the rooms where he'd kicked open the doors. Heat flared in his palms, a reaction to his heightened emotion, and he viciously tamped it down. Adam closed his eyes and took a deep breath of the musty, rust-tinged air.

Jack's boots bit into the grit of the floor as he approached. "Adam?"

Adam ignored him, instead focusing on Claire, the way Mira had taught him. Only blankness and blackness met his efforts. Nothing. It could have been for a million reasons. Most likely it was the wardings in the hospital, which dulled everyone's magick to a mere tired yawn of power.

It could have been his own lack of air magick that made him find only blankness. It could have been because he needed to achieve that certain rhythm of brain wave activity that could only be reached through deep meditation or near sleep. It could have been because Claire was unconscious.

Adam couldn't bring him himself to consider the other possibility.

Then he thought of something. He opened his eyes. "The maintenance areas. I bet no one's checked those yet."

"Let's go," answered Jack.

They descended, past the main floor and into the darkness of the basement. Mold and damp air filled their lungs as they opened the door to the boiler room. Here Adam and Jack were forced to turn on the flashlights they'd brought with them, hanging on the belt that girded the swords sheathed to their backs.

Once this area had been filled with the low, steady hum of the boiler, furnace, and other heavy machinery needed to make a hospital run. Now it was as dead and silent as a morgue.

The hair on the back of Adam's neck rose. Here he could believe the hospital was haunted.

The heavy metal door squeaked when they opened it and shut with a final-sounding click when it closed behind them. They were plunged into darkness, save for the core of light emitted by their flashlights. Something to their left scampered past on small animal feet.

At least, Adam assumed they were small animal feet.

Soundlessly, he moved into the large room, ducking under bare pipes and rounding cold machinery. Here no graffiti marked the walls and no drug paraphernalia littered the floor. He could understand why trespassers had avoided this area.

Carefully, he and Jack paid attention to the path they took, so they could find their way back. With the sputtering, feeble amount of fire magick Adam possessed, he sooted the floor with flashes of heat. Otherwise Adam was sure they'd never find their way out and Thomas would return years from now to find their time-whitened, rat-gnawed-upon bones in a corner somewhere.

Jack could only produce flickers when he called his power, but Adam's magick was more motivated and pushed through the warding better.

Something bellowed.

The sound was so inhuman, so low and filled with rage that it literally stopped Adam's heart for a moment. Both he and Jack came to a perfect, motionless standstill. Both of them switched off their flashlights at the same moment, the velvet darkness around them now more friend than foe.

Unless the ghost-hunting societies had been correct about major spectral activity in this hospital, *that* had been a demon.

Where there were demons, there was Claire.

Slowly, Jack pulled his sword—a bare whisper of copper against the leather sheath and the blade was free. Adam didn't touch his, instead sensing his seat. His will to rescue Claire made it pulse with a strength it should not have had.

A glow of red light caught Adam's eye, cutting through the damp fist of blackness that held them so tight. Adam moved toward it, but Jack caught his upper arm. Adam clenched his fists to keep from rounding on him and punching him square in the face.

"You don't know what's over there," Jack muttered near his ear.

"A fucking demon, that's what's over there. Maybe Claire, too." He paused, drew a careful breath. "Go back, get Thomas and the others. Bring them down here. I'm going to check that out and there's nothing you can do to stop me, Jack."

After a moment, Jack released his arm. "Don't do anything stupid."

A remnant of Adam's former self surfaced, made buoyant by the possibility of finding Claire. He flashed Jack a grin in the reddish light. "Stupid is my middle name."

"Yeah, no kidding." Jack took a step into the shadows. "I'll be back as soon as I can. Hopefully, that will be before you get yourself killed." He retreated into the inkiness and disappeared.

Adam turned and proceeded cautiously toward the red light. The scuffling of feet and low, rumbling male voices met his ears as he drew closer. No feminine lilt joined them. Panic speared through him, making him move faster.

He rounded a furnace and peered beyond the hunk of metal. Claire lay on her side, back to him, wearing a short white hospital gown. She was in a fetal position on a table, not moving.

The demons circled her, teeth gnashing and fists clenching. That body language alone told Adam they were in an agitated state, but beyond that their eyes glowed red and their mouths gaped open, probably to make room for their extended fangs. Apparently, things weren't going according to their plan.

That was either a very good thing for Claire . . . or a very bad thing.

Tevan bellowed again and brought his massive hands down on either side of Claire, shaking the table. The entire building rumbled under the force of his frustration and anger, demon magick spilling out of him and pushing at the concrete walls and ceiling. Dust and debris fell from above Adam, catching in his hair.

On the table, Claire didn't stir. She didn't even twitch. Not even when Tevan turned her to her back and raised his hands above his head, seemingly to bring them straight down onto her unprotected sternum—her seat—did Claire move.

Before Tevan had a chance to strike Claire, Adam strode out from behind the furnace and raised power. Doing it through the wards was like pulling it through two inches of concrete, but rage burned inside him so intense and so strong that the concrete holding back his power simply crumbled.

Adam's magick exploded from his chest and burst down his arms in an almost uncontrollable flash of heat that warmed his skin.

The demons turned toward him, surprise clear on their faces. They had been so intent on whatever torture they were inflicting on Claire that Adam doubted they even knew there were others in the building. He took advantage of their shock and blasted the wall behind them, just like Claire had taught him. The bolt of power ricocheted off the wall and hit them from behind, sidewise.

They were so stunned they didn't even throw up shields. The white-hot fire enveloped them and Adam turned his efforts to holding back the flame from Claire, who lay so near them.

The demons roared, covering their heads with their hands. They shook off the fire magick easily enough, but Adam didn't let up, giving them little time to recover and launch an offensive. He sent blast after blast of it at them, over and over, driving them away from Claire.

Soon his vision blackened a little and his chest ached. He was quickly exhausting all his reserves. Fire rained down from the ceiling and roared up the walls and over the floor, forcing the demons to retreat backward into darkness.

Adam stumbled, trying to get to Claire while keeping up the assault on Tevan and Kai.

Behind him, he heard the approach of the other witches. Reinforcements. The villagers chasing Frankenstein's monster, but instead of pitchforks they carried copper. He didn't know if they could breach the wards like he had through his burst of emotion, but he hoped so. Adam's magickal stores were just about on empty.

Creating a safe pocket in the fire for himself and the Coven witches, he reached Claire just as the others ran past him, chasing the demons into the bowels of the basement. Adam lifted her into his arms and her head lolled to the side, eyes open and unseeing.

Oh, gods, no.

TWENTY-SEVEN

Adam's body coiled tightly with grief. It bubbled up from him like a toxic thing. Disbelief made him shake his head, his expression twist in anguish. Had he been too late?

He put his lips to hers, but her flesh was warm, living. Her breath hit his mouth like the sweetest, most expensive wine made into air. Not dead. He chanted it in his mind. *Not dead. Not dead. Not dead.*

He'd reached her in time.

In his panic, he'd forgotten the venom and the paralysis. The abducted witches in the cargo van had looked like this, too. Tevan and Kai had simply bitten her to keep her pliant and unmoving. The venom would wear off and she'd be fine.

Thomas came up on his side and yelled, "Get her out of here."

He didn't have to say it twice.

Adam tightened his arms around Claire and held her close to his body as he ran through the falling debris dripping from the ceiling, loosened by demon magick and on fire from his rage. His boots pounded on the stairs to the first floor and he carried her through the central lobby and out the front doors.

He didn't stop until they were far into the woods, away from the structure. If he could, he would have run for miles—anything to get Claire away.

He collapsed into a grassy patch, held Claire to his chest, and, breathing heavily, lifted his head to the sky. The waning sunlight, the soft twilight breeze, and the birdsong coming from the treetops seemed so odd considering where they'd just been. Nothing beyond the walls of the hospital hinted at the hellish battle now being waged in its industrial bowels.

He lowered his head and kissed her temple. He smelled like soot, but he'd managed to keep her free of it. "They're never getting you back, Claire," he murmured. "I have you now and I'm never letting go."

After a moment she stirred a little, her arm twitching first and then a leg. Slowly, she regained her ability to move, though not well. That would take some time. "Adam," she whispered in a labored voice. "*Houses*, I'm . . . so happy to see you." She winced, as though pained greatly by the mere effort to form words.

"Don't try and talk, Claire." He rocked her back and forth. "Just rest, okay?"

Fingers gripped his sleeve. "They never got it." She smiled.

"I know." That was clear enough by how frustrated the demons had been.

"You arrived just in time, Adam," she rasped. "They were so angry. If you'd come any later . . ." She trailed off and swallowed hard.

Coldness seeped through his bones at her words, freezing him motionless for a moment. "Don't talk, Claire. *Please*. We're going to get you safe, to a hospital—"

"No! No more hospitals. I hate them." Her voice was as strident as she could manage. "Okay." She smiled and rested her head against his chest. "Now I'll stop talking."

ADAM HAD MADE A PROMISE HE WASN'T SURE HE could keep.

He watched Claire limp across the room and hand Micah a piece of paper. She leaned over and talked to him softly, while Adam drummed his fingertips on a desktop, deep in thought.

Back at the hospital, he'd told her that he would never let demons take her again. Gods, what a stupid thing to say. At any time Tevan or Kai could just pop in and jump her like they did at the gas station.

Quick. Easy. Painless . . . at least for them.

There was no safe place for him to take her, no place to hide. Not even the depths of Gribben, the best warded building on Earth, could stop the demons.

But, apparently, lots of witches could.

Even though Adam had been the only one able to punch through the demon wards at the hospital through the sheer weight of his will and emotion, the witches had managed to beat the demons back . . . even with limited power.

There had been some injuries, but no deaths and the demons had jumped out of there once they realized how outnumbered they'd been.

Thomas said that Adam's magickal display had gone a long way in wearing the *Atrika* down. Thomas had been a little in awe of the whole thing—how Adam had busted the warding and managed to make the demons retreat with his fire magick alone. Adam hadn't even drawn his copper sword. His power had been enough.

Adam only cared that he'd been able to do enough to pry Claire loose from their claws. He hadn't been too late.

It had been a victory for the Coven and they'd celebrated all the way back home to Chicago. The battle had raised the spirits of the Coven as a whole, something they needed after the demoralizing destruction of Micah's lab and the abduction and murder of the witches sent as backup to Minnesota. The Coven was locked in a battle like they'd never known in the history of their record keeping.

The warlocks had nothing on the demons.

Gods help them all if the Duskoff and the *Atrika* ever decided to ally.

Yes, the victory was sweet, but they all knew it was temporary. As they'd returned to the Coven and walked back into the extensive damage still being repaired from the recent attack, the lessening of their spirits had been palpable. The demons were stunned for the moment, sure, but they weren't defeated . . . not by a long shot. And they'd be back.

For Claire.

They needed a miracle.

Micah stood and gave Adam a wary look. It made guilt twinge through him. He knew he wasn't Mr. Good Spirits these days and he'd been especially hard on Micah. "We have a sure-fire way to remove the elium."

Adam bolted to his feet. "What?" Hadn't he just been wishing for a miracle? But why didn't Micah seem happier about it? Standing beside him, Claire looked a little gray.

"So, what's the catch?" asked Thomas from across the room. "I can tell there is one."

"There is." Micah cast another uncertain glance at Adam, like Adam was about to jump across the room and rip his throat out. Adam forced himself to relax his body and facial muscles a little. "And it's a doozy. There's a slight side effect."

"A side effect?" Adam's voice sounded gritty in the cool air of the library. "What kind of side effect?"

Claire had been looking at the polished wood floor. She raised her gaze to his. "It will strip me of *all* my magick, not just the elium. It will, essentially, leave me a non-magickal."

The room went silent.

"It's like surgery." Micah gestured with his hands and avoided catching Adam's gaze. "It's like surgery to remove a tumor. Thing is, in this case, the tumor"—Micah made air quotes—"has inexorably attached itself to another organ, in this case, the seat of Claire's magick. In order to get the tumor, we have to remove everything."

Adam ran a hand over his face. Fuck, he was tired. "Gods."

Thomas shifted and stood. "What happens to the elium in this scenario, Micah? Does the core of her magick stay inter-twined with it?"

Micah shook his head of shaggy brown hair. "Got me. I've never tried anything like this before. I mean, there are spells that will let us make small adjustments to the flow of a witch's power, but this is like a complete . . . complete . . ."

"Amputation," Claire finished for him, her voice dull and dead-sounding.

Micah looked sick. He swallowed hard and continued. "Something like that. In any case, I'm not sure what elemental magick does once it's removed from a witch. The elium is different. It's demon magick, first of all, and was designed in a sort of self-contained ball that can be moved from demon to demon—"

"We're all demon at the heart of us," Thomas cut in gruffly.

"Yeah, but our magick isn't demon magick. Not completely. Our magick is born more purely from the elements than theirs is. That's why Claire carrying the elium was never a good idea. It reacted to her elemental magick by adhering to it."

"Wait a minute." Adam walked toward Micah and Micah took a step back. "Relax, already. I'm sorry I lost my temper with you during the last spell, I really am. Will you chill now? I'm not going to hurt you."

"As long as I don't hurt Claire."

"You got it. That's my trigger, Micah."

Micah touched his throat. "Yeah, okay. If I can, I won't trip it."

"When Claire pulled magick on the demons here in the Coven, it was different—explosive. It felt, smelled, and tasted like demon magick to me, just on a subtler scale. Claire told me she did it by pulling all the threads of the elements together. What if demon magick and elemental magick aren't so different, after all? What if there's another way?"

Micah rubbed his chin. "It's something to look into."

"We don't have time," Thomas put in. "If we intend to save Claire's life, we have to act now. Tevan and Kai could show up here at any moment and take her back."

"They'll kill me right away next time," Claire added. "They tried every other way to take the elium and nothing worked. Now they'll try to take the elium as I die. They're willing to risk it."

"That's why we need to act now," Thomas answered.

She chewed her lower lip. "It *is* possible that when Rue was tweaking my magick, he had a goal in mind. Maybe he was trying to transform my elemental magick into demon magick."

Thomas shook his head. "I don't understand why this is relevant."

Micah turned and walked away, apparently deep in thought. "What they're saying is that perhaps the special brand of magick that Claire possesses isn't that far from demon magick. Perhaps there's a way to push her magick that extra inch, make it truly behave like demon magick. Maybe that way the elium won't react by adhering to her seat and we can extract it without taking away all of Claire's power."

Thomas shifted impatiently. "And how long would it take to figure that out?"

Micah turned to Thomas. "I have no idea, but we have some time."

Adam met Claire's gaze. She'd crossed her arms over her chest protectively, as though the thought of losing her magick was worse than death. "What do you mean?"

"The spell that will extract all the magick from Claire will take a couple days to cook."

Adam blinked and shifted his gaze to Micah, who looked nervous. "Two days? We've got to hope the *Atrika* don't come after her for *two* whole days?"

"There's nothing I can do about it, Adam. These spells, especially the ones using blood magick, have to be cooked under very specific circumstances."

Adam and Thomas asked in unison with strident voices, "Blood magick?"

"Yeah, uh . . ." Micah swallowed hard. "Claire's blood."

Adam laughed harshly and pushed a hand through his hair. "You know, Micah, I might take back my previous statement about not hurting you."

Claire stepped toward him with a staying hand extended. "It's not much blood, Adam. Just a pint or two."

He stared at her.

She laid her hand on his chest and looked up into his eyes. "It's the only way. We do this spell, I get rid of my magick . . . and I live." She paused. "I get to stay with you."

Adam covered her hand with his and held her gaze. *Fuck.* He loved her so much.

Thomas cleared his throat. "Look, this is Claire's call. This is up to her."

Claire held his gaze a moment longer, then turned to Micah. "We can look into this, but only up until it comes time to perform the spell. If we don't have an alterative by then, we take it . . . all." Her voice broke on the last word.

Micah nodded. "I think that's the best course of action."

"I agree," answered Thomas.

"It's late." Micah walked to the door. "And we're all exhausted. Let's pick this up tomorrow morning. I'll start preparations to cook the surgery spell."

Claire nodded as Adam pulled her into the circle of his arms. "See you tomorrow morning."

Thomas gave them a little smile as he also left.

Claire turned in his arms and Adam kissed her. "Let's go upstairs and get some rest. Are you hungry?"

"Starving."

They'd barely eaten or slept since they'd returned from Tennessee. They'd been working nonstop on a way to extract the elium. Too bad the end result sucked so bad.

On their way to his apartment, they stopped in the kitchen and picked up some sliced apples, grapes, cheese, and other various goodies, along with some wine and a couple glasses. Adam tucked it all in a basket he found in one of the cabinets.

They could have cooked a real, hot meal there in the kitchen, but they both were in agreement—they wanted to be alone for a while.

Once they reached his place, he set the basket on the nightstand in his bedroom. A picnic with Claire in bed sounded good to him, never mind the crumbs.

"My last meal?" Claire asked, sliding her shirt over her head.

He turned to her. "Please don't say that."

She finished undressing and slipped a short cotton nightgown over her head. They got into bed together and Adam pulled her close.

They didn't know when the demons would show up, which meant they needed to savor every single moment together.

"I love you, Claire."

She stiffened in his arms and then relaxed. Kissing his chest, she mumbled. "I think I knew that when you came charging after the *Atrika* all on your own, armed with nothing but *aeamon* fire magick . . . through demon wards, no less." She laughed softly. "But it's nice to hear."

He rolled her beneath him and kissed her. "Then I'll say it again. I love you, Claire."

"I love you, too."

Adam closed his eyes and let the words wash over him,

through him. They lightened him. He accepted those words as he accepted the love he felt for her and they lifted something heavy from him.

After a few moments of holding her, enjoying the scent of her skin and the weight of her against him, he pulled the basket onto the bed. "Want something to eat?"

She nodded and they made a meal of bread with butter and fruit. For dessert, he laid a napkin on the bed and spread a few apple slices and some cheese on it. Then he picked up a slice of cheese, laid it on the apple, and brought it to her mouth.

Her soft red lips closed over the end and she bit. Adam couldn't help it, his cock hardened at the sight.

Claire chewed a bit, closed her eyes for a moment, then chewed some more. "Oh, that's good," she whispered after she'd swallowed. "Tart and sweet, creamy and crunchy. Yum."

Yum. That's for sure.

"I have something to make it even better." He reached over, took a bottle of wine from the basket, and poured it into a glass for them to share.

"Wine?" she asked as she took the glass. "I've heard about this."

"Take a sip."

She did. "It's interesting. Not Coca-Cola."

"No." He took the glass from her and took a drink. "It's normally not my thing. Give me a beer instead of wine any day and I'd be happy. Thomas keeps a nice wine stock, so I'm told. Wine's more his thing than mine."

"So, if you're not crazy about wine, why did you take a bottle for us?"

"I took it so you could taste it, Claire."

"I think I like it."

"Thought you might. Thomas tells me you need to develop a taste for it." He raised an eyebrow. "Kind of like me."

She gave a soft laugh. "I really didn't have a problem developing a taste for you, Adam." She took another drink, deeper this time. Wine ran down her chin and dripped to her chest.

Adam dipped his head and lapped it up, taking care to slowly lick her skin until she squirmed beneath him and moaned. He checked to see if her nipples were hard under the cotton of her nightgown and they were—two precious, pink points on her breasts. He pulled the neckline of her gown down low, then dropped his head and kissed both of them.

Claire sighed and almost dumped the glass of wine on the bed. Chuckling, he eased it from her fingers and removed the napkin with the rest of the cheese and apple.

She pulled the nightgown over her head, then settled back to watch him with heavy eyelids, like a warm and satisfied cat. The blankets were pushed down to her waist, revealing her soft breasts with their kissable pink, erect nipples.

He descended on her like she was the main course. Adam pushed the offending blankets the rest of the way off and pulled her beneath him, running his hand over her shapely thigh and the contour of her waist. "Damn, I could live off the feel of your skin alone, Claire. It could sustain me for life."

She sighed and tangled her fingers through his hair. "Let's try. Forget about all this and run away. We can live in the woods in a little log cabin and never see anyone again. Just you and me. That's all we'd need."

Adam groaned and nipped at her stomach. "That sounds good."

"No more demons. No more elium. No more Rue."

"Heaven." He moved down between her thighs, letting his tongue skate over her smooth skin. When he reached her clit and licked, she jumped a little and moaned. "Never mind," he murmured. "*This* is heaven."

TWENTY-EIGHT

HE LICKED HER AGAIN AND HER CLIT SWELLED under the flat of his tongue, becoming aroused and needy for more of his touch. Claire squirmed a little and he parted her thighs and held her down, pinning her to the mattress so he could drink his fill of her.

Her warm, musky-sweet scent intoxicated him as he explored all her silky, soft folds and crevices. He slipped his tongue inside her and groaned at the lusciousness of her flavor spreading over his tongue.

Claire moved on the mattress, sighing and moaning his name. Her sex grew more excited, driving Adam crazier for a deeper taste of her. He slipped one finger inside her to the base, watching it disappear and reappear coated in her cream. Then he added another, stretching her muscles farther, and made her moan. He watched it all, his cock hard. The anticipation of driving his shaft into her hummed through his veins.

While he worked them in and out of her, he settled on her clit, sucking and licking it until she arched on the bed, coming closer to orgasm. When it exploded over her, the muscles of her sex pulsed around his thrusting fingers and his name spilled from her lips.

Gods, he loved to make her come.

As soon as the waves of her climax had ebbed, she pushed him to his back and straddled him. Adam went easily, powerless under her touch and amenable to whatever it was she desired from him. Then she was kissing him—his chest and stomach and then downward with such ferocity that his words and breath were arrested in his throat by pure lust.

When her lips closed around his cock and she sucked him into the recesses of her mouth, Adam bellowed at the pleasant surprise.

Then he groaned.

Gods, it was clear Claire hadn't done this to many men. Any men? Adam was sure she'd only ever been with one besides him. Her inexperience showed in the unpracticed glide of her lips up and down his shaft, but that only made it all the more exciting.

He fisted his fingers in her hair and watched her luscious lips work him up and down, pleasure spiraling through him. Her gaze flickered upward and he saw lust in her dark eyes. Apparently, she wasn't done with him yet.

Thank the gods.

She released his cock and mounted him, her hot, slick sex closing around the head of his shaft and enveloping it. He closed his eyes and groaned as she slid down the length. He gritted his teeth and fought not to flip her and take control, even though his urge was to do just that.

She looked too pretty riding him, her head falling back as she closed her eyes and took him deep into her. Her lovely breasts thrust forward, just the perfect size to fill his hands, and her hips moved rhythmically.

Adam's hands found the nip of her waist as she rose up and down on his cock, the soft, hot clasp of her muscles massaging every inch of his shaft. She moved slow—crazy-makingly so—and held his gaze.

Gods, she was beautiful.

He slipped a hand down and rubbed her clit with his thumb while she rode him. Her breath caught and her eyes widened a bit.

"Does that feel good, baby?"

She caught her lower lip between her teeth and nodded.

"I live to make you feel good. Are you going to come for me?"

She closed her eyes and nodded again, moving up and down on his cock a little faster. He stroked her clit as she rocked, knowing he heightened her pleasure and drove her closer and closer to the precipice of another climax.

Her breathing quickened and she tipped her head back. "Yes, please, don't stop."

He had no such plans. Adam would touch her forever if she wanted him to. Never stop, never let her go.

Her body shuddered and she moaned. The muscles of her sex clamped down around his cock, massaging it, milking it. The look of ecstasy on her face, the lovely sounds issuing from her throat, all of it pushed Adam over the edge.

Pleasure exploded from his balls and deep into her body. He gasped her name, as she enjoyed the tail end of her climax.

"Oh, baby, baby, baby . . ." he murmured as he tipped her to the side and pulled her close to him, kissing her all over. "You're a goddess, my goddess."

"Mmm . . ." she answered with a tired, lazy smile, "I like being called that."

He chuckled and stroked his fingers through her hair. "Sleep, my goddess. I'll be here to keep you safe." She was exhausted and he wasn't going to make her dress. Fuck the demons. Claire could take this night and pretend they didn't exist.

They stayed tangled together until her breathing deepened to sleep.

But Adam couldn't find rest. He stayed up until early in the morning, gazing down at his slumbering beauty . . . and watching for *Atrika*.

CLAIRE AWOKE BEFUDDLED AND HALF-AWARE OF hands and lips on her body.

She became completely conscious on a low moan of needfulness. As she'd slept, Adam had been touching her, priming her. Her sex was plumped, aroused, her clit begging for his touch. Her breasts felt heavy and her nipples were tight and hard.

Moonlight still filtered through the window, painting the floor silver. Morning still hadn't come.

Adam's blond head bobbed between her thighs. He sucked her clit between his lips and she murmured his name.

Without a word, only need laid bare in the deep blue of his eyes, he rose and pushed her gently over onto her stomach, sliding his hand under her hips and pulling her upward so her rear fit into the curve of his pelvis. His hard cock jutted her swollen sex.

"Yes," she murmured, her fingers curling into the blankets. "Please, Adam, yes." Desire knotted low in her stomach. She moved her hips, trying to force him within her.

He swore under his breath and mounted her, rough and needy, pushing the head of his cock into her and thrusting deep. Her breath caught at the sensation of being so filled up, so possessed.

His body came down over hers, teeth finding the tender, vulnerable flesh of the curve of her neck. He bit, just enough for her to feel it, while he began to thrust. He slid easily in and out of her, like he belonged there.

Claire gasped, gooseflesh erupting over her. The bite was animalistic, primal, and it pushed every button Claire had.

His big body pinned hers as he took her, their bodies slapping together in the quiet of the room, their breathing filling the air. A climax flirted hard with her, but remained tantalizingly out of reach.

Adam released her from the bite and pulled her by her hips to all fours. Then he slid a finger to her anus and brushed over it. Claire jerked in surprise at the intimate touch.

"Shh, it's all right," Adam murmured. "Don't tell me Ty never did that to you, baby?"

"No," she said shakily.

"Well, then I'm the lucky guy who gets to introduce you to it." He brushed her again and pleasure tingled through her body. "There are a lot of nerve endings there. You'd be surprised. It feels good to have them stimulated, even better for a woman when she's double-penetrated."

"D-double penetrated?"

Adam gave a low chuckle. "There are so many games we

have yet to play. I can't wait to show you all the things there are for a man and woman to do in bed. In most ways you're mature beyond your years, in others so innocent." He pushed the tip of his finger past the tight ring and inside her.

Claire gasped—but this time not in surprise. Tingles of illicit, forbidden pleasure spread in a wave throughout her body.

He worked his finger out and then in a little farther, slowly and carefully thrusting. At the same time, he speared her sex with his cock. The combination of sensations was breathtaking and confusing, wonderful and . . . wrong, so wrong. But, Houses, it felt good.

"Do you trust me, baby?"

"With all I am."

"Then relax and enjoy this."

Claire let go and moaned, her back arching. Her body eased into it and Adam increased the pace of his play at her rear while he took her harder and faster. The stimulation of her two orifices at once blended together in an ecstasy that she'd never be able to describe in words.

Adam groaned. "Baby, you're so tight and sweet back there. This is making me crazy. We have to take it slow, but one day I want my cock there, deep inside you. I want to make you come that way, with my fingers buried inside your sex."

The words were coarse and the sentiments coarser—how it excited her.

Her climax hit all at once—stronger than any she remembered. It bowed her spine, stole the breath from her lungs, and then gave it back to her in a rush with only one name to cry out.

Her orgasm triggered Adam's and he groaned, thrusting deep inside of her.

Afterward, they collapsed on the bed, both breathing heavy, both sweating, both deliciously exhausted in that satisfying way that happens after truly great sex.

Adam held her close and kissed the top of her head. Claire snuggled close and murmured, "What a way to wake up."

"I aim to please."

"Mmm . . . yes."

"If I could build a career out of making love to you, I would."

She smiled. "Nice thought. Let's take care of these demons and get on that."

Adam remained silent after that comment. She'd mentioned the one thing they'd been able to forget for the night. What was the expression? Oh, yes, *whooops*. The spell was broken.

She lifted her head to see early morning lightening the horizon. "We should take a shower and get ready for the day."

"Only if we can take a shower together."

She smiled and kissed his chest. "Of course."

After a few moments of snuggling and simply enjoying the moment, they rose and went into the bathroom. They turned the water on and climbed into the oversized shower stall.

Reaching in for a thread of water magick, she diverted the warm water to flow around Adam's body like a hug, massaging his muscles. He groaned and closed his eyes at the pleasure of it.

It wasn't long until that ceased to pacify him and the only thing that made him happy was washing her with his big, soapy hands . . . all over her body. It made her sigh and her pulse quicken.

He pushed her against the wall, knelt, and was between her thighs again, pushing them apart so he could greedily seal his mouth to her sex.

Claire's knees went weak watching him there on the tile in front of her, his head between her thighs and his tongue lapping. She had nothing but the slick walls to hold on to as he pushed her to a fast and hard climax that made her cries ricochet off the walls of the bathroom.

"Houses, Adam, you make me come every time you touch me," she said breathlessly.

"Baby," he answered, looking up at her, "making you come is my bread and butter. Your body is my wine."

"I thought you didn't like wine."

He grinned. "I fucking love your vintage, honey. I want another drink, too, a long one."

Adam stood and pushed her face forward against the tile, pushing his big cock eagerly into her sex and took her roughly up against the wall. Claire had to admit that she loved how he didn't ask for permission, he just took her—and he always seemed to give more pleasure than he got.

After they'd both found their bliss, they washed each other thoroughly—hands sliding over curves and calves, breasts and biceps. Adam grabbed a fluffy towel and dried her off.

After they were both dressed and they were back in the bedroom, Adam pulled out the basket from the previous night and rifled through it to find something edible for breakfast. He came up with an apple and held it to her lips.

Claire took a bite and Adam leaned in, slowly licking the juice from the corner of her mouth. The action made her stomach curl with that now-familiar sexual anticipation. She seemed insatiable when it came to Adam. Or maybe it was simply the prospect of impending death that made her seek life-affirming sex with such abandon.

Still, she pulled away with a laugh. "Adam, stop. You're going to make me want you again."

He lifted an eyebrow. "What's so bad about that?"

"The fact that you'll send me off . . . wanting. I have to meet Micah soon."

"Oh, that's right. You plan to spend the day with another man."

"But I'll only be thinking of you."

He mock *harrumphed* and went back to the basket. "Then I guess we better eat some breakfast."

"Just think, if the spell works, we'll be able to do this every morning, and we'll never have to worry about demons interrupting us."

"That would be great. I just wish the cost wasn't so high."

"Yes." A world of grief sat in that one word. "It will be hard to lose my magick, but I would rather lose my magick than my life. I would rather lose my magick than lose you."

CLAIRE SPENT THE MORNING WITH MICAH, experimenting with her magick while Adam hulked in the corner like a protective dark shadow. With the demons loose and no way to ward against them, he wouldn't let her out of his sight for anything beyond bathroom breaks.

She tapped her magick hard and fast, the way she had in the corridor that morning—all four threads together—and magick exploded in her face. Claire fell backward, right onto her ass. That had happened because she hadn't aimed at anything. Shaking her head to clear it from the ringing, she found Adam by her side, one hand on her upper arm.

Micah sprawled near her, also on his ass, looking dazed. "Fuck me!" Micah yelled.

"No way, man," Adam snapped back instantly.

Micah glanced at him and grinned. Claire was content that the tension between them had eased somewhat.

Adam helped her to stand. "What the hell was that?"

"Demon magick, after a fashion," Claire answered, a lop-sided grin spreading over her face. "That was demon magick."

Micah stood and shook his head. "Amazing. All four elements of our magick, when woven together, is their brand of power."

Adam wore a dubious expression. "Didn't seem too controlled to me."

Claire laughed. Houses, it felt good, too. "That's because it wasn't. I can't control it yet, I can only pop out a little burst of it unless I have a direct target."

Adam looked at Micah. "Does this mean anything in terms of the spell you're scheduled to perform tomorrow?"

Claire sobered at the reminder.

"Maybe. I don't know yet." He paused, deep in thought. "The problem is that we need to find a way to combine the elements within the seat of her magick. If we can do that, the power may be enough like demon magick that the elium will stop adhering to it and we can take it out without having to strip Claire of all her power."

Claire bit her lower lip and then turned away. "This is ridiculous, Micah. We'll never find a way to do all that by tomorrow. We don't even have the first clue how."

Adam's hand fell on her shoulder and gave it a reassuring squeeze. "Don't lose hope, Claire. We have to try everything we can, even if we can't be sure it will work."

"She's right about it being a long shot, though," Micah broke in. "I'm doing the best I can, but I'm in the dark on blood magick like this . . . at least in practice. In theory I know a little bit about it, but trying to bind the elemental magick within her seat?" Micah shook his head. "It would be a miracle if we could manage to do that within the next twenty-four hours."

"Way to raise her spirits, Micah," Adam growled.

"I didn't say it wasn't worth a try!" Micah objected, spreading his hands. "I'm just saying, as her acting . . . uh . . . magickal physician here, that the chances of this working aren't very high."

Claire turned toward them both, chewing the edge of her thumb. "And the amputation spell? What's the chance of that one working?"

Micah's silence was answer enough.

Adam shot Micah a look of doom. "Anything is worth a try, Claire."

"I know. And I know Micah is doing his best."

"Yes, Micah *is* doing his best," Micah put in. "So Adam should not kill Micah, who is losing sleep over his girlfriend's problem."

Adam rolled his eyes. "I'm not going to kill you."

Micah looked relieved.

Adam gave Micah a shark's grin. "I might beat you up a little, but I won't kill you."

Claire hit Adam's chest. "Stop it, Adam."

"Micah knows I'm kidding."

Micah shook his head. "No, I don't."

Claire took a step back. "Okay, no one is beating anyone else up and we're going to keep trying."

"Sounds good to me," Micah answered.

They tried allowing Adam's power into Claire once more, in an effort to use his magick to bind the threads of the elements within her. It didn't work.

They tried various spells.

They tried deep, guided meditation.

They worked for the rest of the day, trying everything, ever more cognizant of the deadline looming near.

Nothing worked.

TWENTY-NINE

CLAIRE FOUND A BENCH IN THE MIDDLE OF THE
Coven's conservatory and sat down. The conservatory was a
lovely place, filled with all kinds of flowers, birds, plants, and
trees. A stream ran through the middle of it, and walking paths
with small, picturesque bridges wended their way around the
large space. The area brought together air, earth, and water perfectly. To make sure fire was also included, several tall basins
sat at regular intervals where steady flames burned.

Above Claire's head stars scattered the darkened sky past
the glass ceiling. The moon was full this evening and its light
radiated down and joined the illumination given off by the
small lights along the walking paths. People walked by her
now and again, sometimes couples, all of them talking in low,
muted tones. All of them witches.

It was nice to be among her own kind. She had changed so
much since the day she'd found herself thrust back to Earth.
Now she couldn't remember how—or why—she'd ever wanted
to go back to Eudae.

She was home.

Claire closed her eyes and sank into the silence. This was

the first time she'd been able to get away from Adam. Not that she wanted to get away from him. She thought his constant need to protect her was unbelievably sweet. It was just that, for now, for a few minutes, she needed to be alone with her thoughts.

She wrapped her arms over her chest and breathed in the flower-scented, warm air. It smelled of earth here, the actual ground, and of magick. In fact, she sensed all the magickal elements in this space, just as the Coven founders had intended.

In unison the elements spoke to her—a deep, rich murmur that touched the whole of her. She supposed, oddly, that she had Rue to thank for that. Deep within the heart of her, her magick responded to that cohesive, magick murmur. Air touched air, water touched water, and earth touched earth. Her fire magick reached out and sought fire, danced with it, and retreated.

If only she could bring them all together in her seat.

As they'd worked throughout the day, she'd grown surer that was what Rue had intended all along. She'd always known she'd been an experiment to him, she'd just never understood what kind. Now she thought she knew—he *had* been trying to make demon magick from the elemental magick of an *aeamon*, not just seeing if he could get her to wield all four elements.

But she would never, it appeared, have demon magick at the core of her. On the face it, the very idea made her vaguely ill. So she was slightly relieved. Yet, she'd do pretty much anything to keep her power.

One good thing had come from the day's work. Now, at least, she had a much better control over her new ability. Now she could weave the threads together into a rope of all four as she drew them and could wield her magick in lots of new ways. If the demons did come back, she felt more confident than ever she could fight them.

Of course, unless the demons came for her this night, she wouldn't need to. She'd be losing all her magick the next day. Losing her magick, but gaining Adam.

It would be a fair trade.

"Claire."

She opened her eyes to see Adam. Claire smiled. "Hello."

"You okay?"

She nodded. "I am. I feel better now, a bit more centered." She stood and held out her hand. He took it. "I'm hungry, though. I say we get something to eat and go to bed."

"Sounds good to me."

They made a meal of vegetable soup and cheese sandwiches on thick-cut rye bread in the kitchen before heading up to Adam's room.

In silence, Adam caught her hand, led her to the bedroom, and undressed her slowly, almost with a sense of reverence, leaving kisses over her body as he went that left her breathless. He didn't push her onto the bed, as she'd expected. Instead he slipped her soft cotton nightgown over her head and kissed her lips.

Claire helped him off with his clothes, enjoying the smooth muscle of his arms, chest, and back under her hands. He left just his boxers on and led her to the bed, where he curled up with her and turned off the light.

Held in Adam's arms, under his lips . . . Claire felt loved. No, *cherished*. She felt adored.

She *wanted* Adam. Wanted him to be *hers*.

"You mean more to me than anyone," Adam murmured, his voice breaking. His arms encircled her and held her close.

She swallowed hard and the edge of sorrow rose. "What about Eliza?" Her voice shook on the words.

Adam said nothing for a few moments, and then finally he murmured, "I loved Eliza. She was half of my heart when she was alive and when she died that part of me died." He paused. "Claire, you've brought that half of my heart back to life." His voice held the resonance of wonder. "Only now it belongs to you."

Tears pricked Claire's eyes. She didn't know what to say to that. Anyway, she couldn't speak. There was a lump in her throat.

Adam kissed her forehead. "Eliza was wonderful and I'll always remember her, but I want you, not her, Claire. I love you."

These words were the ones she'd longed to hear from him. These were the words she'd secretly wanted to hear from a man she loved since she'd been a girl.

Like a raindrop into parched earth, his words sank in and nourished her. New buds began to grow.

MORNING CAME, AS IT ALWAYS DID.

Claire opened her eyes and looked out the window of Adam's bedroom. She snuggled back into Adam's arms, taking comfort in the sensation of his smooth, warm skin sliding against hers.

She'd made as much peace as she could with losing her power today, but that didn't mean she didn't feel a pang of sorrow at the morning light on the horizon.

Adam stirred beside her and whispered her name. She turned in his arms and kissed his cheek, rough with stubble.

"Good morning, baby," he rasped in a sleep-roughened voice. "Gods, I love waking up to your beautiful face every day."

She smiled. "And you will continue to do so." He would because she was *going to survive* whatever was coming their way.

A shadow moved across his face, as though he suddenly remembered what day this was. He recovered nicely, though. "I can't wait."

Claire glanced at the clock on the nightstand. "Micah told me to be downstairs at exactly eight A.M. The spell is time sensitive. That gives us just about enough time to bathe and grab a muffin."

He flipped her so suddenly, she yelped. Adam inserted his knee between her thighs and gently slapped her hip, making her yelp again. "No time for . . . anything else?"

She laughed. "Like you don't get enough as it is. No, that will have to wait until later."

"But I can at least grope you in the shower, right?"

She laughed. "I think there's time for groping."

"There's *always* time for groping."

They made it down to Micah's spell lab at the designated time. Both Claire and Adam had been thoroughly groped by each other and they both had muffins in their stomachs. Although, when Claire entered the room, she thought for a moment the muffin might come back up.

Micah stood by a table that held a spell pot, various bowls, and some scattered dried herbs. He looked haggard. His handsome face was drawn and ashen, making him look older than his years. Dark circles marked the flesh beneath his eyes.

The container that would hold the elium sat on a small pedestal in the corner of the room, like a squat, hungry monster. She hoped they'd be able to feed it.

"Didn't you get any sleep, Micah?" Claire asked, making her way into the room. No one else was present. Thomas had chosen to stay away to give them room to work without his sometimes overbearing interference.

Micah turned to them. "A little bit. I was up making sure I had my research right."

"You have me to translate Aemni now, Micah. You should have summoned me. I could have verified things for you."

He shook his head. "You needed your rest more than I did. This spell will mostly count on you expending your energy and will, Claire, not me." He paused. "Anyway, I was okay without your translation help for this. Are you ready?"

Claire held his gaze. "No. No, I'm not ready. I'll never be ready. We just have to do it anyway."

Micah inclined his head. "I understand." He turned to Adam. "I'm not sure you should be here. There's nothing you can do and the spell will look . . . violent when it's working. You have a need to protect Claire and I understand that, but your interference could really screw things up."

Adam tilted his head to the side and his expression tightened a degree. "I'm not leaving Claire."

Micah sighed. "You have to promise to stand back and let things happen like they have to." His voice grew low and strong. "Do you understand?"

Adam looked at Claire, saying nothing.

Claire knew that if she appeared in pain, he'd be hard-pressed not to leap across the room at Micah like the last time. She wanted him here, but . . . "Maybe it would be better if you left the room, Adam."

Adam moved his gaze back to Micah. "I'm not leaving, but I'll promise not to interfere . . . no matter how bad it looks."

Micah shook his head. "Why do I think you're lying?" He turned to the spell pot. "Okay, then. Claire, please lie down on that recliner."

She did as she was asked, lying down on the same inclined chair she'd sat in before. The thing reminded her a little too much of the tooth physician's chair she'd spent so much time in back on Eudae as a child. Plus, memories of the pain she'd experienced the last time she sat here reared their ugly head and made her regret the muffin for the second time that morning.

Adam took a spot near the wall and tried not to look tense. He failed. He shot her an uneasy grin that she returned just as uneasily.

Micah approached her with a bowl in his hand. This was earth magick, an earth spell. A witch like Micah couldn't do anything else. Earth magick was by far the most flexible and useful of the elements, however, so it was fitting he should wield it. The knowledge that Micah possessed was formidable and she was going to enjoy working with him in the future. The bowl smelled of cloves and crushed mugwort and skullcap. She recognized them all from Theo's work at charm-making.

Micah paused above her. "I have to ask you to take off your shirt. I need to put this mixture on your skin over your seat."

"Uh, can I leave my bra on?"

He shrugged. "It's your call. The material will be ruined by the concoction, most likely. It's pretty stinky."

She'd sacrifice the bra. "Good thing it's warm in this room," she muttered as she slid her sweater over her head and dropped it to the floor.

Micah scooped out some of the smelly paste and massaged it into the skin between her breasts, underneath her bra. It tingled and grew warm, immediately sinking into her flesh. The power tingled and pulsed, ready for Micah's invocation.

Micah set the bowl on the table and wiped his fingers off. Then he came back to stand beside her. "Are you ready?"

"Why do you keep asking me that?"

"Okay. Take a couple deep breaths and close your eyes, then. Try to relax as much as you can."

Claire settled back against the recliner and let her eyelids drift closed. She did her best to ignore the bone-deep quiver of fear and dread that vibrated through her. She could act brave all she wanted, but inside she screamed for some kind of intervention, some kind of miracle that would let her keep her magick and her life, too.

Micah led her through a guided meditation. It was the normal sort—where the speaker instructs you to relax your toes, your ankles, yours calves . . . all the way up your body. But around the time she reached her thighs, magick tingled over her skin. Micah's voice grew deeper and more compelling. Once in a while, he would stop the mundane guided meditation and mutter words of power under his breath and the paste on her skin would tingle and pulse even more.

The magick smoothing over her skin intensified and little by little she grew relaxed. Her arm slipped off the side of the recliner and she barely noticed it. Her head lolled to one side. She found herself in the place between sleep and wakefulness, aware but not aware enough to pull herself from the restful stupor her mind was in. Nor did she want to. Again she was under anesthesia of a magickal sort.

Slowly, all her awareness faded. Blackness enveloped her.

WHEN CLAIRE'S OTHER ARM SLIPPED OFF THE EDGE of the recliner, Adam took a step forward. Micah had stopped chanting and he understood that Claire was unconscious.

"When will you start?" he asked, his voice rough with emotion.

Micah glanced at the clock on the table. "In a few minutes. We're right on schedule." He paused and then turned to him. "If this works, if we're able to extract the elium and her magick along with it, you're going to have to help her recover. It will be rough for her both physically and psychologically. Kind of like losing a limb."

"I get that."

Micah glanced at Claire, his voice low. "I don't think she does, not really."

"She's working in survival mode right now. You'd give up your magick to live, right?"

"Yeah, sure. It's just . . . this has never happened to a witch. In all the reading of our history that I've done, I've never heard of anyone losing their power so completely."

Adam looked at Claire, studied the graceful lines of her face. "It's a real pity, too, someone as powerful as she is."

"Yeah, it's sick and ironic as hell. Out of all of us, it has to be her." He glanced at the clock again. "It's time."

"Great." The word, spoken in a flat voice, fell like a stone into the room.

Micah hesitated a moment longer, then turned back to Claire. Adam took a step away, knowing from experience that earth magick was best worked with a little room. Micah closed his eyes and seemed to gather his power for a moment. He'd be drawing a charm he'd already brewed up and magickally ingested beforehand. All he had to do now was utter his invocation.

Power eased through the room like a snake. The heady, turned-earth scent of Micah's magick filled Adam's nostrils and gathered behind his teeth. It wasn't unpleasant, not really. It was like he was out in a garden, planting green things . . . not that Adam was often out in a garden planting green things.

On the recliner, Claire stirred, rolling her head and whimpering. Was she already in pain? Adam's stomach clenched and he forced himself not to take a step near her.

Micah muttered under his breath, a series of words that were incomprehensible to Adam's ears. Earth witches all had something close to their own spell language, special words they used as objects of power for their charms. Magick flared over Adam's skin, stronger now and growing more so.

Even he could feel the subtle pull on the seat of his own magick. It freaked him out, but he didn't back away. He trusted Micah not to draw everyone's power in the room.

On the recliner, Claire tossed her head, writhed, and called for Adam, making him go tense with a sense of helplessness. Undoubtedly, she felt the pull on the seat of her power, too. Even unconsciously, it had to bother her.

Suddenly Claire's body bowed, her spine arching, and she cried out in agony. This time he couldn't help taking two steps toward her. Micah shot him a chilling look, one that clearly said, *Back off*. Adam halted near her, hands clenching at his sides and his body taut.

"It's starting to happen," said Micah. "Little by little, the spell is beginning to draw the magick from her body."

"It's just *starting*?"

Micah nodded. "I created a powerful magnet for her power. It can't resist being dragged toward it. Theoretically, her magick will be yanked out of her seat to the magnet, and the elium will have no choice but to come along with it."

"Theoretically?"

"It's not like this has ever been done before, Adam. I can't find a record of any witch who ever wanted to remove their magick."

Claire screamed.

Adam took another step toward her, stopped, whirled, and paced in the opposite direction. He fisted his hands in his hair, feeling it pull out at the roots. "I can feel the magnet, too, yanking on my seat—"

"It won't get ours, Adam. It's tooled especially to Claire."

"I get that!" Adam rounded on Micah and yelled it. "I'm saying that she's feeling what I'm feeling but a million times worse. This spell is just . . . grabbing her power out of her seat by the roots."

"More or less."

"Fuck, Micah. That's not surgery, that's mutilation!"

Claire cried out again and Micah turned to her, muttering under his breath again.

Adam walked to the wall, leaned against it, and crossed his arms over his chest. He had to do something or he'd go back on his word and interrupt this torment masquerading as a solution.

Micah's mutterings grew louder and more frenzied. Claire thrashed on the recliner and cried out. Over and over she called for Adam until he could take it no longer. Flames born of his high emotion and frustration tickled his palm and jumped from finger to finger, ran up his arms and over his chest. He raced across the room to Micah, but Micah held up a hand to stay him.

"Stop. I'm done. It's finished," Micah said, his face ashen.

Claire moaned and rocked back and forth on the recliner. Adam pushed past Micah and scooped her up into his arms. She nestled against him as if made specifically to fit against his body and laid her head on his shoulder. Her face was deathly pale and her eyelids purple. Her breathing became shallow and she was cold. It was much the same result as the last spell-casting on her.

"It didn't work," said Micah, his face grim. "The attraction between her power and the magnet wasn't great enough."

"The elium is still in her?"

"As is all her magick."

Adam looked down at the woman on his arms that he'd grown to love so much. Why did that sound like a death sentence?

That meant they were nowhere closer to solving this problem than they'd been this morning.

That meant the demons were coming.

That meant they'd kill her for certain this time.

THIRTY

THE ELIUM STILL PULSED DULLY WITHIN HER. Houses, she was almost growing used to the sensation of it there in the middle of her chest.

Claire turned toward the window in Adam's bedroom and pulled the throw blanket more securely around her. It had taken her most of the day to recover from the spell. Still, the seat of her magick ached from the ordeal. She'd been unconscious, but nightmares of the incident had flooded her brain all the same, ones she could still recall. That awful pull on her power, yanking it through flesh, blood, and bone. It had been as if a pair of huge tongs had grabbed hold of her heart and then tried to pull it through living tissue and into the open air.

Of course, it hadn't worked. There was a part of her that had been relieved when she'd awoken to the sensation of her magick still pulsing inside her. She'd been dreading the frigid emptiness that undoubtedly would have met her had the spell worked. *Dry and flavorless as melba toast*. Once she'd heard Thomas refer to non-magickals that way.

The other part of her had been utterly and completely crushed. It had been their last and best hope and it had failed.

Now she was doomed for certain. There were no last-ditch efforts, nothing else to try. Her fate was sealed.

Adam sat in the chair behind her. She heard him rise and approach her. His hand fell on her shoulder, warm, steady, and strong . . . just like him. She closed her eyes.

She'd finally found someone to love her. Someone she could love in return. Someone to invest in, someone to trust. But fate wasn't going to let her keep him. Maybe it would be easier on them both if they just ended things right here and now. The *Atrika* were coming for her. There was no escape.

His breath stirred her hair. "Are you all right? You seem pretty deep in thought."

She shook her head. "No, I'm not all right." Claire gave a little laugh. "I'm kind of out of options." She bowed her head. "I'm sorry."

He turned her to face him. "Sorry? About what?"

"I'd hoped we could stay together. But—" She drew a breath. "I think this should end, Adam. Right now. I should go to my room here in the Coven and we should—"

"Claire, *shut up*." He leaned and kissed her. His lips skated over hers, gentle and commanding, completely possessive. He kissed her for a good two minutes, his hand cupping the nape of her neck and his lips gently skating over hers, once in a while parting so he could flick his tongue against hers.

Even at a time like this he could make her knees go weak with just a kiss.

He rested his forehead against hers. "I don't like those words coming from your sweet lips, and I never want to hear them again. We will stay together through whatever comes our way. We'll meet it head-on and side by side. Okay?"

She sighed and dropped her head to his chest. "Things just look so dark, Adam. Lie to me and tell me everything's going to be all right."

He kissed the crown of her head and rubbed her arm. "Everything's going to be all right. I'm not lying, Claire."

She sighed.

"You're tired, but this isn't over yet. We have a saying here on Earth. It ain't over till the fat lady sings."

She raised her head. "The fat lady? Who's she?"

Adam smiled. "It refers to the last woman to sing in an

opera. Stereotypically all female opera singers are supposed to be fat."

"Opera. I always wanted to see one. My mother used to talk about both opera and ballet."

He hooked her hair around her ear. "Tell you what. If we both come through this in one piece, I'll sacrifice myself and take you to see both." He paused. "But only if you'll come to a Bears game with me."

She wrinkled her nose. "Bears?"

"Football."

"Oh, right." She smiled and kissed his lips. "Here's to future sacrifices, then."

"May they be horrific, frequent, and come soon." He dipped his head and kissed her again.

She sighed against his lips and let him push her backward toward the bed. She laughed. "Again?"

He smiled against her lips. "Why not?"

Indeed, why not? "Well, I guess if there's anything I'd like to spend my last days doing, it's you." She turned him around and gave him a hard push.

He fell back on the mattress and sprawled there, looking up at her in surprise. "Wow, that's so romantic."

She grinned and raised her eyebrows. Comeback all set on her tongue, she readied herself to pounce on him.

Someone knocked on the door.

Adam rose up on his elbows. "Who the hell could that be?"

"I'll get it." Claire wrapped the blanket more securely around her and went to answer it.

Thomas stood on the other side, a grim expression on his handsome face. "Claire, you have to get dressed and come downstairs to the library immediately."

She frowned at the severe tone of his voice. "Why?"

"Rue is here."

CLAIRE NOTICED RUE'S LIPS THIN INTO A LINE OF disapproval when she entered the library hand in hand with Adam. His icy blue eyes hit full-on winter as he noted how Claire stood next to Adam once inside.

Rue was a good-looking male by any female's measure: tall,

broad-shouldered, muscular build. His blond hair came to his shoulders, framing a face drawn in chiseled lines. His mouth was full and his eyes a light shade of blue.

He was handsome. He was a *daaeman*. And he was deadly.

Although he worked by a strict *Ytrayi* code of ethics and morality, he showed no remorse for those he perceived had wronged him. Thomas Monahan knew that firsthand. Ty had died tasting that lack of remorse.

Claire flashed back to the moment when Rue had discovered her relationship with Ty. Fear flicked through her with a sharp, metallic tongue.

"We're not in Eudae," Claire said to Rue, her tone as forceful as she'd ever dared use with him.

Thomas stood near his desk, along with Isabelle. Thomas's gaze snapped to her.

"Your rules don't apply here, Rue," she continued. "I refuse to allow you to even *think* about hurting Adam." She spoke in English. He was well versed in the language and would understand.

Rue tilted his head to the side—like a bird of prey considering a mouse—and took a step toward them. The saliva dried on her tongue, but she stood her ground. She would die before she allowed Adam to come to harm.

"Are these words of protection for this *aeamon* male the first words you have for me after so long, Claire?" He spoke in Aemni. "Do I mean so little to you?"

"That's rude. Speak English, Rue," she snapped.

Rue actually looked chastened. He glanced at Thomas. "Forgive me."

"You're still alive," she stated unnecessarily. She was pleased about that. Her feelings where Rue was concerned were so mixed.

"I managed to escape the spell room and, even though the attack took us by surprise, we were able to fend off the force of the *Atrika*." Now he spoke in English. "I was injured, but I'm recovered now."

"Have you come to take the elium back?" Her voice shook with the hope that he had a way to remove it.

Confusion crossed over his face. "No, Claire." He paused

and seemed to consider her words. "Well, after a fashion. I came to take *you* back."

Adam stepped forward. "That's not happening."

Fury made the veins in Rue's neck pop out. He took a step toward Adam. "You don't dictate to me, boy."

Adam took two steps toward Rue. "Boy? That earns you triple the ass-whipping, *daaeman*. One time for trying to take Claire away. Another for putting her in danger in the first place. And still another for calling me *boy*."

Claire rolled her eyes and stepped forward. *Daaeman* or witch, it didn't matter, testosterone was the same. Right now there was an excess of maleness in the room. She put a hand on Adam's chest. "Adam, stand down." She flicked an annoyed glance at Rue. "Rue, you're not taking me anywhere."

Rue's jaw worked, but he didn't respond. Still, she knew Rue well enough to know that the issue wasn't closed.

She peered around Rue to Thomas. Both he and his wife looked fit to kill. No wonder. This was the man who'd imprisoned and tortured Thomas on Eudae.

Thomas cleared his throat. "He showed up this morning, in the foyer. Isabelle tried to kill him."

Rue unclenched his jaw enough to speak, but kept his gaze focused on Adam, behind her. "It took me a long time to open another doorway. I assumed this was where you'd be if you'd managed to keep away from the *Atrika* who followed you. I tried to get you as close to the Coven as I could when I pushed you through."

"What is the state of Yrystrayi?"

"Badly damaged. The *Atrika* attacked with great force, harder and with more finesse than they have in centuries." He paused. "Something has changed. They've grown in strength for some reason and their will has become stronger. They almost took the palace and they killed a great many of us. We have some of them in custody, but you know what it is to torture information out of an *Atrika*."

Impossible.

"Why did you do it to me, Rue? Why did you force this weapon into me and push me through the doorway into a foreign world?"

Rue finally focused on her face. His expression softened a little. "It was the only way I knew to save the two things I held most dear."

Shock rippled through her. Had he just called *her* . . . dear?

Adam put his hand on her waist and pulled her against his side in a protective gesture.

Rue's gaze shifted to the fire witch who touched her so possessively. "She is like a daughter to me, *aeamon*. I practically raised her."

"Nice way to treat your daughter," muttered Isabelle.

"I had no choice!" Rue shouted, closing his eyes for a moment and clenching his fists. "The *Atrika* would have killed her had she stayed in the spell room. If the *Atrika* had captured me and extracted the elium, all the demon breeds but the *Atrika* would now be exterminated or close to it. I had no idea that the two *Atrika* would lunge through the doorway after you. I did not intend for that to happen."

Claire folded her arms across her chest. "They've killed many witches here." Her tone dropped the temperature of the room. "They were going to kill me. The Coven has paid a high price to keep the elium safe."

"We weren't keeping the elium safe," said Thomas. "We were keeping *you* safe, Claire, no matter what we may have told you." The head of the Coven stepped forward to stand beside her. His black eyes seemed endless with hot fury. "You'd better tell me right now, Rue, that you have a way to take the elium from her safely. I want you to take the elium and then take yourself *the fuck out of my home*." His voice shook.

It was the closest Claire had ever seen the normally well-controlled witch to losing his temper.

Rue fixed his gaze on Thomas. "There is no need for us to be enemies."

Isabelle made a scoffing sound. "You tried to kill him. You tortured him to within an inch of his life! If it hadn't been for Claire, he might have died in your dungeon. You did all this and think we can be friends?"

Rue kept his gaze on Thomas's face while he answered Isabelle. "We never would have killed your mate. We had no idea, of course, the extent to which Claire was interfering." His turned his frosty eyes to her for a moment. "However, we never would have allowed a man as important as the head mage of your people to perish in our care. We simply needed information." He paused. "We still need information."

"You'll get nothing from us," answered Thomas. "Can you take the elium from her or not?"

"Where are the *Atrika*?"

"Still out there, still wanting the weapon. The sooner you take it from her, the sooner she'll be safe from them. If you care about her the way you say, you'll take it from her soon."

Rue jerked his chin at her. "Then we must leave immediately." He reached out, snagged Claire's arm, and jerked her forward.

"The hell you're taking her anywhere," Adam roared.

Rage distorted Rue's handsome face and Claire's stomach twisted in fear. "She is mine, *aeamon*. My property. The fact you've lain with her gives you no right—"

Adam punched him.

Rue went careening backward under the force of it and hit a chair. He stumbled to the side and raised his gaze to Adam's. There was murder on his face. His eyes were red and his fangs had extended.

Claire stalked to Rue and slapped him across the face. "How dare you treat me like a dog to be commanded? I am not property, not anymore. I am home, where I belong." She motioned to Adam and the others. "Among the people I should be with. You say you think of me as your daughter, but you hardly want the best for me, do you? The best thing is to leave me alone, let me stay here with them."

He looked shocked. "Do you want that?"

She closed her eyes in frustration and fisted her hand in her hair. "*Home*, Rue. I just said I'm home. Of course I want to stay."

Rue looked so surprised and, yes, a little bit hurt, that she went to her knees in front of him. "You've treated me well. Without you, I would've died on Eudae. I thank you for that." She pressed her lips together. "But you could've sent me home, right? You could have opened a doorway and sent me back here at any time. Isn't that correct?"

"To what? You had no one here. Your mother was dead and you didn't know who or where your father was. I thought you were happy with your life on Eudae. I didn't think you wanted to come back to Earth."

There had been many years in which she'd most likely have balked at the opportunity to come back here. It was a foreign place to her. Even when she'd had the opportunity to return when Thomas had jumped through, she'd stayed behind. Still . . . "You never asked me. Not once. You never gave me the choice, the opportunity. You just kept me like a pet or a servant—*your property*—and performed your little experiments on me. You denied me the love of a man of my kind . . . love, period. You denied me anything resembling a normal life."

Rue's jaw worked. "I-I'm sorry."

It was the first time in her life she'd ever seen the great Rue, *Cae* of the *Ytrayi*, speechless. It was the first time he had ever apologized for anything.

Rue frowned. "You are so different now. These weeks here on Earth have changed you."

"I am different. I'm changed for the better, Rue." Speaking of the experiments . . . "Were you trying to make me into a demon?"

Rue stared at her for a moment and then struggled to his feet. "In a manner of speaking. I infused you with the other three elements, but I could never manage to get you to thread them all together."

Claire stood. "Why did you want me to learn that?"

Rue shrugged. "It makes a close approximation of demon magick."

"But it isn't *exactly* demon magick," Claire inferred.

Rue shook his head and raised his gaze to hers. "You are *aeamon*, not *daaeman*. You don't have our full blood, so you cannot carry our full power."

"Except for the elium."

"That's different. It's bundled in a way that you can hold it."

"It's seared onto my seat. I managed to isolate most of it, but there are tendrils of the elium clinging to it. No one can take the weapon out of me without killing me. Not even Tevan and Kai."

Rue shook his head and smiled. "You don't understand. That's because—"

Something in the corridor outside the library exploded. The building shook and plaster rained down from above them. Adam yanked her into his arms and covered her head in an effort to protect her. Magick pulsed, deep through their bones.

Demon magick.

"They're here," said Isabelle unnecessarily from across the room.

"And they're mad," Claire finished.

Rue stormed past them, toward the door. Chances were that Tevan and Kai had no idea Rue had arrived.

They were going to be surprised.

Claire pulled from Adam's arms and followed Rue out into the hallway. Tevan stood with his back to the *Cae* of the *Ytrayi*. Tevan turned. If she could have bottled the look on Tevan's face to keep as a memento, she would have.

"You think you've come for the elium," said Rue in Aemni. "But you're getting far more than you bargained for."

Tevan replied by attacking.

Demon magick momentarily bulged the walls of the corridor and Claire found herself yanked back into the library forcibly by Adam. Beyond the doorway power pulsed and destruction reigned.

Another blast of magick made them both hit the floor. Books from the shelves around them slid off and hit the hardwood. The bottles in Thomas's liquor cart rattled until one of them broke in a cascade of amber liquid.

"Houses, I wish Rue hadn't come alone," she muttered. "We could use a few more *Ytrayi*."

"That begs the question. Where is Kai?" said Adam near her ear.

"Looking for me, probably."

"Come on." He dragged her to her feet and they ran to Thomas and Isabelle who stood clinging to Thomas's desk under the force of the battle beyond the doorway of the library. Two *daaeman* in the heat of conflict was like a war, complete with cannons.

"We've got to get Claire out of here before Kai shows up. I don't trust Rue to handle both *Atrika* at once. Hell, I don't trust Rue at all, and I don't think you do either." Adam jerked his chin at the only other way out, the large picture window overlooking the Coven grounds at the far end of the room.

Thomas looked at Isabelle, another blast of magick came from beyond the doorway, shaking the room.

"Why not? It wouldn't be the first time it's been broken," Isabelle yelled over the din with a one-shouldered shrug.

The room shook again and they all grabbed hold of the desk. After the earthquakelike tremors had passed, Adam picked up Thomas's office chair, walked to the huge floor-to-ceiling window, and threw it.

Glass shattered and rained to the floor below.

"That was not subtle, but it was effective," murmured Isabelle beside Claire.

That was Adam.

Adam picked up a long stafflike thing—Thomas had mentioned it was an antique walking stick once—and used it to get rid of any shards of glass still remaining. Then he grabbed a throw blanket draped over one the chairs in the sitting area and laid it over the sill.

Adam held out a hand to Claire. "Come on, let's go."

She went to him and he helped her out of the window. Thomas and Isabelle followed close behind. Another blast of power rocked the house.

In the distance they could see Coven witches spilling from the building, some coughing and having trouble breathing.

Houses, the Coven! Two demons in a fight could level the place.

Claire glanced up at the second floor. "What about Theo?" She stopped short. "He's injured from the battle at the cabin. He won't be able to get out."

"Trust me, Theo is capable of fending for himself even when he's injured," said Thomas, coming up beside her. "But I'm going in the front to help anyone else who might need it. Adam, get Claire to safety." He walked toward the building.

"You aren't going anywhere without me, Thomas," said Isabelle, striding after him.

Adam pulled Claire toward the heavily forested land surrounding the Coven. "Come on, I want you far away from here. Kai is probably in there looking for you and I don't want you anywhere nearby."

They headed away from the Coven, ending up on the far side of the building near the conservatory. It was a beautiful morning, calm. Such a contrast to the battle being waged within the structure.

A woman holding a baby appeared on the other side of the glass within the conservatory. She was coughing, probably from the smoke produced by the fires from the battle of the *daaemans*. Blasts of air magick puffed the smoke away, but it was overpowering her at times.

Claire pointed. "Mira's in there."

Adam followed the direction of her finger, focused, and said, "Oh, shit. We have to get them out of there." He ran to the door leading out into the yard, but it was locked.

Mira caught sight of them and screamed something unintelligible, waving her free hand in desperation. *No, get back! I'm all right!* The words sounded in the air around them, disorienting Claire for a moment. Powerful air magick. *Kai is in here with me.*

THIRTY-ONE

Something made a sound behind Mira and she turned toward it. Through the smoke, Claire could make out a hulking figure growing closer to Mira and the baby in her arms.

"Fuck!" Adam drew a burst of fire and melted the lock on the door. "Claire, get out of here. Run! I'm going to help Mira, but you have to go now!"

Too late, even though she never would've run anyway.

Kai spotted her and came striding toward the door. Mira clutched baby Eva to her with one arm and drew power, directing it at Kai, but he deflected it with a wave of his hand and kept coming. Mira stumbled backward and nearly fell. The cries of her child reached Claire's ears as Adam opened the door and rushed within.

Adam came in with all guns blazing, just as he had at the hospital. He knew how to fight the *daaeman* now and he gave Kai no quarter, sending up a white-hot wall of flame that made the *Atrika* roar in frustration. When Adam was angry, his power seemed greater and he was livid now, probably out of fear for Mira and her child, who were inching toward the door.

Mira hadn't given up, though, and was lending her air magick to making Adam's fire even hotter and stronger.

Kai bellowed again and Claire watched in anguish as the gorgeous plants and flowers in the conservatory caught fire, curled up from the heat, and died. Kai stepped through the wall of flame, letting it sear his skin into blackened strips that Claire knew would soon heal. Fire dripped from his clothes and extinguished in curling bursts of smoke.

Thankfully, Mira extended her hand and removed the air feeding the fire. It died quickly in a rush of hot air that blew Claire's hair around her face.

Kai fixed his gaze on her and Adam drew his sword. He'd strapped it on almost as soon as the name *Rue* had passed Thomas's lips that morning. The soft whisper of copper against the leather sheath sounded loud in the suddenly quiet air. He held it at the ready.

Her own copper blade lay against her skin, hooked on the waistband of her jeans. It was her last resort if one of the demons got so close she could cut him. So far magick had been more effective, but there was always a first time.

"Come here, Claire. I'm sick of chasing you," said Kai in a low voice. He spoke in Aemni. "You know you've got nowhere to hide. Wherever you go, we'll hunt you, and you know better than any *aeamon* the extent of our patience. Mine is at an end."

Claire's rage grew in a swell of power within her. Gathering her magick fast and hard, she drew four threads and wove them together in a heavy chain of force. Then she took that chain and smacked Kai with it face-on. He fell backward, onto the floor, and bowed his head, shaking it. His burnt skin was already healing and Claire could see that his fangs were extended and his eyes glowed a deep, murderous red.

"Don't make me hurt you, little girl," said Kai in a low voice without looking at her. "More importantly to you, don't make me hurt your friends."

Claire stepped forward. "Mira, get out of here. Go now!"

Holding her whimpering child in her arms, Mira didn't hesitate.

Kai laughed. "If I want her and her baby, she can't hide from me. Come with us, Claire, and you guarantee your friends, all of them"—he glanced at Adam—"will live."

Adam unclenched his jaw long enough to tell Claire, "I don't know what he's saying, Claire, but don't let him manipulate you."

Claire switched to English. "I'm through being manipulated. I'm through being scared." She took a step toward Kai. "I can wield my magick at you directly now. I learned how. How about a fight, Kai? Just you and me? Winner take all."

"Claire!" Adam shouted at her. "What are you doing?"

Claire took another step forward. "I'm not being afraid anymore."

"Did you go straight to stupid? Get out of here!"

"No. I'm not running."

Kai took a step toward her. "If you want a fight, Claire, I'll give you one."

Immediately, Claire dropped down and rolled, gathering her power and sending it at Kai in a punch to his solar plexus. The *Atrika* went down with a thud and screeched out a battle cry, an animalistic sound that Claire had hoped in all her years on Eudae she would never hear.

Kai rolled to his side and shot at her. She managed to use her magick to throw up a shield—just like a demon—but the blast still rocked her to her core. Scrambling to her feet, she darted into the still-smoldering foliage, trying to draw Kai away from Adam as far as she could.

Her feet pounded on the soft earth, trampling plants and carrying her over bridges and across streams. She had the advantage; she knew the conservatory and Kai didn't.

Plus, her magick felt stronger here, lighter and easier to control. Even when she threaded the elements together to form the pseudodemon magick, it felt stronger because of the carefully balanced environment.

She had an advantage. She had to keep telling herself that.

The tromp of heavy boots met her ears. Kai wasn't far behind. There were too many trees and bushes in here, though. Kai didn't have a clear shot at her. Although having an *Atrika* chasing her made her heart beat so fast that she feared she'd have a heart attack and save everyone the trouble of extracting the elium. It would just die with her.

She nearly tripped as a possibility rose in her mind. Maybe

she had an ace up her sleeve after all. It wasn't one she actually wanted to play . . . but she could bluff.

Exerting all the physical energy she had left, Claire increased her speed, jumping over bushes and streams until she had a lead on him. Once she'd reached her destination, the open area at the front of the conservatory where there was a fountain and several benches, she hid behind a tree and readied herself.

She wasn't going to use just any magick on Kai, not even her newfound, ever-so-powerful almost-demon magick. She was going to wield the elium, using her magick as the delivery method. The two powers within her could finally find accord, could finally work together.

And it would mean Kai's end, hopefully.

"You want the elium so bad, Kai?" she murmured as the *Atrika* approached. "Here you go."

As Kai emerged from the trees, she drew four threads of elemental power and tapped the elium at the same time. Using her magick to shield herself and Adam, whom she knew was close behind Kai, she directed the demon weapon at the *Atrika* squarely.

It was a gamble. Not only was it a gamble, it was the magickal equivalent of a triple midair twist with a flip and she wasn't working with a net.

The elium exploded out of her and threw her backward to land painfully on the gravel-strewn walkway. Her breath *woofed* out of her and all she could do was lie there for a moment, looking up at the glass ceiling of the conservatory.

THIRTY-TWO

No sound met her ears. No demonic bellowing, no *Atrikan* battle cry. No scraping. No footsteps. Not surprisingly, no birds sang in the trees. Only the gentle noise of the burbling fountain to her left filled the air.

She struggled to sit up, crying out at the pain in the center of her chest. Daggers of it shot through her at every movement and her right arm was numb. Her power was tapped. She'd drained it to the dregs in that one powerful, complicated burst. Claire hoped it had been worth it.

Footfalls on the gravel.

Adam ran to her side. "Are you all right, Claire? Gods, what were you thinking?"

"I'm fine," she wheezed. "Tapped my magick and injured myself, but I'm mostly okay." She swallowed hard and she struggled to stand, her palms pressing into the gravel. "What about Kai?" Her gaze sought the *Atrika*.

Kai lay motionless about twelve feet from them. Adam walked toward him.

"Adam, no, wait," she wheezed. She tried to follow and her knees almost gave out. She managed to grab the granite lip of the fountain with her good arm before she collapsed.

Adam approached Kai warily, sword drawn. He knelt and pressed his fingers to the *Atrika*'s neck. Then Adam called to her, "Do demons have a pulses in their throats like we do?"

She nodded, unable to raise her voice to answer.

Adam rose and gave her a look of incredulity. "Well, this one doesn't have one."

Shock rippled through her. "I killed him?" she half whispered, half mouthed.

"I think so."

"Oh, Houses," she said, her voice going stronger. She'd never in her wildest dreams believed she'd have enough power to take down an *Atrika*.

The doors behind them opened. Adam looked behind her, his expression of surprise closing back down into anger and protectiveness.

Claire turned. Rue and Tevan spilled into the conservatory, both bleeding acidic blood, both reeking of battle and demon magick. Tevan looked at the body on the floor behind Claire and sniffed the air, probably scenting Kai's death.

Rue stopped in his tracks and stared at Claire with utter shock on his face ... which almost immediately turned to pride.

"Elium," rasped Tevan. "You used it."

"Second time is the charm," she said in her trashed-out voice. "This time I knew how to use it. Kai is dead." She didn't sound triumphant, only matter-of-fact. Claire didn't relish taking anyone's life, not even Kai's.

Tevan stared at her for a long moment. His eyes, already red, grew darker. Then he began to shake with absolute rage. "*An aeamon killed Kai li Taelium?*" he roared. "Impossible."

Rue threw his head back and laughed.

Tevan roared and then raised his hand to launch another assault on Rue.

Claire pulled her ace. This had to stop and it had to stop now. The blade slid free easily from the sheath attached to the waistband of her jeans. It didn't press so easily to her throat, but she forced it to go there anyway. She pushed hard enough to draw blood. It trickled hot and slow down her skin.

"Tevan, throw that power and I'll slit my own throat. Then

no one will have the elium. It will wither and die as I do." Her
voice was surprisingly strong and sure.

Both Tevan and Rue looked at her in surprise. It was nice
to know she had the ability to stun the *Cae* of the *Ytrayi* and a
military commander of the *Atrika* into silence.

"I will have the elium!" Tevan roared and rushed her.

Claire gasped at the sight of the *Atrika* in full murderous
rage coming straight at her and took several steps backward,
groping instinctively for her nonexistent stores of magick.

Rue shot a bolt of power at Tevan's back as he approached
Claire. The back of the *Atrika* arched and he stumbled forward. At the same time, Adam stepped up and swung his
sword in a wide, perfectly executed arc, cleanly taking
Tevan's head from his neck. Fire arced along with the blade,
likely from Adam's emotion. Tevan's head sailed into the
foliage with a spray of acidic blood. Claire dove to the
ground to avoid it, but some lightly dappled her clothes,
smoking.

Quiet. No sound but her breathing.

Claire's entire body shook. Knowing she still had Rue to
deal with, she pushed herself back to her feet when all she
wanted was to crawl into Adam's arms.

Adam stood where he had before, breathing heavy and
looking surprised as hell. The sword dangled at his side,
smoking with demon blood. Tevan's head lay on the ground
not far away. She jerked her gaze away from the grisly sight of
his severed head and body.

Hand shaking, she put the dagger back to her throat and
cast her gaze to Rue.

"Claire, put the knife down," said Adam in a taming-
a-wild-animal voice.

"You won't do it." Rue lowered his hand and took a step toward her. "I know you, Claire. I raised you. You would never
take your own life."

She held up a hand. "Stop right there." She pressed the
blade in a little farther. More blood welled. "You're not in a
position to make any sort of prediction about what I might
do. You don't know me, Rue, not really. I was your servant,
your property on Eudae. That was no real relationship, noth-

ing that truly provided a way for either of us to truly know each other."

Rue frowned. He actually looked concerned. "Please stop this immediately, Claire."

"I'm sick of being fought over like I'm some juicy bone all the dogs want. I hold the elium and I can take it away from you in a heartbeat if I choose. Maybe it would be better if the elium didn't exist at all. If the elium didn't exist, there would be nothing for the *Atrika* to covet, nothing for them to use against the *Ytrayi* and the other demon breeds. I could rid the universe, both of them, of this weapon right now. Consider it arms control."

Alarm passed over Rue's face. "No, Claire. The *Atrika* are working on developing their own elium. If you kill yourself and destroy it, we will be weaponless when they eventually achieve their end. We'll have nothing to balance against their threat and we'll be annihilated." Rue visibly tried to relax his body. "We are your people. Don't condemn us all to die."

"My people?" She made a scoffing sound. "You're not my people. You only *took* me from my people, Rue. All these years you kept me from coming home, from having a normal life, from having friends and being loved. Is it any wonder I'm standing here now with a knife pressed to my throat?"

She glanced at Adam. Claire saw in his eyes that he understood she was bluffing.

Adam reached out a hand to her. "Claire, you're starting to scare me."

"Back off, Adam," she said, moving away from him. "All of you, just stay away from me. Tell me why I shouldn't do it, just cut my own throat now? I'm caught between worlds. I belong nowhere. If I live, I'm doomed to a life either as a slave to Rue or running from the *Atrika*."

"You have *that one* who cares for you." Rue jerked his chin at Adam. "You were protective of him just minutes ago. You were holding his hand."

Uh-oh. She lapsed into a steady stream of Aemni. "You know nothing of the customs here, Rue. You don't know what it means when a female holds the hand of a male *aeamon*. You know nothing of what it means when a male defends a female. You know nothing of intimate relationships at all . . . and you made sure I didn't either."

Her voice broke on the last part. It was all true what she said. Adam had taught her about intimate relationships, taught her what it was to truly love.

Rue's mouth snapped shut.

"So this is how it's going to work," she said, her voice a little louder and a little stronger. "You're letting me go free."

Rue stiffened. "You will not dictate to me—"

She rotated the knife, pressed until she winced and saw stars. Adam let out a sharp breath near her. "Yes, I will, Rue. Do as I say and you can have the elium back . . . but you can't have me."

"I thought you liked your life on Eudae." Rue actually sounded hurt.

"I was kept in a very nice cage and given anything I could desire." She paused. "But it was still a cage, Rue. I've had my taste of freedom, of home. If there's anything I have to live for, it's that. Take it away and I want to die."

And that was the unvarnished truth. Not a bluff.

"So," she continued in a calm, sure voice. "If you want the elium back, you'll take it from me . . . and then you'll leave. Promise me, Rue. Give me your word in an *Ytrayi* blood oath right now."

Rue hesitated and she stared him down. If he refused, she wasn't sure what she'd do. Her strength was returning somewhat, but she wasn't sure she could tap the elium again. Anyway, she didn't want to hurt Rue. She certainly didn't want to kill him.

Finally, Rue's eyes grew red and his fangs extended a little. Adam shifted uneasily beside her, not knowing that was exactly how she wanted Rue to react.

Rue bit his wrist and a trickle of blood trailed down his lowered hand and fingers, then dripped to the earth of the conservatory.

He spoke in Aemni. "I, Rue dae Raemish Tor, *Cae* of the *Atrayi*, have shed my blood to show I am bound to complete the following." He paused, raised his gaze to Claire's face, and held it there. "Withdraw the magickal weapon, elium, from the one known as Claire Crane. I release her from her bonds of servitude so that she may live out the rest of her life where and how she chooses."

Claire had stiffened and gone still at the word Crane. "Is that my last name?"

Rue nodded once. "Forgive me for never telling you."

She took several steps toward him, lowering her knife. The oath was uttered out loud, blood was shed. Rue wouldn't go back on that. "What else do you know?"

Rue spread his hands. "That's all, Claire. You simply didn't need to know your last name on Eudae, so I never told you."

Claire bit back a scream of absolute frustration. "Let's do this," she gritted out.

"You must come back with me to remove the elium. I cannot do it here."

"What?" Adam stormed forward. "No way—"

Claire put a hand on his arm. "Rue has sworn an oath in the *Ytrayi* custom. He won't renege."

"I don't want you going back there for any reason."

Rue turned his head and stared at him. "If you want the elium out of her, she must. I don't have the things I need here to accomplish it. You can come along if you're so concerned for her welfare. Claire doesn't need to fear me. I would never harm her."

"Or Adam, right, Rue? You would never hurt Adam either."

Rue sighed. "No. Not now that I understand how much he means to you. I know you care for him, Claire. I know more about *aeamon* relationships than you think I do." He leveled his gaze at Adam. "But he'd better stop attacking me."

Adam replied through a locked jaw. "You first."

Claire turned away and headed out of the conservatory. Her stomach tightened at the damage from the battle. Here and there, witches picked through the wreckage of the corridor. "We're bringing Micah with us, too," she said over her shoulder. "And you won't hurt him either."

Rue, for the first time in all the years she'd known him, simply nodded and followed her.

"Claire . . ." Thomas sighed in relief when she stepped into the library. "You're all right." Jack stood with Mira at the far end of the room, their child held close in his arms.

She raised her gaze and surveyed the damage to Thomas's beautiful bookshelves. "Houses, I'm so sorry, Thomas."

Isabelle walked over and took her by her arm. "Never mind that. It's just a building; they're just books. You're all right and that's all that matters." Her voice trailed off as Rue and Adam entered the room, her gaze fixed on Rue. Isabelle's face shuttered and hatred flared in her eyes.

"He won't hurt you," said Claire. "And I have him oath-bound to take back the elium and free me. The catch is I have to go back to Eudae for him to be able to do it. I thought maybe Micah would want to come."

"I'm going, too," said Adam.

"I don't want any of you to go," said Thomas forcefully. "Are you forgetting what happened to me when I ended up there?"

Rue held up his hand. "Peace, mage. I will not allow any of your people to come to harm. I understand more about your . . . witches now." The word was foreign to him. *Aeamon* were *aeamon* to Rue, at least before now. "The warlocks you fight are like the *Atrika*, but you and your people are akin to the *Ytrayi*. Indeed, I believe you carry our blood. I think it would be wise to form an alliance with you."

Thomas smoldered, his hands fisting. "I don't see how that can be possible. Anyway, to what end? I can't see any reason we would need an alliance."

Rue shrugged. "Your Coven witches carry the *daaeman* genes of the *Ytrayi*. If this is true, I suspect your warlocks carry the genes of the *Atrika*. Don't think our goals might not be in alignment in the future."

Thomas only stared Rue down as though he could light the demon on fire with his hostile gaze alone. His answer was clear in his eyes and in his expression. It made even Claire want to retreat.

Isabelle stepped forward, a little bit in front of her husband in a defensive gesture. Claire understood how Isabelle felt, but Thomas hardly needed anyone's protection. "We don't want an alliance with you or your people for any reason, *ever*."

"I hope you never regret those words," Rue answered.

Micah walked into the room behind the demon. "I heard I have a chance to visit Eudae." He'd probably been called by Mira. Air magick could be handy that way. His voice held an undeniable note of excitement.

Thomas turned away.

"You don't have to go if you don't want to," said Isabelle.

Micah just gave her a look. "Do you know what I would risk for a chance to go there?"

"You have my word they'll be unharmed," Claire said. "I have Rue's word and so do you. I understand why you would be concerned, but in this circumstance, both Adam and Micah will be returned to the Coven without incident."

"Can you be sure of that?" Thomas growled without looking at her.

"I lived with the *Ytrayi* my whole life. Yes, I can be sure."

Thomas pushed a hand through his hair and turned to her. "I trust you."

She smiled. "You should."

"Let's go," said Adam. "I want that crap out of you, Claire. I want us back at the Coven so we can finally relax a little. Take a fucking vacation. Go to Disneyland or something."

"I want that, too." She glanced at him. "Give me a minute."

Claire walked to Jack, a lump growing in her throat. Jack watched her approach with curiosity on his face. "I think I'm your half sister," she said with a quaver in her voice.

"What?" said Mira. Soot smudged her chin and forehead.

Claire raised her voice so it would carry across the room. "Rue, what did you say my mother told you my last name was?"

"She said she'd wanted it to be Crane. But she said it wasn't legal, since she'd never . . . mated . . . no, *married* . . . your father."

"My mother was in the Duskoff, Jack. I think she had an affair with your father." She halted, swallowed hard. "I think *I* was the result."

Jack watched her carefully, shock clear on his face. He said nothing.

"Oh, my goddess," Mira breathed beside him. A smile broke out across her face. "If it's true, that makes you my sister-in-law." She gasped and held up Eva. "You're her aunt!"

Claire let out a sound that was half laugh and half sob. "I know! I can't believe it!" She pressed a hand to her mouth and forced herself to not dissolve into full-fledged tears. She closed her eyes against a sudden swell of emotion.

She'd thought she'd had no family, but maybe she did.

Jack pulled her against him and hugged her hard. "I would be so proud if you were truly my half sister," he whispered huskily.

She pulled away from him and wiped her eyes. "Yes, we can be the two Coven witches with *Atrika* genes." She laughed.

"Yeah," he said conspiratorially, "I'm not sure I'm buying that one."

"Claire." It was Rue. The sound of his voice made her jump. "We should go now."

She turned and followed Micah and Rue out of the library. Adam walked behind her, protective as always.

In the Coven foyer, Rue muttered a few words in Aemni and a doorway shimmered into view. It disturbed the magickal currents, rubbing up against their skin like a cat, and quivered through the air around them. Claire gasped at the vibrational frequency of the doorway as it quavered and then stabilized. Rue's magick was incredibly strong. It was why he was the *Cae*.

"How is it you can do that?" asked Micah in awe. "How can you just open a doorway when it's so difficult for the *Atrika* to do it and it's impossible for us to accomplish it?"

Micah was already asking questions and they hadn't even stepped through yet.

"I can only open this doorway because its mirrored on the other side. I am one of a few *Ytrayi* able to open them, but even for me it's not easy. It takes time and many resources to create a passageway like this one."

"Interesting."

"It's an important part of how the universe works, Micah. If it were easy to open these doorways, there would be utter chaos. War, rape, and pillage. Much death. Much destruction. I keep one established portal in Yrystrayi. All other doorways are forbidden."

Without another word, he stepped through. Micah glanced at them, shrugged, and followed.

Adam took her hand. "Are you ready?"
"To get back here, yes."
He smiled. "Then let's get this over with."
Together, they walked through.

THIRTY-THREE

ADAM PICKED HIMSELF UP OFF THE FLOOR AND realized he could remember nothing from the time he'd entered the doorway hand in hand with Claire until now. He shook the fuzziness from his head and glanced around, finding Claire near him. He sighed in relief and reached out to lay a hand on her arm.

When Erasmus Boyle had jumped Isabelle through his unstable passageway last year, it had made her sick. His trip had not been pleasant, but he wasn't retching on the floor the way Isabelle had been.

Micah was already up and examining the room.

Claire got to her feet and Adam struggled to stand, too. They stood in the middle of a darkened chamber. Symbols were etched into the veined marble floor, and tables, interspersed with tall, carved armoires, lined the room. Bowls and cauldrons sat atop the tables, along with bound sheaves of plants Adam couldn't identify hanging from hooks. Eudae plants, he guessed.

Gods, he was on Eudae.

"This is some kind of spell-casting room, right?" asked Micah turning toward them. His eyes were alight.

"It is," answered Rue. "As a goodwill gesture from my people to yours, I intend to offer you a gift, Micah."

The door opened and a tall, robed man . . . demon . . . entered. He had a thick head of black hair, blue eyes, and a long face. In his hand, he carried a thick book.

The man nodded at Claire and she nodded back.

"That's Domin," she said under her breath to Adam. "He's a *Syari*. One of the keepers of the *Ytrayi* records."

Domin handed the heavy tome to Micah who looked ready to cry tears of joy. Domin spoke in Aemni.

Claire translated. "It's a book of our history, he says. He thinks you'll find lots of interesting information in it."

Micah could only sputter his thanks.

Domin spoke a few more words in Aemni to Rue before he turned and left the room.

Rue turned his gaze on Claire. "I don't want you to leave, Claire." His voice shook.

Claire walked to him, took both his hands in hers. "It's time for me to go back, Rue. It's time for me to go home, to have the life I should have had."

Rue averted his gaze, looking down. He removed his hands from hers. "It will be done quickly, but it will hurt." He flicked his gaze at Adam. "You will need to hold her."

Adam made an irritated sound as he walked to her. "What's a little more pain, right, Claire? You've already had plenty trying to get this stuff out of you. You've had a lot of practice." Anger surged through his veins.

Domin reentered the room with a bowl of a concoction that made Claire wince and wrinkle her nose. The combination of Eudae plants filled the room with a bitter yet sickeningly sweet scent.

Micah approached with interest. "What is that?"

Rue took the bowl from Domin, who left the room again. "It's a paste made of herbs only found on Eudae. The scent of them will aid Claire in releasing her hold on the elium."

"The only thing it's making me do is want to throw up," she answered.

"Please, sit on the rug in the center of the room. Adam, please sit behind her and hold her tight."

They moved to do as he requested while Micah peppered

Rue with questions. The Coven's scholar appeared oblivious to the fact they could all be in danger here. He acted like he was on some school field trip.

"I tried to take the elium from Claire twice without success," said Micah. "Are these herbs necessary to accomplish it?"

"There are other ways," Rue answered. "But you would have been extremely lucky to find one without the help of a *Syari*."

"You said that when Claire pulls the four threads of her magick together and uses it, it acts like demon magick, right?"

"Yes."

"Is there any way for the threads to bind within her seat in order to force her to release the elium?"

Rue stopped short and looked at Micah. "You are very intelligent for an *aeamon*."

"Rue!" Claire said disapprovingly. "That's a backhanded compliment."

Rue let out a rough chuckle. To Adam's ears it sounded like the *Cae* had broken that slight laugh out of a thick coating of rust. "I like this new you, Claire. I will miss you." He turned his attention to Micah. "In order to take the elium from her in that fashion, you would have needed this." Rue motioned to the bowl.

"Ah. Now I don't feel so bad," Micah answered.

Rue knelt in front of Claire. He held the bowl in front of her face and Adam tightened his arms around her midsection. The smell of it made him want to turn his face away, but he forced himself to stay still.

"Breathe deeply, Claire," Rue instructed. "Let it fill your senses. Relax and let my words and magick do their job. This will go very fast."

Claire nodded, closed her eyes, and inhaled deeply. It was clear that she trusted Rue, despite the fact the *Cae* of the *Ytrayi* had a nasty tendency to torture people and rip out the entrails of her lovers.

After a minute of Claire breathing in the scent of the herbal junk, she went limp in his arms. Rue muttered something under his breath and Claire jerked in Adam's arms violently. Adam held on to her as she seemed to go into convulsions.

"Rue!" Adam yelled. "What's going on—"

Rue's spine bowed backward and the bowl flew from his hands to land a distance away, shattering on the marble floor.

Adam pulled Claire into his arms, saying her name over and over, his heart beating hard enough he could hear it in his ears.

She opened her eyes and smiled up at him. "It's gone and I still have my magick."

Rue struggled to his feet, rubbing his chest. "It was successful." He sounded incredibly relieved.

Claire stood with Adam's help. "It hurt, but it was worth it." She glanced at the doorway, still shimmering in the corner with a blue iridescence. "And that means . . ."

"Time to go home," Adam finished for her.

Micah clutched the book to his chest and looked bereft. "Already? That was fast."

"I have something I want to give you, Claire." Rue walked to an armoire and pulled out two small burlap sacks. "One is for Thomas, to pay for the damage to the Coven. The other is for you, Claire, to give you a head start in your new life." He brought them to her and opened one of the sacks. Into his hand spilled several . . . rocks?

"Diamonds," Claire breathed. "Uncut diamonds." She looked up at Rue. "But you need these for warding Yrystrayi. I know how hard they are to find."

Rue shook his head. "We can locate more. I understand that on Earth these are very valuable. You can trade them for your currency."

Micah stared down at Rue's hand. "Wow, that's a lot of diamonds. That many could probably affect our economy in a—"

"Shut up, Micah." Adam growled.

Claire took the sacks from Rue. "Thank you."

Rue placed his hands on Claire's shoulders. "I have wronged you, Claire, wronged you without knowing it. But I want you to know that, no matter what you may think, you have been like a daughter to me."

"Rue . . . I . . . I don't know what to say. You were the closest thing I ever had to a father." Tears sheened her eyes.

"I'm sorry to see you go, but I know of a saying in your

tongue. If you love something, set it free. If it comes back to you, it is yours. I understand that you are not mine, Claire. But I do hope that our paths cross again one day, and I hope that it will be a happy thing for you. It would be a very happy thing for me."

Claire bowed her head. "Thank you for understanding that I must leave."

Rue leaned in and tenderly kissed the top of her head. "My only wish is that you find happiness."

Claire glanced at Adam. "I already have."

Then Rue turned to Adam, his voice growing harsh. "If I ever hear that you hurt her, I will hunt you down and eat your liver like a pâté. Do you understand?"

Adam's eyes widened. "Yeah, I think I got the message crystal clear."

"Good." Rue jerked his head at the doorway. "Now go before I decide to keep you all here."

They moved to the doorway. Claire gave Rue one final, long look, and they stepped through.

The three of them ended up in the middle of the foyer. Adam and Claire were tangled together on the floor and Micah lay not far away. Adam's stomach roiled, but he managed to keep it under control. Oh, *there* was the nausea.

"We're home." Adam closed his eyes and breathed in the scent of the Coven deeply—smoke, destruction, and all. It smelled good.

When he opened his eyes, Claire was staring at him. Warm, intense love suffused her expression, bled into her gaze. It made something deep in his gut grow warm, made it heal.

"Yes, I *am* home," she murmured, then leaned in and kissed him.

Turn the page for a preview of the next book
about the elemental witches by Anya Bast

WITCH
FURY

Coming soon from Berkley Sensation!

SARAFINA MIGHT'VE BEEN NAMED FOR THE ANGELS, but she'd always known one day she'd end up in hell. Her mother had told her that a hundred times while she'd been growing up. She had just never figured it would be while she was still breathing. But here she was—broke, dumped, and grief-stricken. It couldn't get any worse.

Her fingers white and shaking, she released the yellow rose she held and let it fall onto Rosemary's casket. It came to a rest on the polished poplar top, followed by many more flowers released by those around Sarafina. Yellow roses had been Rosemary's favorite. *They match your hair, Buttercup*. That's what Rosemary had always said, holding one of the flowers up to Sarafina's nose.

Sarafina had scraped together every last cent for that shiny coffin. She hadn't been able to afford it. The funeral had almost beggared her. However, her foster mother had deserved the best. And since Rosemary had never had what she deserved in life, Sarafina had made sure she'd had it in death. The only problem was that now Sarafina had ninety-five dollars left in her bank account and rent had been due last week. She'd make it through, though. She always did.

She couldn't cry. It was like all the tears were caught up inside her, stoppered tight. It would be good if she could. It would relieve this awful pressure in her chest.

"Bye, Rosemary," she whispered.

Reverend Evans droned on, but Sarafina hardly heard him. She barely noticed the others around her, either. All of Rosemary's friends who'd come to say their farewells clasped her hands after the funeral was over, squeezed her shoulder, and offered condolences. Her foster mother had had lots of friends.

If Sarafina had still lived here in Bowling Green, she knew she'd have half a million sympathy casseroles on her doorstep by now. As it was, she was headed back to Chicago right after the funeral. Back home.

She couldn't wait.

Still in a daze, she turned away from the grave and came face to face with Nick. His dark brown eyes regarded her solemnly from the handsome face she'd known for years. "You're not fit to drive seven hours today, Sarafina. Stay the night and head out in the morning. You can crash at my place."

A smile flickered over her mouth. "Oh, really? Amanda said that would be all right?"

She and Nick had been sweethearts during high school. Although that fire had long since flickered out and faded to friendship, Sarafina had lost her virginity to Nick. Sarafina strongly suspected Amanda didn't want her on their couch.

Robin, another friend from childhood, came to stand near Nick. "If you don't want to stay with him, you can stay with me." She tilted her blond head to the side in a gesture Sarafina knew meant she was concerned.

Sarafina couldn't swing a cat in Bowling Green and not hit someone from her past. As soon as she'd arrived, she'd been beset by old friends—and other people. Those *other people* were why she wanted to leave so badly. Like, now.

Whispers.

In Bowling Green there were whispers wherever she went. *Hey, that's the girl who . . . Isn't that the daughter of the woman who . . .* She was a walking freak show. Even fifteen years after it had happened, people still recognized her. High school had been hell.

She leaned forward and hugged Nick, then Robin. "Y'all are sweet to offer, but I have to go into the office tomorrow. I can't miss any more work than I have already." She had a funeral to pay off.

Nick shifted and frowned. "They don't give you grief leave?"

Damn it. Caught right in the middle of her subterfuge.

"Yes, a few days." She pressed her lips together. "It's just that—I don't want to—"

Understanding came over his face. "Oh."

Sarafina relaxed. "Yeah."

"It's too bad, but I get it, Sarafina," Robin said, her brown eyes sad.

"I'm glad you both understand. The other reason why I don't want to stay is because I don't want to wallow, you know? I need to stay busy, get my mind on something else. If I don't do that, it'll be worse. The grief, I mean."

If she lost her momentum now and allowed herself to be mired in the loss of the only true mother she'd ever known, Sarafina knew she'd just dissolve.

"This fall I'll come to visit." The words popped out before Sarafina realized it. She'd wanted to appease Robin, but they both knew that had been a lie. Sarafina only came back here when she absolutely had to.

"Will you, really?" asked Robin suspiciously.

"I—I promise to think about it."

Robin patted her back. "Will you at least call when you get home? I'm going to worry about you all day."

Sarafina nodded. "I will." She paused, swallowing hard. God, she wished she could cry.

It wasn't that she wanted to leave her friends. Sarafina loved them, as she'd loved Rosemary, but the town itself held too many bad memories. Once she'd turned eighteen, she'd saved up her money, bought a car, and driven away. Spending time here now, just breathing the air, made her feel suffocated.

"Why didn't Alex come with you, anyway?" Nick asked.

Sarafina looked down at her toes. Ugh. "Alex and I broke up."

"What? When?" Robin exclaimed.

"About a week before Rosemary died. It just wasn't working out." Alex had dumped her, actually.

"I'm so sorry, sweetie," said Robin, cupping her shoulder.

Sarafina probably should've broken up with Alex first, a long time ago. Selfishly, she hadn't wanted to be alone. She'd been *afraid* to be alone, to be perfectly honest. Because of that fear, she'd stayed with him long after the fire had gone out, up until Alex had decided to give the relationship the axe. He'd done them both a favor. It'd been like pulling a dying plant out by its roots. It was a relief not to have to watch the leaves wilt anymore.

"Honestly, I don't miss him much. I do miss you guys, though," she finished, her voice breaking.

Robin hugged her again, making Sarafina let out a small sob. "Well, then, come back," Robin whispered.

Sarafina shook her head and held on to her friend for another long moment. "I can't."

Robin drew back and smiled sadly. "I know."

Sarafina turned and walked away, toward her rusty Honda Accord. "I'll call you when I get home," she called over her shoulder. That was, if her phone service hadn't been shut off.

Robin and Nick stood at Rosemary's grave, waving.

She might be penniless and on the verge of bankruptcy, she might have no family left, and she might be newly dumped, but at least she had good friends. There was always a spot of light in the dark if you looked for it.

The Accord started with a little hitch that made her heart pound.

"God, please, no," she whispered. The last place on Earth she wanted to get stranded was Bowling Green, Kentucky. "If you're going to have trouble, do it far from here, okay?" she crooned at the vehicle. "Or better yet, don't do it all. My bank account can't take it."

Holding her breath, she guided the car away from the curb and out of the cemetery. She'd take the long way back to the highway, avoiding the subdivision where she'd grown up. It was a pretty drive from here to Louisville, full of hills, gorgeous exposed rock walls, and green trees. Kentucky was a beautiful state, but Sarafina couldn't wait to get back to Chicago—where the scent of car exhaust filled her nose, and the honking and voices of humanity constantly filled her ears. Where no one knew her on sight. No one knew her bizarre family history.

Where there were no whispers.

As she drove, a swell of memory assaulted her. Images her brain was able to suppress in Chicago reared their nasty heads here, so near her childhood home. In her mind a memory of her mother flickered. The middle-aged redhead stood on the lawn of their home brandishing a grilling fork, insane words pouring from her lips. Flames licked and the scent of burning . . .

Sarafina lunged for the radio and found a good station that played loud, hard rock music. She opened the window of her car and threw herself into the song, singing the lyrics out loud. She wouldn't allow her mind to go back there; she just couldn't.

Instead, she thought of Grosset, her Pomeranian. She'd left him with her neighbor for the trip south and couldn't wait to see him again. Sarafina smiled. See? Life wasn't so bad. She had friends, a job, and, most importantly, she had the love of a good dog.

Then there was that guy who kept asking her for a date. His name was Brian. No . . . Bradley. Cute, too. He was a UPS guy, came into the office every afternoon and sought her out specifically to sign for the deliveries. What was it about UPS guys? He flirted with her every day, cajoling her to go to dinner with him. It was flattering. She'd been turning him down because of Alex, but now she was free. Maybe the next time he asked, she'd say yes.

She rolled into the northern Chicago suburb in the early evening and parked in front of the beautiful eighteenth-century home where her apartment was located. It was only a few blocks from her office downtown, though she always took the El in to avoid parking problems.

Stopping the car at the curb, she turned off the engine and stared up at the beautiful, huge windows. Sarafina loved this place. The neighborhood was quiet and older, the street lined with stately old trees. Hopefully her landlord would give her an extension on the rent. Most likely he would. After all, this would be the first time she'd ever been late.

She knocked on her downstairs neighbor's door and Alexis,

a college girl, answered. "Grosset? Oh, he's already at your place. Your boyfriend came and picked him up? He's cute!" she squealed. Then said, "Your boyfriend, I mean. Grosset's cute too, though. Ta!" and closed the door in Sarafina's face.

Boyfriend? God, she hoped Alex wasn't having second thoughts. She stared at the closed door for a moment, anxiety making her stomach muscles tighten. Then she stalked up the stairs to her apartment, her mind whirling about what she would say to him. Now that he was gone, she wanted him to stay that way.

Her apartment door squeaked open and she started down the hallway, hearing someone cough in the living room. "Alex, listen—"

She stopped short, and her keys clattered to the floor. Shock held her immobile as she stared at Stefan Faucheux standing in her living room . . . holding her dog. Her mind stuttered.

Stefan Faucheux?

Everyone knew who he was. The rich playboy and CEO of Duskoff International had been the media's darling for a long time. He was everything they loved: handsome, interesting, intelligent, and monied. Then one day he'd disappeared. For a year the world had wondered where he'd gone. Foul play had been suspected and investigations undergone. All the entertainment shows had been atwitter with the mystery.

Then suddenly six months ago he'd simply popped back into existence, taking up where he'd left off as if he'd never been gone. He'd been traveling, he'd explained. Mostly he'd been in Costa Rica surfing. No one had been able to find him because he hadn't wanted to be found. If you had enough money, Sarafina guessed, you could do that, just disappear without a trace. Personally, she wouldn't know.

Most people thought it had simply been a publicity stunt. Maybe they were right. Stefan seemed to like attention.

Right now he really wanted hers.

The bigger question was why? Why was he standing in her living room?

"Wha—" she started and then snapped her mouth closed as Bradley stepped out from her small hallway and stood next to Stefan.

What the hell were the UPS guy and Stefan Faucheux doing in her apartment?

Stefan inclined his head. "Sarafina Connell, it's a pleasure. I think you've already met my associate." He took a step toward her while Grosset panted and smiled a happy doggie smile at her. "We tried the easy way, but you were more resistant than most to Bradley's charms. Women normally just swoon right at his feet, boyfriend or not, making our job so much easier."

"What's going on? What are you—"

"Since Bradley couldn't get you alone, I'm afraid we'll have to do it the less pleasant way. Trust me, we're doing you a favor." He clucked. "Data entry, Sarafina? You're wasting yourself. We'll make the most of your skills where we're taking you. I just wish your initiation could have been nicer."

That was a threat. Stefan Faucheux had just threatened her in her own living room, and he was holding her dog!

Sarafina opened her mouth to scream, and someone grabbed her from behind, a big, meaty hand clamping down hard over her lips. A needle bit deep into her hip, and a thick drowsiness almost immediately closed over her. Her knees buckled, and someone lifted her. Her head lolled to the side, unconsciousness closing over her in a slow wave.

Stefan tilted his head to the side and petted Grosset's silky head, while the Pomeranian panted happily. "Now we have you and your little dog, too."

APPARENTLY, THINGS *COULD* GET WORSE, EXTREMELY worse. Had she considered yesterday to be hellish? Yesterday had been a walk down a lane filled with daisies. Today she wasn't sure if she was even still alive.

Sarafina opened sleep-heavy eyes with colossal effort and watched two men make their way around the small room where they'd locked her. She must still be alive since not even the drugs they'd given her could dull the sharp panic cutting up her throat or the slam of her beating heart. The dichotomy was her worst nightmare. She was a ball of terror imprisoned in a body too heavy to move.

Alive in a dead body.

She'd been drifting this way for over twenty-four hours . . . she guessed, anyway. Just when the drugged lethargy began to ease from her muscles, someone came in and shot her back up again. The time had passed as if she lived in a lucid dream, her consciousness scrabbling against the padded container it was locked within.

As the men left the room and shut the door behind them, her eyelids grew heavy again. Sarafina struggled to keep them open, fought to stay conscious, but she was no match for the drugs wending their way through her veins.

When Sarafina woke next, the first thing she noticed was the absence of the heaviness on her limbs. She could move! Her fear was also gone, replaced by an all-consuming rage.

The second thing she noticed was the man sitting in a chair in the corner of the room, his face hidden by shadow. Creepy.

She bolted upright and addressed the most pressing matter at hand. "Where's my dog? I swear to god if you did anything to Grosset, I will—"

"Please, your dog is fine," came the dulcet voice of Stefan Faucheux, his French accent still audible even though he'd spent most his life in the United States. He stood and smiled, spreading his manicured hands. "What do you take me for, a monster?" His full lips twisted and he gave a one-shouldered shrug. "Okay, so I'm a monster, but not one that hurts children or animals."

"Where is he?"

"He's safe, I assure you, sleeping on a doggie bed in my room. I will bring him to you after we've talked."

Sarafina pushed off the bed and went for the door. "Talk? No way. I'm getting my dog and leaving this place right now."

The door was locked, of course. She used both hands to twist the unyielding knob, and when that didn't work, she hit and kicked the solid oak, yelling at it until she was hoarse.

Stefan stood in the center of the room and watched her with a patient expression on his face. Like she was a two-year-old throwing a tantrum and he was waiting for her to realize the futility of her temper.

Stymied by the door, she whirled and spotted a window.

Ignoring Stefan, she stalked to it, pushing aside the heavy burgundy drapes. They appeared to be in a farmhouse in the middle of absolutely nowhere. Cornfields spread out in every direction she could see. The room they'd put her in was on the second floor, and there was no convenient tree or trestle beyond the pane of glass. Not that Stefan would have let her get that far anyway. Not that she would've tried it without Grossett.

She picked up a tacky porcelain figurine of a milkmaid from the table near the window, turned, and threw it at Stefan. He raised his hand and it burst into a ball of white-hot fire before it reached him, falling to the carpet and smoldering there.

She stared. "What the—"

"You have questions."

She jerked her gaze up from the melting piece of kitsch. "Questions? Yes, I have questions. What the . . ." She knew her eyes were just about saucer sized.

"I can call fire, Sarafina." He smiled. "I play devil to your angel, yes? Although as you will soon see, we're not that different."

Her stomach clenched. Calling fire. *Fire?* It had to be some kind of a trick. God! She had a headache. "You're playing some kind of sick and twisted game with me because you know about my mother. You saw the news articles or the TV show, and now you're doing this for kicks."

Stefan shook his head. "This has nothing to do with your mother, Sarafina. Not directly, anyway. It's not a game we're playing here."

She swallowed hard against her dry throat and mouth, a result of the drugs, she was sure. "What's going on? What do you want from me? *What was that crap you pumped through my body?*"

"We want to help you realize your potential, Sarafina. Nothing dark or sinister. We simply want to tell you who you are. Like many of our kind, you've slipped through the cracks of your heritage."

Sarafina turned to face him. "What are you talking about? Tell me who I am? I know that already. Anyway, if you're going to try and convert me to some cause, why not just ask me out for a nice cup of coffee? Why do you have to resort to kidnapping?"

"If we had asked you for coffee and revealed this truth, you would have caused quite a scene and probably called the police. That's why we don't do it that way." He held out a hand. "We hope you'll forgive the kidnapping, Sarafina, once all is revealed."

She shook her head. "I want to go home. I want my dog and I want—"

"Data entry, Sarafina? No self respecting fire witch would ever work in such a mundane field. What are you thinking? I can make your life so much more meaningful. I can provide a way for you to make lots of money so you can live the life you were meant to live."

The words *fire* and *witch* in the sentence made her vision dim. Her knees went weak and she caught herself on the back of a chair. "What did you say?"

"Don't pretend ignorance, Sarafina. Even if you don't know, you *know*."

She studied him. "The only thing I know is that you're crazy, as bat-shit crazy as my mother was."

Stefan smiled and took a step toward her. "Your mother was crazy, Sarafina. I'm sorry about that. I'm sorry your father went AWOL, too, because he would have raised you correctly. As it happened, your mother, your only living blood relative, went insane and torched herself before she could teach you anything. That's a pity."

Her mother, a highly religious woman, had raised Sarafina alone in a modest middle-class subdivision just west of Bowling Green. Every Sunday her mother had dragged her to church to cleanse the wickedness from Sarafina's soul. Every day her mother had told her she was sinner, a tool of Satan. For a while Sarafina had even believed her.

Her watery light blue eyes narrowed in accusation, Sarafina's mother had said hell would be Sarafina's punishment for being a witch. She'd pointed a thin index finger and declared, *Thou shalt not suffer a witch to live!*

Nearly every single day her mother berated her, up until the time she'd gone straight past crazy and over the cliff to truly insane. After that her mother's berating days had come to a fiery end, and Sarafina had collected a whole shiny new set of nightmares . . . and a foster mother.

Stefan's smile turned predatory. "As it turns out, it's an advantage for us, though."

"What's an advantage?" Her mind whirled. She couldn't track what Stefan was talking about. He made absolutely no sense. It was like talking to her mother at the height of her illness. Sarafina would've said she was on *Candid Camera* or something if the whole situation hadn't been so bizarre and threatening. *Candid Camera* did light and funny, not dangerous and crazy.

"That you're a fire witch, of course. A powerful, untrained, completely oblivious, and vulnerable fire witch." He smiled. "Ours for the taking, if we can convince you to work with us."

"W-witch?"

"I know it's hard to believe. I can imagine what you're thinking given your past and all the things I know you grew up with. It must be hard to comprehend that even though your mother was quite insane, she was also . . . right."

Sarafina shook her head. "This is nuts. This is—" She cut off her sentence, her breath coming faster and faster in an impending panic attack. She whirled, looking again for a way out even though she knew there was none.

"We don't have much time, so I'll prove it to you." Stefan stalked to her, knelt, and forced open her palm.

Power—that's the only word she could use to describe it—poured from her chest, right between her breasts. It bloomed bigger and bigger until she couldn't hold it anymore. It was hot, stinging her to the point of pain. Her head snapped back and something within her swelled in response. It became larger and larger until it exploded from the center of her.

Stefan stepped away and fire—fire!—streamed in an arc from the center of her body to land in a pool of white hot intensity in the middle of the floor.

The stream ended in a tingling rush that made blood roar through her head. Her eyes wide and her heart pounding, she stared at the charred carpet of the room and marveled in the euphoric sensation of the power that Stefan had forced her to wield.

"Oh, my God!" she gasped, staring. The rug crackled.

"Ah, *there* you are. I knew you were in there somewhere." Stefan stared at her for a long moment, a strange smile on his mouth. Then he left the room, clicking the lock on the door behind him.

Discover Romance